Praise for R. A. Salvatore

"An enthralling epic adventure story, it introduces memorable characters and an intricate scheme of magic the readers won't soon forget."
—Terry Brooks
on *The Demon Awakens*

"R. A. Salvatore at his best—and even better."
—Michael A. Stackpole, *New York Times* bestselling author, on *Mortalis*

"As R. A. Salvatore continues to build his detailed and complex history, his readership is sure to build as well."
—Kevin J. Anderson, *New York Times* bestselling author, on *Ascendance*

"Outstanding . . . [*Transcendence* has] a first-rate female high-fantasy protagonist."
—*Booklist*

"A new classic! Wonderfully told! Fans will love it!"
—Troy Denning,
New York Times bestselling author of
Star Wars: Crucible, on *The Demon Awakens*

"Absorbing . . . one of the finest books yet in Salvatore's prolific career."
—*Publishers Weekly*
on *The Demon Spirit*

"Fans of martial fantasy should enjoy his vivid depictions of combat."
—*Library Journal* on *The Ancient*

"[A] swift-moving tale of sword and sorcery . . . Fans of Salvatore's unadorned approach and broad caricatures of archetypal figures should be pleased with this carnival of treachery and medieval feudalism."
—*Publishers Weekly*
on *The Highwayman*

TOR BOOKS BY R. A. SALVATORE

The Highwayman
The Ancient
The Dame
The Bear

DemonWars: First Heroes
DemonWars: The First King

Child of a Mad God
Reckoning of Fallen Gods
Song of the Risen God

R. A. SALVATORE

SONG

OF THE

RISEN

GOD

A TOM DOHERTY ASSOCIATES BOOK NEW YORK

This is a work of fiction. All of the characters, organizations, and events portrayed in this novel are either products of the author's imagination or are used fictitiously.

SONG OF THE RISEN GOD

Copyright © 2019 by R. A. Salvatore

All rights reserved.

Map by Rhys Davies

A Tor Book
Published by Tom Doherty Associates
120 Broadway
New York, NY 10271

www.tor-forge.com

Tor® is a registered trademark of Macmillan Publishing Group, LLC.

ISBN 978-0-7653-9535-1

Our books may be purchased in bulk for promotional, educational, or business use. Please contact your local bookseller or the Macmillan Corporate and Premium Sales Department at 1-800-221-7945, extension 5442, or by email at MacmillanSpecialMarkets@macmillan.com.

First Edition: January 2020
First Mass Market Edition: November 2020

Printed in the United States of America

0 9 8 7 6 5 4 3 2 1

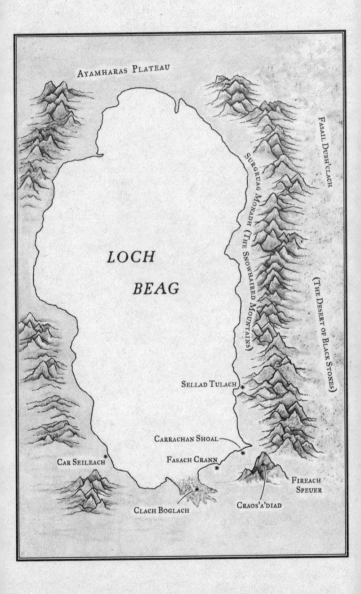

SONG

OF THE

RISEN

GOD

PROLOGUE

The dust of ages greeted Brother Thaddius Roncourt of the Abellican Church when he and his companion at last pried open the stone slab set into the side of the hill. Thaddius tilted his head back, to more fully take in the stale air, and closed his eyes, basking in hope.

Sister Elysant, meanwhile, grunted and pressed harder against her stave, using it as a lever to force the slab—no, not a slab, but an actual door hung on curved metal hooks—open wider. The door was angled, so its weight pressed back against the solid staff.

"Help, if you please, O lazy one," she said through her clenched jaw.

Brother Thaddius didn't reach for the door but instead lifted his hand, holding a large malachite. He fell into the song, attacking the weight of the door with the gem's countering magic.

Elysant stepped forward when she felt the press lessen, and the door swung fully open to fall against the side of the hill.

"Look at these," she marveled, feeling the curved hinges. "Fifth century?"

"Sixth, and beyond," Thaddius replied. They had both seen these types of door hangings at St.-Mere-Abelle, of course, for the old monastery had been fashioned bit by bit across the ages, featuring the architectural designs that spanned the nearly nine hundred years of its existence.

"And nothing we would expect to see out here in the Wilderlands," Elysant added.

Brother Thaddius nodded and stared into the dark hole now opened before him. Was this really a gateway to another time? Was this really a crypt of Abellican brothers? Of saints, even, including one of the greatest Abellicans who had ever lived? He found that he could barely draw breath, and not for the stale air.

For months, Thaddius and Elysant had scoured the foothills of the Belt-and-Buckle Mountains, far to the southwest of the city of Ursal, following the rumors and myths of the people settled about this region known as the Southern Wilderlands. It had been a frustrating, often infuriating journey of discovery, for the ways of these uncivilized folk were quite offensive and foreign to Thaddius. Like the two monks, they were Bearmen, including many who had deserted the kingdom of Honce-the-Bear, seeking the freedom and potential riches of these lands untamed, and many more who had been born in this region, descendants of previous emigrants from Thaddius's homeland.

Even though the wilderfolk, as Thaddius had come to call them, mostly professed themselves Abellicans, few had treated Thaddius and Elysant with any hospitality. Rather, the monks from Honce-the-Bear had been seen with great suspicion. Whispers followed their every step when they ventured through a village, and many, particularly the children, ducked into shadows when they noted the pair passing.

"Do you feel it?" Thaddius asked, and in looking at his

companion, he knew that Elysant didn't have to ask him to clarify.

"The door has not been closed for centuries," she noted. "The growth covering it is not as old as that."

"How long, do you think?"

She moved closer and studied the roots, including some that had been chopped apart at some points. "Decades?" she asked as much as stated, with a noncommittal shrug.

"Twenty-five years?" asked Thaddius.

Again, Elysant shrugged.

"As the old man told us," said Thaddius, referring to the aged villager who had directed Thaddius and Elysant to this nondescript hill hidden in the forest on the very edge of civilization.

"We know nothing yet," she reminded.

Brother Thaddius nodded and fished from his pouch another gem, this one a diamond. He spent only a moment finding the song of the magical stone, then brought forth a rich glow and held it aloft as he might a torch. He took a step for the opening, but Elysant cut in front of him, presenting her staff before her into the darkness with one hand, half turning to put her other hand on Thaddius's chest, holding him back.

"You do your job, I'll do mine," she said.

Thaddius chuckled, amused by her feigned seriousness. "If we are right, it is a place for dead things," he reminded.

"And if there are other ways in, a place for snakes, perhaps? Scorpions?"

Thaddius answered by calling for more magic from the diamond in his hand, the gemstone's glow increasing greatly.

The tunnel went in a short way, through natural stone and dirt, with roots crisscrossing here and there. The floor was of set stones, however, smooth and mostly flat. It bent around to the right, to another door, also of stone, but open. Elysant used her staff to push it wide, revealing a descending stair beyond.

Down they went, their view blocked by a low ceiling that matched the angle of the stairway until they came to a landing and another set of stairs, turning sharply right. This time, the angled ceiling only followed them for a dozen stairs before opening into a chamber of worked stones, roughly square. Elysant crouched low and whispered for more light, the tone of her voice telling Thaddius to hurry. He moved down beside her as he increased the magical diamond light again, and he and Elysant gasped together at the sight revealed.

On the bottom of the stairs lay a body, a skeleton, mostly, in the ragged clothes and hides of the wilderfolk. Another body lay crumpled in the far left corner of the small room, broken and twisted, but neither of the monks gave it more than a passing glance.

For this was indeed a crypt, an old one. A stone sarcophagus was at the center of each wall, all but the one on the opposing wall open. A fifth sarcophagus, the largest of them all, sat in the middle of the room, its lid secured by large stones piled atop it.

"What?" Elysant asked, looking to her companion.

Thaddius could only shake his head and answer with uncertainty. "The robbers, I presume. The superstitions of the wilderfolk run deep."

They went in slowly, Elysant carefully leading the way over the body at the base of the stairs. She moved to the coffin on the wall to her immediate left. Its stone lid was askew enough so that she could see old remains within, a broken skeleton in tattered Abellican robes.

"Closer with the light," she bade, and she bent low to an inscription on the lid and blew hard, lifting the dust from the lettering. She pulled the sleeve of her robe over her hand and briskly rubbed it, then recited the poem inscribed:

Alas for Master Percy Fenne,
Who killed the goblins plenty,

With tiger's hands he felled a score
And piled their bodies twenty.
Alas for Master Percy Fenne,
Whose efforts should have won,
Excepting that his foes this day
Numbered twenty-one.

Elysant couldn't help but laugh. "Even in death, they were heroes," she said.

"Because they believed, and so they did not despair," Brother Thaddius added, and he, too, gave a chuckle at the poem, so wittily macabre and amusing all at once.

Thaddius stood back and turned, and Elysant did, too, and took a step toward that central, most impressive stone sarcophagus. She stopped, though, and motioned to the back wall, where rested the smallest box of all—and one, it seemed, that had not yet been violated.

"By Saint Abelle," she whispered.

"The old man was right," said Thaddius.

Like a black maw, it stared back at them, open and uninviting.

But here they meant to go.

"Give 'em time, what-ho," whispered a large man as he reached out and grabbed a friend striding ahead, bow in hand, arrow nocked.

The others of the gang bristled.

"Let 'em do our work for us, eh?" said the large man.

"The skinny one and the little girl?" a sturdy woman asked skeptically from behind.

"Y'ain't doin' it with a hammer, no matter how hard ye're hittin' it," said the oldest of the group, a middle-aged man, the son of the oldest man in the Wilderlands village, who had heard these tales for all of his life.

"Aye, let 'em do our work, then ye take down the skinny one fast," the large man told his archer friend.

* * *

"As you believed," Sister Elysant whispered when Thaddius had finished his magical work on the small box. Thaddius held his diamond high once more but lowered the intensity of the glow—he wasn't quite sure why that might matter, but it seemed, somehow, more respectful. He stayed back as Elysant carefully slid the now-separated lid from the opened coffer. And it was a coffer, she knew now, and not a funerary, for this one had not been put here to hold a body, as with the other, larger four.

Deceptively strong for such a compact woman, Elysant managed to ease the lid quietly to the floor. She looked over her shoulder at Thaddius for direction, for he had stepped back again and stood unmoving.

"Thaddius?" she asked.

He didn't answer. He could not bring himself to step forward and look in. He recounted the steps that had brought him to this place and this moment—if it was, after all, that which he believed and that which he fervently desired.

"So it was true," Elysant said, barely able to get the words past her shivering lips, and it was not cold in here. The short woman gingerly went up on her tiptoes, peering into the open stone box, but only for a brief moment before turning away. She was feeling the same way as he, Thaddius understood.

"The pagans are good for something, at least," Brother Thaddius said, trying to lighten the tension.

"Pagans?" Elysant asked skeptically.

"You wouldn't consider them Abellicans," Thaddius replied. "Have you witnessed their prayers and offerings? More Samhaist than Abellican—or worse, some blending of the two, which is a greater offense than simply being a Samhaist!"

"Because Abellicanism is so pure?" Elysant asked, flashing a wry grin and letting her quarterstaff twirl slowly in one hand, an unsubtle reminder that she had been trained as a warrior by Pagonel, a Jhesta tu mystic from faraway Behren.

"That is not the same thing," Brother Thaddius argued, but he shook his head and let it go, knowing he could not win the argument here. For a decade, Sister Elysant had been his mental foil, always challenging him and many times (too often for his liking) tying him into logical corners from which he could not escape. It amused Thaddius now to consider that Elysant, three years his junior, not even yet thirty years of age, had become to him his most important teacher.

He hoped that she felt the same of him.

"They believe what they have to believe to get them through the trials of this difficult land," Elysant replied. "And through life itself, for death is ever staring at them, hungry. Was our own faith so ensconced just a few years ago? Was yours?"

"We stand before a great treasure and argue politics," Thaddius replied with a nervous laugh.

"We stand before secrets of the early and great Abellican monks, so we hope," Elysant reminded. "These are treasures only because of politics, and faith."

Brother Thaddius stepped farther back from the open coffer and stared hard at the woman, though his thoughts were judging himself and surely not her. He considered her point more carefully, particularly given his own internal strife during the convulsion of the great civil war that had ravaged the kingdom of Honce-the-Bear a decade before. Brother Thaddius had been a part of the defense of the greatest monastery in the world, the abbey of St.-Mere-Abelle, under the command of Father Abbot Fio Bou'raiy, an Abellican following the tenets of newly sainted Brother Avelyn Desbris. Avelyn's teachings were of compassion and tolerance—even to the point of spreading the beauty of the magical Ring Stones.

Opposing them were the forces of the demon spawn, King Aydrian Boudabras, who led his mighty army to assault St.-Mere-Abelle, the last stronghold opposing his iron rule. That army had included more than a few Abellican monks, led by the fierce and powerful Master De'Unnero.

De'Unnero.

Simply recalling the name brought a wince to the face of Brother Thaddius Roncourt. Marcalo De'Unnero had believed in the old ways, ways of judgment and punishment, of hoarding the Ring Stones within the Church alone and letting the misery of the world serve as a proper reminder to the peasant rabble that their only salvation lay in complete obedience and devotion to the Abellican Church. Father Abbot Bou'raiy's hug of compassion would be met with the slash of De'Unnero's arm, a limb transformed into the killing paw of a tiger.

Both men had died in that battle, one that had included a dragon from the deserts of Behr, and thousands more had perished beside them, but Bou'raiy's side had prevailed. St.-Mere-Abelle had won, with King Aydrian defeated and exiled and gentle Braumin Herde, a friend and disciple of St. Avelyn, elevated to the position of father abbot of the Abellican Church.

The side of goodness and community had won, Brother Thaddius now understood. But he knew, too, as did this woman beside him who had become his closest friend and confidant, that he had begun his inner journey to his current philosophy as a secret follower of Marcalo De'Unnero.

"Hold your judgment of these people about us, Brother," Elysant said, as if reading his mind—which was not likely hard to do at that time, Thaddius realized. "Your consternation weighs on you more than on them. They only know what they know, as we only know what we know."

"And now we are here," Thaddius said lightly and grinned, a proper smile, given the priceless relics now apparently sitting right before them. He hesitantly moved back to the edge of the open casket, the only one of five in this vault that had survived the vandalism and looting of the previous uninvited visitors. The markings on this coffer—the only markings, for it had no inscription like the previous ones—showed that grave robbers had tried to break it open but had failed, as the old villager had recounted. He had told the couple that he had heard tales that one of the coffers would not yield to the determined hammering of the thieves. This one casket among the five, an unmarked and otherwise unremarkable stone coffer, fit that description, and showed exactly those marks.

The other four, Thaddius believed, had held the possessions and bodies of Abellican monks of long ago. All that likely remained now was the scrambled bones and rotted cloth that had survived the looting, as they had seen in the first of the graves. But this one remaining, previously unopened box was no funerary. Those who had buried the others in here had taken special care with this one—or more likely, it had been one of the monks here entombed who had done so, shortly before his death. For this treasure had been magically sealed and could not be forcibly revealed, the stone strengthened and made into one piece by the magical power of the orange citrine stone, and so it could not be opened, not by hammer or mace or brute strength.

Brother Thaddius, however, possessed what the previous intruders had not. He had Ring Stones. He had magic. And he used that magic: First the powerful sunstone to dispel many of the guards and enchantments placed upon this box, and then a polished piece of citrine, the stone of earth, not to break the stone open but to gently separate the top slab from the rest of the coffer.

"Are you going to look?" Elysant said after a long pause.

Thaddius took a deep breath.

"I know," the woman agreed, and then she stepped forward suddenly and faced her fears of disappointment, and stared into the open box. She slapped her hand over her mouth and began to giggle nervously.

"What is it?"

"Come see," Elysant told him. "Oh, come see!"

"Is it?"

The woman never turned from the stone box, and she

began waving excitedly. She gasped again and giggled more loudly when Thaddius approached, diamond held high, showing the true beauty of the sight before her.

For there in the stone box sat three alabaster coffers, decorated in gold, intricately carved with evergreens and other symbols of the Abellican Church, standing on legs that also seemed made of gold. These alone were a treasure, of course, but that only hinted at something even more precious within them.

"These were no ordinary brothers," Thaddius whispered reverently. "This is no simple tomb for lost monks."

"Aye, that's what we've been thinkin' for most o' me life," came a voice from back by the entrance, and the two monks spun about to see a host of ruffians, weapons drawn, entering the room.

The speaker clued Brother Thaddius in to the truth of this, for he recognized that the large man was the son of the very person who had guided him to this place. They had used him and Elysant to get back in and get that last box opened! Now all he could think of was how he might get that cover back on and resealed—but, of course, he knew he hadn't the time for that.

"No reason for the two of ye to get yerselves killed," said the large man.

"Blast, but we ain't leavin' no monk witnesses," said another, and he lifted his bow, aiming for Thaddius.

"More boxes inside, though," Elysant cried out. "You'll not open them without us!"

A woman slapped at the bowman's arms, lowering the weapon.

"So we all got reason to bargain, then," said the big man.

Brother Thaddius wasn't listening. He rolled several gems between his fingers, calling to their magic, readying a strike. He counted five enemies and suspected at least a couple more still on the stairs behind them.

Five enemies, two torches.

Thaddius fell into the vibrations of his moonstone, let the magic tickle his sensibilities, begging release.

"Well?" the big man said, coming forward, just beside the center sarcophagus, lowering his sword to put it in line with Thaddius, who stood barely two strides away. "Ye take out what's in the box and put it down on the floor," he ordered Elysant.

The small woman glanced up at Thaddius, who gave her a slight nod. These two had been traveling and fighting together for a decade, and so nothing more needed to be said.

"Now!" yelled the big man, so Sister Elysant moved, but not for the open stone box.

She leaped forward, her staff spinning, at the man who was twice her size. He squawked and gawked, surely surprised, as she whipped her staff across with such precision and power that it took the sword from his hand.

Elysant halted the swing by loosening her top-hand grip and pulling the staff down with her bottom hand, letting it slide so that she held it, hands apart, near the middle as she turned it vertical. A punch out with her top hand sent the top of the staff crashing down at the man's head. He got his arm up to block, but it didn't really matter, for the strike was a feint, Elysant flipping her top, right hand over to a backhanded grasp and suddenly reversing, pulling that top hand back and down while pressing up powerfully with her left hand, turning her shoulders and stepping forward to strengthen the blow.

Up between the man's legs came that solid stave, crashing into his balls and lifting him up to his tiptoes.

Behind him, the other ruffians shouted out and leaped to action, the archer lifting his bow once more, having been joined by a second bowman, then ducking below the ceiling line on the stairs.

But it was Brother Thaddius who struck next, releasing the power of his moonstone in a great sheet of wind and placing that wind wall perfectly, just in front of Elysant and blowing back toward the stairs.

The large man, already off balance and grabbing at his smashed balls, went tumbling backwards and rolled away, crashing into the side of the sarcophagus along the wall to the right of the stairs. Both archers tried to fire, but their arrows flew wildly and they, too, flew backwards, the man on the stairs cracking hard against the wall, the lead archer stumbling into his bowman companion.

The torches went out in the gust, both of them, and so Thaddius dismissed the magical light emanating from his diamond as well, leaving the vault in pitch blackness. Thaddius went down behind the short end of the central sarcophagus, across from the entry. He felt someone roll near and knew it to be Elysant.

He shuffled about and tapped her on the shoulder, warning her to be ready, then inched his way up the sarcophagus, reminded himself about the stones piled atop it, and released the energy of another magical stone, a chunk of graphite.

A sudden flash brightened the room and showed the ruffians, and then that flash, a stroke of lightning, reached across to strike three of them, including both archers.

Again the vault was dark.

"Now," Elysant whispered, and Thaddius brought forth his diamond light. Elysant leaped out from behind the funerary, driving the end of her staff into the face of the large man like a spear. His nose crunched, his eyes crossed, and he let go of his balls to grasp at his flattened sneezer, blood pouring.

Two others came at the monk woman, though, driving her back from finishing the large man, while the third ruffian, still standing, went around the sarcophagus the other way, charging for Thaddius.

"Behind me!" Elysant cried, backing toward the corner, far right from the stairs and just beyond the smaller box.

Thaddius rushed to the corner, falling into his magic, confident that the finely skilled Elysant could buy him time. She worked her staff brilliantly, slapping aside a woman's spear thrust, then catching a descending sword midshaft and twisting the staff over and out to tangle with the spear-wielding woman.

She even managed to crack the swordsman about the face as she brought her staff back into a defensive position. Still, she knew that she and her friend were in trouble.

"Hurry," she pleaded, for over at the stairs one of the archers was back up, trying to set an arrow to his bow, and yet another, a husky woman, stood tall and shook off the effects of the lightning stroke. Even the large man was steadying himself.

And over toward the center, the man who had charged at Thaddius had diverted and was now standing atop that central sarcophagus, hoisting a large rock over his head.

Across went Elysant's staff, right to left once more, to intercept a sweep of the spear. Pressing out and down, the monk ducked low and left, just avoiding the stab of her other opponent's sword.

"Dismiss the light!" she cried, snapping the staff back the other way to drive back the swordsman.

Brother Thaddius certainly understood her sentiment, but he disagreed with her choice, for it was too late. The man on the sarcophagus was already throwing the rock, and the darkness would only stop him and Elysant from dodging.

The rock arched in over the two ruffians, forcing Elysant to desperately duck, and Thaddius, behind her, had to turn fast, instinctively slapping at the rock with his hand to help guide it aside so that it only clipped him, doing no real physical harm beyond a bloodied finger and a bruised hip, before it cracked against the corner and fell to the stone floor.

More troublesome, though, was that Thaddius had slapped it with the hand holding the magical gemstones, and two of them fell from his grasp, including a healing soul stone, leaving him only the diamond and one other!

Elysant fought furiously, holding the two at bay, meeting the rush of the third, the woman coming from the stairs, with a sudden stab that stole her breath and his momentum.

Thaddius looked about for his fallen treasures.

"The light!" Elysant yelled.

"No, not that one!" the large man with the splattered sneezer yelled, apparently at the man on the center grave. "No, put it back!"

Thaddius glanced back. The man on the sarcophagus already had another stone lifted up high. Stealing the light wouldn't help.

The man with the rock paused, gawking in surprise at his unexpectedly frantic friend, and that gave Thaddius all the time he needed to throw forth another gust of wind.

It blew the rock holder back off the far side of the casket. He fell hard to the floor, his rock falling hard to slam him about the shoulder and head, with the other rocks, all smaller, also tumbling atop him.

Thaddius growled at the win. If only he could gather his other stones.

As he resumed his search, though, a loud crash turned his head back around almost immediately, and he stared in shock as the lid of that central sarcophagus slid to the side and fell away.

The vault echoed with screams.

"Run!" the large man howled.

Up stood the contents of that coffin, a withered corpse wearing Abellican robes, its shriveled face and now permanently lipless grin staring out from under a fine black hood, its almost skeletal hands clutching a stave that seemed made of polished stone.

The large man, limping still, bolted for the stairs, but the ghoulish newcomer leaped out of the coffin to land beside him, the staff flashing across to crack the man on the side of the head, shattering his skull and sending him skidding down to the floor in a spray of blood, bone, and brain.

The archer at the stairs let an arrow fly, almost point blank, which seemed to Thaddius a sure hit, but somehow it flew wide of the corpse's head as the undead thing only dodged slightly.

The archer didn't wait even long enough to see it, though. He turned and fled up the stairs as soon as he had fired. His companion, too—now somewhat recovered from the shock of Thaddius's blast, hair dancing, clothing smoking—tried to climb.

But the stairs before him suddenly began to glow, and the second archer shouted in pain as he stepped upon them.

The zombie ghoul turned away from him.

Thaddius didn't know what to do. The fighting in front of him had stopped, the three battling Elysant scattering to either side of the room, ducking, trying to find a way out. And Elysant seemed uninterested in pursuing them, now that this new and greater monster had appeared.

"Do something," she begged her magic-using friend.

Thaddius had no idea what that something might be. He thought to dismiss the diamond light, hoping that he and Elysant might find their way out in the darkness before the monster caught them.

The man on the stairs yelled in agony. He had fallen across the steps, the stones red hot, and his clothing ignited, brightening the room. He writhed and fell from the stairs, landing atop the sarcophagus on that wall and then tumbling to the floor, where the flames ate him.

The zombie turned right, where the first two of Elysant's attackers had circled and were now rushing for the stairs. The third, the last woman into the fray, inched along the right-hand wall, scrambling over the open stone box; then, as the ghoulish monster went for her companions, she sprinted for the stairs.

Elysant, though, ever the ferocious warrior, leaped for the zombie.

Thaddius wanted to tell her *No! Run!*, but he couldn't get the words out of his mouth, and he came to see the order as useless anyway as he watched the robed zombie dispatch the other two men along the far wall with effortless speed and power. The stone staff crashed through the shield of the swordsman with stunning force, slamming him in the shoulder and throwing him into the air to slam against the wall.

The woman with the spear stabbed the zombie, but the staff came across in a vicious downward chop to shatter both the prodding weapon and the arm holding it. Up came the stone staff again, the tip flashing under her chin, and with what seemed like a simple shrug, the zombie sent the ruffian flying away. She landed, kneeling, beside the casket along that wall, her head upon it.

The zombie lifted the stone stave to execute her.

"No!" yelled Elysant, and she cracked the zombie across the back of its head with all the force she could channel through her own wooden staff, a blow that would have felled almost any man.

She did save the ruffian woman, for the wraith paused. The woman yelped and flung herself to the side, then scrambled to get her feet under her, running for the stairs, where the other woman was now yelping in pain as she skipped and jumped across the molten field.

Elysant fell back as the ghoulish monster slowly turned about.

"Run!" she yelled—to Thaddius, to the man who had been sent flying, and to the fellow still on the floor behind the central sarcophagus, who was only then extracting himself from the rubble.

"And you, go back to hell!" Elysant growled, setting her staff into a wild and powerful flurry, stabbing, striking, sweeping it across.

The stone staff turned and dipped, rose fast and then set vertically against the floor, defeating the skilled woman's every attack with practiced ease.

Elysant fell back defensively. "Run," she said again, though with less confidence, surely. She growled and steadied herself and added more powerfully, "For your lives, I say!"

The man against the wall slipped past behind the zombie. The man on the floor scrambled past, or tried to, as the zombie moved to crush him with the stone staff.

Elysant's staff intercepted, the monk deftly turning it as a lever to buy the wounded man enough room to get by.

The zombie stepped back and put up its staff, its dead, lidless eyes staring at the woman. The monster seemed to smile wider somehow, and slowly nodded, as if in approval.

The man ran up the stairs, yelping, his boots smoking when he stepped on the still-glowing area.

"Mercy," the undead thing said, still nodding, and though the word was strained and sounded more like *"Erce,"* Elysant understood it.

"Thaddius, run," she said, setting herself in better balance.

But Thaddius hadn't moved, hadn't even looked for his gems. He stood, half bent to the floor, diamond still in hand, looking back at the zombie with his jaw hanging open.

"Run!" Elysant yelled, as if trying to break him from a trance.

"Waited," the ghoul gasped. ". . . inally fre . . ."

Elysant moved as if to strike.

"Wait!" Thaddius yelled at her.

"It didn't hesitate to strike our attackers," Thaddius continued when she stopped. "Why? Why is it standing passively now?"

"Fi . . . nal . . . ly frrrrr . . . eee," the ghoulish monster forced out. "Guar . . . di . . . an . . . take . . . all."

"What does it mean?" Elysant demanded.

The zombie extended a hand and opened wide its bony fingers, two stones falling from its grasp: an orange citrine, much like the one Thaddius had used to open the stone box, and a shining red ruby. It let go of the staff with its other hand, the stone item falling hard to clang against the floor at Elysant's feet.

"Take," the zombie intoned, reaching up to unfasten the cloak and hood, which fell to the floor. "Take all."

Thaddius and Elysant recoiled when the thing then untied its robe. "I . . . am . . . free . . . rest."

The robe fell to the floor. The naked corpse shivered violently for a few moments, then crumpled to the floor in a pile of jumbled bones and paper-thin gray skin.

Elysant fell back a step. "By Saint Abelle," she breathed.

Brother Thaddius stepped past her to retrieve the citrine and ruby. He stayed low, eyeing the staff, narrow and long. "Stone," he said, shaking his head, for how could that be? He moved to touch it, but hesitated, and instead stood up, staring in shocked disbelief at his friend. "The staff looks like stone, like fine marble. How?"

Elysant dropped her own staff, stepped over, and, with a growl, lifted the unusual weapon, gripping it strongly in both hands. Her eyes went wide immediately.

"What?" Thaddius demanded.

"Power," she said. "The enchantment. I feel it." She put the weapon through some movement, twirling it and stabbing left, then sweeping it behind her back to catch it and present it defensively before her. "Perfect balance."

"Such a stone is too brittle!" Thaddius reasoned.

In response, Elysant brought the weapon up over her head and drove it with all her might against the open rim of the middle sarcophagus. It struck with enough force to take a small chip from the funerary stone, but the staff itself showed not a scratch.

"Apparently, not so," said the woman, shaking her head, obviously beyond impressed with this treasure.

"'Take it all,' the monster said," mused Thaddius, as Elysant bent to inspect the damage to the sarcophagus. "He was guarding—"

"No monster!" Elysant interrupted, her gaze now removed from the sarcophagus as she stared wide-eyed at the lid that had been pushed aside.

"What do you know?"

"Belfour Albrek," she read softly, as if she could barely get the words past her lips. "The Rock of Vanguard."

"Saint Belfour," Thaddius breathed, immediately falling to his knees. He began to sob, overcome. They had been saved by the undead specter of St. Belfour!

Elysant followed him to the floor, gasping and laughing, not crying, but every sound came from the same place of reverent disbelief.

After a long while and many prayers, the two gathered up the corpse carefully and moved to the open coffin. There they paused, however, for the box wasn't empty. A second staff lay within, and a small pouch.

Thaddius took the pouch and opened it, nodded as he discovered a small trove of sacred Ring Stones. When she took the staff, though, Elysant wasn't similarly nodding.

"What is it?" Thaddius asked.

"Not for fighting," the woman replied, and she held it forth.

Thaddius brought the magical diamond closer and increased its radiance. The staff was of wood, but like none he had ever seen before. Green and shot with lines of silver, the body of the light staff was marked by six sockets made of silver and connected by a line that resembled a thread, if that thread had been fashioned of the stuff of soul stones. One of the sockets held another diamond.

"I have never . . ." the monk remarked, taking the staff from Elysant. He bit short the remark with a gasp, for as soon as he gripped the staff, he heard clearly the song of that diamond, as surely as he heard the one in his other hand, as if he had already coaxed its magic into a usable state.

He looked at Elysant and smiled widely. "Not for your kind of fighting, perhaps," he said wryly, and he couldn't wait to find some time to more properly test this treasure. "Let us be done here and let the dead properly rest."

The companions reverently arranged the body of St. Belfour in his sarcophagus. Thaddius then used Belfour's own citrine to seal the funerary box, again uttering many prayers.

They gathered up the two staves, the robe, the cloak, and the hood, and Thaddius recovered the rest of his fallen gems, putting them in the pouch beside the newfound ones. They took the three coffers from the small stone box, and then that container, too, Thaddius resealed with the magical stone.

"He is at rest now," Thaddius said, looking back one last time from the stairs, which had cooled to normal once more.

"He was waiting for Abellicans to come and retrieve the items," Elysant said. She looked at the robe she was holding. "We should have dressed him."

"He dropped the robe as another treasure for us," Thaddius replied. "Why would he have done that if he wanted us to simply put it back on him?" He smiled at his companion. "You follow the fighting style of Saint Belfour. Wear it."

Elysant looked at the robe skeptically.

"He wasn't much taller than you," Thaddius teased.

"It should be put under glass," she argued. "We cannot let it rot!"

"If that was truly the robe of Saint Belfour, it has been down here for more than two centuries," Thaddius reminded. "Do you doubt the magic of it, given everything else we have found, given the saint's insistence that we take everything? Put it on, my friend." He looked at the sarcophagus in the middle of the room, drawing Elysant's gaze with his own. "If I understood it correctly, the ghost of a saint bade you to wear it."

Elysant's hands trembled the entire time she was changing. She was putting on the very robes worn by the legendary St. Belfour of Vanguard.

"Well?" Thaddius asked when she had the robe tied about her. The fit was loose, but not terribly so.

Elysant smiled and took up the stone staff. She started to

speak but then just kept smiling, wider and wider, and shaking her head as if in disbelief.

Thaddius understood. She could feel the power, the magical energy, the holy glory.

"Let us be far from this place," Thaddius said.

"What of the thieves who fled?"

Brother Thaddius shook his head. They didn't matter, he knew. They didn't matter at all.

PART 1

THE WESTERN WINDS BLOW

There is a beauty to this mountain—Tzatzini to the xoconai, Fireach Speuer to the humans—that goes beyond its physical features, and one that remains constant whether looking below to the vast lake called Loch Beag, or now, the golden city of Otontotomi. For the real beauty of the mountain lies below its rocky spurs and lines of evergreen trees in caves filled with crystals and crystals filled with sparkling stones which carry within them magical energy beyond the strength of a warrior, beyond the power of an army.

The xoconai claim this place as holy, as their own, the rightful domain and magic of Glorious Gold, their god Scathmizzane.

The humans who lived here for centuries untold claim this place as holy, as their own, the rightful domain and magic of their god, Usgar.

To the xoconai, the humans confuse their fake god with the demon Cizinfozza, which they called the fossa.

I wonder, then, was this god, Usgar, truly the same as Cizinfozza? And so, a god or a demon?

Or are they the same thing, god and demon?

As I grow familiar with the similarities between the humans and the xoconai—the social and family structures, they way they go about their days in their respective villages and cities—I find that question coming to mind more often, and it is one that troubles me greatly. I was raised to favor a god, and to hate those who favored a different god. Or to pity those misguided others, at least, and to recognize that if we conquered them and showed them our god and our ways, they would be better off and would come to gratitude.

Perhaps that is the case, perhaps not, or perhaps it fluctuates back and forth as the respective societies change and evolve.

But none of that really has anything to do with the gods, or demons, or whatever they are.

The humans of this conquered land surely do not appreciate the coming of the xoconai at this time. Hundreds were killed, thousands taken as prisoner, to now work hard under the merciless eyes of the xoconai augurs. What love can any parent, xoconai or human, hold towards an invading army that stole a child and destroyed a home? Even if the xoconai show this conquered people a better way of life, that sting is profound and lasting.

Will the eventual outcome dull the desire for vengeance? How many generations will need to pass, I wonder, before there can be any true mending of the relationship?

Or will that not matter to the xoconai? Perhaps the augurs will demand that the humans be wholly eradicated, worked to death in slavery or sacrificed to Glorious Gold. Perhaps in the end, Tonoloya, the nation of the xoconai, will stretch from sea to sea as Scathmizzane demands, and within that vast nation, humans will be erased, first chased to the edges of civilization, then hunted down and murdered.

Then will Tonoloya know peace from the humans.

But I see these humans, their ways, their familial love, their hopes, and know they are akin to the xoconai in all of these things, person to person. And in that truth, how is Cizinfozza an evil and monstrous demon, but Scathmizzane a wonderful god, Glorious Gold?

I have come to see, to my hope and my sadness, that if the distinction is merely that this god or that god is my god, and that I am little different from my enemy who serves a different god, and if our gods demand that we two peoples do war, then perhaps we are both better served with no god.

To everything I learned in my youth, this is blasphemy. And were I to speak it aloud, my end would be certain and painful and the memory of me would be erased except in whispers among those few who might agree.

To deny it in my private ruminations, however, is to kill the truth of myself, of who I am and what I believe and hold dear, and that truth is more important to me than the body that holds it.

I sign this your student, forever in your debt,

—*Ag'ardu An'grian*
Sunrise Face

1

THESE SONGS
OF MAGIC

Aoleyn looked back from the windswept bluff to the small group winding down the rocky decline.

So small. A hundred, perhaps, no more.

The tears in her eyes were from the wind, the woman told herself. Yes, the previous night had brought amazing and dramatic changes, a wall of mountains melting, a huge and deep lake pouring forth across the flatland low desert.

Yes, her world had so suddenly turned upside down. Not for the first time—or the last, she knew, wiping some moisture from her cheek.

It was just the wind, she told herself, trying desperately and futilely to put aside the reality that, for every one of that band of refugees moving down from the Ayamharas Plateau, thirty other men, women, and children had been slaughtered in the course of a single day.

Yesterday.

Aoleyn hadn't many friends in the world—no close ones beyond Bahdlahn, who was now among the refugee group fleeing the conquered plateau—but that didn't lessen the pain, however she tried to hide it. The sheer scale and suddenness of the destruction overwhelmed her.

The woman pushed a long strand of her black hair out from in front of her face, blinked her dark eyes determinedly to push the sadness and the tears away, and then put a hand on her bare belly, feeling the chain she had fastened there and the multiple gemstones set upon it. Her finger brushed the smoothness of one, a moonstone, and there her hand lingered, connecting her more intimately to the magical energy within that small stone.

She coaxed the power, bit by bit, until her fingers trembled with the magical vibrations, until the song of the gem filled her thoughts.

She called upon the magic, she leaped away, and she began to fly, like a bird on the wing. Around the side of the great chasm, which had only yesterday been a mountain lake, she went, staying low, not daring to go over the rim and expose herself to the conquerors, who were already as thick as ants along the southern rim of the bowl.

Not daring to expose herself to the giant among them, a huge and beautiful and terrible creature she had seen riding a monster, a snakelike dragon that seemed to swim through the air.

Sometimes no more than her own height above the ground, sometimes weaving about clusters of trees, she sped along the new canyon's western rim, avoiding any signs of movement, giving wide berth the one village on this side, a place that had been sacked even as she and the others had made their desperate escape across the deep and dark waters. In a very short while, she had traversed the length of the canyon and come to the thicker trees and sheltering rocks of the foothills of the great mountain looming above the southeastern rim. Fireach Speuer, it was called, thick and tall and casting long shadows each morning across the waters of the lake that had been. The huge and hulking mountain that had been her home. One area of flat ground, more than halfway up those slopes, had served as the summer camp for her people, the Usgar, and a stony plateau at the mountain's high peak had been their winter home, the seat of their power, the source of their magic, of the Coven's magic, of Aoleyn's magic.

Aoleyn had to set down in those foothills, to pause and consider her luck—or was it, perhaps, fate? For only because she had been fleeing her people, running away from the Usgar and all that they believed, had she escaped the tide of strange-looking conquerors that had crested every mountain pass and ridge like a great wave of death breaking over Fireach Speuer itself.

She wasn't even sure how she felt about the obvious conquest and destruction of the Usgar. Had these invaders done her a favor, done the world a favor, in ridding everyone of the foul barbarian tribe and their murderous ways?

No, Aoleyn found that she couldn't bring herself to think like that. She had not hated all of the Usgar, after all, and had considered many, particularly the tribe's subjugated women, to be victims beaten into acquiescence. She had wanted to save them all from the ways of Usgar, not from these strange invaders, who, after all, she hadn't known existed until she had flown over them as they destroyed the lake village known as Fasach Crann. Only when Aoleyn had come to understand that she could not save the Usgar from themselves had she fled.

Aoleyn grimaced, which looked much like her crooked little smile, when she thought of Tay Aillig, the leader of the Usgar, her tormentor, whom she had brought down from on high in an avalanche of stone in the midst of her escape. She looked down at her hand, now the small and delicate hand of a young woman, tattooed with the pad markings of a cloud leopard's large paw.

She felt the vibrations of that tattoo, of the bits of gems she had implanted to make the image, and the magic they contained, a power that had transformed that hand and arm into the limb of a cloud leopard. She imagined those long claws now, and saw again the last look of horror on Tay Aillig's face as he lay there, trapped among the fallen stones. She had shown him no mercy.

She grimaced again as she remembered the killing move—her sweeping claw taking the man's throat so easily, so fluidly; the blood, so much blood, gushing down the front of Tay Aillig; the shocked expression of a confused man who had thought himself a god—frozen forever in the mind of Aoleyn.

So be it.

A deep breath blew the memory aside for the moment and brought Aoleyn back into the present, where she quickly realized that she was not as alone as she had hoped. She ducked fast amid a tumble of boulders.

She heard them. Their voices, melodic, a bit higher-pitched, undeniably beautiful, sounded not so far away.

Aoleyn crouched lower in the shadows of the boulders. She called upon the magic of the diamond set in her belly ring to absorb the nearby light and deepen the shadows about her.

Many enemies were nearby, she quickly realized. Her thumb rolled across the band set on her ring finger, feeling the ruby and the serpentine set there.

Serpentine to protect her from flames, ruby to create fire.

Aoleyn winced yet again, remembering the smell of the charred corpses she had left in a cave. Men, Usgar men, guarding her and taunting her.

Then melting before her.

I did what I had to do, she stubbornly told herself, and though it was true, the image haunted her still.

And then she forgot it, in the blink of a surprised eye, when she saw him, a tall, golden-skinned man whose nose was as red as the blood that had gushed from Tay Aillig's neck, and that patch lined by blue streaks as brilliant as the waters of the lost Loch Beag under an autumn sun. He wore a shirt of armor, rows of golden bars, it seemed, and shot with lines of brilliant silver. So, too, was his helm of gold. How could it be anything else, for what mundane metal might have been worthy of this beautiful golden-skinned man?

Aoleyn's trance broke when she scanned to his lifted arm, for he held a spear above his shoulder—no, it was at the end of a Y-shaped throwing stick!—and was aiming it right at her.

Aoleyn had not yet coaxed to a crescendo the magical song of any of her gemstones.

Aoleyn had no fire or lightning to throw.

Aoleyn had nowhere to run.

His wounds would not kill him. He knew that now. He looked down at the golden cast that had been poured over his hip and side.

Poured! Liquid gold!

It should have killed him, of course, and surely it had hurt, bursts of agony the Usgar warrior had never imagined possible. But whatever the wrap was that these strange, tall, painted-faced humans had placed on him before pouring had kept him from melting under the molten metal.

Now he was feeling better, too much better to deny. His strength was returning, though one of his legs obviously had been broken in his fall. They were going to pour gold on that injury, too, he believed, judging from the way the shaman or priest or whatever he might be had been indicating the course to his helpers. He couldn't feel any pain down there, couldn't feel anything at all, and he desperately hoped that their medicine would fix that, as well.

He propped himself up on his elbows as one woman passed him.

"Do you know who I am?" he declared imperiously. "Tay Ail—"

She punched him across the face, then put her foot on

his throat and slammed him back down to the ground, her weapon, a flat wooden paddle with the teeth of some animal lining both its edges, hovering threateningly just above his face.

Tay Aillig is my uncle, Egard finished in his thoughts, but he wisely said no more.

He closed his eyes and tried to fall far, far away.

The woman's return, with another of these strange-looking people, surprised him. They grabbed him by the shoulders and hoisted him up to a sitting position.

"What—" he started, but then he shrieked as the woman drove something sharp into the back of his shoulder. He turned fast to look at her, then shrieked again as the man did the same to the other shoulder.

They each stabbed him again in a different location—no, not stabbed, he realized when the woman got him in the back of the arm. They weren't simply stabbing him; they were hooking him!

A third stranger, or perhaps more than one, pulled on ropes behind him. Up went his arms, above his head, then up went Egard, hoisted by eight separate hooks driven into his flesh. He was standing then, though his legs remained numb and were not supporting him, and then he was off the ground, hanging there helplessly, shocking bolts of pain, blisters of agony, shooting through him.

Barely, through the pain, he felt pieces of that same healing cloth being set about the hooks, and he watched, mesmerized and horrified, as these handlers poured more liquid gold, sealing and supporting the hooked areas, stopping his flesh from simply tearing and thus dropping him to the ground.

He screamed and writhed, twisting furiously, which only made the pain even more intense.

They brought before him a long piece of metal, shining golden, polished so that he could see himself.

A full-length mirror?

It made no sense. None of this made any sense!

Another came up behind him and, from over his shoulder, peered at him in the mirror.

Egard recoiled at the sight, the shock of it overcoming his agony for just a heartbeat. For this one's face was hidden behind a mask, if it was a mask, of a human skull, as if that skull had been pressed right through the flesh of his face.

Egard tried to turn his head to get a better look, but the stranger cupped him about the ears and forced him to stare into the mirror.

And in that reflection, Egard's eyes met those of the stranger, locked gazes drawing him deeper into the image, deeper into this monstrous man.

He felt the intimate invasion, the stranger boring in, as keenly as if fingers were pushing through his eye sockets. He writhed and cried out and closed his eyes, but too late.

For the skull-faced augur was in there, in his thoughts, probing.

Aoleyn threw her hands out in front of her defensively, desperately, and turned her head so fast in terror that she didn't even notice her arms transforming.

She leaped, instinctively, straight up, and she was high above the ground before she even realized the transformation. Suddenly she loomed twenty feet above her attacker, who stared up at her in shock. Down she dropped, and she braced herself against the fall.

She landed lightly and pounced immediately, burying the golden man beneath. She slapped him on the ground repeatedly, hitting him several times before she even realized that her arms, like her legs, were those of a leopard and not a woman.

Aoleyn pulled her head back and looked down at the mauled stranger, trembling, gasping, covered in the blood pouring from deep, raking wounds.

What had happened? How had it happened?

Her tattoo, she realized. The leopard paw–like gemstone that she had used to mark her body had somehow taken over, or her terror had called to it on a level below her consciousness. Pure survival had demanded the swift change, and so it had come to her without her even consciously willing it!

Aoleyn, too, trembled, her thoughts spinning as she tried to sort through this shocking transformation.

Her tattoo? Was the connection truly so powerful and intimate? It had taken over in that moment of desperation, as if she had become something else, something animal, something monstrous.

Like the fossa.

She looked at the torn man before her, expiring, certainly, as his blood continued to flow.

"No!" Aoleyn growled, and she forced her own limbs back to those of a young woman. She called upon the wedstone immediately, demanding of it the healing magic that would allow her to save this stranger.

She knew she should be away—other enemies were about her and had likely heard the commotion. But she stayed, and she demanded the magic. He was an enemy. He had tried to kill her. She was justified in killing him, she knew.

She knew, but she didn't care. Not this time, not when it had been done by something within herself that she simply didn't understand, and something she truly feared. She stayed and sent the waves of magic forth, over and over. She shifted the focus of the wedstone and used it to free her own spirit to go within the mind of this wounded person, to possess him.

A barrage of images and names flashed before her.

Xoconai.

Scathmizzane.

Golden temples . . . domed pyramids . . . a vast basin to the sea . . .

So many images assailed her—no, not that, she came to

see. So many images *informed* her. She went back to her own body and took a deep breath. She heard others approaching. She had to leave.

The man was breathing again, lying still and barely conscious. He was no goblin, she realized, not physically at least.

"It's not paint," she whispered of the red and blue markings on his face.

But he was a man, she knew now. Some type of man, though she could not begin to understand in that moment. Nor could she remain. She had to hope she had done enough to save him, for her own sake and not just for his.

She called upon the moonstone in her belly ring and flew away.

An exhausted and drained Egard lost himself, with his reflection in the mirror, like some golden ghost of Egard, mocking him from the other side of death. It seemed to float about as he twisted a bit on his hooks, and for a while, the man, delusional in his pain, actually thought that he was in there, in the mirror, and not within his own body, as if he were walking the fine line between the living and the dead.

That notion grew stronger when Egard again noticed the second image in the mirror, a skeleton or a floating skull, hovering behind him. He wasn't afraid. He was too lost in agony to be afraid.

The skull came up right behind his shoulder. A hand, of flesh and not of bone, was raised up and set against the side of his face, and then a second was placed on the other side, holding his head still.

The skull began to hum, or moan, or something in between.

"Pixquicauh," Egard said, though he didn't mean to and had no idea what that word might mean.

Then, suddenly, horrifically, Egard knew that he was not

alone, not in this room and not even in his own mind. This monster, whatever it was—Pixquicauh?—stared at him through the eyeholes of the skull, invading his very soul.

He felt its presence within and only then remembered the experience from before. It asked him, it probed him, and it took from him the answers before he could even respond. He realized a violation more profound and painful than the eight hooks that had been plunged into his skin, as if his very identity, not his physical body, were being torn open by this monster.

He shook and thrashed, trying to expel the possessor.

But it stayed, and it smiled behind the mask.

Egard began to lose himself to the jumble of his own breaking mind.

Then, suddenly, he was free, jolted back to the present reality. He was Egard, nephew of Tay Aillig, hanging on hooks before a golden mirror.

The monster remained, leering at him through the skull's eyeholes, over his shoulder.

It demanded of him.

"Pixquicauh," he recited.

The monster smiled behind the skull mask and walked away.

Egard swayed on eight hooks.

She was not hindered by the steep incline, for it was no more difficult to fly up the side of the mountain than to soar above level ground. And here, with the many ridges, tree lines, boulder tumbles, and uneven ground, Aoleyn did not have to worry as much about being seen, particularly since the mountain, this early morning, was hugged by a thick mist, not quite a fog.

She did remain very cautious, though, in stark comparison to the day before, when she had flown openly down the slopes of this same mountain, defying the Usgar to catch her. Now, however, columns of these strange-looking invaders lined the trails of Fireach Speuer, from Craos'a'diad at the peak to the lake-turned-canyon below.

Aoleyn paused at one point and used a small lens her friend Talmadge had loaned her to look across that canyon to the far northern rim of the bowl. She breathed a sigh of relief when she noted none of these invaders there, and she took heart that her friends and the refugees continued to move swiftly away. She had come back here to scout, to garner information, and they would need that to get away, she reminded herself.

But she wasn't quite sure of how she might get it.

She moved her hand to the left side of her head, to a cuff she wore over that ear. A small gem, a cat's-eye, was set in the cuff, granting her clear vision in the dimmest of light, but the cuff itself, made of turquoise, was also magical, powerfully so. Aoleyn closed her eyes and sent her thoughts into it, hearing the calm song, using it to guide her senses to a nearby tree, where a small bird perched upon a limb.

Into that bird went Aoleyn's thoughts, easily taking control, and off it flew, swinging around the mountain, more in line with the main trails leading down to the lake. She felt the tension in the small bird and understood, through its senses, that it had detected an owl, and so she too spotted the predatory fowl.

Aoleyn's spirit abandoned the small bird and flew fast, moving to her favored host, and a moment later the owl took wing, guided by the distant woman.

Now she could hear, so keenly, so crisply, and she caught a voice soon enough, melodic and smooth—she thought perhaps it might belong to one of the Usgar women. But no, when she came into sight of the creature, she discovered the pitch of the voice was deceptive, for it belonged to an invader male, a tall and strong man carrying an armload of firewood, moving for a saddled lizard that was tethered to a tree not far away.

Now she had her target. She swooped the owl down low, claws extended, to startle the man, and she took some pleasure when he dropped the wood in reaction, spouting words she did not understand, though she did recognize them as curses. She noted the area and the landmarks, then released the owl, immediately coming back to her sensibilities. Now Aoleyn called upon another gemstone. She placed her hand on her hip, fingers covering the large gray backing of the orange stone in the center of the pendant that hung from her chain belt.

Again she left her body, but this time it was more than the simple ray of thoughts she might use to briefly inhabit the sensibilities of an animal. This time she was fully removed from her corporeal form, spirit-walking out from her own flesh, bone, and blood.

She looked back at her physical form and considered her concealment, then flew up and scanned all about, making sure that no enemies were near. Off she went for the firewood gatherer, and she found him easily enough, sputtering a stream of invective, loading the logs into his arms once more.

Aoleyn entered him like a sudden gale, overwhelming him before he could begin to realize the possession, assaulting his mind and his spirit. She had achieved complete surprise and quickly dominated her target, fast cordoning his spirit deep in a pocket within his own mind. She began scouring that mind for what she wanted: expansions of the glances she had found in her melding with the other sidhe—no, not sidhe, but xoconai.

It was not long before she found her answers. Images of war, of conquest, of the complete domination of the world, filled her mind's eye. A massive column of these strange humanoids, tens of thousands strong—more beings than Aoleyn had ever seen, had ever conceived of—all gathered to make war. And at their head, a shining golden god, huge and beautiful and terrible.

One she recognized.

One she had seen riding a dragon that seemed to swim in the sky.

Aoleyn recoiled.

You will not succeed, she imparted to the xoconai in his own language—and she was amazed at how easily that language had come to her through the intimate thought-sharing with this stranger.

She felt the xoconai's confusion and understood much of the ensuing barrage of silent questions, the snippets of bewilderment.

Aoleyn then fled the creature's mind and returned to her own body. She knew the invader, the xoconai, would be dazed after her vicious assault and likely wouldn't ever truly sort through it. Soon she was physically flying again, farther up the mountain. She had one last task to accomplish up here before she returned to her companions—such as they were—and told them what she knew.

And then she and the others would have to leave and go far, far away.

She climbed to the top of Fireach Speuer, along the western rim of peaks, moving along the same areas, she noted, where she had first seen the demon fossa on that long-ago night, far away, from her perch in a pine tree in the sacred grove of her people. She came to the edge of one ridge and looked back that way, her old home in sight.

The Usgar winter plateau teemed with invaders. Nearer to her, but still distant, within the sacred grove and the meadow called Dail Usgar, she noted movement and heard soft singing. That intrigued her but also terrified her. Were her people still alive, any of them? Was Mairen there along with the other witches? Or had the xoconai taken the ceremonial place as their own?

Early that same morning, after all, she had seen their god figure fly from Dail Usgar on his serpentine dragon.

Aoleyn resisted the urge to investigate, reminding herself

of her other purpose here, one that she hoped would help her many refugee companions truly escape this region. Besides, she thought, nodding as the memory came clear, she could get a more complete understanding of the events in Dail Usgar from a much better and much safer angle. Off she went, to the east, to the highest peak of Fireach Speuer.

The Usgar called it Craos'a'diad, the Mouth of God, but to Aoleyn, the gaping hole in the high plateau atop Fireach Speuer seemed no more than an execution pit—though one that led to a series of crystal-encrusted caverns that were marvelously magical. For all her thoughts about the beauty below, though, it was hard for her to consider her next move in entering the chasm, because it was indeed a place where the Usgar performed their sacrifices.

Her own, among many others.

Aoleyn approached carefully from behind cover and glanced down cautiously. And it was a good thing that she had taken the precautions, she knew immediately, for a surprising number of xoconai invaders were up here this day, some building structures Aoleyn could not identify, others placing golden ornaments all about. Aoleyn noted that all, from those who seemed to be warriors to those moving more like common folk, men and women alike, had those distinctive markings, the red nose with the blue central face about it. Some of the colors were bright, some paler, but all so incredibly distinctive.

They weren't guarding the chasm, but getting down there without being seen presented a challenge.

She wondered if perhaps it would be better to leave and return at night.

But no. Aoleyn shook her head determinedly. She had gone into the lair of the demon fossa. She had faced the wrath of Mairen and the Coven and had thrown them aside. She had met Tay Aillig in battle and he lay dead now, and she unscathed.

She reached to her moonstone once more, bringing it to

its fullest power. She called upon the graphite bar in her anklet and threw its magic into that of the moonstone, swirling and churning. A thundercloud formed and she guided it above Craos'a'diad.

As one, the xoconai looked up, obviously surprised by the suddenness of the small storm, though such events were of course not unknown in the mountains.

Aoleyn willed her storm to rain on them. She added lightning blasts, sending the xoconai scrambling—some rushing for cover, others moving to protect the items they had brought to the plateau.

Aoleyn smiled at her cleverness, then reached to her diamond and, again, her moonstone. She marked her angle and created a globe of darkness about her form, blurring it.

She called another lightning bolt from her storm cloud, cracking down upon the stone, as she flew off suddenly and swiftly, and then for a third bolt, to steal the attention as she dove for the chasm, slipping into its dark depths without slowing.

Down in the chasm, she released and reversed her darkness, giving herself some light. The pit went down a long way, but there were layers of caves above its bottom. Aoleyn went into the highest of these, caverns lined with giant crystals growing from their walls. She had walked this way during her first visit here, in her trials to determine if she had the capability to serve in the sacred coven of thirteen witches dancing for the god Usgar.

She had made her magical jewelry from the stones in these crystals and in these very caves.

Now she needed more.

She let go of the powers of her own jewelry stones, except for one, a red garnet hanging on her right earring, and began calling to the vibrations of magic all around her, lighting diamond-flecked crystals like torches as she passed. Through the power of the garnet, a stone that showed her magic, Aoleyn listened for variations in the music of the stone vibrations, seeking those with powers different than the ones she had thus far collected.

The caverns were long and winding and the process took time, but every time Aoleyn thought it was time to quit, she came upon another crystal teeming with energy she had not before utilized, like one with thick flecks of smooth green and red striations, a bloodstone. When she called upon its energy, Aoleyn felt her muscles tighten. At first she feared that she was becoming again leopard-like, but no, she was merely growing stronger—much stronger.

She kept looking.

The day turned to night outside the caves, and Aoleyn kept looking. When she grew tired and hungry, she moved to the chasm. She didn't go up, though. Instead, she traveled down to the lower tunnels, to a room she had known in the weeks she had remained here, recuperating from the attempt to sacrifice her. In a deep cave, she entered a warm chamber, one with a pool fed by a small waterfall and full of fish. A chamber whose walls vibrated with magical power. She bathed and ate and slept, but only briefly, and was back at her work before the next dawn had broken.

That second day passed, and Aoleyn kept looking, now with a handful of small crystals in her small pack, each thick with different gems.

Despite the fear that she might have trouble finding her fleeing companions, Aoleyn would have kept going—there were even more variations, she was sure—except that her journey was interrupted by a song, a harmony different than she knew, perhaps, but sung by voices that she thought she recognized.

The Coven was singing more loudly this night, more intensely and forcefully.

Curious, Aoleyn headed down again to the pool chamber, for in there, she knew, there was a better way to spy upon the Coven in Dail Usgar. With the power of the wedstone, the powerful witch left her corporeal body beside the underground pool and flew up to the ceiling. She found the magical vein of crystal near the waterfall and entered it, traveling up past the higher caverns, up to the surface, entering the God Crystal itself, the leaning obelisk the Usgar named as their god, in the center of the sacred lea where the witches danced and sang.

And they were dancing, though there were only twelve, she noted, after a long while counting the spinning bodies as they danced in a circle about her host. She could see out of the crystal, but not clearly, and so she wasn't sure who might be missing. It wasn't Mairen, though, that much she knew, for the leader of the Coven, the Usgar-righinn, stood in her usual place beside the God Crystal, directing the song in a voice loud and clear.

Soon after, Aoleyn felt a deep discomfort, a profound chill, coming over her.

She had felt this before, near the chasm, where the ghosts of the dead had been captured and held. She wasn't in her mortal body, so he didn't have any breath to hold, but Aoleyn kept her thoughts very still, her spirit on edge here, feeling a threat.

A xoconai walked onto the plateau. But not just any xoconai. No, this was a giant one, tall as the trees, lean and beautiful.

And terrible. Aoleyn could feel its power.

More coldness filtered through her, and she came to understand, to her horror, that souls were passing around her, within the crystal beside her, but spreading forth like the seed of a man onto the sacred lea. There they grew and took form, specters, like men and women formed of mist, their faces twisted in agony.

They, too, began to dance, very near the crystal, and Aoleyn saw them, saw their faces—and knew their faces! Some of them, at least, for they were the Usgar, her own tribe.

She saw Tay Aillig!

And she saw the ghosts of xoconai, too, many, and of lakemen, many.

They danced and they twirled along a winding line, ending up before the tall xoconai god. And there, they faded, their essence diminishing, seemingly absorbed by the giant being before them.

No, not absorbed, Aoleyn came to understand. No, they were being obliterated of the thing they were, their essences stripped of identity, their souls turned to . . .

To what?

Aoleyn felt the God Crystal thrumming with power, growing stronger, collecting the energy of souls destroyed.

All around her, the witches of the Coven danced, singing reverently to this creature, this monster, this glorious golden god.

And the being looked at the God Crystal—nay, at her!— and it smiled, and Aoleyn knew that it saw her despite the fact that she should have been invisible.

She fled. For all her life, for all her soul, for all her eternity, Aoleyn fled.

She fled back to her body by the pond in the cave far below. She fled on foot through the tunnel to the chasm, then brought forth the power of her moonstone and flew up as fast as she could manage, coming clear of Craos'a'diad, not even worrying about any who might see her emerge—and fortunately no xoconai or anyone else was up there in this dark hour.

As quickly as she could manage, she fled back down the mountain and soared along the western rim of the chasm, heading for the place where she had left her companions.

Aoleyn had only ever known life here, on Fireach Speuer, but now she knew the only thing to do was to flee.

To run away as far as she could.

2

THE ENEMY
OF MY ENEMY

"Stay together," Tamilee recited, more to herself than to her two lifelong friends, the brothers Asef and Asba. They had grown up as neighbors in the small fishing village of Carra-chan Shoal, living their lives in each other's company, hunt-ing, fishing, playing, and exploring their boundaries, their hopes, their fears together.

Tamilee loved them both as brothers—no, as more than brothers. She had often fantasized about raising a family with one or the other. She knew that she could be happy in the arms of either. They were so much alike. They even looked alike, with their single-hump elongated skulls, brown hair and beards cut similarly, and piercing eyes—eyes as blue as any in the village other than Tamilee herself. Asef was leaner and swifter, while Asba was among the strongest men in the village.

And now, with most of the village slaughtered, with the village itself destroyed . . .

"They're all about us," Asba quietly replied, to Asef's agreeing nods.

The three moved in a group of more than twenty refugees, padding through the light forests along the western
rim of the mountain crater—the crater that had been a lake,
upon which they and all the others had been sailing, fleeing
the massive invasion of these strange-faced monsters. They
hadn't seen any of the invaders since coming ashore, but
they knew. They all knew.

The monsters were all about.

"We should've kept going across the lake," Asef whispered,
moving between the other two. "Foolish turn to the west."

"Only the fast boats made it," Tamilee reminded. "We
were overladen and slow."

Asef started to respond but then closed his mouth fast and
nodded—and what else could he do? What argument could
be made? Their boat was built for a dozen passengers and
had twice that number pushing it low in the water, plodding
along. They had seen the carnage behind them, both from
the eruptions on the far bank and from the appearance of
the great lake monster. The only way their boat could have
paced those that escaped to the far northern bank of Loch
Beag would have been to throw half the people overboard to
drown or be eaten.

So they, and many other boats, had turned to the much
nearer western bank of the great lake, coming ashore and
rushing for cover, huddling in fear throughout the night of
explosions and fiery stones flying high into the air. The magical cataclysm created by a beam of power shooting down
from Fireach Speuer had destroyed a large part of the mountains hemming the lake on the east, and that had opened a
great chasm down thousands of feet to the Desert of Black
Stones—a desert that was now, because of the draining of
Loch Beag through the mountain breach, a vast lake.

So suddenly, their entire world had changed.

"We should be going north, not south," Asba offered, and
not for the first time. Before the dawn, the passengers from
their boat had set out, and after several arguments, the el-

ders among them had determined that they would go south, toward the village of Car Seileach and in the direction of those other refugee boats that had beached nearby.

"We must join with the others, and with the folk of Car Seileach, to find a way to fight back," said Asef, but Asba was shaking his head through his brother's entire reply.

"We three should be going south," Tamilee said, supporting the very arguments Asba had made during that early morning gathering. "Just we three and not all of us. We'd move faster."

"We'd move quieter," Asba interjected.

"Aye, and we could catch up to them before they ever reached the folk who sailed to the northern bank," Tamilee went on. She looked around at those hiking to either side, ahead, and behind. "Too many, too loud, too slow."

"And the painted-faced sidhe are all around us," said Asef. "I can feel them."

Dread, sheer dread, settled on Connebragh's shoulders. She knew she couldn't stay in the small cave beneath some exposed tree roots, but where was she to go? She couldn't return to her tribe, the Usgar on the mountain, for her tribe had been slaughtered.

Or perverted, enslaved, she reminded herself, thinking of the other women of the coven of witches, likely still dancing about the God Crystal, serving that hideous giant sidhe monster with intoxicated glee.

She considered her one valuable item, the spear she had taken from the fallen Ahn'Namay, one of the leaders of her lost tribe. She had gathered it from his body, which had been riddled by the spears of the invaders, missiles hurled with frightening power and accuracy.

She sent her thoughts into the crystalline spear tip, seeking the magic, the song of Usgar, contained within. She heard two distinctive whispers: the green flecks that lessened her weight and allowed her to run fast down the broken ground of the mountain, and the sparkles of tiny diamonds, the stone of light and darkness. She felt, too, the wedstone—all of the Usgar spears had a bit of this stone of healing, the keystone to all the magics—but it was not strong in this particular spear.

And she found no offensive magic available, no lightning or fire, which was probably a good thing, for she had little idea of how to actually use a spear in a fight. Unlike in the lake tribes, among the Usgar, the warriors were men, only men. Connebragh winced as she recalled the scene up on the sacred plateau, where the painted-faced invaders had rained spears upon her people to devastating effect. She was no warrior, but would that even matter? Even if she could match Tay Aillig himself in battle prowess, she would have no chance against these foreign monsters—and they, Connebragh reminded herself, were only part of her problem. She was surrounded now, all sides, by monsters and enemy uamhas, the lake people the Usgar raided and killed and took for slaves. With their skulls elongated from birth into a long single hump reaching back and up, or even in two humps, and sometimes two humps that were not identical, leaning left, leaning right, Connebragh found the uamhas uglier than the invaders, even.

And would they hate her any less?

Could she even think of uamhas as people?

The woman closed her eyes and heard again the screams in the night, the cries of lake folk being caught and murdered by the invaders. She hadn't seen those murders but had heard them, and the uamhas had screamed as an Usgar would scream, sometimes calling for friends, calling for their mothers.

The sounds had pierced Connebragh's heart and soul, had brought a river of tears to her as she huddled in that impromptu camp beneath the exposed tree roots. She had felt every death, keenly.

The woman took a deep and steadying breath and gripped her spear tightly. She looked all about. Where was she to go? She thought she might go back to the mountain to find more spears, more magic, perhaps even other Usgar, but that notion washed away when she looked to the southeast, to the hulking mound of Fireach Speuer, for, from that very direction, she heard them, the sidhe invaders, coming in a swarm.

She called upon the green flecks to lighten her step, to make her faster, and she ran to the north, moving from shadow to shadow, from tree to tree.

Only a short distance later, the woman was glad of her caution, for she spotted some of the sidhe, their faces shining brilliant red and blue in the morning sun. They moved in a column east of her position, near the rim of what was now the great gorge. Their lines and cadence showed discipline, a large force moving perfectly as one.

Connebragh sped along, determined to get far ahead, but stopped again beside one weeping willow, peering through the hanging strands of leaves flowing in the morning breeze. She had spotted a group of uamhas, two dozen perhaps, moving south.

Connebragh glanced back the way she had come, the direction of the approaching invaders.

These people were doomed.

She reminded herself that these were lake people, uamhas, less than human, good only as simple slaves. Were they any better than the invaders moving now to slaughter them?

Connebragh's sensibilities answered that question before her conscious thoughts could catch up.

She ran to the east, still in the shadows, but more concerned with speed, trying to formulate the best way to shout a warning.

"We should turn them around," Asef said, shaking his head. The troupe had passed several of the beached boats of their kin and kind but had found no sign of their fellow refugees. "This is without hope. You heard the screams from Car Seileach when we were still out on the lake."

"Yes, and there we'll find our friends," answered an older woman.

"And drive these monsters back over the mountain," a middle-aged man agreed.

"And if the town is dead?" Tamilee interjected. "As the sidhe overran Carrachan Shoal and Fasach Crann? Have ye any reason to think it's different here?"

"Bah!" the man snorted. "And where would ye have us go?"

"North!" Asef and Tamilee said together. Behind them, Asba just sighed and nodded his agreement.

Tamilee started to argue some more but stopped before uttering a complete word, for out to the west something flew at them through the willows. All gazes followed hers, and people scrambled. The item looked like a piece of a willow branch the size of an arm, moving across the sky, leaves trailing, except that it was flying as if thrown, floating as if caught on unseen breezes.

The folk moved aside as it came in above them and then stopped its progress suddenly and dropped to the ground.

"A branch?" Asef remarked.

"Run!" came a voice from an unseen woman somewhere out among the willows. "Run! They're coming! For your lives, run!"

"What?" Asef remarked.

"What was that?" Tamilee agreed, moving to stare down at the branch—and that's all it was, a willow branch. A willow branch that had floated out from the trees to garner their full attention.

"Magic," the middle-aged man growled, and he lifted his spear high and shook it.

"Usgar," the old woman agreed.

The group shifted and shuffled, friends finding trusted

friends, creating several impromptu defensive formations—scattered, though, and nothing that could withstand a sizable onslaught.

"She said run," Tamilee reminded, edging back to the north. "She said run!"

"Who was she?" more than one asked.

"An Usgar chasing us away!" said the old woman.

"Why would they?" Asba said above them all. "Do the Usgar even survive? The monsters came down Fireach Speuer, a swarm, every trail!"

"Might be that the Usgar bringed them!" the old woman said, shaking a crooked finger at the young man.

The three young friends turned to each other, all unsure.

"Half the people here can't fight," Asef whispered. "We'll be overrun."

"What would you have us do?" said Tamilee.

"We can'no leave them to die," said Asef.

A shout from the front of the troupe ended the conversation, and the three friends turned to see their worst fears realized. Through the trees ahead came enemies, bright-faced, red and blue, holding high their deadly spears and riding the lizards, green and golden collared, running fast, tongues flicking, long backs swaying side to side with each twisting stride.

"Form!" the middle-aged man shouted.

"Run!" Asba and Tamilee shouted above him in unison, for they knew they couldn't possibly stand against this force.

"We can'no leave them!" said Asef, leaping past them, lifting his spear just as the first volley from the invaders soared in.

The first devastating volley.

Almost half the lake folk went down, Asef among them. He spun in a descending spiral, growling in pain, impaled just above his right hip.

Tamilee was to him first, diving upon him to stop him from rolling over in his writhing, which would have twisted the spear inside him. She forced him over onto his back and, crying for her brother, grabbed the spear and tugged it free, a gout of blood and some twisted entrails coming with it.

How poor Asef screamed!

Asba fell back, horrified, and Tamilee pulled off her shirt and fell over the wound, tucking the guts back in, holding back the blood.

Asba recovered fast and grabbed his brother by the arm, hoisting him up over his broad shoulders, then running off, Tamilee close behind.

All of the remaining folk were scattering then, most to the north, some to the east, but the three went the other way, west, toward the voice that had warned them. They wound their way through the willows, glad for the cover, running, stumbling, scrambling, searching for no direction but away.

Just away.

Behind them came the screams, a few all together at first, but then one at a time, and they could only imagine their villagers, their friends, in those last moments before eternal darkness fell.

Asba and Tamilee didn't even slow enough to look back. Caught in terror, they just ran for their lives, for Asef's life, dripping away in lines of blood with every stride.

They didn't know how far they had run, how many strides they had put behind them, though the now occasional screams sounded distant.

The ground grew rougher, with more stones and fewer trees, and Asba stumbled down to one knee.

"We can'no stop," Tamilee told him, and he nodded, gasping too much to answer aloud, and forced himself back up to his feet.

She led her friend a bit farther from the battlefield but stopped short, cursing, as the ground fell away into a hidden ravine, so common among the jagged Ayamharas Plateau. She looked for a way down and noted some possibilities— but were they possibilities with Asef slung over Asba's shoulder? Tamilee glanced back at her friends, trying to gauge how much Asef was still bleeding and whether they could find a way down. She turned, expecting to ask Asba his thoughts, but the words got caught in her throat.

They had not escaped.

She saw the lizard-riding invader coming from the side, noting the lizard's tail from behind a tree. It was running straight for Asba. The notion that the attacker hadn't even seen her flashed in her mind.

Asba turned fast and went down low, rolling the groaning Asef off his shoulder and to the ground.

Tamilee leaped forward to intercept. She wouldn't get there, she knew, so, in desperation, she grasped her spear at the base of its long handle and whipped it across like a bat. Her timing was lucky, and perfect, the rider crossing her path just as the spear came swinging around. It didn't hit him hard, and it barely slowed in its swing, but it crossed right at the rider's neck height, its sharp edge slicing through golden-colored skin. The swinging spear followed through to bang against the trunk of the willow, jarring it from Tamilee's hands.

The rider gasped and made a half turn, grabbing at his throat. He kept turning, unintentionally it seemed, and twisted himself right out of the saddle, dropping to the ground on the far side of the still-running lizard.

Tamilee turned, stifling a shout in case other enemies might be about, but horrified as the lizard bore down on Asba, the vicious thing clearly needing no guidance to continue the attack.

Asba darted out to the right, toward the drop, waving his arm and making himself conspicuous—trying to keep the lizard off his brother, Tamilee realized, and that broke her from her shock and had her scrambling for her spear.

She grabbed it up and spun, thinking to throw it, but she sucked in her breath when she saw that she had no time.

For the lizard cut fast and leaped at Asba, who also seemed surprised by its agility.

Through the air it flew, and Asba tried to get aside, stumbling down to one knee along the uneven ground, then trying to bring his spear around to bear on the living missile arching right for him.

Tamilee's desperate expression—Asba's, too—twisted in confusion, though, for the lizard did not descend from the apex of its arc; suddenly it seemed more as if it were floating, not leaping, as if some invisible hand had grabbed it. The lizard began to thrash weirdly in the air, its claws having nothing to grab on to. Thus, it couldn't change its trajectory and just kept floating, past Asba and beyond, out over the drop, far from the declining slope. There it held and hung in the air, managing to look back and hiss viciously at Asba.

Then it fell, just dropped, as if that invisible hand had simply let it go.

Asba turned to Tamilee, who shrugged and shook her head, with nothing to offer. As Asba ran for his brother, she moved to the fallen attacker, towering over him as he lay still on the ground, her spear hovering over his throat.

"Who are you?" she demanded.

The stranger, blue eyes shining out from the edge of brilliant blue on his face, just beyond the central red stripe that encompassed his nose, stared at her hatefully but made no move to respond.

"It's not war paint," Asba said, coming up beside her as she and the stranger just stared at each other. "Tattoo?"

He bent low and shook his head. "No," he said with open disgust. "I don't think so. I . . . I think it's his skin."

"Who are you?" Tamilee insisted.

The prone man tried to say something, some growling curse, it seemed, but the movement had more blood pouring from the wound, which left him scowling hatefully up at her.

"We've got to be away," Asba said to her.

Tamilee returned the fallen stranger's scowl, then drove her spear down, through the fingers over his throat and through his throat, pressing down, leaning on the weapon and rolling her shoulder left and right, twisting the thick, embedded tip.

The stranger thrashed only briefly, then lay shuddering for a few heartbeats, his last heartbeats, before lying very still.

"I know," Tamilee told her friend.

The two exchanged grim nods and Asba ran for his brother, gently lifting Asef into his arms while Tamilee moved back to the drop. She saw the lizard far below, still alive but on its back, thrashing and broken.

She tried to pick a way down, then glanced back as Asba approached.

Asef was bleeding again.

Asef was dying.

"Go!" Asba said to her, and the quiver in his voice told Tamilee that he knew it, too.

It didn't seem possible to Tamilee for them to get Asef down this slope, but she moved down to the first ledge, a jut not far below that allowed her to see Asba's approach and help him down beside her.

Tamilee slipped to the side, bending low, nearly sitting, and using her hands to help her drop to the next ledge. This one was much narrower, and angled, and the loose stones slipped out from under her so much that she only remained upright because she had a firm grasp on the stones above.

She lost her spear, though, and it went sliding, then falling fast down the ravine.

"How do we do this?" Asba asked, unable to find a way to join her.

It wasn't possible. He had to hand Asef down to her, but even that seemed problematic, for the woman had no solid footing down there. He gently rolled Asef down in front of him and took his brother's arms, hoping to stretch him down.

But as Asef stretched, his wound pulled open wider, blood spilling and entrails again showing.

Asef wailed and Asba pushed him down to the ground on

this top ledge. Tamilee rushed over and climbed up as much as she could to aid her wounded friend.

"Leave me, leave me," Asef said over and over, every word forced out through obvious agony.

"No! Never!" said Asba.

"Go! Run!" Asef implored him, summoning the strength to prop himself up on one elbow and grab Asba's collar with his other hand. "Go!"

He fell back almost immediately, groaning, but still whispering, "I'm already dead. Go . . . run."

Tamilee looked at Asba, who stared back in horror as the realization sank in. They couldn't get Asef down this slope.

"We have to find another way," Asba stated, but as he ended, they heard more sounds of approaching enemies, and not far away.

Asba half slid, half ran back across the small ledge and looked back the way they had come. He saw movement, not far away, and started for his spear, but stopped and ducked when the person came into a view. No bright-faced stranger, this one, but an unwelcome sight anyway.

Tamilee crouched by the lower ledge, staring at her friend, who had his back to the wall, looking back at her, sweating profusely and mouthing, *Usgar!*

"Leave me," Asef called out with all the strength he had left, and the effort left him convulsing, blood pumping from his garish wound.

Asba leaped for him, falling to his knees beside his brother.

"Go! You must go!" came a harsh whisper, but not from Asef, not from any of the three companions. Tamilee and Asba glanced up and saw her, straw-colored hair, a head unshaped by swaddle cloths, an Usgar woman, holding one of the cursed tribe's trademark and deadly crystal-tipped spears.

Asba scrambled back to his feet, or started to, for as he

rose, his foot slipped out from under him on the loose dirt and stones, and down he half slid then stumbled.

Tamilee grabbed at him, trying to catch him, but the added weight and her already unsteady footing had both of them sliding down the angled ledge, then dropping hard to the ledge below. The two managed to catch themselves there, scraped and bruised but not badly injured. Together, they looked up, seeing only Asef's feet hanging over the top ledge for a moment, wondering how to get to him. But then they saw the Usgar, popping her head out beside those feet, and then her arm waving at them frantically to flee.

A spear flew over the ledge above her.

Tamilee and Asba had no choice. Down they went, as fast as they could, Tamilee pushing Asba before her, urging him to hurry and not look back. Tamilee did glance back, just once, to see the Usgar woman coming over the top ledge.

She didn't know what to make of any of it.

She knew in her heart, though, that Asef, her friend, her lifelong companion, was certainly dead.

Connebragh realized that she had little time and understood that she should abandon this gravely wounded man.

But she could not.

She told herself that he was just an uamhas, and so what did she care? But she did care. With all of the horror of the last two days, with all of the upheaval and the arrival of these bright-faced monsters, she had nothing. She had no one.

She had to hurry.

She fell into the song of the spear tip again, the same green flecks she had used to heighten the lizard's leap and send it flying out over the ledge. Now she lessened the weight of this fallen uamhas and slid him toward her. She kept her focus strong on the song as he came into her arms, used it to lighten them both, and they slid together, then dropped, but gently, to the third ledge.

But the bright-faced sidhe monsters had arrived, she knew from the sounds high above. They were right up there, soon to look down.

The third ledge had an overhang, and under it went Connebragh and the wounded man. The Usgar woman went to the spear tip once more. She was exhausted, physically and spiritually, but she couldn't fail now. She needed the magic.

She heard the sidhe coming down.

A ball of darkness surrounded Connebragh and the man. He groaned and she slapped her hand over his mouth.

"If you make a sound, we both die," she whispered to him, and she pressed harder to silence him.

She changed tactics immediately, though, and called to a second song in her magical crystal spear tip, the thinnest of the three magics by far. Wedstone was the conduit to access the powers in these spears, and it was also the stone of healing. Connebragh brought it forth with all she could manage, at the same time maintaining the darkness globe.

The wounded man calmed and quieted almost immediately.

Connebragh focused, holding her breath. She could sense them above.

Then they were right before her, out on the third ledge! She heard them, not two steps away, a pair, at least, with more above.

She felt the man tense up—he sensed them, too, she knew.

But he stayed quiet, and she stayed quiet, and somehow, beyond what she thought her limits, she held fast to the magical song. Desperation overcame exhaustion. With her life so obviously on the line here, Connebragh found strength she did not know she possessed.

She held on.

The bright-faced monsters moved away.

Soon after, the magical darkness faded. Connebragh,

barely able to summon the strength to move, crept out of the overhang just enough to look around.

All was quiet.

Behind her, the uamhas groaned.

Connebragh sighed. He would surely die, she thought. She had no strength left, and the healing magic in this spear tip was minor, only minor. She thought of leaving then, of going far from this dying place.

But no. Connebragh shook her head in defiance and crawled back in beside the man. She inspected his wound. She tucked his guts back in.

Then she fell over him, demanding of the spear.

She wasn't sure if she was doing this to save the man's life or simply to deny the bright-faced monsters the kill.

It didn't matter. She went at that wound with purpose and anger.

"So I'll bury him, then," Asba growled back, and Tamilee backed away. "I'm not leaving my brother for the vultures."

Tamilee understood and didn't want to upset her friend any more than they both already were. They had spent a sleepless night hiding in the forest, invaders all about for half of it, and even after they had left the area, neither could find any rest.

Not with Asef lying back here. Not with Asef likely dead.

They crept back to the base of the gully and ducked low. For they saw her up there, the Usgar, on the top ledge, her back to them as she peered back to the east over the side of the gully.

Asba took up his spear determinedly. She was too far for a throw, some forty feet above them at least, but he sorted his way and started off quietly, Tamilee right behind.

Up they crept, almost close enough to throw a spear into the Usgar's back, watching her.

She shook her head and turned back, then saw them, saw

Asba lift his spear and let fly. He missed badly, the missile striking the ledge below the woman.

Tamilee ran past him, long-striding, jumping, determined to get to the enemy before she could properly set herself. To the third ledge from the top Tamilee jumped, rushing.

Then skidded to a stop.

For there, before her, feet toward her, lay Asef.

Up above, the woman began to cry. "I tried," she pleaded. "I tried, but I . . ."

Tamilee scrambled up and fell to her friend's side, with Asba closing a short way behind her. She inspected the wound and saw that it was closed, the skin knitted but still swollen and purple. She moved to Asef's face, calling to her friend, begging him to answer.

He was cold.

He was dead.

Tamilee let out a wail. She had expected this, of course, but having it so real before her had proven too much for the shocked and battered woman.

Behind her, Asba made the ledge, growling in denial.

"I tried," the Usgar said above them. "My magic . . . it couldn't . . ."

Asba jumped up and slapped his hand over the second ledge, grabbing his spear.

Above him, the Usgar woman sank to the ground, sobbing.

Asba moved to throw, but Tamilee grabbed him by the arm. "Usgar magic," she said, urgently motioning to the body lying under the overhang, to the revealed wound, which had obviously been closed, somewhat, with magic.

"I think she tried," Tamilee whispered.

Asba rushed past her to fall over his brother. Tamilee stepped out to confront the Usgar woman.

"Who are you?"

"Connebra—"

"Why are you here?"

"All dead," the woman answered. "They killed all. The bright-faced sidhe demons."

"Demons like the Usgar!" Tamilee answered.

The woman slumped pitifully. It seemed to Tamilee as if her backbone just melted as she rolled her shoulders and face forward to fall into her hands, and there she bobbed with sobs.

Tamilee gripped her spear more tightly. She even lifted it as if to throw it into the woman—she could have killed this one easily at that moment.

She lowered the spear.

Asba came out beside her, his face red and puffy, tears streaking his cheeks. He looked up at the Usgar, then back to Tamilee, who slowly shook her head.

"Come down here, then," Asba barked up at her. "Come down and tell us all, or we'll stick you with our spears and yank you down and kill you."

The woman moved slowly, like a broken thing. She unwound and straightened her back just enough to slide forward, hugging her spear close. She went over the ledge and half fell, half floated to the one below, then again seemed to float and slide to the lip and over, coming down right before Tamilee and Asba, with Asef lying dead behind her.

"I tried," she said through sniffles and tears. "All night. I could not. I could not."

3

OVERCOMING REPUTATION

"We'd have to stay near the lake," Talmadge told Aydrian, the two out ahead of the refugee group, which had moved fully off the Ayamharas Plateau earlier that morning. Scouting out in front now, Aydrian and Talmadge had traveled past the foothills east of their descent to come to the banks of the wide lake that had been formed by the fissure cut through the mountains. It stretched far to the south of their position and out of sight to the east.

"There's no cover," said Aydrian. He ran his fingers through his curly black hair, then cupped them over his eyes and peered to the east.

"But there is food and water, and we'll need both to get this many across the desert," Talmadge replied. He was taller than Aydrian, but much lankier, and nowhere near as formidable as the exiled king of Honce-the-Bear. Aydrian wasn't wearing his brilliant breastplate now, but he was still far thicker than Talmadge, with muscles tight from years of rigorous training. "But I understand your concerns," the frontiersman added. "Were it just we two . . ."

Aydrian turned to regard him. "If they spy us along the lakeside and come out, where might we run?"

"They'll have a long way to get to us, though."

"A long way for a flying dragon?"

Talmadge had no answer to Aydrian's question.

"Perhaps we should not have let the Usgar witch take the farseeing crystal," Aydrian added. "It would be good to look back on our enemies, and good to see if the far side of this new lake empties into a river that might afford us passage."

"Aoleyn will return," Talmadge insisted, and looked back up at the towering plateau. "She has to."

Aydrian stared at the man, locking his gaze, and gave a slight nod. "If you trust in her, I trust in her," he said. "I hope she will return soon. It would be good to know." He turned back the way they had come and added resignedly, "We cannot wait."

Aoleyn stayed mostly low, more in a series of nearly weightless hops using the malachite stone than the actual flight offered by her moonstone. The descent from the northern rim of the chasm seemed obvious enough at first, but with trails splitting many times as she moved down the mountainside.

She feared she might lose the trail, and feared even worse. She kept telling herself that she had been gone more than a full day and so her friends could be far along, but that didn't much help her anxiety here. If they had been caught and killed, Aoleyn would be alone, truly alone. Only then did the young woman feel the weight of that possibility, terrifying and chilling.

Those thoughts stayed with her and grew heavier with each stride. Where were they?

"No signs of battle," she whispered, but her litany sounded hollow to her. She had seen the enemy, so many, so fierce. She had seen their god, and the dragon upon which he rode.

She paused at one high point, glancing desperately to the north, to the east, even back to the west. "Where are you?" she whispered.

It was a good question. Aoleyn pulled a small implement from her pouch. She held it up and called to its magic, peering through it, sending her vision far and wide. First to the west, then around to the north, and finally to the east, to the base of the mountain plateau.

Aoleyn breathed a sigh of great relief when she at last came in sight of the refugee band, nestled among the boulders at the base of the mountains, already down at the level of the desert.

She replaced the implement and called to her green malachite and her moonstone, running with great leaps, sometimes flying, taking a straight line toward the camp instead of the winding trails the refugees would have had to walk around the many broken ravines and boulders. Still, they had made great progress, and Aoleyn expected that her friend Talmadge had led the way.

She went down to the ground, back to walking, as she came upon the last straight run to the camp. She didn't need to flaunt Usgar magic to the uamhas, certainly. Her unstretched skull was enough to keep her dangerously distanced from them already.

She walked into the camp tentatively, head down, glancing about only enough to make sure the scowls didn't turn into dangerous action. There were no Usgar here, and only three others who were not of the lake tribes. And there was a fourth, a young man she at last spotted, whose head had not been elongated in infancy.

"Bahdlahn," she breathed, rushing for him, and how his face brightened when he saw her, his arms going wide to catch her and draw her in for a great hug.

"I thought you would return before the night," he said breathlessly. "I thought . . . I feared . . ."

"Shh," Aoleyn implored him, putting her finger over his lips. "I had much to do." As she spoke, Aoleyn looked past Bahdlahn to another woman who was not of the tribes, though she had lived with the lakemen for some time. Using her hands to claw along the ground, the dark-skinned, black-haired woman forced her roller board across the broken ground.

"Talmadge will be glad to see you," the woman, Khotai, said. "And if you've half the power he says you have, I guess we're all glad you've returned."

Aoleyn grinned as she looked down at Khotai, someone she had not forgotten during her time in the caves. Outwardly, and to those who did not know her, Khotai seemed a pitiful thing, with one leg bitten off by the monster in the lake and the other rendered useless. Now her hands, too, seemed broken things, from all her clawing about the ground in the years since the attack.

The return look from the woman was not a reflection of Aoleyn's mirth, though, but a frown, and Aoleyn realized that Khotai believed her smile to be condescending, as she looked down on the crippled woman.

Aoleyn quickly fished about her pack, seeking specific crystals, turning the opening to catch the sunlight so she could see the colors of the flecks. She brought a small armful up, clutched them close, and closed her eyes, hearing the song of Usgar.

"Ah, Usgar witch!" one nearby woman yelled, scrambling away so frantically that she fell right over. Others took up the call.

Aoleyn ignored them, focusing on the song. She opened her eyes and held her hand out to Khotai, who, along with Bahdlahn, was staring at her curiously.

Khotai looked at the offered hand.

"Take it," Aoleyn said.

Khotai's eyes narrowed.

"Please?" Aoleyn begged, and she moved the hand a bit.

Never releasing Aoleyn from her gaze, Khotai gingerly reached up and grasped Aoleyn's hand.

Khotai rose, floating up, her remaining leg unwinding below her. And there she was, standing, or seeming to stand, though her leg below her found no solid placement on the ground. Gasps arose all around the two women, though not from Bahdlahn, who merely smiled widely, not surprised by any miracles Aoleyn might enact.

"Bahdlahn," Aoleyn said, though she kept looking at Khotai, "find me a blanket that we can make into a dress, and two straps of leather, two belts."

"What do you mean to do?" Khotai quietly asked her.

"I mean to make you a belt with these crystals I hold. One that will give you the power to do this for yourself."

"Do not tease me . . ."

"Follow with me," Aoleyn said, and she took a step aside.

Khotai twitched her leg, and she floated along, settling right beside the woman.

"Hurry, Bahdlahn!" Aoleyn called after the young man, who was already off into the crowd.

Aoleyn led the way for a bit, Khotai easily pacing her, then she bade Khotai to lead, and the woman did.

"If this doesn't work as you're promising, I'll have your head," the fierce To-gai-ru woman warned, but confident Aoleyn only smiled in return.

Aydrian and Talmadge noted the commotion when they came in sight of the refugee camp. They exchanged a concerned look and picked up their pace, side by side, jogging the rest of the way up the last slope to the gathering. Both grew more alarmed, their expressions tightening, when they heard the word *witch* being thrown about.

"What did you bring to us, Talmadge, you fool?" one man called. He even started for Talmadge, quite threateningly, but a strong woman grabbed him by the arm and pulled him back as she stepped up before him.

"It's good that you're back," Catriona of Fasach Crann greeted him.

"What is the trouble?"

"Your Usgar friend, Aoleyn, has returned," Catriona explained, glancing back. "She displays her magic."

"It is the same as my own," Aydrian answered, his command of the regional language growing quite strong now. "The magic which healed so many of your people. The magic that allowed me to walk out to the capsized boat, to—"

"You are not Usgar," Catriona curtly interrupted. She turned her attention right back to Talmadge. "Come and see."

She led the two through the clusters of people, around the strewn boulders of the small plateau, then within a ring of onlookers, who stood shoulder to shoulder.

There sat Aoleyn and Khotai, with Khotai fastening the last ties of a makeshift skirt and Aoleyn weaving a line of some thin material through a pair of leather straps, fastening them together into a double-thick strap.

"Khotai?" Talmadge asked.

The woman looked up at him, offered an unusually sheepish smile, and held up her hand to keep him back.

"Now?" she asked Aoleyn.

Aoleyn ran the tie, a wire of wedstone like those she had used to fashion her own jewelry, back through the two leather straps, then up and over to tightly bind them together. After a quick look at the completed belt, she leaned forward to help fasten it about Khotai's waist.

"I'm no witch," the woman whispered into Aoleyn's ear when they came very close together.

"You do'no have to be," Aoleyn quietly replied. "You'll feel the magic and hear the song. Just tell it what you want it to do."

Aoleyn leaned back and fastened the belt in front. "This

will hurt a bit," she warned, lifting Khotai's shirt to reveal her belly button.

That was the place, Aoleyn knew from her own experience. Of all the jewelry fastened to her flesh through wedstone wires, that one was the most omnipresent, as it was attached to her very life energy. She pierced Khotai's navel, enacting a bit of healing within the wedstone wire to heal the wound about it as she stitched Khotai to her belt.

Khotai's expression changed. Aoleyn understood that she was indeed hearing the magic song.

"Close your eyes," Aoleyn said, and she shifted back, then stood up and stepped back. "Just tell it what you would have it do."

"Aoleyn, what—" Talmadge started to ask, but Aoleyn hushed him.

He said nothing more, but gasped indeed, his eyes going wide, his mouth hanging open, as Khotai lifted from the ground, floating up to stand on her one twisted leg. She rocked back and forth for a moment and Talmadge made a move toward her, but Aoleyn held him back with an outstretched arm.

Khotai steadied and stared at Aoleyn, her face beaming.

"How long?" she asked.

"Until you're tired," Aoleyn replied. "If you even grow tired." Aoleyn stepped forward and put her hands on Khotai's shoulders, staring the woman right in the eye. "Your days on the ground are over, my friend."

Khotai's smile broke then, as she tried to respond. No words came forth, though, just tears, and she fell into Aoleyn's arms.

"It will work forever," Aoleyn whispered to her, promising her.

The gathering didn't know how to react. Villagers turned to each other and shrugged, stared, some laughing, some crying, some shaking their heads, though whether in disbelief, denial, anger, or some combination of all of those emotions, none seemed to know.

Bahdlahn began a cheer for Aoleyn, which was met with a tepid response. Talmadge rushed to Khotai, the woman he loved.

"You seem unsurprised," Catriona said to Aydrian, who was outwardly reacting the least of anyone to the remarkable events.

"You cannot begin to understand the magic of the eastern lands," he told the woman. "Both in spell and in item. The magic of my sword or breastplate, the gems that allowed me to walk across the water. I am surprised that one such as this Usgar woman, who is not of the Abellican Church or not of the elves, has found such affinity to the gemstones, but not surprised at all at what those magical stones have accomplished here. The magic is powerful, Catriona of Fasach Crann."

"Powerful enough to stop *them*?" the woman asked, glancing up toward the mountains beside them, to the conquered Ayamharas Plateau.

"We shall see," Aydrian replied. "I fear that we shall *have* to see."

The refugee band set off soon after, moving along the northern bank of the new lake. Aydrian used Talmadge's quartz crystal to scan behind to the continuing waterfall, running much thinner now, as it fed the new and vast lake. He scanned ahead to the eastern shores and discovered a small river running away from the lake, running east.

"The crossing will be easier along the lakeshore," he told Catriona and the others. "We've water and food to get us across the desert to lands Talmadge and Khotai know well, and from there we'll be long away from the invaders."

"If they do'no catch us," the woman replied.

Aydrian had no answer for that.

"They won't catch us," Aoleyn replied from a few ranks back in the procession. "And if they try, they'll be sorry for the choice."

Even the lake folk who didn't trust her, who harbored hatred for her because she was Usgar, nodded at her declaration.

Aydrian was glad of that. He looked to Khotai, who was already moving smoothly, effortlessly pacing the others, and who could easily outrun them now with that curious step-and-glide motion offered by the magical belt Aoleyn had fashioned. Even with her singular twisted and damaged limb, the one-legged woman was able to plant that foot and push away enough to cover twenty strides in her nearly weightless hop.

Between that, Aoleyn's continuing work with the healing stone, and Khotai's determined declaration, Aoleyn was breaking down the hatred, certainly.

That gave Aydrian hope.

Not hope for Aoleyn, for he was confident that the woman would find her way through this turbulent uprooting, but for himself. Aydrian knew what he had to do, and he could easily enough guess what resistance he would face in Ursal from King Midalis, and even more from the Abellican Church.

It occurred to him quite often that he would be walking to his death by going back there. His exile had offered no leeway in its conditions: He was never to return to Honce-the-Bear, under penalty of death.

Even though he was bearing the tidings of such potential danger in the west, Aydrian feared that those terms would not be ignored.

So be it.

They set camp along the lakeshore, not far from the plateau's foothills, for they could not safely continue in the dark. Catriona allowed no torches, no lights at all, though Aoleyn was able to use her ruby ring to warm up stones for the camp and keep the folk comfortable against the nighttime desert chill.

Also, as she had promised, Aoleyn's work with Khotai was not yet finished. She used her healing powers on the woman's damaged right hand, but the left proved more problematic, for the years of crawling had twisted her ligaments and reshaped her fingers.

"I can fix it," she told Khotai. "But it will hurt, perhaps as much pain as you've ever known."

"Oh, don't you doubt that I've known lots of pain, friend," Khotai replied, throwing a wink to Talmadge as she spoke. "Got one leg bitten off and the other shattered by a lake monster that now seems to be a dragon."

Aoleyn laughed and nodded.

"When?" Khotai asked.

"Whenever you're ready," Aoleyn replied.

"Now," the woman answered, without hesitation and without a single tremor in her voice.

Aoleyn motioned to Talmadge and Aydrian. "Give her something to bite on, and hold her tight."

"Are you sure?" Bahdlahn whispered to Aoleyn, for she had told him his role.

"Have you stopped trusting me already?" she replied, drawing a nod and a smile from the young man.

"As soon as he strikes, use whatever healing you can summon," Aoleyn reminded Aydrian, who was wearing his gem-studded breastplate for just this occasion, and he, too, replied with a nod.

The two men held Khotai tightly, her ruined left hand out to the side. Talmadge grasped her forearm tightly to keep it over a flat stone that Aoleyn had chosen for this event.

Bahdlahn carefully set a second flat stone atop the hand.

Aoleyn put her hand on her hip, over her largest and strongest wedstone, and fell into the song. When the notes rang true and strong, she looked up and motioned to Bahdlahn, and the young man, who had spent the last months working the stones of a stairway far up the side of Fireach Speuer, a man whose muscles had been honed by endless days of chopping and shaping and carrying stone, brought a hammer up over his head and snapped it down with frightening power and accuracy atop the stone that lay atop Khotai's hand.

The woman bit and growled and howled, her bones shattering.

Aydrian sent her healing magic from the soul stones in his breastplate.

Aoleyn attacked her pain with a powerful wave of warmth and healing, using the same type of stone, a hematite, which she knew as a wedstone.

It went on for many heartbeats before Khotai had calmed enough to spit out the leather bit they had given her to chomp.

Talmadge and Aydrian let her go.

"Aye, that hurt," she admitted to Aoleyn. "Oh, but that hurt."

"And now?" Aoleyn asked.

Khotai smiled easily.

"Do'no move," Aoleyn bade her, and she motioned for the three men to leave them, then continued the healing for a long, long while. When she had finished, she carefully wrapped the hand tight with cloth, using sticks to keep the fingers straight.

"Do'no try to use it," she bade Khotai.

"How long?"

"Soon," Aoleyn promised.

To Khotai's surprise, Aoleyn then reached down and unfastened the magical belt, freeing it.

"You'll see," she promised and moved away. "Just rest—try to sleep. You'll be getting it back in the morning."

"A problem?" There was no missing the concern in Khotai's voice. She had been given back her mobility only that same day, and it was clear that any hint that she might be losing it again terrified her.

"No, but I've an idea. You'll see," Aoleyn promised, her voice upbeat.

When Khotai awoke the next morning, Aoleyn gave her back the belt. It felt much the same, and she rose easily and in balance.

"I will heal the hand again as we move," Aoleyn told her.

"What about the belt?"

"It is the same for walking," Aoleyn said, a mischievous grin spreading wide. "But now you can walk across the water, if you choose."

Khotai giggled nervously. "Across the water? Atop the water?"

Aoleyn nodded, grinning widely.

"I owe you my life, Aoleyn of Usgar."

"And I owe Talmadge mine, and Talmadge owes his to Khotai," Aoleyn replied. "I would say that we're all the better for our debts."

Not far away, Aydrian overheard the conversation, and he found himself agreeing with the sentiment. All the world was better off with such debts, he mused.

He thought of his own history, of his time with Marcalo De'Unnero and the evil road he had walked, the demon dactyl strong within him.

He was free now of that vile presence, an entity that had been injected into his spirit when he was not yet even born, a demonic influence that had been exploited by bad men to horrific ends.

Alas, though, Aydrian could not forgive himself his history.

He had to hope that King Midalis and Father Abbot

Braumin Herde could forgive him, though, at least enough to heed his warnings, for he simply did not believe that these bright-faced invaders meant to stop at the mountain plateau. They had come from the west, and their road of conquest was almost certainly east.

East lay Honce-the-Bear and a million innocents.

4

FLIGHT AND FIGHT

He was alone. Hanging, swaying, with only his reflection in the mirror to keep him company, other than the occasional guard who came in to replace the torches.

They wouldn't give Egard darkness. They wouldn't even afford him that dignity. They wanted him to see himself in that golden mirror, hanging there helplessly. They wanted him to witness his every attempt to bend his arm enough to try, futilely, to grab at one of the hooks stabbed into his upper arm. They wanted him to see the grimace of agony on his face every time frustration overcame him and made him thrash about, trying, again futilely and pitifully, to tear himself enough on those hooks that he would simply fall.

Their lack of any recognition of him, as if he mattered not at all, might have been the worst of all for the captured Usgar warrior. When the last guard entered with new torches, Egard had screamed and pleaded, threatened and twisted almost all the way around, before the pain drove him back to face the mirror, to hang limply with agonized exhaustion.

That guard hadn't even turned his red and blue face up to glance at Egard, hadn't even started in the slightest at the bellows of the tortured man.

They didn't even care.

Except for one occasional visitor. Except for the priest whose face was half skull, who leered at him over his shoulder and then tortured and violated him more profoundly than any physical implement could ever hope to achieve.

Whenever that skull appeared in the mirror, Egard knew what was coming. The creature stared through the eyeholes of its skull mask, locked its reflected gaze with Egard's, and invaded his very soul through those eyes.

The violation was beyond Egard's darkest fears, a complete stripping of his soul and his thoughts, his very identity, everything that made him Egard, laid bare for the pickings of this monstrous creature. And in those moments of forced and brutal intimacy, the priest tickled him with terror, gave back to Egard images horrible and horrifying.

The demon priest took pleasure in taking from him his secrets, his fears, his failings, and then took greater pleasure in turning all of that personal knowledge back against him.

When the interrogations—no, more than interrogations; these were mental, emotional, and spiritual scourings— were finished, when the priest had extracted as much as he could garner, he would leave Egard alone to hang painfully for a few more hours. But only after promising to use the information Egard had provided against everything that Egard held dear.

"Kill me," Egard whispered after this most recent invasion of his soul.

For once, surprisingly, the priest responded. "No," he said, in Egard's own language, a language he had stolen from the Usgar prisoner. "You are not empty yet. Once you are hollowed out, then you may die."

And he walked away, uncaring. And Egard hung his head and hoped to die.

"Beyond your pleasure, what purpose do you see in this?" Tuolonatl asked High Priest Pixquicauh when the old augur exited the prison. Unlike the man she addressed, Tuolonatl carried no formal title, though many called her *cochcal*, a rank recognizing her as the general of the xoconai forces. She didn't need it. The middle-aged woman was known to every living xoconai the length and breadth of the combined xoconai nation of Tonoloya. She led the elite mundunugu cavalry, the highest warrior caste of the bright-faced people, deadly warriors astride their collared cuetzpali mounts. As the God King Scathmizzane had chosen the old augur to serve as the high priest, his mortal voice among the people, so too had he chosen Tuolonatl to lead this glorious march of the xoconai nation to its promised restoration, a Greater Tonoloya in which the sun would rise over one sea and set over the other. They would march east until the land itself ended.

There could have been no other reasonable choice to lead the armies. While the xoconai had many heroes, none shone as brightly as Tuolonatl.

However, the old augur, now called High Priest Pixquicauh, wished his Glorious Gold had picked someone else. He found Tuolonatl insufferable and irreligious.

"You do not think it important that we gather as much knowledge of our enemies as we can?" he asked the woman.

"There are better ways to interrogate. Ingratiate, make of them friends, earn of them their trust. Then they will tell you so much more."

Pixquicauh snorted and thought her terribly naive. He wondered how someone so soft could have risen to such a lofty perch among the fierce mundunugu.

"It is tried and true," she answered.

"I speak their language," the old augur boasted. "Do you?"

He saw that he had put her back on her heels with that revelation, and that made him glad. He wasn't lying. Scathmizzane's golden mirror had allowed him deep into the thoughts of the captured man, and those thoughts were translated as they were discovered and scoured, giving the old augur the man's language as fully as if he had been speaking it his entire life.

Another miracle of Glorious Gold!

"And I need not search to determine if what he tells me is truth or falsehood," Pixquicauh added. "He has no place to hide from me. If he thinks to deceive in his answers, then I hear him thinking that."

"So you need to hang him on hooks?"

"The torment weakens him. It makes my task easier. Does that bother you, great Tuolonatl? To learn that the edicts of Scathmizzane are made easier?"

The woman scowled and, in that pose, wrinkles showed about her eyes and tightened lips, a reminder of her age. Few would think her near to fifty, Pixquicauh realized more fully, when he looked upon that scowl. Her muscles remained firm, her movements full of the grace associated with youth, her hair still thick, her face still carrying a measure of youthful luster and innocence, despite the indisputable fact that this woman had slain scores of enemies.

"It is curious to me that you care so deeply," he said. "Are the tales of your bloody macana untrue? Is the pile of javelins celebrating the kills of Tuolonatl an exaggeration?"

"You will not bait me, High Priest," she said. "We together serve Scathmizzane, the Glorious Gold, the God King who rides Kithkukulikhan. By his blessing are we given our place."

"Then you should remember yours, and remember mine," Pixquicauh scolded, hardly believing her claim of devotion. "I will empty the human, the child of Cizinfozza, and when I am done with him, I will sacrifice him, that his spirit may feed the power of Scathmizzane." He led the woman's gaze to the north, to the rim of the chasm that held the sacred xoconai city of Otontotomi, now reclaimed from the waters that had covered it for centuries. The xoconai had taken hundreds of prisoners, and now they worked, cleaning the stairs and removing the sediment that had settled on the structures, repairing the buildings, polishing the gold.

Thousands of xoconai worked, too, but not like the slave humans, their every wrong move responded to with the crack of a whip.

"They will be worked to their deaths," he told Tuolonatl, savoring every word because he sensed that the notion bothered her more than a little. Pixquicauh enjoyed Tuolonatl's apparent weakness, as it reinforced his own belief and desire that he, not she, was the prime subject of Scathmizzane's court. "And their spirits will be summoned up the slopes of Tzatzini to the crystal symbol of Glorious Gold, and there the humans' own sisters, once their witches, will usher them to the belly of Scathmizzane. Their bodies will be broken in life, their souls will be eaten in death. Does this bother you?"

"It is not just the souls of the humans," she whispered in reply.

It was true enough, Pixquicauh, of course, knew. The xoconai who had fallen in the fight were also given to Scathmizzane, of course!

"I cannot imagine a more glorious service to the God King," he said. He added, in a tone heavily edged in accusation, "Can you?"

Tuolonatl didn't respond, and the old augur could see the conflict within her. She wasn't going to speak out against the edicts of Scathmizzane, but they horrified her. The passage from life to death and from death to ingestion by their God King was something that many people could think about positively only when it was a distant prayer.

Now that prayer had become reality, brutal reality, and for people like Tuolonatl, for all of her battle prowess and ferocity, witnessing that glorious truth was no easy spectacle.

The old augur smiled but did well to suppress his laughter. She couldn't answer him—what could she say?

He was the chosen of Scathmizzane. She was being used as the tip of Scathmizzane's spear. Would she even survive the war?

Pixquicauh hoped she would not.

Tuolonatl lingered about the long stairway leading down the gorge that housed the ancient xoconai city of Otontotomi. In only a couple of days, the work down below was beginning to show remarkable process. The xoconai had several hundred slaves, but it was more due to the efforts of the forty thousand xoconai warriors working tirelessly to reclaim the beauty and grandeur of Otontotomi.

And working, too, to quickly make the city self-supporting, the most critical factor if the xoconai were to press eastward. Right down along this staircase of more than two thousand steps before her, Tuolonatl saw the progress: the stairs fully cleared and squared, the temporary rope railings already in place, with more permanent safeguards already under construction.

For all her misgivings expressed to the high priest, the xoconai cochcal could not help being prideful and pleased by the discipline of her forces. Far down the staircase, three large boats descended. The xoconai were assembling and organizing a fleet from the craft procured from the lake towns. The next morning would see many fishing boats on the new lake, and others sailing to the banks to map and note the currents and winds.

Already. In just a couple of days.

Tuolonatl signaled to one of her attendants, who rushed over with her cuetzpali, the reptilian mount, already saddled and waiting. She noted that the young woman handler seemed quite eager here, as if she knew something Tuolonatl did not.

Tuolonatl hopped into her seat gracefully and sent the lizard running down the long staircase. She wasn't fond of riding these collared lizards, with their side-to-side swaying, but she had to admit that, in going downhill, particularly in a steep decline along steps such as these, the lizards, with their low center and sticky padded feet, were much handier than horses.

Her handler followed close behind on a second mount, with a horn in hand, one she blew whenever they neared someone lower on the stairs. Without hesitation, those xoconai, even the teams handling the heavy and awkward boats, rushed aside to let the great Tuolonatl pass unhindered—after all, any little thing she needed to do was far more important than anything they might do.

The day was warm, the sun bright, and the lizard's energy levels high, so the great mundunugu warrior made the floor of the chasm in short order. She headed for the massive central pyramid of Otontotomi, part temple, part city hall, where both the high priest and the city sovereign of this recovered city, if one was appointed, would reside and hold court. Tuolonatl suspected that Scathmizzane himself would take his place within.

"Great cochcal, pray hold," the handler behind Tuolonatl said, surprising her. She pulled up the reins, drawing a hiss from the cuetzpali, and swung about in her seat to note the trailing rider, who directed her gaze to a sand mound beside another of the structures, which had nearly been reclaimed.

Tuolonatl didn't understand the significance at first, until a handsome young mundunugu walked out around that mound, one whom Tuolonatl surely recognized.

She began to hail Ataquixt, the man she had named as her lead scout, a man she had come to consider a friend and, if she managed to find her way, a lover, too. Before she got the

name out, though, Ataquixt tugged on a bridle he held, and
from around the mound of sand came another dear friend,
perhaps Tuolonatl's dearest friend of all.

"Pocheoya," the woman said, bursting into a happy giggle
at the sight of the brown and white, blue-eyed pinto horse,
its proud brown shield patch covering the muscled chest. Pocheoya was not tall, not fifteen hands, even, but could run
with the finest horses of Tonoloya. And, low to the ground
and so very strong, Pocheoya could outmaneuver and out-
muscle any in the barrel races, when guided by the skilled
hand of Tuolonatl.

In contrast to any other horse she had known, and certainly compared to the stupid cuetzpali lizards, Tuolonatl
never felt as if she was Pocheoya's master. When she was on
this one's broad back, they were more than master and beast,
more than a team, even. It was almost as if they became a
singular being, each understanding the other so very well.

"How did you get him down that mountain and to Otontotomi so quickly?" she asked Ataquixt as he approached with
the horse. Tuolonatl handed him her cuetzpali's reins as he
handed Pocheoya's to her.

"I knew you wanted him," Ataquixt answered, smiling,
seeming quite happy at giving Tuolonatl such obvious pleasure.

"Ataquixt was up all night and took great care in sneak-
ing Pocheoya past you in the village at the rim," the female
attendant explained.

Tuolonatl smiled warmly at her lead scout, who shrugged
rather adorably, she thought. The woman's gaze lingered
longer than she intended, caught by the beauty of Ataquixt's
face. There was something about it, she thought, about the
way the colors mixed. His nose was bright red, but not near
the base. There it faded to pink, and then to an almost yellowish small line before being met by the blue skin on either side. She imagined him lying on his side in the early
morning, looking back at her, and she thought that his face,

either half, might resemble the softening colors of sunrise or sunset.

His colorful face softened in the morning light, he would be quite beautiful.

There was something else, too, that had her studying this young warrior. He had expressed such eagerness for the war, shouting encouragement to the other scouts, promising glory, but Tuolonatl sensed a conflict within him, as within herself. She had no doubt that the eastward march of the xoconai would better the world, but she was not eager for the puddles of blood through which they would march.

She wondered if the same reservations niggled at Ataquixt.

Ataquixt offered his cupped hands to help Tuolonatl up into Pocheoya's saddle, then moved over and climbed atop the cuetzpali she had been riding.

"To canahuac?"

Tuolonatl looked at him slyly. "Canahuac or tepachoni?" she asked. "Temple or governing hall?"

"Canahuac," Ataquixt said without hesitation. "Scathmizzane is there in the great pyramid. It is his place, and he fills it with his augurs. The sovereigns have not been invited, other than singular audiences at his demand."

Tuolonatl settled lower on Pocheoya, falling within herself as she tried to sort through the implications of Ataquixt's revelation. She knew well from previous experiences that there would be a push-pull between the augurs and the more secular sovereigns who ruled the great cities of Tonoloya, for the goals of the augurs were often not in alignment with pragmatic governance. It made sense to her that the augurs would be gaining in this eternal struggle—their God King had come to them, after all—but hearing it so clearly now shook her more than she would have expected.

"Perhaps we should go first to the ixnecia," she said, turning her horse to the east, to face the great fissure that had been cut into the mountains.

She started along the eastern-running boulevard at an easy pace, looking left and right with every stride to take in the progress of reclaiming the city, which was going on all about her. Still quite far away, though, Tuolonatl caught a flash of light from up high, on the right side of the ixnecia, then another, lower down, then responding flashes from the left wall of the giant fissure.

She hadn't been expecting the signals and so didn't register them quickly enough to properly decode or even count the short and long flickers from the signal mirrors reflecting the sunlight, but she knew enough to realize that something important was going on over there.

She urged Pocheoya into a trot, then a canter, the lizards of her two companions struggling to keep up.

By the time they arrived, they found quite a gathering on the right-hand side of the mountain river that ran along the southeastern rim of the chasm, flowing out through the base of the ixnecia and into the great and wide lake beyond. The xoconai had already built a bridge over that river, but it wasn't yet fortified or widened enough to bring a horse across. Tuolonatl dismounted and motioned for Ataquixt to join her and for the handler to hold the mounts.

On the large, flat rock at the other side of the bridge, every xoconai bent the knee when they noted the identity of the woman hustling to join them.

"What do we know?" Tuolonatl asked Zhorivemba, a veteran and scarred mundunugu she recognized as the leader of this company.

He pointed out through the fissure and out over the lake to the northeast. "Runners," he answered. "Children of Cizinfozza. A large band it would seem."

"How large?"

"They are too far to know, Great Cochcal Tuolonatl," Zhorivemba answered.

"I would know."

Zhorivemba nodded. "I and mine will ride." He began

motioning to his commanders to gather the cuetzpali and form up.

"It will take you days to catch them, if you can even quickly locate the trail they used to climb down from the plateau," Tuolonatl said.

"But we will catch them," answered the man, who was about Tuolonatl's age.

Tuolonatl said, "No," even as she tried to sort through this new development. For some reason, the idea of a mundunugu brigade charging out from the captured plateau seemed reckless to her. How far would they be from Otontotomi when they at last caught up to the fleeing humans? How far from supplies and reinforcements?

"The humans are running in the belief that we are unstoppable," she said, thinking out loud to draw the others into her planning. "In a matter of a day, all that they knew was swept from them, including the lake they thought of as their home. This is a good message to let them carry to the other villages, wherever those might be. Their fear will be our advantage."

"Then we will let some continue and only kill half," Zhorivemba declared.

His words sounded so wretchedly bloodthirsty to Tuolonatl, like a last and desperate attempt to allow him to cover his macana in blood, for no reason other than him wanting to do so.

"No," she stated again, and she glanced back to the southeast, to the great stair descending to Otontotomi, and to the captured boats being carried down.

"We sail after them?" Ataquixt asked, noting her expression.

Tuolonatl smiled. "Scare them, keep them running," she reasoned. "Then track them secretly, from the shadows. Let them lead us to the next villages."

Ataquixt grinned widely. He hailed from the westernmost reaches of the xoconai nation, from a city that watched the sunset each night from the very edge of the great ocean. Tu-olonatl knew this, of course.

"You can sail by the stars," she stated more than asked.

"Here? On a calm lake beneath an open sky?" Ataquixt replied with a laugh.

"One ship, thirty warriors, no cuetzpali," Tuolonatl told him, but then she quickly corrected herself. "One cuetzpali. Only one, for my trusted scout alone."

Ataquixt nodded solemnly. He wasn't simply leading the mission; he would be the mundunugu entrusted with guiding the next march of the xoconai. As he had led them here, to Tzatzini and Otontotomi, so too would his eyes guide them eastward, ever eastward, until they watched the sun rise out of the other ocean. Ataquixt believed in the mission of a Greater Tonoloya. The xoconai were good, and they would bring light to the world. Though greatly skilled in battle, he didn't enjoy the killing.

"For a better world," he reminded himself.

That very sunset, the industrious xoconai had a boat set-tled upon the shores of the new lake, and the handpicked crew, all loyal to Tuolonatl, set off, sails wide and full of a favorable southeastern wind.

Ataquixt remained at the prow, steering, peering, watch-ing. He set others all about with long poles, feeling for the bottom, for the lake was not deep. This had been a desert only two days before, after all, and the deep, deep waters of what the humans had called Loch Beag had spread far and wide.

But it was deep enough, and rocks large enough to threaten the boat were few and far between.

The winds blew strong, the prow kicked up white spray, and soon after the night had passed its midpoint, the low light of a sheltered fire came into view.

Aoleyn stood by the lake, cloak wrapped tight about her, star-ing at the reflection of the stars in the mostly still water. She appreciated the power of that water. This had been a mostly flat desert of black sand and black stones, but the surge of water from the fissure, the tremendous force of the giant Loch Beag thundering down thousands of feet, had dug a hole and pushed and shoved the sand and stones in its irresistible press. The shoreline all the way from the mountains was broken and uneven, with piled stones, water-plowed berms, and many areas of rivulets and small streams as the continuing flow from the fissure overfilled the new lake.

"The wind is chill this night," Bahdlahn noted when he caught up to Aoleyn, not long after.

"Warmer than up above," she replied, looking back to the west and the distant plateau, which was glowing with the fires of the invaders.

"I have found a quiet place," Bahdlahn softly added.

Aoleyn noted the tremble and timidity in his voice, a bit of nervousness, which explained to her his subtle suggestion. A quiet place like the mountain ledge to which she had led him, not long ago, and where she had made love to him under a sky not so different than the one this night. It was the first time Bahdlahn had made love, and the first time for Aoleyn, too, for she could not—could never—consider what her husband had done to her on the day he had been killed by the demon fossa to be such.

A pang of guilt struck Aoleyn. She had initiated the events of that night and had guided the innocent Bahdlahn through them. She had wanted to make love to him, because she did indeed care for him and because she needed to know what lovemaking, and not rape, would be like. And truly, Aoleyn had enjoyed that night, and she treasured the memory of it.

But, to her surprise, Aoleyn didn't want to repeat it.

She loved Bahdlahn and treasured his friendship and wanted nothing but the very best for him in his journey from slave to free man.

"We start this journey together," she said to him, taking his hands in her own, "but we will not end up in the same place."

"You do'no know that," he replied, and she gathered from his confident and reassuring tone that he wasn't understanding her quite yet. "We may find a new place to live, to build new homes, all of us together."

"No, Bahdlahn," the woman said softly. "You and I. You have so much to learn and to know and to grow. You have barely tasted freedom and what it is to be a man."

"What do you mean?" She noted a tremor in his voice, different from the nervous quiver when he was hoping they would make love again.

"Your road is undecided," she tried to explain. "You can'no know where the wide world will take you."

"Nor can Aoleyn."

She conceded that with a nod, but went on, "I suspect much of what lies before me in the wider lands to the east, and I expect that my journey will be dangerous and will return me to this place."

"And I will be beside you and will fight for you."

"No."

"How can you deny—"

"No."

Bahdlahn took a step back, his hands falling from hers.

"Our journeys diverge. The road will soon fork," she said. "Your way and mine will not be the same, for the good of us both and the good of those around us."

She pulled her hands from his, held them up, and, with a thought, transformed them into the paws of a leopard.

How Bahdlahn's eyes widened!

"The magic consumes my thoughts and my heart, Bahdlahn, my friend Bahdlahn," she tried to explain, though she realized that anyone who was not experiencing the beauty of the spiritual song could not truly understand. "I can'no know who I am until I have come to fully understand what it is within me. This will be my journey, and mine alone. It would not be fair to you."

"I do'no care."

"It would not be fair to me."

Bahdlahn winced. "I thought you loved me."

"You are my dearest friend," Aoleyn said, sincerely and without hesitation. "I would give my life protecting you."

"Then be with me this night."

Aoleyn closed her eyes and let her hands become those of a young woman once more. She almost gave in to the plea, but before she opened her dark eyes, she was already shaking her head. "What we did was wonderful," she said. "It gave to me confidence. Making love to you showed me that I—I and no one else—control this body that holds the spirit of Aoleyn. It showed me that intimacy can be beautiful and calming and joyous. I wanted that gift from you, and to give that gift to you, that our first experience would be one of trust and respect and comfortable joy. Nothing that might have happened in that night we spent in each other's arms could have lessened my respect for you—and your respect of me, I trust."

"I love you," he said breathlessly. "Then and now."

Aoleyn was shaking her head again, hardly even aware of the movement. "Then be my friend, Bahdlahn. Because that is what I need now as I sort out the puzzles before me. Be my friend and trust in me, and let me trust in you. And promise me that you will not let these feelings you have for me stop you from learning who you are. If Talmadge's words are true, we will meet many new people in the coming weeks. We will find our way in a new world."

"Together."

"Our roads will separate, perhaps forever."

He started to shake his head and argue, but Aoleyn stepped forward fast and put her finger over his lips.

"You are no warrior. That is not yet your place. But I am. With my magic, I am. I killed the fossa. I killed Tay Aillig. I have already learned the language of our enemies and will soon know more about them, and more about how to defeat them, than anyone alive. A great fight looms before me and

I'll not spend it worrying about Bahdlahn, who is no warrior."

"I will learn to be a warrior," he said, through a determinedly clenched jaw.

"Of that, I do not doubt."

"I would spend this night in your embrace. Just holding you. Just being held by you."

Aoleyn was actually surprised by her level of resistance to that plea. In that dark place not long ago, she had needed Bahdlahn, and sensed that he had needed her. But now she didn't feel that need, and now she didn't want that complication. Again, those pangs of guilt brought a slight wince to her. She feared that she had used Bahdlahn selfishly. She tried to respond several times but couldn't find the words.

Bahdlahn rushed forward and crushed her in a great hug, then moved back to arm's length.

"You saved my life many times," he said, and his voice grew strong and confident. "You showed me friendship when I had none. You showed me love when I did'no think it could be." He paused and took a deep breath, looking down, trying to find some balance, she thought.

"Aoleyn," Bahdlahn finished, "I will be your friend."

He lifted her hand and kissed it gently, then turned and walked back to the larger camp of refugees.

Aoleyn turned back to the lake and closed her eyes, trying to steady her swirling emotions. She thought that it wouldn't have cost her much to go and be with the man—she did indeed trust him and cared deeply for him. But no, how could she if it was not in her heart?

"Your pardon, good lady," she heard behind her, and she turned to find Aydrian walking her way—and from the side, along the rocky lakeshore, not from the camp.

She sensed the discomfort in his voice.

"How much did you overhear?" she demanded.

"More than I should have, I expect," he answered. "But I did not wish to interrupt."

"Then I will trust your discretion." She turned back to the lake.

"Of course." Aydrian moved up beside her and said quietly, "That hurt you."

"It hurt Bahdlahn."

"He will recover," the large man said, drawing a side-eye and a scowl from Aoleyn.

"It is good, then, that it hurt you too," Aydrian added. "It is good that you care deeply about the effect your choices have on others."

Aoleyn glanced back to the camp and caught the silhouette of Bahdlahn still moving away.

"But it was still your choice and only yours," Aydrian offered. "If you had lain with him, then what of the next time? Or the time after that?"

"I do'no see how this is your affair."

"It isn't," the man admitted, but Aoleyn caught his knowing grin when she couldn't help but continue.

"Bahdlahn is only now knowing freedom, for the first time in his life. He barely knows what it is to have choices, never mind what it is to be a man, never mind the responsibilities of being a lover or husband."

"Bahdlahn?"

"Yes," she answered, surprised.

"Aoleyn," Aydrian corrected. "You speak for Aoleyn, not Bahdlahn. Do not hide behind what you think are your responsibilities toward Bahdlahn."

"You think to scold me?"

"I deign to tell you the truth, for I hope that you will come to trust me, for all our sakes," said Aydrian. "It was not for Bahdlahn that Aoleyn refused his bed. It was for you. If in your heart you wanted his embrace, if your body tingled for him, you would have gone with him."

"I . . ." She stopped short and turned to the lake, closing up defensively.

"That choice is yours alone, and Bahdlahn's alone for Bahdlahn. That is honesty," Aydrian said.

"The tingling of my body is no concern of yours!" Aoleyn scolded, turning, but that only drew a grin from the warrior, who was a decade her senior. She turned back to the lake yet again, so imperiously that she surprised herself by not stomping her foot.

"It is not," he agreed.

Aoleyn was glad the discussion was over, except that it was not, and after a long pause Aydrian added, "I notice that you did not deny my observation."

After another pause, during which she digested the words and privately admitted the truth of them to herself, she turned to Aydrian.

"And what would you have me do, O wise one?" she asked, her sarcasm masking her very real desire for an answer.

"You did the right thing, for yourself and for the young man," Aydrian said. "You never owe such intimacy to another. It must be freely and willingly given, by both."

Aoleyn turned back to him yet again, locking his gaze with her own.

"It's either there or it isn't, so I have been told," Aydrian said.

"So you've been told? And what about for this man named Aydrian?"

He gave a chuckle, one that seemed almost pitiful to Aoleyn. "I spent the first twenty years of my life with a dactyl demon inside me, a cancer put there in the womb when my valiant mother did battle with a most foul fiend."

"Like the demon fossa," Aoleyn said under her breath, trying to put aside her fears that the magic of the beast was also within her, calling her to become an animal wholly, as the fossa had once been. She thought of the bright-faced enemy and her instinctive transformation to save herself from his spear. How easy it would have been to tear out his throat . . . how warm his blood would have felt . . .

"And the last ten years in exile among the Touel'alfar," Aydrian went on. Then, seeing Aoleyn's confused expression, he explained, "The elves." He held his hand out at about waist height. "This tall. Not human. The only human company I've had for a decade, other than a chance meeting with Talmadge and now with you people, was my own mother."

"You were lonely, then?"

"No, not at all," he replied. "For the one person I didn't know was myself. How could I think about joining with another in such intimacy when I wasn't even certain of who I was?"

Aoleyn felt as if he was talking about her in that moment, and she relaxed, realizing then that this stranger did understand her inner turmoil.

"I was more than satisfied with the company I found," Aydrian went on. "With the elves, with my mother—oh, no one could ever ask for a more wonderful mother than Jilseponie—and with Bradwarden the centaur."

"A centaur?"

"Half man, half—"

"Half horse. Yes, I know from our old tales—tales told to frighten the children."

"Oh, they are very real," Aydrian assured her. "Larger than life, and none who ever met one, particularly Bradwarden, would ever forget him."

Aoleyn pondered that for a bit. "I would like to meet him, I think."

"Maybe someday I will introduce you," Aydrian said with a warm smile. "And then you will have a reason to be mad at me."

He couldn't hold a straight face, and soon Aoleyn joined him in quiet laughter, recognizing the joke.

"Someday," she said, and Aydrian nodded.

"You should go and rest," Aydrian said a moment later. "I came out to relieve you. I'll watch the lake."

Aoleyn nodded. "You know the magic songs?" she asked.

"I know how to use the gemstones, yes, if that is what you mean."

Aoleyn produced a crystal she had slid into her belt, holding it up. "When I went back to the mountain, I found this one," she explained, holding it up to her face and peering through it into the water. "Through its song, I can sense the fish. If I had been using it, you would not have overheard my conversation with Bahdlahn, because I would have sensed your approach."

"It tells you when life is about?"

"It does. When we heard the coyotes as the sun set, I counted them through the magic of this crystal and knew they would be no threat to us. And here, on the lake, in the dark of night . . ." She held it up and looked to the west, the way they had come.

"You can see a long way, then?" Aydrian asked, and Aoleyn nodded and slowly turned, first to her right, inland, then back around and to the lake, as if taking a final scan of the area before retiring for the night.

She stopped short, however, and continued to stare out across the lake waters, and sucked in her breath in surprise.

"What do you see?" Aydrian asked.

"There is something out there—some*one* out there," she replied. She kept peering out across the water but held the crystal out for Aydrian to take it and pointed with her other hand to show him the way.

Aydrian did take the crystal, but, to Aoleyn's surprise, he didn't bring it to his eyes. Instead, he crouched low, then moved lower, finally lying on the ground and looking out over the lake.

"What are you doing?"

"Come down here," he bade her. "Get your eyes as low as you can and look up just enough to put the blackness of the mountains below your sight."

Aoleyn did as he asked, staring hard, and was about to ask what the point of it might be. But then she knew, for a patch of stars disappeared, then more, and she followed the silhouette and surely recognized it.

"A sail, a boat," she gasped, sitting up.

"Aye, coming fast," said Aydrian.

"One volley," Ataquixt quietly told his warriors. "Send them running, but we do not engage."

"We can defeat them," an older mundunugu argued.

"More slaves for Scathmizzane," said another.

Ataquixt calmed them, reminding them how easily sound carried across open water. "One," he whispered, emphatically holding up one finger. "Send them running, that I can get ashore."

Some scowled, some sighed, but most nodded their reluctant agreement. This was a scouting expedition, not a war party, they had been told before setting off. And that scouting would not end at the new lake's edge. Quietly, the twenty warriors set spears to their atlatl throwing sticks while the pilot maneuvered to bring the boat in close and then turn her sidelong to give the spearmen more room to throw.

The winds had not diminished. Sails full, the boat rushed toward the shore and then, with a call of warning, cut fast to the target, turning parallel to the shore.

The xoconai lifted their arms to let fly, aiming for the glow of the sheltered campfires not twenty paces inland.

Then they saw her—most of them did, at least—a small human woman, standing on the water's edge, her arms outstretched, her cloak flying in the wind behind her.

"Fly!" Ataquixt commanded, and the arms came forward and the light spears flew out from the boat, many of them aimed at that clear and obvious target.

* * *

"Go. Get them running," Aoleyn told Aydrian.

"Come with me!" Aydrian bade her.

"I will slow them."

"You will die." He grabbed her by the arm.

Aoleyn flashed him a dangerous scowl. "Trust me," she demanded. "Go!"

Aydrian let her go, offered a nod of respect, then sprinted for the camp, which was already stirring, for others had now obviously noted the incoming craft.

Aoleyn spun back to the lake and listened for the song of her gemstones. She clearly saw the boat now, rushing for the shore and then turning fast, bending low in the water. She understood. She didn't even need to see the uplifted spears to understand.

Every instinct within the woman told her to throw herself down behind the rocks, told her that she was too late, and that she couldn't hold back this barrage.

But she heard the song of Usgar, a song she had come to trust, and she called upon the moonstone set in her belly ring, creating a wall of wind. Twenty spears flew out from the boat and twenty spears were slowed, deflected, defeated, by Aoleyn's magical gale.

The boat continued its turn away from the shore. Aoleyn stamped her foot and a bolt of lightning shot out at it, but it couldn't quite catch up to it and dispersed with a bright flash in the lake water. In that flash, she saw them clearly, their red-and-blue-streaked faces.

And she heard them yelling and knew their words—one voice, in particular, above the others, calling for a turn, a turn and a charge and a second volley.

Calling for the others to kill her, to kill the sorceress.

"Yes, come," Aoleyn whispered. She turned back toward the refugee camp and called out to Aydrian and Talmadge to hurry them all away.

Aoleyn had no intention of following. Not yet.

She settled back to staring out at the boat, which was

coming fully around now, its sails suddenly filling with the trailing wind, making it seem to almost leap forward. Now it was speeding in, straight for her, and Aoleyn realized that their turn would be much closer to shore this time, too close for her to fully blow aside the volley.

But she didn't run.

She heard the song and trusted the song, and had the enemies on the boat seen the small woman's crooked smile, they might have understood their folly.

Set in Aoleyn's anklet was a large blue gemstone, one that she had used in a desperate situation before and whose power had shocked and frightened her.

Now she wasn't frightened.

She felt the song rising, powerfully, its notes filling her frame with shivers of power and cold.

On came the boat.

She watched for the turn of the sail.

And as it began, as the boat suddenly broke again to her left, Aoleyn called forth the magic, aiming not for the boat itself but for the water in front of the boat, turning it into a sheet of thick ice.

Halfway into its turn, the speeding boat struck the berg, wood splintering, the craft lurching so violently that most of those aboard went flying over the side, some landing hard on the iceberg and sliding, tumbling, twisting across to plop into the water on the far side of it. Those who had somehow managed to stay aboard were not much better off, for half the prow had caved in from the impact, swamping the small craft, which listed hard and groaned as it settled against the ice.

Aoleyn heard the songs, several songs, and brought them spinning together as she had done to Tay Aillig up on the rocky outcropping. Above the crashed boat, above the ice, above the flailing enemies, the magics joined in wind and lightning and a sudden deluge of stinging sleet.

Aoleyn stamped her foot, calling down a lightning bolt

from that tempest. The streak flashed into the water, where it became like a fireball, spreading in all directions, shocking the fallen xoconai and stealing from them their coordination so that they would flail and drown.

The young witch stared coldly, accepting the horrible reality of what she had to do. She brought down a second bolt, then spun on her heels and started away.

She called a third stroke of lightning, and then she was running. She called a fourth, from far away, the fleeing lakemen in sight, moving inland across the desert.

She would stay between them and the enemies, she decided, and any of the bright-faced invaders who made it to shore and gave chase would be dead before the dawn. Aoleyn mouthed her litany against the revulsion of such carnage.

"So be it."

He only got out from under the tempest because of his cuetzpali mount, the strong-swimming lizard resisting the shocks of lightning enough to keep its course.

Ataquixt heard the cries and shrieks from his crew, saw them flailing with every bolt of lightning, saw others simply bobbing facedown in the area of choppy water. The boat was fully on its side by then, mostly submerged, and useful only for a few who somehow managed to hold on to it in the churning, shocking waters.

Every passing heartbeat seemed like a tortured hour to Ataquixt, and, he knew, likely longer still to those caught under the magical storm.

Finally, the swirling black cloud broke apart, and Ataquixt guided his cuetzpali mount back to the boat. There, he began towing those still alive to the nearby shore. Then he brought in the bodies, a half dozen dead.

"We will find her and kill her," a mundunugu promised through teeth still chattering, though whether from the cold, his wounds, or the residual shock of the lightning, Ataquixt could not know.

"You will carry our brethren back to the west," Ataquixt told them. "You will give them to Pixquicauh as heroes, that they may be offered to Scathmizzane, and you will tell Tuolonatl the story of the battle and the human sorceress."

"The cochcal will not be pleased," a woman warned.

"Great Tuolonatl knows war," Ataquixt replied confidently. "She will think our battle a great success."

Many of the others looked to each other skeptically, he noted.

"We have learned much about our enemy this day," he explained. "When we came over Tzatzini, we slaughtered them too quickly for them to reveal to us their true powers." He looked back out to the lake, to the ruined boat floating free on its side in the waters that now seemed clear of ice.

"Now we know."

"And I, Ataquixt, will learn much, much more."

The scout, entrusted by the great Tuolonatl, tugged his cuetzpali's reins and turned the beast, then padded off into the desert night.

5

WILDERLAND WANDERING

The weather and the season were with them for most of the journey. On makeshift rafts, they rode the rivers from the new lake and far to the east, to lands Talmadge and Khotai knew well. And with their magical powers, Aydrian and, particularly, Aoleyn kept the band safe from bears and great cats and any other threats in the wilds through the central regions of the continent. With only one notable accident of a capsized raft—one mitigated greatly by Aoleyn's powers, when she levitated three children from the rushing waters and floated them to the riverbank—the journey had been as smooth and safe as any could have hoped. A hundred and fourteen people had started from the Ayamharas Plateau and a hundred and nine remained.

Five deaths in two months, out in the wilds, with threats all about.

But now the season had turned. Summer had come on with blazing heat, and the rivers had greatly thinned, meaning that the troupe would walk now almost all the time.

Two weeks, Talmadge had told them that first day away

from the last river, trudging through a region sparse with trees and other shade and thick with coyotes, hyenas, and gigantic monsters called birch haunts, which could cleverly hide in a stand of small trees, only to come forth as raging giants. *We will make Matinee in two weeks.*

Alone, the man would have made it in ten days, easily—he had done so many times before.

But with this group, tired, haggard, blistered, and beaten by the elements, downtrodden and without a home, the two weeks passed and Matinee remained a long road away.

Another person, an elderly lakewoman with two humps on her elongated skull, gave in to her exhaustion and died in the night. The next day, a teenage girl spotted what she thought was a bird's nest and climbed a tree in search of eggs, only to discover that it was a nest of plains wasps, which swarmed and stung her, causing her to lose her balance and crash down through twenty feet of branches. She landed hard against the lowest branch, which snapped, the jagged edge catching the skin of her side and tearing it, all the way down the side of her leg. She dropped, broken and bleeding, to the ground, her long strip of skin hanging above her like the shed skin of a large snake.

Aoleyn blew the wasp swarm away with a hot and fiery wind, but it took her the rest of that day to save the life of the poor girl, who would need to be carried on a litter the remainder of the way, for it would be weeks before she recovered enough to walk, and never again without a noticeable limp.

Three more grueling, hot days passed. The morning of the fourth found three refugees dead in their grassy bedrolls, a mystery that lasted until Aydrian found and killed a nine-foot viper.

The next day brought a terrible thunderstorm, but the battered caravan continued on. Late that afternoon, the storm blew past, building a rainbow in the east before them, and under that rainbow loomed a small settlement with a huge hall at its center.

"Matinee," Khotai told Aoleyn and the others. "At last, Matinee."

Aoleyn glanced back to the west with a look of concern. She knew what was coming. "Not the end of our road."

"A short respite, and valuable allies to be found," Khotai explained. "These are the people who know these lands better than anyone. They are skilled trackers, hunters, fighters, scouts. If the pursuit comes—"

"The xoconai have no intention of stopping," Aoleyn interrupted.

Khotai nodded. "When they come, we will know. From any direction and in what numbers."

Aoleyn offered a return nod, but there was nothing in her expression to show that she considered that declaration important.

"The east is powerful," Khotai explained. "Honce-the-Bear is a kingdom of many people. Thousands, hundreds of thousands of people, with great warriors like Aydrian and monks with magical powers not unlike your own. They have strength and a single king. They will stop these bright-faced murderers."

Aoleyn managed a smile and another, more decisive nod. She appreciated Khotai's optimism, and when she thought about it, she understood the source more clearly.

A few weeks ago, this woman was barely mobile, crawling at best, and could not stand or move at all without pain. Now she had endured the long and trying journey better than any, moving with such grace that she seemed more a spirit transcending the mortal coil than a weary traveler weighed by it. While others had trudged, Khotai had leaped and floated, in complete control of the magic and of her own body in her nearly weightless form. Indeed, everything about her seemed lighter: her step, her smile, her attitude each and every day. Even her grooming had gone back to her days of freedom before her ghastly wounds, and her unique beauty, born of strength and competence and tamed by compassion, shined through her brown skin and her dark eyes.

That made Aoleyn happy, and hopeful. They would need Khotai's optimism, she knew. The haggard and homeless survivors of the disaster at the Ayamharas Plateau would need whatever cheering they might find, and more.

Soon after, a small group of four headed down to Matinee to prepare the frontiersmen for the coming surprises. Aoleyn was surprised when Talmadge and Khotai, who knew these people, asked her to go along. She walked behind the two, with Catriona of Fasach Crann, unsure of her place here and more than happy to heed the orders of Talmadge that she speak little and listen a lot.

And she heard a lot, indeed, even before they got into the large hall, where the drinking, gaming, betting, and playing was heaviest. She heard many quiet remarks directed at her, almost all complimentary, and more than a few referring somewhat suggestively to her bare midriff and sparkling belly ring. At first, Aoleyn felt self-conscious, as she wasn't used to such attention, but she quickly reminded herself of the gravity of the situation around her and of her own chosen role here and decided that it didn't much matter. In that moment, perhaps more than ever before, Aoleyn felt comfortable in her skin, in who she was, and confident in her ability to make anyone and everyone respect that, whether they liked it or not.

She had faced the demon fossa and had won. She had not allowed herself to be intimidated by Tay Aillig or Mairen— and he was dead by Aoleyn's hand, while Mairen was a prisoner in a faraway land.

These strangers, though some were thrice her size, would not intimidate her.

Nor was she the focus of their whispers, laughter, or gasps, and after seeing the prime target of the surprised frontier folk, Aoleyn better understood why Talmadge and Khotai had asked her to come along. She grabbed Catriona's arm and pulled the woman close, whispering reassurances in her ear and translating some of the excited babble going on all about them.

Aoleyn thought Catriona quite beautiful, with her golden-tanned and unblemished young skin and her solid, well-muscled frame—supple, strong, and nearly half a foot taller than diminutive Aoleyn. The woman's braided hair was thick and golden, her eyes bright and sharp, to aptly reflect her mind. Despite her youth, Catriona had been the one most of the villagers had looked toward when disaster had befallen the lake tribes.

She inspired confidence beyond her years.

And yes, to Aoleyn, the young woman was indeed beautiful, but Aoleyn had become accustomed to the head shaping of the uamhas. She was no longer shocked by it and had come to see it as nothing demeaning or ugly. In fact, in Catriona's case and many others, quite the opposite.

But could these frontier folk even see the woman as human? They were aghast, clearly, and Aoleyn better understood the reasons that Talmadge and Khotai had chosen this specific makeup of the introduction group.

Two men, in particular, seemed to be fully intrigued by—or horrified by—Catriona's elongated skull. They talked loudly, though their motions were similar to what Aoleyn would expect if they were whispering; they even covered their mouths as they spoke. They pretended to be looking all around, but their eyes would not turn away even when they turned their heads, both sets locked on the spectacle of the long-headed stranger. One of them even pointed at Catriona, more than once.

"They do not understand," Aoleyn said to Catriona, when she saw that the woman had taken note of the two.

"They all look like Usgar to me," Catriona replied steadily and disparagingly.

"We are not all bad," Aoleyn quipped, and Catriona giggled with embarrassment, for she had obviously forgotten Aoleyn's own heritage when delivering her insult.

The laugh was a perfect antidote to the unwanted attention.

"I am glad that you found your way with us," Catriona said to Aoleyn. "I am glad that you stand here with me."

The profundity of that compliment was not lost on Aoleyn. The hatred between the lake villagers and the Usgar ran deep through uncounted generations, yet the sincerity in Catriona's voice was easy to hear.

"I am sad that it took the invading xoconai to show us that we are alike and not enemies," Aoleyn said.

"But Aoleyn knew that all along," Catriona replied, surprising the dark-haired woman.

"I have spoken much with Bahdlahn," Catriona explained. "He told me of Aoleyn and of the other prisoners. Of his mother and of all that you did. He says that if the bright-faced invaders had not come, Aoleyn would have defeated the chieftain of the Usgar and would have brought peace between our tribes."

Aoleyn shrugged. "Sometimes Bahdlahn thinks too highly of me."

"But you would have tried?"

Aoleyn locked on to the woman's gaze. "Yes."

"I am glad that you found your way with us," Catriona repeated. "I am glad that you stand here with me."

"Would young and fierce Catriona have answered my calls for peace, I wonder?" Aoleyn asked.

Before the woman could answer, a loud communal gasp stole their attention, and the two women watched all heads in Matinee lifted to see the short flight—or rather, the long leap—of Khotai, the one-legged To-gai-ru woman who was floating wall to wall across the huge open-floored building.

"She did that?" one woman called above the others, pointing to Aoleyn.

"She did," Khotai replied, and she bounded back the other way, to land beside Aoleyn and Catriona. "I owe my life to Aoleyn of Usgar."

"And it is a debt we must all repay," Talmadge said, moving to join his three companions. "For our own sakes. It is good to be back with you, my friends, but know that I will never again go to that mountain lake of which you have so often heard me speak, for that lake is no more, and no more are the people I knew about it. I did not bring back Aoleyn for your cheers—she deserves them but does not need them. And I did not bring back Catriona that you could gawk and laugh at her strange skull."

He glanced to the three woman and nodded, offering a look to tell them that he thought this was all going well, then turned back to the room more seriously. "I ask that the drinks be withheld now, for I have a story you must hear, and at once."

Some protests erupted at the call for the drinks to be stopped, but Talmadge and some others managed to quell that immediately, and Talmadge continued, "And I have a hundred more just like Catriona here." He moved over and put his hand on the woman's shoulder. "We did not come here to amuse you. We came here because there was nowhere else to go, because we are pursued by a vast army intent on dominion."

"You led an army to us?" one woman complained.

"We could have gone straight past this place," Talmadge told her. "And you would have died. All of you."

Aoleyn noted that there remained no smiles in the room. They were listening. At least they were listening!

"Where are these hundred?" another man asked.

"Not far," Talmadge replied. "They are hungry, they are homeless. Many are wounded, all are weary. Some are very old, some very young. I would not bring them into Matinee without the agreement and permission of all here."

"You think us a monastery tending the infirm?" a woman's

voice yelled from the back of the gathering, but she was hushed quickly and loudly by many others.

"I think you good people who prefer to be alone but not from a lack of responsibility to others in need," said Talmadge. "These people need you."

"Are they all ugly like that one?" asked a large man, one of the two who had been joking about Catriona, Aoleyn noted.

"She looks different, and that unsettles you," Aoleyn loudly interjected, stepping in front of Talmadge to address the man directly.

A collective gasp filled the large room.

"And where are you from, lass?" the man asked in reply, and in an accusatory tone.

"Fireach Speuer, the mountain shadowing the Loch Beag."

"Before that."

"There was no 'before that.'"

"You speak—"

"I taught myself your language," Aoleyn said to him. "I am not like you. I do not fear that which is different. I learn from it."

"Why is your head like that and not like that?" he demanded, poking his finger at Aoleyn, then at Catriona.

"Why is your hair brown but her hair is red?" Aoleyn asked, nodding toward a red-haired woman not far from the large man. "Why is Khotai's skin dark but your own light?"

"She is To-gai-ru," the man answered.

"Is she the first of her kind you ever saw?"

"No!" he insisted.

"Yes," said the man he previously had been whispering with. "First for me."

"And what did you think when first you saw Khotai?" Aoleyn asked the second man. "Did you think her beautiful or did you think her strange?"

"Well . . ." He stammered a bit, and that brought some titters of laughter all about. "Aye, strange!" the man admitted.

"And now?" Aoleyn pressed him. "You were all so thrilled when Khotai entered the hall. I watched it. You thought her dead these last years, but here she is, and you welcomed her back as if a friend."

"She is a friend!" the man insisted, and the first agreed loudly, as did many others.

"Well, then," Aoleyn said, walking right up to him and staring him in the eye, "tell me—tell us all, tell Khotai—do you still think her strange looking, or beautiful?"

"Take care your answer, Marley Bruuin," Khotai said. "I've but one leg left, aye, but it's enough to kick yer fat ass."

The hall erupted in laughter, all aimed at poor Marley Bruuin, who, along with his mate, took it in stride. He leaped forward and fell to one knee before Khotai. "She's beautiful!" he said. "Ah, but she's a dark-skinned beauty!"

"Huzzah!" cheered the hall.

"The people with us are beautiful," Aoleyn said when the noise calmed. "And they're desperate. They've lost their tribes, their families, their friends. They need the good-will of the good folk of Matinee. And all the folk of all the lands need the skill of the folk of Matinee now, because the golden darkness of the xoconai is coming, do'no doubt, and led by a god of murdering light riding a dragon that swims through the air."

"Talmadge!" shouted a man from the side of the hall, presiding over the stacks of kegs of ale and wine, which made him a very important voice in Matinee. "Go and get your . . . our friends and bring them in. You've a story to tell us in full and in haste, so it seems, and one we need to hear and hear fast."

"I do, and I will," Talmadge answered.

Aoleyn rejoined him and the other three, and Khotai took her hand in a warm embrace as she neared.

"Now you know why I told you to bring her," she said to Talmadge, all the while beaming a smile of gratitude and admiration at Aoleyn.

"Now you know why I didn't need to be told," Talmadge replied. He put on a stern expression and turned to Aoleyn. "I thought I told you to speak little and listen a lot," he scolded.

"I had better things to say than you were saying," Aoleyn replied.

"You do'no know your place," Talmadge teased.

"I do know my place," Aoleyn shot back. "And so I make it."

Talmadge blinked and took a moment to digest that, then came forward and kissed Aoleyn on the forehead. "Please do not ever change," he whispered to her.

"I'll go get the others," Khotai said.

"I'll come with you," said Talmadge.

But Khotai looked at Aoleyn, both their smiles widening. "You'll only slow me down," Khotai reminded, and a flick of her leg sent her floating for the door.

A tired and annoyed Brother Thaddius lifted the ridiculously large door knocker ring and thumped the chapel door yet again. He knew the place wasn't empty, for he had seen the candlelight moving about from window to window on his approach through this small town still far from the borders of Honce-the-Bear.

"It's probably vagrants in the place," Sister Elysant told him. She looked around at the small village. "They've probably had no chaplain here for many years."

Her words were proven false even as she finished the sentence, though, as the large door of the small chapel swung open, revealing a large, round, balding man of at least fifty winters wearing the robes of an Abellican brother. He seemed quite annoyed at Thaddius for just a moment, but then his eyes went wide indeed when he realized that these were fellow Abellican monks come calling.

"Yes? Umm, brrr," he asked, and cleared his throat. "But what have we here? Who and why and when and how?"

"Greetings to you, too, Brother," said Thaddius.

"Master," the man corrected rather importantly. "Abbot, actually. Cornelius Chesterfield. Abbot Cornelius Chesterfield."

"Greetings, then, Abbot Cornelius," Elysant said.

The large man—and he was thrice Elysant's weight, she figured—scowled down at her, seeming rather unpleased to see her, or perhaps to see that this second monk was a "her."

"Abbot Chesterfield," he corrected.

"As you wish, Abbot Chesterfield," said Thaddius. "I am Brother Thaddius of Saint-Mere-Abelle, and this is Sister Elysant of Saint Gwendolyn-by-the-Sea."

"Saint Gwendolyn was sacked, was it not?"

"It was," Elysant answered.

"I was asking him," Chesterfield insisted.

"Saint Gwendolyn was sacked, yes, and many of her brothers and sisters slain," Thaddius answered.

"But not all," Elysant added, against the abbot's scowl. "And that was a decade ago."

"We have been on the road for many weeks," Thaddius said. "May we enter?"

"On the road to find me?" Chesterfield asked, not moving out of the way, and though it was a wide door, the large man more than blocked it.

"No," said Thaddius.

"We did not know who you are, nor where we are, nor that there was an Abellican house of worship to be found here," Elysant said. When Chesterfield again scowled her way, she added, with not a little sarcasm, "A fortunate find for us all, yes?"

Grumbling under his breath, the large man moved aside, holding open the door, scowling all the while. He watched every movement, Elysant noted, as she and Thaddius each took an end of the wooden box they carried, one they had bought to hold secret the three alabaster coffers they had taken from the tomb. Chesterfield glanced at Thaddius only briefly, and at the curious walking stick the brother carried, which Thaddius had wrapped in leather to conceal the gems he had set into the sockets of the strange and wondrous item. The large monk then turned his stern gaze on Sister Elysant.

She wasn't surprised. The reign of Father Abbot Braumin Herde had brought many women into the clergy, but not without many objections from the traditionalists—or, at least, from the men who conveniently and self-servingly claimed a patriarchy as "traditionalist" within the teachings of St. Abelle. Many of the Abellicans, she knew—and not even only the ones who had followed the ways of Marcalo De'Unnero—had been secretly pleased at the downfall of St. Gwendolyn-by-the-Sea, preferring their order to be one of brothers alone. Elysant wasn't bothered by the attitude, or by Abbot Chesterfield's obvious disdain, as she had witnessed it so many times before.

She simply took private pleasure in her confidence that she could put Abbot Chesterfield down to the ground with little effort.

"If you're not here with any mission to find me, then tell me why you've come," the large man said to Thaddius. "You're a long way from Saint-Mere-Abelle, Brother."

"And a longer way, we were," Thaddius answered. "A meal, perhaps? Let us break bread that I might find the strength to tell you of our journey."

"First you tell me why you've come to the chapel of Appleby-in-Wilderland. I doubt you've arrived unseen, and more than a few of the suspicious folk of the village will come knocking and wanting to know why."

"We did not know that there was a chapel of Appleby-in-Wilder . . . ness?" Elysant interjected.

"Wilderland," Chesterfield gruffly corrected.

"Wilderland, then," Elysant went on, before Thaddius could jump in. "We didn't even know that there was an Appleby-in-Wilderland. We saw the distant fires and figured to find a cluster of hunting lodges, or farmhouses perhaps. We're tired from the road and so thought to find a brief respite in a comfortable bed or even a bale of hay."

"One you two would share?" the large man asked, looking accusingly from Thaddius to Elysant and back again. He ended on Thaddius, as if expecting an answer from the man, but all he got was a great sigh from Elysant.

"Abbot," Thaddius then said, "we are fellow Abellicans, monks of the Church and strong in our faith. We come to your door seeking respite and the hospitality one Abellican must expect from another. Nothing more, nothing less. Are you of a generous nature?"

"Piety, dignity, poverty, charity," Elysant said, the first pledge of any Abellican, and a stark reminder to Chesterfield of his duties here to any traveler who happened upon his door with good intent.

The large man harrumphed, then pulled himself away to gather some plates and bread and stew for his uninvited guests.

"Take care how much you reveal to that one," Elysant warned Thaddius when they were alone.

"He has been too long out here, perhaps," Thaddius replied.

"I care not why, but take heed of your words. We carry with us great treasure, and so great temptation. Abbot Cornelius Chesterfield seems a man who has long given up resistance to that which he covets."

Thaddius started to nod, but his expression changed suddenly and he stared at his diminutive companion. "And you take care," he warned.

Elysant snorted and tapped her stone stave on the floor. "He'll be standing straighter with this halfway up his fat arse," she promised.

"Well, come on, then!" came a shout from one of the side rooms of the evergreen-shaped nave of the chapel. "I'm not about to bring it to you!"

The two moved across the way and into the side room to find Abbot Chesterfield standing beside a table, staring at them, particularly at Elysant, every step of the way. He motioned to the table, where he had set two small bowls of stew, a torn lump of bread beside each.

"Your robe's ill-fitting, Sister," he remarked as Elysant took her seat.

"It's newly acquired," she replied, not making eye contact.

"You're new to the order?"

"Eleven years."

"And they haven't found you a robe that would properly fit?"

Elysant looked up. "I have another robe. One that properly fits. I prefer this one. It's newly acquired."

"And the staff you carry?" he asked, his suspicions quite obvious. "What is that?"

"A staff."

"Strange wood."

"It would be, if it were wood."

"Strange metal."

"Do you wish to hear our tale or not?" Thaddius interrupted.

"It is stone," Elysant answered anyway. "A staff made of stone."

"Ridiculous," said Chesterfield.

"If you've one of wood, perhaps we can see," Elysant said with a little smile, one that had Thaddius sucking in his breath.

"I've a rather large sword," Chesterfield replied. "One of strong steel."

"I am sure you think it large—" Elysant started, but Thaddius cut her off.

"We have been away from Honce for the better part of a year," he said, lifting a spoon for his first taste of the stew.

He motioned to the chair across from him, and Abbot Chesterfield, after a pause to stare some more at the woman, finally sat down.

"On an exploration," Thaddius went on. "Seeking the veracity of some old writings, at the request of Father Abbot Braumin Herde himself." It wasn't exactly the truth. The father abbot hadn't sent them on a mission, but neither had he stopped them, and the abbot of St. Ursal had been quite excited to let them follow the leads they had uncovered. The Abellican Church remained in a precarious position, and the world needed heroes, after all.

"Do tell me of your exploration, if it was that important," Chesterfield said sarcastically.

"For a lost chapel in the foothills of the Belt-and-Buckle," Thaddius replied. "An ancient place, so hinted the clues, and so it was, far to the south and the west."

"There is a chapel southwest of Appleby?" Chesterfield replied, doubtfully. "I know of no brothers southwest, or west at all."

"Ruins," Elysant explained. "Ancient ruins."

"A pair of monks sent so far to look at pocked and broken stone? Foolishness!"

"And tombs," said Elysant. "Do not forget the tombs."

"Tombs?"

"Abellican tombs," she replied.

"And knowledge," said Thaddius. "Knowledge, most of all. For that was our purpose, to confirm the rumors, to seek the truth, and to return the truth to Saint-Mere-Abelle."

He stopped there and went to the stew, laughing when Elysant tore off a piece of bread, the jolt of her sudden movement sending a bit of thick broth flying into his cheek.

"And . . . ?" Abbot Chesterfield asked, when neither of his visitors moved to add to the story.

"And? That is all," said Thaddius. "We were sent to learn the truth and return that truth, and that return brought us, by happenstance, to this place and to your door. So, greetings once more, good abbot, and thank you for the food, and for the beds we expect you'll offer."

Abbot Chesterfield rubbed his thick chin and nodded. "Indeed."

"You're all welcomed to stay at Matinee for as long as you're desiring," Marley Bruuin announced to Talmadge and some others, a couple of days later. The refugees had told the story of the fall of the Ayamharas Plateau and the destruction of Loch Beag, to many sympathetic nods, that first night in Matinee, and the gathering had asked for privacy that they could digest the news and offer a unified response.

"Stay?" Aydrian answered, before Talmadge could respond. "Did you not hear what we told you?"

"Aye," said Hawker Fief, another of the hunters gathered for Matinee. "We heard, and so we're opening our larders for you. We've got the food and drink, and all we'll ask in return is that you and yours do your part, and that your part includes a bit of the magical healing yourself and that small girl there promised." He nodded toward Aoleyn, who was off to the side with Catriona and some others, and only then took note that the frontiersmen had come out.

"We should all be on the move to the east," Talmadge replied.

"With all haste," Aydrian agreed. "All, save a few clever scouts and those supporting them to relay the news."

Marley and Hawker looked to each other with clear skepticism.

"You don't believe us?" Talmadge asked.

"We believe you got overrun by a swarm of strange-looking men, aye," said Marley.

"And from your tale of your journey here, we know it to be, what, a thousand miles? Two thousand?" said Hawker.

"Closer to two," said Marley. "And that's what you've said in the past, aye, Talmadge? Months of river riding, months of walking?"

"It is a long way," Talmadge agreed. "But there isn't much between the plateau and here."

"Goblins and giants, bears and snakes, deep snows and hot suns," said Marley.

"We made it," Aydrian reminded.

"And you rafted half of it," Marley said. "Spring melt's lowering already. Moving a hundred folk ain't moving an army of thousands."

"More than thousands," Talmadge insisted.

"More than you could ever know," added Aoleyn, walking over and shaking her head. "And they're coming, a swarm like you'd no e'er imagine. They're no stopping—they've no need to stop."

"We've sent eyes to the west," Marley Bruuin said to her, patting his hands in the air as if that would calm the obviously agitated young woman. "Most hunt in the west, and they'll be watching for signs, don't you fear."

"And then it will be too late," Aoleyn snapped back at him.

Aydrian stepped before her and looked down at her, quietly begging her to be calm.

"How many people did you say got killed?" Marley asked Talmadge. "Few thousand?"

"Three thousand or more."

"These red-and-blue-faced monsters swept over the mountain and overran the villages."

"Yes."

"A swarm."

"A swarm?" Marley asked. "Ten thousand? Fifty? Five hundred thousand?"

"I don't know! Too many! They swept us from the mountain, chased us onto the lake, and eight tribes fell, wiped away, other than these few from each who managed to run off with us. Aoleyn is the only Usgar left, I expect, and hers was the strongest of the eight tribes by far."

Marley and Hawker again exchanged those skeptical looks.

"We're not lying," said Aoleyn.

"We don't doubt you," Hawker replied without hesitation. "And we're sorry for your great losses, lass. Nor do we doubt that you think this the greatest army you've e'er seen. But that's because you've no understanding of the lands to the east, of the cities a hundred thousand strong, with walls as tall as your mountain."

"I know them well," Aydrian said, but in a whisper, and he lowered his gaze. And when he considered it, he really wasn't surprised by the reaction of the folks of Matinee. He should have anticipated this, he realized. A hundred people fleeing for thousands of miles from an enemy they had seen for but a single day? An enemy they could not name in any way to properly convey the danger to these men and women who had never heard of the xoconai, a name Aydrian only knew because of Aoleyn, and who had never seen a man with a bright red nose lined by bright blue cheeks riding a green and golden lizard?

"They have a dragon, a great flying serpent!" Aoleyn shot back at Hawker.

The man directed her gaze to the south. "You see those mountains? Closer than your home, aye? Much closer. Just beyond them there's a dragon, Agradeleous by name, and that one's flown about the lands to the east before, oh aye."

"Big dragon, from all the tales," Marley Bruuin added.

Aydrian nodded. He knew Agradeleous well, and the woman who had ridden the beast into the battle of St.-Mere-Abelle.

"We'll keep an eye aimed west for your dragon and the red-nosed enemies," Hawker assured them. "A thousand miles of wilderness is a long way to move an army, and two thousand's a lot more, eh? No fields of grain, no towns to sack, no fights to keep the soldiers in line."

"And you're welcomed, any or all, to stay," Marley added.

"Our road is east," Aydrian said. "Aoleyn and I will continue the healing for another few days, and then we're away. Horses and some wagons would greatly help."

"We've some to spare," Hawker assured him.

"Fools," Aoleyn said, when the two frontiersmen had gone back inside.

"We should have known," Aydrian told her. "The threat is too distant."

"These folk have lived on the edge of disaster for many years," Talmadge added. "Many have been killing goblins and giants longer than you've been alive. They know this ground, all of it."

"But only Talmadge knew Loch Beag," said Aydrian.

"Not only Talmadge," Khotai said, and Talmadge looked to her with obvious surprise, to which she merely shrugged.

"Talmadge and Khotai," Aydrian corrected.

"And one other," Khotai reminded.

Talmadge nodded, remembering Redshanks, an old man now, who was a legend among the frontiersman but who had stopped his wilderness ways and joined the Matinee several years before. He lived in one of the many communities in the region known as the Wilderlands, just west of Honce-the-Bear's western borders, a town called Appleby-in-Wilderland.

"Our road is east," Talmadge agreed.

"I'm not going to continue this game with you," Elysant told Abbot Chesterfield the next morning after breakfast, when she found herself alone with the always-scowling man, sitting across from him at a small table.

"You are leaving, then?" came the sarcastic reply.

"I am an Abellican sister," she replied. "I have as much right to be in this chapel as you do."

"I am the abbot," the large man protested.

"Because you are here alone, and only because of that. It is a title you've given yourself, where a simple rank of chaplain would more than suffice. You err in believing that you are superior in the eyes of God and of the Church to Brother Thaddius Roncourt."

The man snickered.

"He has the ear and confidence of Father Abbot Braumin Herde," Elysant told him. "He fought at the Battle of Saint-Mere-Abelle among the titans and the dragon. He was sent to the aid of Saint Gwendolyn by the father abbot, above all others."

"Brother Thaddius," Abbot Chesterfield said, emphasizing the first word. "Not even a master, but merely a brother."

"He is a master," Elysant assured the man. "He could be an abbot, if he had so chosen that course. Instead, he has chosen the road, wide and long, to search for the truth of the world and his heart. You would do well to recognize that, perhaps to learn from it."

"You think to teach me?"

"I think someone should. Take note of Brother Thaddius's staff, if you will. Ask him to show you what is under the wrappings he placed upon it."

The man could not hide his curiosity.

"Few in the order are more proficient with the Ring Stones than Thaddius of Saint-Mere-Abelle," Elysant explained. "He is far more likely to elevate to the position of father abbot than Abbot Cornelius Chesterfield, of course, and may well be next in line, once we have returned to the mother abbey with our find."

Chesterfield snorted and waved his hands as if dismissing the entire conversation.

"I cannot ask you to treat him, or myself, with respect, Abbot. Respect is given, not demanded. But your hospitality is demanded. We will remain as long as it suits us, and you will be tolerant of our company, if not glad of it. This is the way of Abelle."

"And if I refuse?"

"We'll stay anyway."

"Big words from a small girl."

"Abbot, if you wish to take up your sword, then pray get it," Elysant replied. "Perhaps you will quickly understand why I was chosen to accompany Brother Thaddius in his travels."

"I thought you his whore."

Elysant smiled, trying to hide the tension in her face.

Chesterfield returned that grin tenfold and reached across as if to stroke the woman's light brown hair. He almost touched Elysant's locks before her left hand shot up, slapping backhand against his palm, her thumb hooking around his as she made a fist, then turned and punched ahead, rolling the man's hand under, locking his elbow and nearly driving his face down to the table.

Elysant slowly rose and stepped around the side of the table, increasing the pressure, forcing Abbot Chesterfield lower.

"Sister . . . Sister," he said. "I am an abbot."

"Would you like to be buried as such?" she asked sweetly. "If you ever try to touch me again uninvited, I can promise you that much, at least."

"Well now, have I missed all of the fun?" came a voice from the door. Elysant turned to see a man entering, a most curious man, indeed, with a huge gray mustache and unkempt long silver hair sticking out from under a strangely bright red beret. He wore a blousy white shirt with a plaid sash running right shoulder to left hip, blending there with the similar tartan of his kilt.

His kilt? Elysant thought, and nearly said aloud, in her surprise. She tried not to stare at his bony old knees or the bright red stockings rising as if to hold them together. Even his shoes held her attention, black and polished, low cut and thick-heeled and tied with a large golden buckle.

"Pray, don't break him, lass," he said. "He's fat and quite stupid, but he's all we've got."

Elysant gave a slight twist before letting the man go and stepping aside.

"Why didn't you tell me you had company?" the newcomer asked Chesterfield.

"I hoped to spare you the drear of meeting them."

That brought a hearty laugh. "But, my friend, I'm liking this one already."

"I am Sister Elysant of the Order of Blessed Abelle," the woman declared.

"Redshanks," the man returned with a low bow, sweeping his right arm out wide.

"Brother Thaddius," came a greeting from the room's other door.

"Greetings to both!" Redshanks said, in such an exuberant way as to make Elysant wonder if the man ever carried a lower level of animation. "I watched your arrival—or at least, my friends did so and told me. And my other friends told me your names and from whence you came."

"Saint Ursal," Elysant said, at the same moment that Thaddius answered, "Saint-Mere-Abelle."

"More recently," said Redshanks, and his gazed drifted to the wall near Elysant, where rested her new stone staff.

"Is there a problem?" a clearly confused Abbot Chesterfield asked.

"Yes, do tell," bade Brother Thaddius.

"I've no problem," Redshanks assured them. "Just curiosity."

"As much as you provoke?" asked Thaddius.

"Redshanks here is the most well-known and revered man in the Wilderlands," Chesterfield explained. "A legend to those beyond Honce-the-Bear's western border, and one with many friends, including me."

The older man shrugged rather sheepishly. He looked directly at Thaddius. "I listen more than I talk, good brother. Hard to believe, I know."

"And what have you heard, with all of this listening?"

"A tale of some old, old graves, and of a plot to deceive a pair of monks, and of some fools walking gingerly on burned feet."

"What is this all about?" Abbot Chesterfield demanded.

"And of specters and ghosts," Redshanks finished.

"You've heard one side alone, and that side is incomplete, I expect," Brother Thaddius replied, and he looked to Elysant and shook his head slightly, and she knew that he had noticed her inching for her staff.

"I was hoping to hear the other side and a tale more complete."

"Hope is a good thing, whether it comes to fruition or not," said Thaddius.

"Then I hope you will stay and we will get to know and trust each other. I am curious how you escaped that tomb." He looked to Elysant and grinned knowingly. "Fine staff," he said with a wink.

"I prefer a man who speaks directly," Elysant said. "Are you accusing us of something?"

"Hardly," Redshanks said with a laugh. "Well, I am accusing you of having a fine and worthy adventure. In my younger years, I attended the Matinee of the frontiersmen each spring, where the tales grew long as the drink grew short. It has been years since I've heard tales of a worthy adventure, so I hope we will come to be friends."

He ended with a wide smile and another bow, then bade Abbot Chesterfield to follow him and took his leave.

"We should gather our things and go," Elysant said, as soon as she and Thaddius were alone.

But the brother shook his head. "No, I have waited too long already to open the alabaster coffers. I would not return to Ursal until I better understand that which we have found."

"Keep your soul stone full of energy, then," said Elysant. "Abbot Chesterfield tried to touch me, and if he does so again, you will need the power of the gem to reattach his arm to his body."

Thaddius looked at her curiously. "You should have called for me," he said.

"You think I need your help?"

"I think I would like to watch," he replied.

6

THE MARCH OF LIGHT

The summer sun blazed off the golden domes of the recovered xoconai city. The work continued, but most of the repairs were nearing completion, and the sheer beauty of the place had been restored.

Tuolonatl stood down by the lake and the new docks being built on the eastern side of the mountain fissure, looking across the wide waters, contemplating the best ways to move her large army. They needed to march soon, she knew, for more and more warriors kept streaming in over the peaks of Tzatzini, the great mountain that shadowed the valley and city of Otontotomi. The lake could supply this burgeoning place, but the xoconai were running out of room.

Tuolonatl had learned enough of the immediate region about the lake and the rivers running from it to know that the hot sun would not hinder their passage. Once that area had been a great and barren desert and summer travel would have been difficult, but no more.

The question, of course, was where and how far? What conquests awaited them, what resistance might they find?

Even Pixquicauh, with his divination, even Scathmizzane himself, in those rare moments when he appeared among them, offered little insight beyond the immediate area.

So Tuolonatl was pleased indeed that morning when word came to her that Ataquixt, her prime scout, had at last returned.

He came right down to the docks to meet with her, and the two rowed out onto the lake in a small boat to privately discuss his findings.

"We will find weeks of empty travel," he told her. "Lands untamed and mostly uninhabited, with more goblins than the human children of Cizinfozza. But not enough of either to slow us."

"Or to make the journey worth the trouble," Tuolonatl finished.

"The fleeing humans made it," said Ataquixt. "I followed them all the way to a small village. I think it was a celebration, where the humans who hunt these wilderness lands come together before the season begins in full."

"How many?"

"Around an equal number to the hundred refugees from this land."

"We will not need much of an army, then," said the woman. "We could hard ride a group of mundunugu and take the place swiftly."

"I moved beyond that small village," Ataquixt said. "I found high ground that I could survey, further to the east."

Tuolonatl cocked her head and stared at him expectantly. She could tell from his voice that he was saving the best news for last.

"I saw the lights of other villages across the plains and along the lower foothills of more mountains," the scout explained. "More and more villages further and further to the east."

"Enough to sustain an army of a hundred thousand?"

"I cannot say, and because I cannot speak the language of

these humans, I cannot know if my suspicion is correct, but I believe that the true nations of the humans lie even further to the east, and what I saw was much like Skithivale and Hashenvalley, or Romaja to the south."

Tuolonatl leaned back in the boat, digesting that. North of the great cities of Tonoloya lay the valleys Ataquixt had just referenced. These were the borderlands of Tonoloya, full of independent-minded xoconai who held allegiance to Scathmizzane and to one or another of the city sovereigns nearest their regions only for practical purposes. They were farmers and hunters and vintners and needed the trade with the greater cities.

Romaja, to the south, was even wilder and less populated, and with fewer interactions with the southern sovereigns of Tonoloya. Why should the humans be any different in their social constructs, she wondered? In every kingdom, every nation, every group, there were always some who preferred the less tamed lands, who sought space above convenience, and who preferred the dangers of the wilderness to the suffocating rules of the tamed lands.

"You did not see the eastern sea?" she asked.

"I saw mountains in the south, running east beyond my sight," Ataquixt answered. "Great and tall mountains, as tall as Tzatzini and more. My journey to the east, like that of the refugees I pursued, was mostly on the waterways, and the water flowed swiftly, with few falls or rapids. An easy journey with my cuetzpali hunting for me, may Scathmizzane forever bless that fine mount. The journey back was more difficult and took me twice as long—nearly six weeks of riding, dawn to dusk."

"A thousand miles?

"Half again, and I do not believe that I was anywhere near the eastern sea. The boundaries of the land beyond Tonoloya are immense, my leader. Vast lands."

Tuolonatl sighed and rubbed her face, not thrilled at all by the report. Moving an army through civilized lands was far easier than across the wilderness, even if every week brought battles. How could she feed an army the size of the one leaving Otontotomi without fields of grain and cities with huge storerooms to conquer along the way?

"It would seem that the children of Scathmizzane and the children of Cizinfozza were separated by more than the mountain wall of Teotl Tenamitl," she said.

"The rumored great cities of them, if they exist, then yes," Ataquixt agreed.

Tuolonatl looked to the west, to the towering mountain range the xoconai called Teotl Tenamitl, God's Parapet. She had thought that range the dividing line of the world, with the xoconai to the west, the humans to the east, and while that might be true, she had never imagined that those lands to the east were so much larger than the basin of Tonoloya, a strip of fertile land from the mountains to the western sea that was only a few hundred miles of ground east to west, and perhaps thrice that north to south. How many Tonoloya-sized journeys would they have to undertake before they even looked upon the rumored great cities of the humans?

"We must go to the great pyramid and tell this to Pixquicauh," she told Ataquixt. "Let us hope that he has the ear of Scathmizzane this day, that we can find guidance. I would not lose the whole of the summer in empty wilderness."

"Will we even march?" the scout dared to ask.

That had Tuolonatl looking to the east, the seemingly endless east. She nodded her head, though. Whatever surprises the land beyond the conquered plateau might hold, whatever trials they might face in their long journey, whatever years might pass in their conquests, she understood the will of Scathmizzane.

The god would see the sun rise over his kingdom from the beaches of the eastern sea and would see it set behind his kingdom from the beaches of the western sea.

Of that, she had no doubt.

* * *

"He is still providing valuable information?" Tuolonatl asked High Priest Pixquicauh, when she caught up to him on a high balcony in the main temple of Otontotomi. She had expected that, by this point, Pixquicauh would have executed the human she had captured on the mountainside, but there he was, in a chamber below them in this very temple, hanging from his hooks in front of a golden mirror. Curiously, the room was filled with other augurs, all staring into mirrors of their own.

"He has no valuable information for us," Pixquicauh said. "His knowledge of any lands beyond this plateau is weaker than our own. It would seem that he and these other Cizinfozza spawn typically spent the entirety of their lives in their miserable little villages. This one, Egard, though the nephew of a chieftain—"

"Chieftain?" Tuolonatl interrupted.

"A sovereign of his tribe," the augur explained. "This one knew the northwestern face of the mountain and the few villages immediately beneath it, along the lake. Nothing more. He had never seen the desert that is now a lake from anywhere but the high peaks of Tzatzini."

"Yet he lives."

"Because he does possess one thing of value to us: he speaks the language of the humans."

"These humans," Tuolonatl replied. "I am slow to believe that the language found here in this place is common throughout the lands to the east."

"Why?"

Tuolonatl couldn't see much expression in Pixquicauh's face, of course, since most of it was covered by an embedded skull, but she was fairly sure that her remark had shaken the augur.

"My scout has returned from his travels behind the escaping humans."

"Only now? More than two months?"

"More than a thousand miles of wilderness each way, and even the lands he came upon were full of no more than small and scattered villages. It is a vast world east of us, high priest."

Pixquicauh nodded slowly, digesting the information, and Tuolonatl recognized the same doubts within him as she had known when Ataquixt had reported to her. How were they going to march an army of a hundred thousand warriors, perhaps even more, across thousands of miles of wilderness?

"You have learned the language of the humans from this one?" she asked at length.

Pixquicauh nodded. "Much of it. It is easy with the mirrors."

Tuolonatl didn't hide her confusion.

"His mirror reflects to the others," the augur explained. "When they look into their mirrors, they look into the mind of Egard, where his every thought is translated to them. In but a few lessons, every one of them will speak enough of the human language to interrogate a child of Cizinfozza."

"I should like to learn this language."

"Of course." He gave her a sly look, a grin under the skull's teeth, and narrowed clever eyes behind the empty bone sockets. "If the God King orders it of me."

"And where is the Glorious Gold?" Tuolonatl asked. "I have seen neither Scathmizzane nor his dragon in many days."

"He will come forth soon. Otontotomi is nearly to its full shining beauty. He is up on the mountain with the other humans. I know not why, or what is so important to him up there, but I share this warning with you: Bring no harm to the human women dancing about the crystal obelisk. I thought to bring one in to question, as I have done with this wretch, but the God King would not hear of it. He needs them—all of them."

"Xoconai females will not suffice?"

The high priest shrugged. "We will march soon, of course," he told her. "The lands to the east might be vast, but there is no amount of ground that will save the children of Cizinfozza. We will reach the eastern sea."

"I would like to learn their language before that march," Tuolonatl pressed.

Again, the augur shrugged and grinned.

"A tactical necessity," the warrior woman insisted. "I do not think the God King will be pleased to have his army delayed because his high priest was afraid to make an easy decision."

That took the smile from his face, she saw, and was glad.

"They are nearly done this day," he said grumpily. "I will have a mirror in there for you tomorrow."

"And one for Ataquixt," she instructed. "If my most skilled and trusted scout is versed in the human tongue, he will be far more valuable to us all."

A hard stare took a long time to turn into an agreeing nod, but it came at length, and Tuolonatl left the great temple feeling that she had won that round.

More than a week passed before Tuolonatl glimpsed the God King again. Scathmizzane, in giant form, rode his dragon Kithkukulikhan down from the great mountain Tzatzini, across the city, and down to the docks in the east, where Tuolonatl had gone with Pixquicauh at the old augur's bidding.

The dragon settled down in the water—it had been a lake monster for many generations before Loch Beag had been drained—and Scathmizzane shrank down to the size of a large xoconai as the beast swam for the dock, moving close enough for the God King to easily step onto the wharf to join his high priest and his cochcal.

"It is time to begin our journey," Scathmizzane told them. He looked around at the many boats that had been assembled, many carried down from the lake villages on the rim of the chasm but some newly built by the industrious xoconai.

"We can ferry a thousand at a time across the lake," Tuolonatl told him.

"That is good," he congratulated. "But unnecessary." He looked to Pixquicauh. "You have brought the two mirrors?"

The old augur looked around and nodded to some other priests, who scurried to retrieve the mirrors, the one from the top of the great temple and the one Scathmizzane had given to Pixquicauh for his personal use, the same one he had used to torment the captured human named Egard.

"These are the purest gold," the God King explained to Tuolonatl. "It lessens the risk."

The risk? the woman mouthed under her breath, but she dared not ask aloud.

"This is your favored man?" Scathmizzane asked her, indicating the young and tall xoconai by Tuolonatl's side.

"Ataquixt, God King," she said, pushing Ataquixt forward.

"You are a fine mundunugu, I am told," Scathmizzane said to the man, who kept his gaze deferentially to the ground.

"Do you think you can guide Kithkukulikhan with your steady hand?" Scathmizzane asked him, drawing several gasps from those around, including one from Tuolonatl.

Ataquixt's gaze rose quickly, the mundunugu staring into the eyes of Glorious Gold. "I . . . I . . ." poor Ataquixt muttered, surely overwhelmed.

"We will see," Scathmizzane said and, turning to the water, called for the dragon.

"Two augurs," the God King instructed Pixquicauh, "and the mirror from atop Otontotomi. Fear not, we will replace the mirror presently, and if Kithkukulikhan eats the augurs and this young warrior, they will be replaced."

Pixquicauh glanced back and motioned to two of the priests, young men both, bidding them to bring forward the desired golden mirror. Both hesitated, staring out at the dragon with clear trepidation, but Ataquixt's chuckle mocked them, especially when Glorious Gold joined in.

Scathmizzane guided Ataquixt to the appropriate spot on the dragon's huge back, then helped the priests to settle behind him. "Guide Kithkukulikhan to the spot where the fleeing children of Cizinfozza left the lakeshore," he instructed Ataquixt. Then, to the two augurs, he said, "And there, set the mirror aiming back to this spot. Recite your prayer to the rising and setting sun. Catch the rays of the rising sun and redirect them to us back here on this dock."

Away went the dragon, half of it in the water, half above, propelled by the snakelike body and the small, beating wings.

"Bring your mirror, Pixquicauh," Scathmizzane told the high priest. "And you," he said to Tuolonatl, "use that mirror to track the reflection of Kithkukulikhan."

None of them understood what this might be about, but neither were they about to question their god. The second mirror was brought forth and set on the edge of the dock. Tuolonatl stood before it, just a bit to the side, directing the priests to turn it a bit left, then right, so that she could see the reflection of the dragon, which by then was nearing the spot far across the lake.

She couldn't make out the movements, exactly, as the three xoconai debarked the giant mount and the dragon started away. The woman told the priests to turn the mirror to follow.

"No, watch your chosen scout in the reflection," Scathmizzane instructed, and the mirror was quickly realigned.

"What do you see?"

"Flickers of the mirror, nothing more," the woman replied. "They are far away, my Glorious Gold."

"Look deeper," Scathmizzane told her. "Let yourself flow into the mirror more fully. Trust in the image."

Tuolonatl stared at the distant image and, to her surprise, it did seem to grow a bit in the mirror. She knew that the trio and the other mirror were too far away for this to be possible, but she could indeed see them, moving about, the augurs flanking the golden sheet, Ataquixt behind them, directing.

They grew bigger still when their mirror was turned correctly, catching the light of the rising sun and turning it back so that the glare became intense in the mirror before Tuolonatl.

So intense! A bright flash, blinding, washing away all other sights.

No, there they were again, the woman thought, looking at Ataquixt over the top edge of the mirror he had taken across the lake. So large now, and appearing so near! Tuolonatl felt as if she could reach out and touch—

The woman gasped and spun about.

She was across the lake, standing with the shocked trio of Ataquixt and the two augurs. Looking back the other way, she saw clearly the fissure of the ixnecia and the distant, tiny boats and their swaying masts, the docks, the Glorious Gold, Scathmizzane.

A flash in the mirror across the way became one in the mirror beside her, and then Pixquicauh was there.

"Glorious Gold," he muttered repeatedly, shaking his head and seeming fully overcome with awe and shock.

"He comes!" Ataquixt said then, pointing out over the lake, and the others turned to see Kithkukulikhan flying toward them, with Scathmizzane, once more a giant, riding the dragon. He flew right up to them, hovering above them, towering above them.

"This is how we will move the legions," Scathmizzane explained to them. "Flash-steps—we will cover a hundred miles a day, easily. And those trailing will erect pyramids, one facing behind, one forward, each with a mirror to keep this magical trail open to us. Go back now the way you came, Tuolonatl. Get the boats laden with supplies and sailing at once. Get my warriors and their cuetzpali to the docks and through the mirrors.

"Go back now the way you came, Pixquicauh," Scathmizzane continued. "Gather the augurs and twenty-two more mirrors that we can begin a dozen points of flash-step travel. Quickly, before the sun climbs too high."

"How many, God King?" Tuolonatl dared to ask.

"A hundred legions," he answered.

The woman tried to quickly calculate how long that would take, given a thousand warriors in each legion.

"Only in the sunlight?"

"The sunlight is your mount," Scathmizzane explained. "For now. There are other ways, but the sunlight will be enough at this time."

More calculations swirled about the commander's thoughts. She would have to get the mirrors across as quickly as possible, then send twelve lines in orderly flash-stepping. They would have to move in fast march to keep the bank area clear. They would have to take more mirrors ahead for a second hop, and a third. Would the most efficient process involve twelve on either side of the intended step or a line of mirrors allowing the warriors to frog-hop along, stretching the lines?

She tried to consider the logistics in light of this new and remarkable magic, and more than once shook her head, dismissing this arrangement or that.

"You will discern the best way, great Tuolonatl," Scathmizzane said to her, drawing her from her contemplation and causing a gasp of embarrassment.

"This is why I chose you as cochcal," the Glorious Gold told her. "You will find the best arrangement of the mirrors, and you will keep the mundunugu and the macana marching, or perhaps rafting, when the mirrors are not enough, when the sun cannot be caught to give passage. A hundred miles a day."

Tuolonatl nodded subserviently. There was no room in Glorious Gold's tone for her to argue or question or perform any less than had been demanded. Still, she had no idea of how they might accomplish this. Even going as fast as they could, it would take many hours to simply get the legions flash-stepping to the next spot, and many hours more if they lessened the mirror portals. She could get her mundunugu to sprint forward spot to spot with fresh cuetzpali, even a total of a hundred miles in a day, but that, too, would be no easy task.

"I give you one more gift to complete your task," Scathmizzane said, as if reading her confusion and doubts. "I, upon Kithkukulikhan, will fly the mirrors and their handlers, a dozen at a time, to the next point in line."

The woman nodded, the process becoming clear, the task seeming suddenly far less daunting.

"A hundred miles a day," Glorious Gold reiterated. "Go assemble my legions. Fill their packs, bring the supplies. The children of Cizinfozza will find no rest, and the nation of Tonoloya will see the sun climb from the eastern sea and sink into the western sea each night for its sleep."

"Yes, Glorious Gold," Tuolonatl said, and bowed. She could hardly catch her breath. In only two weeks, they would come to the small village Ataquixt had scouted. How much longer, she wondered, would pass before she stood on the beaches of the eastern sea?

And what carnage would a hundred fierce xoconai legions leave in their wake?

7

THE BIG, WIDE WORLD

Aoleyn perched atop a ridge, watching the somber procession as the beleaguered refugees continued their journey to the east from Matinee. They had been traveling for more than two weeks. The eastern mountains Aydrian had named as the Barbacan were now to the north, while the southern mountain range, the Belt-and-Buckle, loomed ever nearer in the south. They had encountered only a few scattered clusters of houses along the way, enough to resupply, but Aoleyn had been told that was about to change. In only a few days, they would reach the next, larger village in line, but then the traveling would supposedly get easier, with villages spaced roughly a day's march apart.

Would it get easier, though? Aoleyn had to wonder. She had watched the expressions of the frontier folk at Matinee—a truly generous and kindly lot, a collection of independent-minded people who appreciated individual differences. Yet even they could barely contain a wince when they looked upon the uamhas who composed almost all of this caravan, with their elongated heads and double-humped skulls. Aoleyn wasn't at all sure that the refugees of Ayam-haras would find peace and hospitality in the lands east, where everyone looked more like her, Talmadge, Khotai (other than her much darker skin), Aydrian, and, she was thankful, Bahdlahn.

She scanned about, looking for her closest friend. She had been getting the sense that Bahdlahn had been somewhat avoiding her since that evening beside the lake, and memories of that conversation pained Aoleyn profoundly. It would have been easier for her—so much so!—to simply continue her intimacy with Bahdlahn, to give him her love and the security he likely desired. Easier for her, perhaps, but in the end, not so much for him. In many ways, Bahdlahn had to grow, to experience more, to learn more about himself before giving himself wholly to anyone else. Aoleyn did not at all regret spending that night in intimacy with him on the high mountain perch under the stars—it had truly been a magical and wonderful experience for her, a healing encounter in which she had shaken off the last vestiges of pain from the domination of Brayth and Tay Aillig.

That night on the high perch, Aoleyn had found so many answers, and confidence. And freedom, a more genuine and lasting understanding of her own physical independence.

It had been good for Bahdlahn, too, in many different ways. Most of all, they had shared the bond of trust, something neither of them had ever truly found outside of each other. She had not taken advantage of him that night, had not used him selfishly. And certainly, Aoleyn had never intended for things to progress between them in this manner and at this pace, for, at that time, she had no expectation of the great events that would so quickly undo their entire world!

"I never meant to hurt you," she whispered, though she knew he could not hear.

She smiled when she at last spotted him, on the far side of the caravan, going through practice movements with a most amazing sword, under the direction of Aydrian.

The smile disappeared when Aoleyn considered that she might be grinning more about Aydrian than Bahdlahn. The man from the east had taken up the void, had filled the hole in Bahdlahn's heart after the rejection by Aoleyn, by asking the young man to serve as his squire. Aydrian would train him in the ways of the sword and the bow, and even teach him the language of the east.

Aydrian knew what Aoleyn knew: Bahdlahn had great potential but remained far from a finished man ready for the severe challenges they were all likely to face soon.

She smiled again and didn't care about the source. They had escaped, for now at least, and the road ahead was both promising and terrifying. A new challenge, she thought, and she nodded and smiled wider when she noted Khotai leaping all about in great and easy bounds.

Aoleyn had given her that gift. Aoleyn had made Khotai's life better, and Talmadge's life better by extension.

She had shared a great gift with Bahdlahn that night on the mountainside, one they had given to each other and that had lifted them both in confidence and purpose. And she had given him another, equally important gift that night by the lake.

She had given him his freedom, that he could discover himself fully.

Regrets could not take hold in the thoughts of the young witch. She looked back to the west only rarely and briefly. Her gaze was to the east, mostly, to the future, to the adventure.

She would survive this, she told herself, and she would do to her enemies as she had done to Tay Aillig.

She thought of him then, only briefly, lying among the fallen rocks, dying painfully, begging her for help.

The woman lifted an arm and watched it transform into the paw of a leopard. She flexed her claws, marveling at their length and delicate curve, and though her thoughts were grim and that memory of Tay Aillig's ending was full of blood, Aoleyn nodded once more.

And grinned.

So be it.

The arrow flew from on high, speeding down to hit its target, though a bit to the left edge.

"You are drifting again," Aydrian told Khotai as she descended from her seemingly impossible high leap.

"How can I not, when the breeze captures me and flings me like a dry leaf?"

"I mean with your eyes," Aydrian explained. "Teach your body to hold fast your aim, though it is shifting aside."

"I hit the target," the woman countered.

"So you did, indeed!" Aydrian said with a laugh. He looked to Talmadge, Bahdlahn, and Catriona, the latter two having taken a break from their sparring to watch Khotai's amazing leaps and her newfound skill with the bow, Hawkwing, that Aydrian had loaned to her.

"I still prefer the spear," Catriona said.

"Fair enough," said Talmadge. "But consider that Khotai will not be shooting as a distraction against her charge. With the magic Aoleyn has given to her, she is too light for close fighting, with no weight behind her blows and no way to stand her ground."

"Even shooting an arrow sends me drifting," the Togai-ru woman said with a helpless chuckle.

"Do not despair," Aydrian said.

"Despair?" she echoed incredulously. "A month ago, I was crawling about on the ground, ruining my hands from clawing, filthy from the dirt I could not escape, and dependent upon all around me. Now?" She stopped and sprang upward, her foot coming a dozen feet from the ground, and let fly another arrow, this one hitting nearer the center of the distant target.

"Now I can silence Talmadge from thirty strides when he annoys me," she said, touching down easily on that one foot. She paused and glanced to the side, then smiled more widely still and said, "Because of her."

All of them turned to follow that gaze, to see Aoleyn off in the distance, upon a ridge, watching, as she ever seemed to be watching.

And, they knew, protecting them with her magic.

Bahdlahn stabbed his practice sword into the soft ground and wiped the sweat and grime from his hands as he stepped aside.

"So you're thinking that we're done, are you?" Catriona teased, leveling the dulled spear that had put more than one bruise on the young man's body this morning.

"I have to go," Bahdlahn said seriously. He looked to Talmadge, then to Khotai. "I have to go and tell her."

"We will make Appleby-in-Wilderland in three days," Khotai reminded him.

"She should know before," Bahdlahn replied, walking away.

"We have caught three of them," Ataquixt told Tuolonatl, the pair sitting astride their mounts, the scout on a cuetzpali, the commander astride her beloved horse, Pocheoya. "They fight well and know the region, and they do not speak the same tongue as those we captured on Tzatzini."

"I feared that," Tuolonatl replied. "We are a long way from that land. I doubt these humans have had much contact with the villages we conquered, in many years, if ever."

"Why are the children of Cizinfozza so disparate? Our Glorious Gold would never allow—"

"Because they are wider spread," Tuolonatl explained. "And, from what High Priest Pixquicauh has learned, they are further removed from their god. Pixquicauh claims that the villagers on the lakeshore with the strange heads did not even worship the same god as those on the mountain, and that they shaped their heads simply to be different from those mountain humans, whom they considered demons."

Ataquixt shook his head.

"What plans, then?" he asked, motioning down the wide expanse before them, where a massive building stood among many tents.

Tuolonatl spent a long while considering their next moves. The forward legion had flash-stepped through the mirror some twenty miles to the west, but the march from that point had commenced on foot and on cuetzpali, as Pixquicauh had ordered the forward golden mirrors to a new task. With the line they had to string to secure the movements of those still far behind, Tuolonatl had fewer than two hundred mundunugu this far east, and, by all accounts, nearly that number of humans—and humans who would fight well, by Ataquixt's account—were certainly within and about that building.

"Keep a wide perimeter," she decided. "Do not be seen."

"More prisoners? They come out often, usually singularly or in pairs."

"No," she replied, clearly surprising him.

"We can whittle down their numbers."

"Their numbers will be irrelevant when the legions catch up to us in but a few days."

"That is the place Scathmizzane told us to go," the scout reminded. "A hundred miles a day, he commanded, and so we have done over these two weeks. Will he tolerate our hesitation?"

"He named me as cochcal," Tuolonatl reminded. "If he is angered, it will fall on me."

Ataquixt gave her a look that sent shivers through her, a look of great concern. "I would not like that," he admitted.

She returned a smile to comfort the man. "We need no more prisoners. We need not worry about diminishing their numbers—we will overrun them with ease as our ranks grow. Take the three prisoners back to the augurs at the mirrors. Bid the augurs to bring forth Pixquicauh, that we might learn this new language the children of Cizinfozza use."

Ataquixt seemed perplexed.

"Do you think we should simply burn down their building and their tents, with them inside? Kill them all?" Tuolonatl asked.

The man's expression barely changed.

"We have many weeks ahead of us, with tens of thousands, perhaps hundreds of thousands, perhaps millions of Cizinfozza's children standing between us and the eastern sea. We will not kill them all. We will not even battle them all, and fewer still if we can speak with them and coax subservience without too much blood. To build the greater kingdom of Tonoloya does not mean eradicating the children of Cizinfozza, my young mundunugu. It means subjugating them. And who knows? They are not stupid beings. Perhaps we will coax them to see the light of Scathmizzane."

"Steal them from Cizinfozza?" asked Ataquixt, and he seemed quite intrigued.

"Cizinfozza is destroyed. So Kithkukulikhan showed us, when he ate and vomited the sun. Cizinfozza's children are orphaned. Glorious Gold is great."

"Tonoloya will need slaves," Ataquixt mumbled, nodding as he regarded the distant building and tents.

Tuolonatl didn't disagree, though she wasn't really thinking along those lines. Not slaves, she silently considered.

She looked more carefully at Ataquixt, and had a notion that he, too, wasn't pleased by his last declaration.

Tuolonatl was glad of that.

She clutched Talmadge's lens tightly, but she wasn't looking through the item as she had before. Using the power of the quartz gemstone set within it, Aoleyn was casting her vision farther than the lens had ever before shown her. She looked to the south and saw the mountains so clearly, running east and west beyond her sight. She looked to the mountains in the north, the beginning of the range that ran straight north from her position and again out of sight.

She looked to the east and saw the next village in line, and then some northeast, some southeast, many more scattered about, larger and more impressive than all the lake villages she had known, most containing more people than all of those lake villages combined. And these were the Wilderland towns, according to Talmadge and Aydrian—tiny villages compared to those farther to the east in the kingdom known as Honce-the-Bear.

Aoleyn couldn't resist, and she cast her vision farther still, glimpsing vast areas. In one such glance, she noted the high walls and towers of a city, on a scale beyond anything she had ever seen before. She went there with her sight, but only briefly, for it was far, far away, and the magic taxed her.

And she hadn't yet even used it in the most important way.

Still, she did go there, and she saw the towering walls, the huge docks on a great and wide river, the castle, and another massive stone structure that could have housed all of the Usgar and more, with ease—perhaps all of the uamhas as well. A single structure!

The young witch blew out her breath and let the magic expire, then took a few deep breaths to collect her thoughts and focus.

She grasped the quartz again, tightly, but took still more steadying breaths. She was afraid now, as she faced the west.

With a growl of defiance, Aoleyn sent forth her magical sight, looking back along the trail that had brought the caravan to this point. Three blinks showed her the structure called Matinee and the tents around it, and Aoleyn breathed a sigh of relief to see that it seemed as it had been when they had left. Men and women mulled about peacefully and at ease, with no bright-faced enemies to be seen.

She pushed farther, but just beyond Matinee her vision blurred and became a haze of light, as if she was looking at the sun itself through a dense fog. Aoleyn pressed with all her magical strength, but to no avail.

She let go of the quartz magic and found herself gasping as she tried to hold her balance.

She looked to the west again, but not with the magic, wondering what had blocked her way. Perhaps it was her own exhaustion, she mused, and she muttered curses at herself for not having had the courage to look to the west at first. Even in that mind-set, though, the woman held doubts. How curious, she thought, that her power and sight should reach its end precisely at Matinee.

Determined, she spun back to the east and called upon the magic, and soon she again glimpsed the great city on the river.

That city was much farther away than Matinee.

She turned, growled, and threw all her power into the quartz, and she managed again to see Matinee—and nothing beyond it.

Aoleyn found herself trembling when she stepped out of the magic once more. Something strange was happening in the west, and she feared that she knew the source.

"Aoleyn?"

The call caught her by surprise. She jumped a bit and turned quickly to see the approach of Bahdlahn.

"You frightened me."

"It is open ground," the young man said, looking around. "I called to you over and over."

Aoleyn gave a sheepish laugh and shook her hair, then pulled it back from her face. "I was busy," she explained and held up Talmadge's magical lens. She noted Bahdlahn's movements and realized that he seemed somewhat unsure of himself here, nervous even.

"What did you see?"

"Matinee," she told him, but paused there, before recounting the wall of light that had stopped her at that place. No need to get him uneasy, she figured, until she knew more about what had happened. "Oh, and I looked east, Bahdlahn, to the villages we will pass, and a city, a great city! Greater than anything you could imagine, with tall walls and more people than we could count if we had years to do it!"

"Aydrian has told me," he said.

"Oh, but hearing about it is not the same," Aoleyn promised. "Wait until you see it, Bahdlahn. The world is bigger than we thought, than we dreamed. There is so much for us out there—I know it."

Bahdlahn nodded but didn't seem nearly as enthusiastic as Aoleyn would have expected. She hid her wince well enough, fearing that she had brought on this apparent melancholy.

"We will learn so much in that place," she said, trying to bring him up emotionally beside her. "You will grow, I will grow. We will—"

"I'm not going there," he interrupted. "Not now, at least."

"It will be weeks still, yes."

"No," he said with a suddenness that surprised her. "The next village is called Appleby."

"Appleby-in-Wilderland, yes."

"Talmadge and Khotai have a friend there they will introduce to Aydrian," Bahdlahn explained. "That friend will guide Aydrian beyond Appleby, and will lead you and the caravan."

"Bahdlahn?"

He stared into her eyes and she saw the sorrow there, but also a determination.

"Guide us where?" she quietly asked.

"East?" the young man asked as much as answered. "To that city you saw, maybe."

"What are you saying? Speak it plainly."

"I'm going south with Talmadge and Khotai," he replied, his voice strong and confident. "They agreed. South to the mountains, and over the mountains, to the land Khotai called home."

"Why?"

"She would warn her people, as Aydrian wishes to warn his."

Aoleyn wanted to argue, and she almost said that the caravan, too, would then go south, before realizing how foolish that would be. The mountains to the south towered great and tall, snow-capped, though summer was upon the land. The journey would be difficult, much more so than traveling the flat grounds toward the east, with villages all along the way.

"Khotai's people are protected by a wall of mountains," she argued instead.

"The bright-faced enemies crossed mountains to get to us," Bahdlahn reminded.

Aoleyn had no counter. She felt like her world was melting away before her. She wanted Bahdlahn to invite her along—why hadn't he done so immediately? Why would he leave her? She had known him since the day he was born, had grown up beside him, had become his only friend, his dearest friend, even his lover.

"Bahdlahn, oh Bahdlahn, you don't have to go away."

"I do," he said softly, the strength and confidence in his voice beginning to crack.

"I . . . I didn't mean . . ." the woman stuttered.

"I know," he said. "I know what you meant, and why."

"Do'no hate me," she begged.

"I could'no," he said. "I could'no do anything but love you."

"But you're leaving."

"I have to," he said.

"The world is too big," she whispered, trying as much to make sense of all this as to convince Bahdlahn. "I'll not ever see you again."

Bahdlahn came forward and hugged her, and whispered in her ear, "You will. My word, you will. And maybe . . ."

He stopped and stepped back, staring at her, trying to talk but unable to force any sound from his trembling jaw.

Aoleyn fought back her tears and once again reconsidered

her choice, that night on the lake. She was surprised at how terrifying she found the thought of Bahdlahn leaving her side, and this would not be happening if she had—

But no. She put that thought aside. She remembered Aydrian's words and remembered the other side to her decision, the emotions and needs that had led her to realize that she had no room at that time for holding Bahdlahn so close to her. It wouldn't have been fair to him. This journey with Talmadge and Khotai would show him marvelous things, she expected. He needed to learn about himself through his own eyes and not hers. She didn't doubt that he loved her. How could he not?

That was part of the problem. Aoleyn had been his dearest friend, along with his mother, for all of his life. Aoleyn had been his strength and his salvation—she had saved him from death on more than one occasion. Everything he knew about love and trust and intimacy he knew from her. Of course he loved her.

Did she love him? On so many levels, that answer was a screamed *yes* in her heart and mind, but, as with Bahdlahn, what choice did she have? She was Bahdlahn's only friend, and he, hers. They were two entwined by harsh circumstance as much as by anything else, and yet here was a wide world, full of so many mysteries and wonders, suddenly spread before them.

Aoleyn didn't have the answer, as she hadn't found any answer that night on the lakeshore. She didn't know what she didn't know, and that, she understood so clearly, was very much about the world and about herself.

"I go back to fight with Catriona," Bahdlahn said after a long silence. "Would you join us?"

Aoleyn shook her head.

Bahdlahn accepted that with a nod, turned, and started away.

"I don't want you to go," Aoleyn whispered, but under her breath so that he could not hear.

"Bahdlahn!" she called then, more loudly, stopping him and turning him about.

"I'll never let go of the memory of our night on the mountain," she told him.

His jaw moved as if he meant to respond, but he just made some weird gesture—part shrug, part head shake, part throwing his arms up in surrender—and spun about, walking more briskly away from her.

Aoleyn thought that it shouldn't hurt this much.

But it did.

8

REVELATIONS

Connebragh opened her eyes, then jumped up in panic, only relaxing when she realized that her darkness barricade was still in place. She had dozed only briefly. The witch rested back against the stone wall of the shallow cave and took a deep breath, trying to come to terms with the hopelessness and the horror. She admitted to herself her moral failure of the previous night: she had been glad when she heard the other voices, terrified screams of men and women being chased down by the ruthless, bright-faced invaders—glad that it was them and not her.

None of the trio had gotten much sleep, for patrols had been all about their little hiding place all through the night. Connebragh had used her diamond to keep their hole darker, but the flip side of that magic was that they couldn't know if the bright-faced sidhe were lingering right outside.

"How many more nights?" Asba said from across the small floor, barely three strides from Connebragh but invisible to her in the darkness of the cave.

"Is the night even over?" Tamilee whispered in reply.

"I think it is," said Connebragh.

"Have you heard anything?"

"No."

"Release your magic?" Tamilee offered.

Connebragh took another deep breath and clutched her crystals closer. For all she knew, the sidhe could be right outside, ready and waiting. Still, the three certainly couldn't stay in here for much longer.

She called to the diamond-flecked crystal, ending the song. The darkness diminished quickly and sunlight streamed in. It was late morning, for the bright sun was obviously already over the peaks of Fireach Speuer.

Connebragh looked to her uamhas companions, lying in each other's arms, naked under a flimsy fur that barely covered their torsos. When the immediate danger of patrolling sidhe had passed them by, the two had fallen together for comfort. Connebragh understood, surely, and wished that she had someone, anyone, to clutch.

Asba sat up and reached for his clothes. Tamilee crawled to the entrance of the cave and peered out. She looked back at Connebragh. "Clear."

Connebragh pulled herself from the wall and crept up beside Tamilee, even rested her head on the woman's bare shoulder for a moment to take yet another deep breath, this one of relief. She was the first out of the cave, with the other two joining her after they had dressed.

It wasn't hard to find evidence of last night's commotion. They were still among the willows on the southwestern reaches of what had been the shoreline of Loch Beag, and the ground was soft enough to show the passage of booted sidhe, of their clawing lizard mounts, of running lakemen.

By the time Asba and Tamilee caught up to Connebragh, she was able to point out a stretch of muddy ground where a person had been dragged, heels dug in determinedly but futilely.

"Another group caught," Asba muttered, anger thick in

his voice, his fists clenched in frustration. "We should have come out to help."

The two women exchanged looks, both understanding and neither believing a word of it. They couldn't fight the bright-faced invaders, and even if they did, and somehow won a skirmish, the area would soon flood with warriors. They had seen it before, after the fight that had brought the two refugees and their dying friend from Carrachan Shoal to Connebragh.

Two weeks after that, from afar, they had watched a group of refugees, probably from Car Seileach, the town nearest their position, chase off a band of sidhe. Before the three could get near those victorious humans—indeed, before the villagers had even lowered their hands from cheering—the sidhe had returned with a hundred reinforcements.

"How long can we do this?" Connebragh asked, as much to herself as the others.

"What choice?" Asba replied. "There is nowhere to go."

"I was glad to hear others caught last night," Connebragh admitted, looking down in shame. She sniffled back a sob and looked up sharply, expecting consternation, but to her relief, and also her resigned horror, she found Asba and Tamilee nodding their agreement.

"What is this doing to us?" Connebragh asked. "What is left of us?"

"Were you glad because they were just uamhas?" Tamilee asked.

"No!" Connebragh blurted. "No . . . even if it was Usgar . . . I was glad it wasn't us."

Tamilee came over, nodding, and gave the witch a much-needed hug.

"We have to get out of here," Connebragh whispered.

"There is nowhere to go," said Tamilee.

To the south, along the rim of the gorge that now held a glittering city of gold and bright colors, a gong sounded, followed by a blast of many horns.

The three moved cautiously through the willows, heading that way, carefully picking their way along smaller paths they had come to know well in the weeks since the invasion. They slowed as they neared some high ground that they knew bordered Car Seileach on the north. Strangely, no sidhe seemed to be about.

They crept closer, compelled. They heard crying, a plea for mercy, another blowing of horns.

Asba led the way, belly-crawling up to the top of a nearby ridge, daring it, though it was a place they had often seen sidhe sentinels.

From the top, they could see the ruins of the lakeside village, though many structures had been rebuilt and many of the bright-faced invaders now milled about, gathering about a long and sparse structure consisting of a raised platform covered by a series of posts and pillars, with many crossbeams, from which hung many ropes.

A sidhe in robes stood atop the platform, preaching to the gathering, rousing them. He spun about, and Connebragh gasped, then planted her face in the grass, in a panic that she had been too loud.

"Shh," Asba whispered in her ear, but she could tell from his touch that the sight of that one had unnerved him as well, for the priest's face was a skull, and seemed little more than that!

They had seen him before, only once, and knew him to be an important figure, for he had been riding the dragon along with the giant being, up from the city to the sacred Usgar grove far above.

Connebragh composed herself and looked back, just in time to witness a parade of captured, miserable humans being marched up the stairs to the platform. Men, women, even children were set in lines, one to each rope. Other sidhe were up there, too, working fast to bind the prisoners' ankles to the hanging ropes and then to different ropes coming up from the floorboards.

"What are they doing?" she whispered.

Her answer came a moment later, when a line of sidhe took up a rope behind the platform and ran back with it. The feet of a woman tied to the line flew out from under her, and she slammed down hard to the platform, but only for a moment, before she scraped along and was inverted, going upside down into the air, stretching to her limits, the second rope holding tight about her wrists.

The tugging sidhe pulled until she groaned in agony, then wrapped the end of the rope around a cylinder. Another sidhe ran up with a pole, sticking it into a hole on one side of the cylinder, then he and two other sidhe leaned on it, tightening the rope, eliciting a scream from the prisoner.

They locked it in place, to the cheers of the crowd, the inverted woman stretched beyond her limits.

The pulling group went to the next rope in line and soon had a man hanging beside the woman in similar fashion. And so it went down the line, until the platform looked like something that might be used to hang dressed deer after a great hunt. Connebragh counted thirty people, upside down and stretched in agony.

The crowd cheered.

The priest pontificated and walked among the prisoners, a scourge in his hand. Randomly, brutally, he whipped them and shouted at them, and the three onlookers were shocked indeed to hear him speaking their language, and perfectly!

He was looking for other refugees, demanding that the prisoners speak, and when one didn't, or didn't give an answer he liked, he whipped that person and motioned to the team, and the crank was turned another notch.

A woman's elbow dislocated with a snapping sound.

Connebragh melted back down the ridge, gagging. She climbed off the back side and ran off, hand over her mouth, trying unsuccessfully to hold back her vomit.

By the time Asba and Tamilee caught up to her, she was far, far away.

"You have sympathy for my people," Tamilee said.

Connebragh looked at her curiously.

"What do you think your people did to us when they came down on their raids?" Tamilee scolded.

Connebragh held up her hands helplessly. "I did'no know," she said.

"Did'no know what?" Tamilee demanded.

"What they did?" added Asba.

"That you were people," Connebragh blurted. She flailed about, stuttering, trying to explain, thinking that these two might finally be rid of her. But, to her surprise, Asba embraced her and Tamilee joined him, the three sharing a needed hug and cry.

"Brother Gilbert of Annacuth!" Brother Thaddius announced triumphantly. He looked up from the scroll he had been reading, which came from the first of the alabaster coffers he had taken from the tomb.

"The name is not known to me," Elysant answered. She sat on the far wall of the small antechamber in the chapel of Appleby-in-Wilderland, which Thaddius had set up as their study, against the disagreement of Abbot Chesterfield. "Is he the brother referenced by Saint Belfour?"

Thaddius nodded excitedly. "It truly was the tomb of Saint Belfour. Now I am certain of it."

Elysant motioned incredulously to her stone staff, to the new staff Thaddius had set by the door, to the robe she now wore, reminding him of their most extraordinary encounter.

"I know, I know," the monk argued, against her expression. "But I had to be certain before we went all the way back to Ursal, and to Saint-Mere-Abelle beyond that."

"Saint-Mere-Abelle?"

"The documents of Saint Belfour's intended journey south, too few by far, spoke of Brother Gilbert. This Gilbert, Gilbert of Annacuth, I believe."

"Where is Annacuth?"

"North of Palmaris, along the gulf, I believe, but I don't think it survives to this day. But here, too, Saint Belfour, or one of his brothers on the journey, writes of Brother Gilbert and references his writings. If the village of Annacuth is gone, as I believe, then any surviving writings would be—"

"In the catacomb library of Saint-Mere-Abelle," Elysant finished.

"Our journey and quest are just begun, my wonderful friend," Brother Thaddius stated.

Some commotion out in the main chapel caught his ear, then, and he and Elysant closed up their work quickly, gathered their staves, and headed out to investigate. They found Abbot Chesterfield and the old man named Redshanks standing by the door.

"Ah, we meet again, Brother Tad," Redshanks said.

"Thaddius" the monk corrected, though Redshanks wasn't looking at him anymore.

"And the beautiful Sister Elysant," the old scalawag said, with a wink at the woman. "Aye, but there's a name I won't soon forget. Ah, but when I was a younger man . . ."

"I would knock you down and make you apologize to my friend," Elysant sweetly assured him, drawing a great bout of laughter.

A tall and lanky stranger and a dark-skinned woman in a long dress entered the chapel.

"My friends," Redshanks explained. "Old friends, from the far west. They've come with a hundred refugees, ones stranger still, seeking shelter and guidance."

Elysant noted that Thaddius's gaze was locked on the dark-skinned woman. It was a stare not of lust but of disturbed curiosity.

"I am Talmadge," the tall man introduced himself to the abbot.

"Yes, I remember when you came through here a few years ago."

"And now I am returned, and will not go back to the west, I expect. I come with grim tidings and a dire warning."

"We should bring some of the village leaders and all sit down," Redshanks said. "You need to hear what my friend Talmadge has to say."

Some commotion out in the street interrupted the conversation and had them moving for the door—all except for Thaddius, Elysant noted, who was still studying the dark-skinned woman. Elysant looked at her, too, and only then understood her friend's curiosity, for her movements were not natural. She seemed to be more floating than walking.

Thaddius caught her gaze and gave a slight nod, and Elysant understood. She fell in behind the other five and produced a red garnet that she had been using in the study, one that would show her any magic working on the woman.

They came to the door, and the abbot and two monks then understood the commotion, for in the street stood the strangest group of people they had ever seen: men, women, a few children, all with elongated, oversize heads!

The villagers of Appleby were all about, some gasping, some even praying.

"What is that?" Abbot Chesterfield demanded.

As Redshanks began to explain, Brother Thaddius gasped loudly, which seemed strangely delayed, until Elysant realized that he wasn't looking at the strangers with the weird heads but at another man, tall and muscular, with dark hair and a fine-looking sword on his hip, who was milling about the gathering.

"It cannot be," Thaddius mouthed, almost silently, and Elysant realized that only she took note of it. She took her friend by the arm.

"I know him," Brother Thaddius whispered to her. "The whole of Honce-the-Bear knows him."

* * *

The look on Asba's face told the two women all they needed to know.

"Dead," Tamilee said, as he approached.

"They're feeding them to their lizards," he replied, barely able to get the words out.

"I want to kill them all," said Connebragh. She looked to her left, to the east, and the rim of the gorge that was not so far away. Many times she had thought to gather up stones as heavy as she could find and throw them at the city far below. Someday, she vowed, she would find the courage to do just that.

"They're bringing more," Asba said. "They're killing many."

"Then we have to hide," Tamilee said, expressing the frustration of all of them.

They were helpless here, utterly so. It took all of their wits and wiles to simply stay ahead of the patrols while finding enough to eat, let alone trying to find some meaningful way to strike back or to help the doomed prisoners.

The three were a long way from their cave, but the sun was setting, and to this point, at least, the sidhe weren't sending any patrols out in the dark of night. So they dared to stay where they were, in the hollow of a willow's base. Connebragh didn't even bring up her magical darkness at first, taking some solace in staring at the moonless sky above.

How many times had she stared at that sky up on the slopes of Fireach Speuer?

How many times had she danced under that sky with her sisters of the Coven?

She could almost hear that song now, as twilight fell and the stars began to twinkle above. She could almost . . .

She *could* hear that song.

The woman blinked out of her trance and leaned out of the hollow, feeling the night breeze as it flowed down the mountain, carrying with it the melodies of the Coven. But not the words. She did not understand the words.

Compelled, the woman crawled out of the hole. Her two companions warned and complained but then came out behind her and flanked her as she stared up at the distant mountain and a growing orange-hued light up near its peak.

They had not seen this before, or heard it, though they had only rarely been this close to the mountain.

"It is part of the sacrifices we saw this day and last," Connebragh said, somehow knowing.

She turned left with a start, as did the others, as a glow emanated from the crater of what had been Loch Beag—white light, growing brighter with every note from above.

"What . . . ?" Tamilee whispered, and led the way, for they had to see.

They crept to the rim, peered over, and gasped as one.

The city was lit as if in daytime! Sparkling lights decorated every building, lined every boulevard, and the walls.

Oh, the walls!

Right below them, they saw the source, saw crystals growing out of the stone walls, growing and glowing with magical diamond light.

"Usgar," Asba breathed, but Connebragh shook her head. She thought of the cave up above, beneath the God Crystal, where she had trained for the Coven. Full of crystals, magical all. She had called upon them to light her way through a maze of caverns much like this, though not near the scale.

Far below, torches exploded with small fireballs, then burned in their tall lampposts.

"What is happening?" Asba asked.

A boom of thunder shook the ground beneath them, followed by a communal cheer from far below. They looked up to the mountain to see a huge, dark cloud swirling above the peak, repeatedly flashing with lightning.

"The crystals," Connebragh said, trying to make some sense of it all. "The caverns . . ."

She looked to her two companions and shook her head, at a loss. She swallowed hard. "We can'no stay here."

"We've nowhere to go," Tamilee reminded.

"They're using the crystals," Connebragh explained. "They're bringing them forth from the earth itself and calling their powers." She locked their stares and added, slowly, "There are crystals that sense life and tell you where and what might be about."

"Your darkness," Asba replied.

"There are crystals that find magic." Connebragh tried to compose herself. "We can'no stay here."

"Then, where?" asked Tamilee.

"Where there are less of them," Asba answered suddenly and with conviction. He nodded toward Fireach Speuer. "Up there."

Brother Thaddius paced the small side room, rubbing his face, muttering under his breath.

"The abbot's guests have arrived," Elysant told him.

"I know."

"They await us."

"I know!"

Elysant furrowed her brow, and Thaddius forced himself to calm down.

"Are you sure?" the woman asked.

"It is him, King Aydrian Boudabras," Thaddius insisted. "I know him. I was there at the battle of Saint-Mere-Abelle, when he was defeated. I was among the brothers who accompanied him and his mother down to the docks to put them on a boat that would take them far away, never to return."

"Never to return to Honce-the-Bear," Elysant said.

"Yes," Thaddius started to answer, before he realized her point.

"We are not in Honce," Elysant confirmed. "He is doing nothing against his exile. If that is even—"

"It is him," Thaddius declared. "I would never forget him.

You know that I was in favor of Marcalo De'Unnero. It is to my great shame, but I cannot deny it. I thought De'Unnero and that man, Aydrian, would bring the discipline needed by church and crown. I did not understand until that very last battle that they were monsters. And now I see a monster in an Abellican chapel, and I am sickened."

"Father Abbot Braumin chose mercy for Aydrian," Elysant reminded.

"Only because of his mother—once the queen, ever the hero. There is no one more revered in Honce-the-Bear than Queen Jilseponie, still to this day, and that is well deserved."

"Then maybe he saw hope for her son."

Thaddius rubbed his face yet again, brightening the blotchy marks against his pale skin.

"Your hope is mere conjecture."

"Everything in here is mere conjecture," Elysant said. "Even your identification of the . . ."

She stopped and held up her hands, telling Thaddius that his scowl was enough.

Thaddius walked over to the table where sat the three alabaster coffers and picked up a pair of dark red garnets. He tossed one to his companion. "Pay attention to his sword. I know that sword—its name is Tempest. It was made by the elves for Aydrian's great-uncle, then claimed by Aydrian's father, Elbryan. King Aydrian added gemstones to it. It was a topic of great interest at Saint-Mere-Abelle."

"And on the woman, too," Elysant said. "She floats and does not walk. There is something magical about her."

Thaddius took another deep breath, trying to compose himself.

"Are you ready?" Elysant asked, and Thaddius nodded.

They found the gathering in Abbot Chesterfield's large audience chamber, just behind the main hall of the chapel. Chesterfield was there along with Redshanks, three other prominent Appleby citizens, and six of the visitors—the five who did not have misshapen heads and the young woman with braided blond hair and an elongated skull, the one Chesterfield had called Catriona.

"Ah, at last," said Chesterfield. He moved to his seat behind the desk at the back of the room and motioned to the other collection of chairs and benches set haphazardly about the room. "I am not used to such large gatherings," he said. "Not outside of the chapel proper, at least, so please excuse the less than hospitable trappings. But I thought it better that we speak in here, given the gravity of the claims of these visitors."

Thaddius was hardly listening. He scanned the dark-skinned woman and chewed his lip when he detected the powerful magic set about her waist. He turned to the man he knew to be Aydrian, but stopped short of the mark when his gaze passed across the smallish woman with the dark hair and darker eyes. His attention was caught by her clothing, first of all, or lack thereof, for she wore low-cut, short-legged breeches that left most of her lower legs bare and revealed a thin anklet set with stones. Her shirt was cropped short, leaving her entire midriff bare, revealing a three-tined belly ring set with various gemstones.

Thaddius couldn't take his eyes from that bare belly, and not for any carnal reasons.

The belly ring, the pendant hanging from her waist chain, the anklet above her right sandal, the earring on her left ear, the ring on her right hand, even the skin—nay, not the skin, but the markings!—of her hands and bare arms, all of it tingled with magic.

This stranger, this woman supposedly from a land thousands of miles to the west, was decorated in Abellican Ring Stones!

She noted his stare, then, and the monk turned away, embarrassed. He washed that notion aside quickly, though, for there sat Aydrian on a bench, and yes, his sword emanated magic, as did the man's torso. Thaddius closed his eyes and took note: King Aydrian was wearing his magical armor, the breastplate at least.

"Now, my friends of Appleby," Abbot Chesterfield began, when all but Thaddius had taken a seat. "You know of my guests, Brother Thaddius and Sister Elysant, of course, but I have asked you here because of these new visitors here, who are friends of—"

"Where did you get those?" Thaddius interrupted, standing, staring hard at the small woman, and pointing at her belly.

She looked over at him and narrowed her eyes but did not respond.

"Brother," the man he knew to be Aydrian replied.

"Brother Thaddius, take your seat," Abbot Chesterfield ordered.

"Those gemstones you wear," Thaddius pressed on. "Where did you get them?"

Still returning his stare with a hard look of her own, the woman stood up.

"And you!" Thaddius said, spinning about to point accusingly at the dark-skinned woman. "That belt you wear! You two, both of you, are thick with Abellican magic."

Abbot Chesterfield slammed his large fists down on his desk and stood up, shouting, "Brother!"

"Brother, sit down," another man implored him.

"I know who you are," Thaddius answered that man. "Why are you here?"

"That's what we're looking to learn, I'm expecting," Redshanks remarked.

"I do not deny who I am," the target of Thaddius's ire said, standing. He looked around and then opened his overcoat, revealing a beautiful breastplate, silver, edged in gold, and set with a line of sparkling gemstones.

Gasps arose throughout the room, with most leaping to their feet in surprise.

"I am Aydrian, son of Elbryan and of Jilseponie, now of

Andur'Blough Inninness, trained by the Touel'alfar in the ways of the ranger."

"You are Aydrian Boudabras, defeated and exiled king of Honce-the-Bear," Thaddius corrected. "Do you deny?"

"I deny nothing."

"Abbot Chesterfield, you have in your house heretics and traitors," Thaddius insisted.

"I would ask that you calm, Brother," Aydrian said. "The news we bring is larger than your ire."

"You were exiled!"

"I am not in Honce-the-Bear."

"They wear—"

"Those are not Abellican gemstones," Aydrian said, coming forward to stand immediately before the man, though he assumed no threatening posture. "They came from the west, not from the island of Pimaninicuit."

"You cannot speak that name," Elysant said from the side, but Aydrian didn't even turn to regard her.

"Those gems were not blessed by any Abellican monk," Aydrian continued. "Indeed, I expect that you, the good sister here, and Abbot Chesterfield are the first of your order who have ever looked upon these stones."

"That cannot be."

"Oh, but the world is wider than you'll ever understand," said Talmadge from across the room.

Thaddius turned on him.

"Do not be a fool," Talmadge said. He held out his hand for his female companion, who took his hand and stood up beside him—and again, the way she moved reminded Thaddius of the magic.

"Show them, my love Khotai," Talmadge said to her. With a smile, Khotai lifted her long dress, pulling it up high enough to reveal her missing leg and the debilitating damage to the other. To further the display, the woman then lifted off the floor, just a bit.

All seven of those who had not come in with the refugee

caravan seemed to want to say something, but none seemed to have any words they could get past their shock at that moment.

"Wondrous, is it not?" Aydrian asked them all. "This woman here, Aoleyn, no Abellican, who never met an Abellican or ever heard of Saint Abelle, created this belt for dear Khotai, returning her mobility to her."

"And dignity," Khotai added.

"You never lost your dignity," Talmadge corrected.

"How is this possible, Brother, Sister, Abbot?" Aydrian asked. "How is it possible that one who is not Abellican—who came from lands the Abellicans know nothing of, from wilderlands far to the west—how is it that she could craft such an item, and that she, yes, wearing magical gemstones all about her body, is possessed of power that would be the envy of all, or at least of most, of your sacred order?"

Thaddius stumbled for a response. He looked to Elysant, to Chesterfield, and finally to the dark-eyed woman.

"She is an Usgar witch," said Catriona with a laugh. "One who learned your language through magic and taught it to me and all of my people through magic. One who gave a great gift to Khotai, who is our friend. One who healed us and helped us escape. One who destroyed the ship of our bright-faced enemies, the sidhe, when they pursued us. She is Aoleyn of Usgar, and she is good, I say."

Catriona and Aoleyn exchanged smiles then, and Thaddius could only stand, flummoxed, trying to digest all that had been thrown at him this evening. Through it all, one word above all struck him and stuck in his thoughts. "The sidhe?" he whispered.

St. Belfour had gone south to find the people written about by Brother Gilbert of Annacuth. A race, a people, called the sidhe.

"You came all this way to show us this new magic?" Abbot Chesterfield asked.

"We came here to tell you that you must look west,"

Aydrian answered. "With all eyes, all scouts. These people here are refugees, chased from their homes by a great army, one that we fear will continue their march. We came that you might help these refugees, but mostly we came to warn you."

"We warned Matinee," Talmadge told them, mostly Redshanks. "Our friends there gave us the horses and wagons."

"Matinee is gone," Aoleyn stated, drawing all eyes her way.

"How do you know?" Talmadge asked.

Aoleyn held up Talmadge's lens. "I looked again just before we arrived this night," she explained. "Matinee is gone."

"You're certain?" Redshanks asked Aoleyn later, after Abbot Chesterfield had cleared the chapel of all but the monks, Redshanks, Aydrian, and this strange young woman from far away.

"No, not certain," she replied. "I have been looking back to the west with the magic. Last time, I found a wall of golden light behind Matinee. I thought it the end of my vision. This time, I found that wall blocking my sight just before Matinee."

"But you've come farther, so . . ."

"It is not the distance," Aoleyn told him. "It is our enemies. They have magic, and they use it to hide from my vision."

"So you don't know that Matinee is gone," Thaddius said.

"If they are all the way to Matinee, we must know," Abbot Chesterfield remarked, his voice shaky.

"We cannot risk—" Aydrian began, but Aoleyn cut him short.

"I can find out," she said. "There is a way." When all eyes turned to regard her, she added, "I can send my spirit."

"What do you mean?" Thaddius asked, at the same time that Elysant said, "The soul stone."

"You will send your spirit out of your body and travel back?" Thaddius deduced, his voice growing sharp.

"Spirit-walk?" asked a shocked Abbot Chesterfield.

"That is not allowed," Thaddius protested.

"It is allowed when needed," Aydrian corrected. "I would say that now it is needed."

"But—" Thaddius started to protest.

"She is not Abellican," Aydrian told him. "She is not bound by your rules."

"You use the magic?" Aoleyn asked Thaddius.

He held up his hands incredulously, as if telling her that she had no right to even question him about this.

"Then come with me," Aoleyn challenged.

"One does not simply spirit-walk," Thaddius scolded. "The threat of possession . . ."

"If you are afraid, I will go alone," Aoleyn told him. She turned away from him, walked over to take a seat on a bench at the side of the room, and took a deep breath as she put her hand over the large wedstone, which the monks had called a soul stone, hanging from the chain she wore about her hips.

"Wait!" Thaddius yelled at her. "You cannot do this."

"Come with me or do'no," Aoleyn calmly replied.

Thaddius stopped, obviously at a loss. He looked to Elysant for support but found Aydrian intercepting that gaze.

"Go with her," Aydrian told him. "You must see this to understand."

"Only the father abbot can permit such a thing," Thaddius told him. "The risks are too great."

"Now is the time for courage."

Thaddius glanced over at Elysant, who nodded. After a few moments to take it all in, Thaddius went to the bench to sit beside Aoleyn. He lifted his staff. He had filled the sockets with his most important gemstones, including a soul stone of the highest quality.

"You have done this before?" he asked Aoleyn, who nodded.

"Then you know the temptation."

"It is not so great," Aoleyn replied.

"Many have succumbed to it and lost themselves in the mortal body of another, or lost their way back to their own bodies, and so have wandered the spirit world without anchor."

The woman's responding gaze was one of incredulity. She paid him no more heed and instead fell into her song, her hand clutching the large gray wedstone on her hip.

Moments later, the spirits of Aoleyn and Brother Thaddius flew to the west, side by side, untethered by the restraints of the physical world. Propelled by thought, they moved across the miles with ease and soon enough saw the magical barrier, a wall of golden glow extending north and south as far as they could see.

They came to the base tentatively.

This is where my vision failed, Aoleyn warned, making a telepathic connection.

Thaddius faltered, near panic. *Do not! Go back!*

Do not do what?

Possession is evil!

There is no possession, the woman assured him, and he was truly caught off guard, for his magical training and history had never shown such communication between spirits unless within the corporeal form of one of them, which meant a fight for control of that body.

I do'no know if we can safely pass through, Aoleyn imparted, and then, immediately, she added, *Wait*.

And she went through, and Thaddius was certain that his corporeal form back in the chapel of Appleby-in-Wilderland gasped aloud! He could not believe her courage, the fearless way in which she had just plunged through the unknown.

It is safe, he heard in his thoughts, and still it took him a few moments to find the courage to plunge through that magical barrier.

Then he understood, and they both knew, for before them

lay Matinee, fully captured by creatures Brother Thaddius had never before seen, with faces lined bright red and bright blue. Miserable human prisoners moved about at various tasks, often shying from the hiss of giant lizards—lizards the conquerors used as mounts, as the refugees had claimed.

Aoleyn telepathically implored him to follow her farther to the west, and only then was the scope of the invasion revealed to them—rank upon rank, legion upon legion, soldiers uncounted stretching back to the horizon. The pair traveled many more miles, soaring up and to the side of the vast, unending columns, and saw one point, one pyramid, which had been newly constructed, for it had not been there in the weeks before, when Aoleyn and the others had passed this way.

More bright-faced soldiers exited the doors of that structure, laden with great packs. Lizard riders came out, wagons pulled by horse teams came out! Too many exited—they could not all have fit in this place! How could this be?

A golden mirror atop the structure flashed repeatedly, to a corresponding flicker of light many miles distant.

Aoleyn led the way to that second light, to a second pyramid set within a large village—again, newly built. In this one, lines of soldiers, cavalry, and wagons streamed into the pyramid, too many to fit.

Teleporting, Thaddius thought, but Aoleyn seemed to not understand, and he didn't have the time then to look deeper or to explain it.

On they went.

They found several more of these magical relay points, and it became clear that this great army was marching across long stretches of ground to supply points, then transporting magically to the beginning of the next march, with frightening efficiency.

On they went, coming to a river Aoleyn knew and had ridden in her flight from her conquered homeland, and soon the mountains came into view, still far to the west.

Surgruag Monadh, Aoleyn's spirit told him. *The Snowhaired Mountains. That was my home.*

Thaddius's corresponding thoughts were a jumble of confusion, following the realization that he and this strange witch had just spirit-walked nearly two thousand miles!

Before he could respond coherently, though, and even as he realized the danger of being so far away from his corporeal form and noted the exhaustion that was beginning to creep through him, both he and Aoleyn discovered something new and quite confusing.

They were not alone here as disembodied spirits.

We must return! a panicking Thaddius imparted.

But Aoleyn soared away from him, flying across the river to the southwestern side, and there she froze.

Thaddius started to follow, but here his previous fears came into play, for he felt suddenly a great compulsion, a spiritual calling, a summons that he could barely resist. Across that river went a procession of spirit-walkers. Nay, he realized to his horror, not spirit-walkers but the dead—humans and these strange conquerors alike moving slowly, inexorably, to the west.

An image of beauty filled Thaddius's mind, of a huge and glorious being. *Glorious Gold*, he thought, and he knew it to be a title, a name. He saw an obelisk, a huge crystal sticking out of the ground at an angle. He didn't understand it, he didn't know the godlike being standing beside it, but he knew it to be good and kind.

It was a call to heaven.

A wave of pure revulsion hit the monk. This was not his god. This was not the promise of St. Abelle!

Before he could hear the coercion once more, he was back across the river, and once there he understood the deception more completely.

But the witch . . .

Thaddius flew back across the miles, his spirit traveling like a bolt of lightning back into his body in the chapel. He blinked open his eyes and stumbled from the bench, to be caught and supported by Elysant and Aydrian.

"What did you see?" Abbot Chesterfield asked, but Thaddius had no time to answer. Not then.

Exhaustion flooded through him. He felt more weary than he had ever known, and he took up his staff and looked at the wedstone doubtfully. He wanted to get Elysant to do this, but she had no affinity for the Ring Stones and would never be strong enough. He looked to Abbot Chesterfield, but dismissed that out of hand. The man was a bumbling fool.

Thaddius issued a series of short gasps, then dove back into the magic of the wedstone. He left his body but did not fly off. Instead, he flew into the corporeal form of the strange woman known as Aoleyn.

The beauty was undeniable. She had to go to it, to touch the crystal, to give herself to this god, Scathmizzane.

How did she know that name?

He called to her, and his voice was like the song of life, the harmony of celestial spheres, the truth of . . . everything. And he was offering himself to her, calling her to his side.

Her and thousands of others. Aoleyn and all those who had died and whose souls had not yet departed.

Scathmizzane called them. The crystal, the God Crystal, called them, and it was too beautiful to ignore.

Images of souls being consumed flitted about the woman's consciousness. She had been there. She had seen the procession of the dead, coming to a feast not as guests but as the meal.

But those memories could not break through with any force against the beauty.

She walked along, hearing the song.

But then it hit her, a profound violation, an unwanted intrusion that sent Aoleyn's thoughts careering back to that terrible day with Brayth, who had been named as her husband.

Her sensibilities jolted, insulted, the woman did not think but simply reacted instinctually and defensively.

In mere moments, she saw a speck of light in the dark distance and she flew for it, enraged. She arrived like a thunderstorm, assailing her attacker with a wall of defiance and an undeniable cry of *Get out!*

The body of Thaddius hung limp in the grasp of Aydrian and Elysant, as if the man had simply died.

On the bench against the wall, the form of Aoleyn, sitting cross-legged and serene, eyes closed, hands at rest on her knees, suddenly stirred, just a bit.

"Aoleyn?" Aydrian whispered.

The woman thrashed suddenly and sprang from her seat with such force that she pitched right over to the floor.

Thaddius, too, shuddered violently. The pair holding him felt the spirit reentering with brutal suddenness, his eyes popping open wide as he pulled away from them and stumbled.

Aoleyn came up to face him, murderous intent clear in her eyes.

"Aoleyn!" Aydrian cried, jumping in between the two and grabbing the woman even as Elysant took hold of Thaddius and tugged him back.

"What did you do?" Aoleyn yelled at him.

"Sister. Friend," Thaddius blabbered. "I did not mean . . . I had to . . . You were . . . You were . . ."

Aoleyn calmed suddenly, took a deep breath, and moved back from Aydrian, her hands uplifted to show that she was not a threat.

"The compulsion," Thaddius tried to explain. "I feared that you were—"

"I was lost," Aoleyn admitted, and she whispered, "Scath-mizzane?" She shook her head, then lifted a hand to pull her long, thick black hair back from her face. It took her a long time to steady herself, unwind the shocking bits of informa-tion here, and finally look Brother Thaddius in the eye.

"You saved me," she said.

"I had to try," he replied. "The others . . ."

"Others?" Aydrian and Elysant said together.

"The dead," Aoleyn explained. "Scathmizzane will eat the dead."

"Who?" Abbot Chesterfield asked. "What is she babbling about?"

"The end of the world," Brother Thaddius said seriously. "They are coming."

"What do you know?" Chesterfield demanded.

"Run," answered the shaken, exhausted monk. "Run east. Ever east."

PART 2

THE
WAKE OF
GLORIOUS
GOLD

It did not surprise me to learn that the seven tribes about the lakeshore and the one on the mountain knew not the name Cizinfozza, or that their respective religions did not in any way resemble the xoconai knowledge of the children of Cizinfozza. They all recognized a creature they called the fossa, however, and this, it seems, was the vessel of the god.

None of them worshipped the fossa. Quite the contrary— they feared and fled from the monster.

Rightly so.

Those tribes on the lakes named a multitude of gods and a course through a mystical barrier to the world beyond death. The tribe on the mountain worshipped a god called Usgar, manifested in the giant crystal that carried the magical power of Tzatzini to them. That crystal, the heat it generated, was the only way they could remain on the mountain through the winter months, after all.

It is, then, no surprise that they elevated it to god stature.

It also did not surprise me to learn, as I probed deeper, that the differences between the Usgar god and those of the lake were more semantic than profound, the emphasis of one word over another to justify behavior supporting the present top caste in the tribe. For the Usgar, the emphasis remained on the patriarchy, surely. Even though the witches of their Coven controlled all the magic, and that magic offered them survival and primacy in the region, those women were never considered equal to the men. I suspect that this came about, as happens in many societies, because the women were simply too valuable to be out on the dangerous mountain slopes, hunting terrible beasts or doing battle with the lake folk far below. The tribe was not large, was never large, and the loss of a few women of childbearing age could have dire consequences regarding the very survival of the Usgar.

So, they studied those sermons—sermons also in the ancient writings and songs used by the lake folk—and emphasized those which supported their practical consideration, and lessened, or even ignored, those that did not.

Isn't that ever the way?

Similarly, the Usgar used the power they believed given them by their "god" to exploit the lake tribes, yes, but that divine intervention was not really very different than one lake tribe or another catching a favorable wind out on the lake and seeing that as a sign to justify an assault on another boat in a favored fishing spot.

It is all semantics, a point made clearer to me when I heard the respective prayers and sermons of the eight tribes, for those prayers were practically identical, save the name given the supreme being. Those prayers, like most I have ever heard from any religion, were mostly an instruction on how to maintain a civil society, even detailing what food to eat and what to avoid or the advice offered by a ring of clouds about the moon. As much as a belief in an afterlife, these were the instructions for survival.

No surprise, then, the similarities.

At the place called Matinee, there is little prayer or proselytizing among the gathered humans. These were the most individual of the people east of the great mountains, and if they followed this god or that god or no god at all, that was a matter kept private.

Not so further east, in the kingdom of Honce-the-Bear, where a dominant religion was shared by almost all the folk, and those who did not ascribe did not speak openly of their disbelief.

Again, it is no surprise to me that of these four groups, there was little practical difference. All of the religions, and even the lack of religion, called for the same ethics (at least within the selected group) and comradery, the same path for being "good" and so being allowed into paradise.

The differences remained around the edges, not the core, and usually those differences depended upon interpretation, and in such a way for one group or another to hold power, whether the monks of Honce or the patriarchy of the Usgar (and of Honce).

What did surprise me, however, were the similarities between all of these groups and the singular religion of the xoconai. Xoconai prophecies of Scathmizzane echo the goodness of the one God of the Abellicans, and the promises of both of those god figures present a society wished by the unbelievers I encountered at Matinee!

Strangely, to read the sacred texts, all of them, of every land, xoconai and human alike, proved an exercise of losing my religion.

Not my ethics.

Not my hopes.

Just the particular rituals and particular names associated with those rituals.

Those seem to matter less to me now that I know that all long for the same paradise, the same heavenly kingdom, the same wonderland, the same promised land.

My suspicion of those who reject this wider commonality roots in my question of what the doubter gains with such a proprietary attitude. Pride, I think, is the source, as so often is the case. If my god is stronger than your god, if my god is true and yours false, then I, by extension, am above you.

And thus, I am justified in waging war on you, in taking that which is yours, in spreading the truth at the end of a javelin.

Yes, this war between xoconai and human has taught me a lot, but has raised more questions than answers, I fear.

Or I hope.

Ag'ardu An'grian
Sunrise Face

9

TWO KINGS

Aoleyn peered out the window of the small upper-floor room of the dirty tenement building in the city of Ursal. Truly, the place assailed the young witch's sensibilities. So many people, stacked on top of each other in what seemed to be man-made caves. She didn't know there were this many people in the entire world!

And how could they live like this, she wondered? She, who had grown up on a mountainside, with sweeping vistas and distant horizons, could not begin to imagine ending every day with this sort of a view. They were on the third of four stories in the building, with windows on two different walls, and she couldn't see anything beyond twenty feet, other than the walls of other cramped buildings.

Even being within this building, regardless of the view, made the walls close in on her, the exact opposite of her favorite thing in the world: to fly in the open sky, either with her mind, within the borrowed body of a bird, or flying fully with her moonstone, feeling the wind across her body.

She closed her eyes and sent her thoughts out wider,

wondering what had become of Bahdlahn. He and a dozen other refugees, including Catriona of Fasach Crann, had gone south from Appleby-in-Wilderland with Talmadge and Khotai, intent on crossing the mountains to Khotai's homeland to alert her people. Khotai claimed they were great warriors—and after what she had seen rolling in from the west, Aoleyn hoped that was true.

Her thoughts now, though, focused on Bahdlahn. She had hurt him with her rejection, but she felt better about it now. She had done the right thing, for both of them. Bahdlahn needed to come into the wider world on his own, without constraints—and any relationship with Aoleyn, particularly given the role she was now being forced into, would surely impose a constraint.

He was in good and capable company, the young witch told herself. Besides, she strongly believed that the xoconai weren't going south to cross any mountains. They were coming east, all the way, until they were stopped.

Or maybe a second army of the bright-faced people was also moving east to the south of the mountains.

Aoleyn shook her head, pointedly telling herself to remain focused on the task at hand and to trust in Bahdlahn and his very capable companions.

She heard Aydrian mention her name and turned about to regard the man and the monk Thaddius.

"'Like Aoleyn'?" she asked, echoing Aydrian's words.

"I was explaining to our friend here that there is more magic in the world than he and his church will ever know," Aydrian replied. "Brother Thaddius still believes that the gemstones you wear came from the brothers of his order."

"They came from crystals," Aoleyn said.

"Crystals?" Thaddius asked.

"Large crystals, in a cave atop a mountain far to the west, a cave beneath the great God Crystal that warms the mountaintop throughout the winter snows to keep the Usgar alive."

The two men exchanged curious looks.

"Talmadge mentioned the same thing to me," said Aydrian.

"Beneath that giant crystal obelisk, one larger than a man, are caves, long and winding and full of crystals that are full of stones, like these I wear. My sister witches use the crystal, our warriors tip . . ." She paused and sucked in her breath. "Tipped," she corrected, for what Usgar warrior remained alive, after all? "Our warriors tipped their spears with crystals, some that crackled with lightning, others for fire, or healing, and almost all possessed of some green flecks to lighten their steps along the dangerous mountain trails."

"Malachite," Thaddius said. "Like the one hanging on your belly ring."

Aoleyn nodded, her hand reflexively going to the ring. "I harvested the stones and put them upon my body to feel their song more keenly."

"Typically, a monk must hold the stones in his hand," Thaddius explained.

"I need not. I hear every song of the gemstones upon me."

Thaddius motioned for her to come across the room to him, where he sat on a bench against the wall. His eyes locked on her bare midriff and belly ring as she neared. He even reached up as if to touch her.

"May I?" he asked, suddenly embarrassed by his forwardness.

Aoleyn studied him, locked his gaze with her own, then nodded.

Thaddius gingerly lifted the strands of that belly ring, closing his fingers gently over the gemstones hanging on those strands.

"You can use them right now?"

"Any of them," Aoleyn answered.

"You need not close your hand over them? You need not touch them?"

"They touch me," the witch answered. "They are woven into my skin with a strand made of wedstone."

Thaddius looked at her closely and mouthed, *Wedstone?* His fingers moved from the gems to the strands holding them, and a moment later his eyes opened wide.

"Soul stone," he gasped, finally grasping the woman's meaning, that wedstone was in fact the hematite stone, the stone the monks called soul stone.

He let go and fell back, jaw hanging open. "You have joined with the stones through those threads?"

"Yes," Aoleyn answered, one hand going to her belly.

"Is it so different, I wonder, than the staff you now carry?" Aydrian asked. "You do not hold the six socketed gems directly, yet they are ready for your call, are they not? Might it be that the staff, too, is shot with wedsto—soul stone, and that is offering you the magic?"

The monk considered it for a moment, then nodded.

"And this?" Thaddius asked, grabbing the hand Aoleyn had placed on her belly and turning it about to show the woman's leopard paw tattoo.

Aoleyn pulled away and eyed the monk carefully. With a nod, she held up the hand in question and demonstrated, quickly turning her arm into that of a cloud leopard.

"Like De'Unnero," Aydrian whispered, his voice suddenly raspy.

Thaddius could only shake his head. He looked to Aydrian, mouth hanging open.

"As I told you," the former king replied, in response to that look, "there is more magic in the world than you shall ever know. More forms and more powers." Aydrian moved a step to the side and collected Thaddius's remarkable staff, running his fingers over the six energized gemstones set into its sockets before handing it to Thaddius.

"Who do you think made this?" he asked the monk.

"Brothers. Those about Saint Belfour. They were skilled . . ."

"Where do you think they found this wood? Have you seen it before?"

"No," the monk admitted, lifting up the staff to examine the burnished shaft more closely.

"Yes," Aydrian corrected. He moved across the room to the cot he had claimed as his own when the group had secretly put up here in Ursal, then returned with Hawkwing, his extraordinary bow. He set its bottom tip against the floor right before Thaddius, right beside the monk's newfound staff.

The wood appeared to be identical, more dark green than brown and subtly striated with fine lines of silver.

"Darkfern," Aydrian explained. "It is the most important crop of the elves. Since you found it along the Belt-and-Buckle in the south, I would guess that it was more likely fashioned by the Doc'alfar than by your long-ago monk brethren, or perhaps fashioned in concert between both."

"The xoconai wear that wood," Aoleyn said, and both men turned to her suddenly.

"Their armor," she explained, moving her hand down before her chest to indicate a breastplate. She held out one hand, fashioning a circle with her thumb and index finger, about an inch in diameter. "A string of wooden poles strung together tightly, hanging front and back on the xoconai warriors."

"More magic in the world than you or I will ever know," Aydrian whispered to Thaddius. "If the xoconai have fields of darkfern for harvest, their weapons will—"

A knock on the door interrupted him.

Brother Thaddius motioned to Aoleyn to gather up the cloak he had given her. "Pull it tight," he reminded. "Cover that belly and that leg."

It wasn't modesty motivating the man, Aoleyn knew, for he had told her repeatedly that she had to keep her magical gemstones secret in this great city. The monks here would not understand or accept one who was not of the Abellican Order wearing such treasures, he had warned her often.

Aoleyn complied. Thaddius had gotten them into the

city through a network of connections. They had come in
quietly a few nights before, ahead of the main caravan of
remaining refugees from the Ayamharas Plateau and those
few who had heeded the warning and abandoned Appleby-
in-Wilderland, and several other towns they had crossed
through during the ensuing weeks, on their way to this
greatest of Honce cities. With the help of friends of Thaddius, the small group of companions had entered through
the docks, not the guarded gates, and had skulked through
the shadows to this tenement, where a room waited and the
landlord asked no questions.

Aydrian, too, took a moment to hide Hawkwing once
more, along with his sword, helmet, and breastplate.

When they nodded that they were ready, Thaddius opened
the door to Sister Elysant, who entered in front of an older
man who was sharp-featured, scowling, and dressed in robes
similar to Thaddius's, but much finer and cleaner.

"Abbot Ohwan," Thaddius greeted. "I am glad you have
come."

The man nodded, but his gaze went over to the side, to
Aydrian, and he sucked in his breath suddenly.

"So it is true."

Aydrian nodded.

"My king," Abbot Ohwan said, and bowed, and the eyes
of Aoleyn's three companions all opened wide with surprise.

"Do I know you, Abbot?" Aydrian asked.

"I was a mere brother here at Saint Honce when you ruled,"
the man explained. "I was known to Master De'Unnero."

"And now you are abbot, and serve Father Abbot Braumin Herde," Aydrian said.

"I serve Saint Abelle," the man replied.

Aoleyn noted the expressions of her companions, particularly of Elysant, who looked as if the old man had just
slapped her. There was conflict and subterfuge here in this
great kingdom of strange men, Aoleyn realized.

"I have arranged for your audience with King Midalis,"

Ohwan said. "He does not know, of course, and cannot know, until it is just we three in the room."

Aydrian nodded and collected a cloak, one with a large cowl.

"Just Aydrian?" Thaddius asked.

"It would be better," said Abbot Ohwan.

"He will be safe?" Aoleyn dared to ask.

The old man looked over at her as if he only then had even noticed her. "Who are you?" he asked, and when she started to reply, he cut her short. "You are nobody. You do not dare address me unless I first address you, foolish girl."

Aoleyn looked to Aydrian, who nodded for her to remain calm and proceed cautiously.

The young witch looked down at the ground, feigning obedience. She had grown up among the Usgar.

She knew how to feign subservience.

And while she was staring at her feet, she chewed her lip and fantasized about throwing wide her ridiculous robe, calling upon her belly ring, and blowing this old fool out of the room with hot winds.

He couldn't see them from under the low flaps of his large cowl, but Aydrian could feel the stares upon him as he moved through the castle beside Abbot Ohwan. They didn't know who he was, he believed, and certainly the guards who had initially searched him when he entered the castle had not recognized him.

A wave of emotions rolled back and forth through the man as he walked across those mosaic floors, tile patterns he had seen daily and that had been burned into his consciousness. He was home, and yet he was not, for this was the place where Aydrian Wyndon had fully become Aydrian Boudabras, a king he now despised, a tyrant who cared only for his own power and the desires of the awful Marcalo De'Unnero.

Aydrian had spent more than a decade trying to forget this

place and his role here, but long before he had returned to the castle in Ursal, he knew in his heart that he never would.

Now he had to spend the rest of his life trying to make whatever amends he could. That was his role, his only role, and he went at it with relish.

Still, it didn't make this solemn walk any easier.

On a signal from Abbot Ohwan, a castle guard opened a side door that was cleverly concealed within the patterns on the audience hall walls. Aydrian knew what to expect when moving through it—so little had changed in this place—and knew, too, the man he was about to face.

He kept his cowl low and peered under the brim to see King Midalis dan Ursal sitting at his desk, stamping the royal seal onto hot wax to secure a rolled parchment.

"Abbot Ohwan of Saint Honce," the sentry announced, "and Tai'ma . . ."

"Tai'maqwilloq," Aydrian answered, the name he had been given by the Touel'alfar during his decade of training.

Midalis looked up curiously. He didn't know the name, Aydrian believed, but he, who had been a friend to Aydrian's parents, certainly knew enough of the elves to recognize it as one of theirs.

"Tai'maqwilloq?" he replied. "A ranger?"

"Leave us," Abbot Ohwan told the guards, and Midalis waved his hands at the sentries in agreement.

As soon as the room's door closed, Aydrian reached up and slowly pulled back his cowl.

King Midalis leaped up, hands slamming the desk, his face a mask of surprise and anger.

"Aydrian," he breathed. "What treachery is this?"

"No treachery, my king," Ohwan said.

Aydrian lowered his head and held his hands out unthreat-eningly. "I come only because of the news I bear."

"You should have sent a courier."

"I could not. Not for this."

"You enter Ursal on pain of death," Midalis reminded, but

Aydrian could hear the man's tone softening. King Midalis certainly had great reason to want to see Aydrian dead. Aydrian had killed his uncle, King Danube Brock Ursal, and Danube's two sons, an act that put Midalis next in line for the throne of Honce.

Aydrian had claimed that throne as his own and so had started the great civil war, one splitting the secular and religious kingdom into two bloody factions. The war had culminated in involving the monastery St.-Mere-Abelle in the bloodiest battle of all.

But Midalis had spared Aydrian and had sent him into exile, because of Midalis's respect for and love of Jilseponie, Aydrian's mother, who had been both a bishop of the Abellican Church and King Danube's queen. King Midalis had heard Jilseponie's claims that Aydrian should be shown leniency because the man who had caused the trouble, the darkness who had brought war to Honce-the-Bear, had been possessed by the spirit of the demon dactyl itself.

"If you must kill me, then I only ask that you make it as quick as you can," Aydrian answered. "And more than that, I beg of you to hear what I have to say, for the sake of all your lands."

"You come to Ursal to tell of a threat to my people?" Midalis asked incredulously.

"A threat not from me, my king."

"I am not your king."

Aydrian bowed respectfully. "You are not. And I ask nothing more of you than that you hear my words."

"You should have sent your mother."

"Alas, Jilseponie left this world more than a year ago."

He couldn't miss Midalis's wince at that. Yes, the man had loved Jilseponie—everyone, it seemed, had loved Jilseponie, and that made Aydrian feel comfortably warm.

"She was wonderful," Aydrian said quietly. "I owe her everything—my life, my freedom. I think of her every day, a reminder to me that my work must continue."

"Your work? A ranger? What is your work, Aydrian?"

"To do good wherever I can," he answered simply. "I can never make amends, but what a lesser person I would be if I did not try."

King Midalis sat back down, his gaze never leaving Aydrian's.

"Strangely, I find that I believe you," he said. "This is why you came, to tell me of Jilseponie? To be sure, all of Honce-the-Bear will spend a day and more of mourning at this news."

"You haven't time," Aydrian replied. "For no, that is not the news that brought me to your court. I never again intended to walk this city, not for my own sake but for the sake of those in the city and the memories they should not recall.

"I have seen an army," Aydrian went on, filling his voice with all the gravity he could manage. "An army greater than anything you or I have ever witnessed, even if we combined both of our forces at the ill-conceived Battle of Saint-Mere-Abelle."

Midalis looked to Ohwan, who shook his head. "It is his word," the abbot explained. "I have sent forth the magical eyes of my underlings but have seen nothing as of yet. I did not wish to wait for confirmation before you would hear the words of Aydrian, my king."

Midalis nodded and turned back to Aydrian.

"They are far in the west, likely now somewhere in the region between the southern spurs of the Barbacan and the slopes of the Belt-and-Buckle," Aydrian told him. "And they are coming, all the way, and are led by a giant being of great power who rides a dragon that swims through the sky. This, too, I have seen, in a faraway place."

"A dactyl?"

Aydrian shrugged. "I know not. But darkness is coming, King Midalis. A greater darkness, I fear, than Honce-the-Bear has known in many years."

"Greater than the darkness of Aydrian Boudabras?" Midalis asked sharply.

"Yes," the man answered without hesitation. "For this is not an army of humans but of xoconai."

That brought curious stares from the other two men in the room.

"Once, they might have been called the sidhe, but I cannot be sure," Aydrian answered. "I know of them only what I saw in fleeing from them, along with the refugees who came to your gates earlier this week."

"With the strange heads?" Midalis asked.

"Yes, it is a cultural tradition and nothing more. They are all who remain of several large tribes of people, overrun by the xoconai."

"They have told us similar tales of these invaders," Abbot Ohwan added.

"The xoconai are coming," Aydrian declared ominously. "I do not know that anything can stop them."

Midalis brought his hands up before his face, his fingers tapping as he tried to sort through this extraordinary news. "What do you next plan?" he asked Aydrian.

"I am free to leave?"

"Quietly, yes," the king decided. "I would hope for your sword in this war, if there is to be a war, but I would not dare to put you among my troops, given . . ." He let it go there, holding up his hands.

"Saint-Mere-Abelle," Aydrian answered. "I would go to Father Abbot Braumin with this dire news. The coming enemies are not without magic of their own, but I have witnessed the power of the Ring Stones against them. We will need the monks."

"We?"

"You," Aydrian corrected.

"No," said Midalis standing and nodding. "We. If all that you say is true, son of Jilseponie, then I thank you for your warning and your courage in coming here. If it is not true, I will . . . Well, enough of that. I will write you an imprimatur to ease your access to Saint-Mere-Abelle, where the father abbot need not fear the anger of the Crown if he allows you admission. What else would you need from me?"

"I will need transport to speed my journey. Perhaps horses and a carriage."

"How many?"

"I am with three companions."

"Saint Honce will send emissaries beside him. A royal guard might be prudent," Abbot Ohwan said.

King Midalis nodded, but there was no missing the sudden conflict on his face, as if in epiphany or reconsideration.

"King?" Aydrian asked quietly.

"We were enemies," Midalis answered. "I remember what you did to my uncle and my cousins. Now here I am, with two young children of my own, being asked to accept your word."

"Not his alone," said Ohwan, to which King Midalis gave a little laugh.

"So clams Brother Ohwan, who is no friend to Father Abbot Braumin Herde and who sided with Marcalo De'Unnero in the war."

"That is history, my king. I am a loyal subject to King Midalis and to Father Abbot Braumin, who has allowed me to serve as Abbot of Saint Honce for this last decade and more."

"Only because it would cause him more trouble to try to remove you, I expect," Midalis replied with a grin, but it was clear to Aydrian that the king was only partially joking.

"If you wish me to leave Honce-the-Bear, I will go," Aydrian said. "If you wish me to remain here, even in your dungeon, that is your choice. In that event, I only ask that when the xoconai attack the city, you give me a sword, that I might fight them."

Midalis gave another little chuckle, helpless and resigned. "I find that I believe you," he said, "I know not why, but my heart is to believe you."

Aydrian bowed.

"But truthfully, this is not about only my belief," Midalis went on. "This is about my responsibility. You will remain here while the brothers of Saint Honce seek to confirm your tales. Abbot Ohwan, go and gather Aydrian's three companions that they, too, will be my guests here in the castle as we seek the truth."

He stood back up and looked Aydrian straight in the eye. "I am sorry—sorry to your mother—but a million souls depend upon my judgment, and I need more than the word of a man who brought civil war to the kingdom. If that proof comes, I will provide the imprimatur and an escort to speed you to Saint-Mere-Abelle."

"I pray you do not delay in this search, either of you," Aydrian said, accepting the judgment with a nod. "King Midalis, they are coming."

Aydrian paced the comfortable suite King Midalis had given him, awaiting the arrival of his companions and fearing greatly for Aoleyn. Ohwan had been a follower of De'Unnero, which meant that he had once, and probably still, believed that the gemstone magic was the sole province of the Abellican Church and of those whom they alone deemed worthy of gifts from the Church, like the breastplate that had been fashioned for Aydrian, with its set gemstones granting him enhancements and healing when he did battle.

Abbot Ohwan wouldn't accept Aoleyn's jewelry, he feared, tempering that only because Brother Thaddius, too, had been a De'Unnero disciple but had come to accept Aoleyn.

People could change—was there any better example of that than Aydrian himself? But Aydrian had not gotten the sense of any great transformation from Abbot Ohwan of St. Honce.

He stopped short and turned when the door to his main chamber opened. He was surprised to see King Midalis enter alone and close the door behind.

The man looked haunted. He moved over to Aydrian deliberately, but there was no spring in his step.

"You saw," Aydrian reasoned.

"Saw?"

"The army in the west."

King Midalis shook his head. "The monks continue their search but have found nothing, though some have spoken of a wall of light halting their vision."

"That is the enemy's front rank," Aydrian explained. "Tell Abbot Ohwan that the only way to see beyond that foreign magic is to spirit-walk, but tell him to take care, because—"

"Spirit-walk? How would you know this?"

"Because my companion Aoleyn did it," Aydrian decided to admit. "And Brother Thaddius of Saint-Mere-Abelle beside her."

"Such acts can only be sanctioned by the father abbot."

"He was not available in the lands beyond the Wilderlands."

Midalis snorted at the sarcasm.

"We had no choice," Aydrian said. "We had to know. For your sake as well as our own."

"Brother Thaddius would find himself in serious trouble if the father abbot learned of his indiscretion."

"Then Braumin Herde is not the man he used to be. Did not Saint Avelyn, too, bend the rules out of necessity?"

Midalis relaxed a bit at that, for it was an undeniable truth. Braumin Herde had been a devoted follower of Brother Avelyn in the years of the demon dactyl, standing shoulder to shoulder with the great monk, and against the Abellican Church itself, in that time of schism.

"And this other companion?"

"I need you to protect her," Aydrian said, drawing a surprised arch of Midalis's dark and bushy eyebrows. "Her name is Aoleyn. She is with Brother Thaddius and Sister Elysant of Saint Gwendolyn. And she is very formidable, and very young, and very naive regarding our customs and laws."

"Why would she need protecting, then?"

"Because she carries upon her many . . . Ring Stones, except that they are not . . . not in the manner of those collected by the Abellicans far out on the sea, at least. It is a long tale, and one that perhaps we will share when we find a proper time and less urgency, but it is enough now to say to you that the Abellicans might not understand the source of the woman's magic stones or her magical power."

"Considerable power?" King Midalis asked, and it seemed to Aydrian as if he was not grasping the depth of this matter.

"In my life, I have seen one person to rival the magical power of this young—very young—woman, and that is my own mother, Jilseponie," Aydrian said.

Midalis's expression changed quite dramatically.

"I am not exaggerating. Perhaps a few others, myself included. Saint Avelyn, too, I expect, though he was long dead before I was born. If the brothers of Saint Honce learn the truth of Aoleyn, they may well try to fight her, and if they do, they will likely defeat her, but I expect that their church will lie smoldering and half of their brothers will be well on their journey to eternity to learn the truth of their faith."

"You tell me openly of a companion who is in violation of Church law and who presents a danger to my citizens? Why?"

Aydrian paused and took a deep breath. "Because I trust that you will do the right thing."

That brought an unexpected chuckle from Midalis. "The right thing," he echoed. "That is ever the pursuit, but so often it is hard to know which choice that might be."

"You are speaking to a man who very often chose very wrongly," Aydrian reminded.

"Because you were possessed by the spirit of the demon dactyl, so claimed your mother."

Aydrian shrugged.

"And still you are haunted," said Midalis.

"Forever I am haunted."

"Many who would admit such a thing about their past would have ended their lives."

"I will die in service, as I live in service. I cannot make amends, but I cannot help but try."

King Midalis nodded and walked to the side of the room, where sat a tray on a table, set with a bottle of the elvish wine known as boggle and a pair of wineglasses. He popped the top and poured two drinks, then walked back to hand one to Aydrian.

"To making the right choice," the king toasted, lifting his glass, and Aydrian did likewise.

"And to your mother and your father," Midalis added. "May the world never need heroes of their caliber again, and if we do, may those heroes emerge."

"I understand your dilemma," Aydrian said.

"I expect it was quite clear in our earlier discussion with Abbot Ohwan," Midalis replied. "My first instinct was to send you on your way to Saint-Mere-Abelle, but how can I?" He shrugged and gave a little helpless laugh. "I can because I know I must, nothing more."

"You do right by your people," Aydrian said, tipping his glass in a deferential toast.

"I do right by my people because that is my intent, and thus I do right by my people by following the course I know in my heart to be true." He reached under the fold of his cloak and brought forth a rolled parchment, fastened with the royal seal.

"Go," he told Aydrian. "I have decided against the horses. A ship and crew await you at the docks. Collect those you must and sail fast to Saint-Mere-Abelle. I will instruct Abbot Ohwan to double his efforts to see what is happening in the west. My own scouts have been dispatched, as well."

"What of the other refugees who came in with us from the west?"

"They will be treated with all the hospitality Ursal can

show, of course. And if this war comes, as you fear, is there a greater stronghold in Honce-the-Bear than this very city?"

Aydrian took the imprimatur, offering another tip of his glass before draining it. He might have argued that St.-Mere-Abelle was a greater stronghold, but he took King Midalis's point as valid, anyway.

Because if mighty Ursal fell, what castle or city in all of Honce-the-Bear could hope to stand?

Soon after, a ship sailed from the docks of Ursal, catching favorable winds and current, with a skilled crew and captain and a team of ten Allheart Knights for protection. Aydrian, Aoleyn, Thaddius, and Elysant stood at the taffrail, watching the city fast recede behind them. They had a long sail before them, hundreds of miles, but, for Aydrian, the most difficult part of their journey, by far, would be the last few steps, from the docks of the great monastery to the great chapel of St.-Mere-Abelle, the mother church of the Abellican Order.

The place where King Aydrian Boudabras had been thrown down.

10

IMPENETRABLE

Talmadge began to reconsider his decision to explore this particular region alone.

The mountain peaks were distinct, and he had found a hidden ravine leading to a low forest and a bog, and thus he was fairly certain that he was in the area Aydrian had privately told him about, an area that included a reclusive band of elves who called themselves the Tylwyn Doc but were more commonly known as the Doc'alfar.

Until less than two decades before, no one knew of these elves, but the recent wars in Behren and Honce-the-Bear had changed all of that, for the Doc'alfar had been involved, a bit at least, and had helped the eventual victors.

Still, Aydrian had warned Talmadge repeatedly, this was a reclusive people, and one known for dealing with intruders with extreme measures and, often, finality. Despite the warning, Talmadge had felt the side excursion worth the danger, for here, or hereabouts, was a tunnel through the towering peaks of the Belt-and-Buckle Mountains, a shortcut that would ease their journey to To-gai tremendously.

The skilled frontiersman carefully put one foot in front of the other on the muddy ground, quite aware that a misstep would likely get him swallowed by the bog. The smell of death hung all about him, and the rich odor of peat, of rot. The deeper he moved, the thinner grew the trees, all dead and skeletal in here—and yet it was darker here, for a constant pungent steam rose from the swampy ground, giving the area a mysterious and ghostly appearance.

Talmadge stopped abruptly, his head snapping to the side.

Something or someone had moved over there.

His head snapped back the other way at the sound of a slurping footstep.

The man moved closer to the nearest tree trunk and crouched low, trying to hide. He wasn't alone, he knew.

"Aydr—" he started to call out, but he had to pause and catch his breath and clear his throat.

"I am sent by Aydrian Wyndon of Andur'Blough Inninness," he recited, as he had been instructed, though he remained unsure of what or where Andur'Blough Inninness might be.

More movement to the left, to the right, and then right before him, and Talmadge clutched the tree tighter, trying to prevent himself from shaking. He peered ahead anxiously, silently cursing the fog, and gradually, so teasingly, a humanoid shadow came into view.

One shoulder hung much lower than the other, he noted, and it shambled weirdly, though perhaps that was just the sucking ground of the bog altering the gait.

Talmadge didn't really believe that, but he kept telling it to himself.

Because he had to.

"Aydrian Wyndon," he repeated, standing up and forcing himself away from the tree, which was no easy emotional task. "I am sent by—"

The words caught in Talmadge's throat as the humanoid came more clearly into view—a human, a dead human, covered in the dripping yellowish mud of the bog, rotting and filthy, shambling awkwardly with one arm swaying limply at its side.

Talmadge gasped repeatedly, trying to hold to his sensibilities. He had faced goblins, giant bears, the bright-faced sidhe invaders, the Usgar, even the demon fossa. But this . . . this was a dead man, a dead man walking, a zombie coming for him. He wanted to run, but his legs would not hear the silent screams in his mind!

Closer it came, its one working arm reaching out for him. To the side came another.

Talmadge screamed, finally, and spun, and stabbed his own forehead onto the tip of a sword, angled down from above, held by a person half his size, though he doubted not at all that this creature could put the fine edge of the weapon right through his skull.

He froze and held his hands out and up unthreateningly.

"Aydrian Wyndon sent me," he said, and then again.

"You do not belong here," came a melodic response. Talmadge managed to lift his gaze to more fully see the creature, who was of course a Doc'alfar, an elf, he supposed.

It was a girl—no, a woman, he realized, reminding himself not to be confused by the diminutive size. Her skin was pale, so very pale, her hair raven black, her eyes the lightest blue, her entire appearance a study in contrast that lent itself to an undeniable and exotic beauty.

A sting in Talmadge's back told him that she was not alone, and a third sword, slender and fine, came in at his side, resting just above his hip. He managed a glance that way to see a second elf, a male, with dark hair and dark eyes and that same pale skin and undeniable beauty.

"I came to warn you," Talmadge managed to stutter with some conviction, though it was only a half-truth. "Enemies are about, bright-faced, red and blue . . ."

"No one is about that we do not see," the elf woman assured him.

"The sidhe," Talmadge started to explain.

"Xoconai," the elf corrected, and Talmadge's eyes went wide.

"Then you know."

"The memories of the Tylwyn Doc are long," she said.

"They are coming," Talmadge said. "A great army."

She nodded. "They will not find us. They have no business with us."

"But—" he started to reply, but was cut short.

"*You* have no business with us," she said, and poked her fine sword a wee bit harder for emphasis.

"Please," Talmadge begged, closing his eyes. "I am with friends. We must get through the mountains to warn—"

"You do not belong here."

"My friend is from To-gai . . ."

"Do not return," the elf warned.

Talmadge looked up at her and, to his surprise, she smiled, then blew him a kiss and waggled the fingers of her free hand.

A wet ball of mud splattered into the man's face, a heavy blow that had him staggering back a step—and for a terrifying moment, he feared that he would impale himself on that second sword.

But he felt nothing behind, just the wet mud caked on his face.

He felt a sting, then a second, and suddenly a dozen more, as if the bog mud itself was alive and trying to eat him!

Desperately, Talmadge flailed and slapped at his face, trying to clear it. Through blurry eyes, he looked at a patch of peat in his hand, to see small white worms wriggling there, one crawling across the flesh below his thumb, then biting him.

He slapped it away, he slapped them all away, and he ran, stumbling.

Zombies moved at his sides, zombies followed behind, so Talmadge put his head down and ran for all his life.

* * *

"There!" Bahdlahn said. He grabbed Catriona by the arm and tugged her down with him as he fell behind a large stone.

Catriona managed to extract herself enough to kneel, that she could peer over the rock. "Khotai," she whispered. "Oh!"

Bahdlahn came up beside her, nodding. In the distance leaped Khotai, the woman crossing large tumbles of stones with a single, magically enhanced bound. The people chasing her, their blue-and-red-striped faces visible even from this distance, could not pace her, but they had spears and sent them flying from their atlatl throwing sticks.

Khotai descended behind a rocky ridge—these foothills of the Belt-and-Buckle seemed nothing more than one rocky ridge after another—but right behind her came a line of spears.

Catriona gasped and started over the stone, but Bahdlahn grabbed her and held her back. At least a dozen of the enemies were coming fast up the slopes, and they were well armed and armored, with several riding those huge and terrible lizards.

"We have to . . ." the fiery Catriona said, ever the warrior.

Her desire to help, to almost certainly go to her death for this woman she had only known for a few weeks, touched Bahdlahn profoundly, but it was not enough to make him ignore the reality of the situation, or their responsibility to those back in the camp down to the northeast.

"What of the others, many of them your people, if we get killed out here, too, and so they are given no warning?" he asked.

Catriona growled a bit under her breath, but clearly had no answer.

"We can'no," Bahdlahn told her. He thought back to that day he had witnessed the execution of his mother at Craos'a'diad, when the Usgar named Aghmor had held him back. How he had wanted to leap over the rocks and run down at the gathered Usgar, to send as many as he could into that deep pit behind his beloved Innevah!

But if Bahdlahn had gone over those rocks, if Aghmor had allowed that, then Bahdlahn would surely be dead. He wouldn't have known love with Aoleyn. He wouldn't have tasted freedom.

"We can'no," he said again to Catriona, with more conviction and a tightening grip. "We've got to get back to the camp at once and hope we're in time."

"The mountains crawl with the bright-faced bastards," Catriona agreed.

Bahdlahn couldn't disagree, at least among the foothills. It appeared that the xoconai were flanking the towns like Appleby-in-Wilderland here under the cover of the Belt-and-Buckle's many ravines and shadows.

The young man and Catriona picked their way carefully down the slope, hiding and sprinting. They breathed a bit easier when they came in sight of the encampment, a collection of bedrolls and lean-tos set up in a small copse of trees, but that relief was short-lived as they neared, for there were forms moving about the shadows of the camp. They at first thought them some of their fellow dozen refugees who had come south with them, but no, they now realized.

Their companions were lying on the ground, or kneeling, bound, and facing the spears and macana of the enemy.

The two moved behind another ridge, lying on the back side, peering over.

"What can we do?" Catriona whispered, and Bahdlahn could only shake his head helplessly. Several enemies moved about the camp, and off in the distance, Bahdlahn spotted another group of them, riding those lizards hard to the north. He held his breath when he saw the reason: a pair of fleeing refugees.

He closed his eyes when he saw the riding warriors lift their spears.

Catriona hugged him close, burying her face in his shoulder.

Khotai closed her eyes, throwing all of her concentration into her belt as she noted the lines of spears coming down at her. She pictured them in her mind and threw the magic of the belt at them, the magic of the malachite and the moonstone, anything, for she hadn't the time to dodge.

She opened her eyes and swung her bow back and forth before her, swatting away the spears, which seemed now to be floating more than flying, slowing quickly against the moonstone wind emanating from the woman.

She got hit more than once, but there was no weight to the strikes. She did bleed a bit, though, and she quickly spread the red liquid to amplify its appearance, then lay back with a spear sticking up as if impaling her, though in truth Khotai was simply holding it under her arm, pressing it tightly against the side of her chest.

She kept her eyes closed as she heard the approaching footsteps. She heard the xoconai speak, to be answered by a second, who sounded as if it were back up by the top of the bowl.

Khotai held her nerve and sorted her path, both in terms of her movements here and where she would next try to run.

The warrior grabbed the spear shaft.

Khotai called upon her belt with all her strength and pushed off with her leg and arm, rising suddenly, weirdly, unexpectedly into the air. She opened her eyes to see the surprised face of the enemy soldier. She brought her other hand across, brought her knife across, to take the xoconai's throat before it could cry out.

She shoved the dying thing down and to the side, the push sending the woman floating back the other way, as she had planned. For she turned as she drifted, lifting her bow, setting an arrow.

The warrior up on the lip saw her and threw its spear, shouting out in surprise.

But Khotai kept moving and the spear missed.

The hours and hours of practice with Aydrian all came to fruition in that one moment, when Khotai's arrow flew true, stabbing the spear thrower right in the forehead, his head snapping back as he fell backwards to the ground.

Khotai leaped away to the north and west, pushing with all her might, calling upon her magical belt with all her magical strength. The other xoconai cried out and took up the chase quickly as the woman bounded away.

But now Khotai knew where she might go, and soon enough she came to the banks of a small pond fed by a waterfall and feeding another waterfall.

She had to trust in Aoleyn. She went to her belt again, this time focusing on the third song she heard there, one from an orange stretch of crystal within the leather wraps. She leaped out onto the pond, touched down lightly but securely, and ran across the water.

She heard the protests from the pursuers as they came up behind her, heard the splash of spears landing behind her, and spun about in her next leap.

She saw three of them, on lizards. They entered the water and swam at her, but they couldn't pace her, and she made the far bank well ahead of them.

Up she went, scaling the cliff beside the waterfall with the help of her belt. When she came to the top, she looked at a long and majestic view before her to the south, with many more mountains to cross to be sure, but with her beloved To-gai beyond them.

Khotai glanced back to the east, to the north. Talmadge was there, along with the others, unless they had already been killed.

But the way to To-gai was south.

She had no time to consider the choice, for she knew that

those lizards with their sticky footpads could easily bring their riders up the cliff.

With a heavy sigh, Khotai took a giant stride.

Bahdlahn nearly jumped out of his shoes when a hand slapped on his shoulder. He spun to strike but found a filthy Talmadge there beside him, the man tapping a dirty finger emphatically against his pursed lips, begging the other to remain quiet.

Bahdlahn leaned back and scrunched up his face as he considered his friend, for poor Talmadge's face was covered in red welts like bee stings and he was as disheveled as if he had face-dived into a mud puddle.

"What happened to you?" Catriona whispered, moving to Bahdlahn's side.

"Doesn't matter," the man said. He nodded toward the captured encampment. "All?"

Bahdlahn held up his hands and half nodded, half shrugged.

"Khotai?" Talmadge asked desperately.

"She is out," Catriona answered, and Bahdlahn didn't miss the halting manner of her deceptive reply.

"We know not where," the young man played along, and it was true enough, but still he had to work hard to keep his voice steady. "The enemies are in the foothills, thick about. We cannot cross."

"Did you find the tunnel?" Catriona asked.

"No," Talmadge answered. "There is no way to be found. We cannot go near the lands Aydrian told to me. We are not welcome."

"We have to try," said Catriona.

"We cannot," he answered. When the woman seemed less than convinced, he added, "There are worse things than death, and I think I've just seen one of them."

Bahdlahn and Catriona exchanged a look.

"We have to get back to Appleby and warn them," Talmadge said. He moved to the rock and peered over, Bahdlahn moving right beside him.

"We can'no fight them," Bahdlahn told him.

"When it gets dark, we run," Talmadge said.

Catriona nodded her agreement.

"But what of Khotai, then?" Talmadge suddenly added, and Bahdlahn saw the man's grimace and felt his pain.

"Trust in her," he told Talmadge.

"I left her once before," Talmadge whispered. "I cannot again."

"We saw her," Catriona admitted.

Talmadge glanced from the woman to Bahdlahn, who looked back at Catriona and nodded.

"They were pursuing her," Catriona went on. "She ran down over a ridge, chased by spear throwers on their lizards. We could'no get near her. She is caught or she is dead, I fear."

"Then we have to find her," said Talmadge.

"But what of them, then?" Bahdlahn asked, pointing over the stone toward the distant camp and the other refugees.

"We cannot help them."

"We can'no help her," Bahdlahn retorted. "Your love for her doesn't change that. She is dead or she is not. She is caught or she is not, and if she is not, then Khotai can move faster than any of us, especially over the mountain ground. Trust in her, I beg. We have to get out of here, to Appleby, to warn them."

"You two go, then, and I'll—"

"We'd no even find our way back," Catriona interrupted.

"It's due north . . ." Talmadge replied, but his voice trailed away and his words became a resigned sigh. These two would never find their way without him, especially with so many xoconai about. He looked back at the rising foothills behind him, then to the camp.

He took out his lens and held it up, then peered through to get a better view.

He saw the dead and the captured and the bright-faced enemies milling all about.

"As soon as it gets dark," Talmadge told his friends. "Keep a watch."

He went back to his crystal and turned his attention to the mountains, catching glimpses of places far away, hoping against hope that he might see Khotai up there.

Somewhere.

The three crept out as twilight deepened around them. The larger encampment was empty by that point; several of their fellow refugees had been dragged off by the xo-conai, tethered to lizards and running behind, stumbling, falling, dragged along, until the poor folk could not get back to their feet.

Talmadge, Bahdlahn, and Catriona went into the destroyed camp cautiously.

Three bodies lay where they had fallen, two of them from Fasach Crann and well known to Catriona.

"I convinced them to come with us," she said, standing over them.

"And I convinced you," Bahdlahn told her, moving close and draping his arm about her.

"Coming south was my idea," Talmadge reminded. The two turned to him, and he just shrugged helplessly.

"He's right," Bahdlahn said, nodding to show that he had gleaned the man's point. "Placing blame is foolishness. We all chose this path of our own accord, and we knew the risks."

"And we do'no know that those we left behind have fared any better," Catriona added. "Our enemies have come fast and far."

"We should bury them," Bahdlahn said.

Talmadge was fast to shoot that notion down. "No," he said. "We should leave them where they lie. If that were me dead on the ground, I'd not want those who found me to further risk their own lives by tarrying here or by telling the sidhe that they missed a few targets in their raid. Say your prayers over them. Catriona, bid your friends farewell. Then we leave, with all haste, back to Appleby."

He had spat the word *sidhe* with utter contempt, an emotion Bahdlahn could certainly understand at that dark moment.

"Or to To-gai, as we had planned," Bahdlahn surprised him by saying. "As Khotai desired, to warn the To-gai-ru."

"We can't get through."

"We can find that tunnel," Catriona offered.

"No!" Talmadge bluntly and emphatically replied. He thought of the zombies rising all about him, dripping mud, reaching for him with rotting hands. "I'm never going near that place again. We can't go there, and we can't hope to get over the mountains, crawling as they are with our enemies."

Before Catriona could argue, another voice chimed in. "He's right."

The three spun, eyes wide, faces brightening as Khotai glided into their midst. She had barely touched down when Talmadge threw a great hug upon her, Bahdlahn and Catriona quickly joining in.

"We thought you dead," said Bahdlahn.

"So did I," the woman admitted. "The value of Aoleyn's gift to me can'no be measured. It kept their spears from my flesh and kept me moving far ahead of them."

"We need to go, now and swiftly," Talmadge said. "Appleby-in-Wilderland."

No one argued this time, and the four set off to the north. Khotai took the lead, repeatedly springing up into trees to better scout the region, while Talmadge used his crystal lens as often as he could manage to try to see the path ahead. They found a place to hide and sleep before the dawn, but, with no signs of the sidhe anywhere about, broke that camp soon after midday and started out again.

Every day brought more confidence that the way was clear, and soon enough, early one evening, they came in sight of the window candles and hearth fires of Appleby-in-Wilderland, with one other, open campfire, burning brightly near the southeastern corner of the town.

The place appeared peaceful and quiet—perhaps too much so.

"They should have sentries set about," Catriona remarked, when the small group pulled up in a copse of trees not far from the campfire.

"Unless they didn't believe our tales," Bahdlahn replied. "I cared little for that Abbot Chesterfield, and less still for some of the townsfolk I met."

"Redshanks," Talmadge said.

"Aye," Khotai agreed. "Redshanks knew to believe us, and he's a convincing fellow."

"No," Talmadge interrupted, and when the others looked at him, he pointed to the north, to the fire, and smiled. "Redshanks."

Following his lead, the others, too, spotted the distinctive old man, limping before the bonfire, playing with the embers with his cane.

"Ah, so they've sentries about after all," said Catriona.

"Not very good ones," Bahdlahn remarked.

"For all we know, Redshanks knows of our approach and is tending the fire for a warmer welcome," said Khotai, and she started for the man.

With a smile on their faces, the four came into the light before the man, who seemed not at all surprised to see them, bolstering Khotai's thought.

"Ah, the way was closed," Redshanks said.

"Aye," said Talmadge, and he felt uneasy suddenly, noting that this whole meeting seemed off kilter somehow. He started to go on, but paused and looked closely at the old frontiersman. "What do you know?"

"I'm sorry," Redshanks replied. "I know that I'm sorry."

Before he could explain, before any of the four could ask him to explain, other forms, tall and lean, walked into the firelight, some with spears, some with those deadly tooth-edged paddles.

As one, the four reflexively crouched and moved quickly to form some defensive posture.

But they heard the hissing of huge lizards in the darkness all about them, and more xoconai came into view at the edges of the light.

Staring at them helplessly, Redshanks shook his head.

A female warrior walked up beside him. "I am Tuolonatl," she said, "who commands the army of light. If you choose to fight, we will kill you here and will go back into the town and kill a child to avenge any xoconai who has bled. This is your choice."

"They got us all," Redshanks told the four. "They got us all."

Talmadge was the last to drop his weapon to the ground but the first to get the back of his legs buckled by the whack of a macana, which drove him to kneel. He closed his eyes and let go of hope as enemies fell over him, yanking his arms painfully to bind them behind his back. He was barely aware of the movement as he was roughly hoisted to his feet and shoved away. Each of the four was pushed in a slightly different direction, each moving with xoconai escorts toward a different building.

The veteran frontiersman, who had escaped death so many times, believed that he could hold on to this resigned internal surrender, could simply let go and let happen whatever might.

He might have done that, until he noted Khotai being handled roughly, the monsters pulling at her belt.

Talmadge didn't fear his own death nearly as much as he feared seeing his beloved once again cast down to crawl about in the dirt.

11

MORAL BOUNDARIES

The morning came bright and warm, the summer sun finding just enough clouds to duck behind now and then to keep it all quite comfortable.

Still haunted by his decision to let Aydrian leave, King Midalis bade his wife good morning and left their tower suite, moving out onto the parapets that ran the whole of the high wall enclosing the capital city of Honce-the-Bear.

The castle was set near the southeastern corner of the city, so Midalis walked the eastern wall first, enjoying the orange and pink glows of sunrise, catching the bottom of the clouds in long runs of color. It had been a long time since he had traveled to the east, years since he had looked upon the seaport of Entel, his kingdom's most populous city, with its blend of Honce and Behrenese architecture. He should go there as soon as whatever business Aydrian was speaking of had been settled, he thought. Entel was a city of two minds, reflecting the colorful culture of the desert people of Behren as much as the more stoic and somber mood of Honce-the-Bear. The city was only a short sail around the edge of the Belt-and-Buckle from the greatest Behrenese city of Jacintha, after all, a sprawling collection of tents and painted buildings forming a vast city larger than both Entel and Ursal combined.

Most of Entel's commerce flowed up and down the coast, with far more goods coming and going from Behren than from the interior of Honce-the-Bear, including Ursal.

Even with regard to the Abellican faith, Entel remained of two minds. It was the only city with two major monasteries, ever rivals, and bitterly so since the war, when the brothers of St. Bondabruce, loyal to the throne, had sided with King Aydrian and had routed the less traditional monks of St. Rontelmore—an abbey with many brothers, whose families had come to Honce-the-Bear from Behren.

Yes, he should go there to see the great city, and perhaps find his way to Jacintha, as well. He would like to look upon the sands of Behren and to see again Brynn Dharielle, the great ranger warrior who had ridden the great dragon in the war that had deposed Aydrian.

"King Aydrian?" the man muttered under his breath, the question lingering. He looked back to the sunrise, soaking in the glow. The war seemed like a million years ago and yesterday all at once.

As he neared the northeastern edge of the city, the king's focus shifted to the great Masur Delaval, the river running north and east to the Gulf of Corona. The docks were awake below him, with hands scrambling all about to ready the ships that wanted to catch the morning "breath" of the river, whose flow depended to no small degree on the tides of the gulf.

Midalis slowed as he crossed the midpoint of that northern wall, past the great waterfalls that flushed the city's waste, past the huge warehouses of the docks. He tried to keep his focus as he headed back into the city, which was now awakening. The people would grow uneasy, if they hadn't already—so many innocents depending on him to make the right choices in these dangerous times.

When the sun climbed higher in the eastern sky, the shadows shortening, he caught a glimpse of the long, golden glow in the west and all thoughts of the past, of the war, of Entel and Behren, of Aydrian even, were washed away.

For there loomed the wall of light, a wash of golden glare, as if some great mirror were scattering the reflection of the sun into a defined and tangible barrier.

Unable to delay or deflect his concern, King Midalis picked up his pace, moving swiftly to the large guard tower anchoring the northwestern corner of the city.

The soldiers snapped to attention when he entered, the lone Allheart Knight, Sir Julian of the Evergreen, coming swiftly to greet him.

"It seems closer this day," Midalis said to the strong young man, all splendid in his shining breastplate, fine sword on his left hip, helm tucked under his right arm.

"Whatever is causing it has advanced, my king," agreed Julian, whose mouth and cheeks always seemed to be smiling, whose eyes always seemed lost in wonderment, whose curly brown locks always bounced, even when he was standing still.

Midalis paused a moment to allow himself the chance to bask in the youthful energy and joy of this young man, much as he had taken in the sunrise when first he had stepped onto the wall. Even among the Allhearts, the greatest fighters of Honce, loyal and dedicated, this one stood out to Midalis. He was of the new generation of Allheart Knights, who had been children during the dark days of the war and had come to the call of new King Midalis to serve the people of Honce-the-Bear with courage and mercy, an ethical grounding, and a determination that the darkness that had befallen the kingdom in the days of the demon dactyl would never again take hold.

These were the Allheart Knights of King Midalis alone, different than those of his uncle and of the bloodline before him, and far different than those who had served in the court of King Aydrian. For many generations, the Allheart

Knights had been simply the sons and daughters of the various dukes and earls of Honce-the-Bear, a collection of scions from the families that lorded over the various counties from their hilltop castles across the land—families with the wealth to fashion fabulous weapons and suits of armor and to hire the proper instructors in the etiquette and battle prowess required of such an elite order. There still were many in the order, particularly the older Allhearts, who had chosen to remain in service when Midalis had dethroned Aydrian, but these newest recruits had been formed "more of the heart than of the coin," as Midalis had put it in his decree—which had been met with more than a little consternation. It took more than generational wealth to become an Allheart Knight during the reign of King Midalis dan Ursal than during times previous.

It took merit with the sword and with the heart. It took empathy.

Julian of the Evergreen might prove be the greatest of this generation of Allhearts, Midalis had often thought. He had been recommended to the Allheart Order by Master Viscenti of St.-Mere-Abelle, dear and valued friend to both King Midalis and Father Abbot Braumin Herde. His title, "of the Evergreen," referred to the fact that Julian had joined the Abellican Order, recruited into St.-Mere-Abelle to become a monk. But while his heart and temperament had shown the proper humility and grace, his piousness had proven . . . less. Still, Master Viscenti and the father abbot had remained so enamored of the young man that they would not simply dismiss him back to the small village of his birth and had gone to great lengths to keep him in service to the people of Honce.

"What is it, Julian? What is it?" Midalis leaned on the sill of a west-facing window and stared hard at the golden wall of light far in the distance.

"The monks haven't been able to see through it yet," the young knight replied.

"I'm not asking the monks," Midalis said, standing tall and turning back to stare into Julian's gray-green eyes. "I'm asking you. What do you think it is?"

"I've met the refugees from the far west," the young knight answered. "I've no reason to doubt their words. So it is the front rank of a great army, I believe."

"What did you think of those refugees, with their strangely shaped heads?" Midalis asked.

Julian smiled and shrugged.

"Difficult to look at, yes?"

"At first," Julian admitted.

"So what did you think of them when you got past that obvious distraction?"

"I believed them," he answered. "And so I find them extraordinary, and brave. They walked halfway across the world, and then kept walking, because they knew that we should be warned."

"Perhaps it is in their interest, too, that we should know," Midalis dryly offered. "There is an army chasing them."

"There is an army coming for us, so they claim."

"But they were between that army and us," Midalis reminded. "Their choice to enlist us in the fight seems prudent."

"They could have turned aside, north into the valleys and dark holes of the Barbacan, and let the invaders pass them by."

"Ah, but I don't know," Midalis replied, leaning back on the windowsill and staring out to the west once more. "So much I don't know. If that is the leading edge of the invading army, Sir Julian, then where are the rest?"

"The rest?"

"The rest of the refugees," Midalis explained, not looking back. "That line of light stands before the Wilderlands and most of Westerhonce. How many towns? Dozens of settlements, scores, hundreds even. Why are there not lines of subjects rushing to our gates ahead of the pursuit?"

When no answer came forth, he glanced back at Julian, who stared blankly and again could only shrug.

"So much we do not know," King Midalis muttered. "I do not like not knowing."

Tuolonatl found Ataquixt at the church in Appleby, arguing with an augur. As she neared the heated discussion and recognized the man behind the vulture-skull condoral, she grew less surprised, for this particular augur, Matlal of Ixquixqui, was perhaps the most disagreeable person she had ever met, worse even than the old augur who had become High Priest Pixquicauh. At first, she had thought Matlal's constant shrieking and running about with his arms flailing no more than a facade, a tactic, a bargaining technique to get his way, and also a display of passionate devotion as he tried to ingratiate himself with the high priest. Matlal was certainly an ambitious young man, and a smart one, though damaged in the heart and soul.

Yes, very damaged, she reminded herself, as she physically interjected herself into the conversation, stepping between the two.

"Commander," the augur greeted, with obviously feigned respect, offering just enough of a bow to fulfill his obligation.

"This is not a holy place of Scathmizzane," Tuolonatl replied. "If you wish to speak with me, remove your condoral."

"This is a symbol of our god. Would you disrespect—"

Tuolonatl turned her back to him and addressed Ataquixt directly. "There is a problem, it seems. Explain."

"Commander!" Matlal interjected, before Ataquixt could begin.

Tuolonatl turned on the augur with such a scowl that he backed away a step. "Another word . . ." she warned.

Matlal reached up and grabbed his condoral by the beak and pulled it from his head.

Such a homely man, she thought, and almost said aloud, and she wondered how much his appearance contributed to his wretched attitude, or how much was influenced by his inner ugliness. He had a huge forehead, his hairline receding far back on his skull despite his young age. His nose was more pink than red, and the blue lines beside it were blotchy in appearance, not a beautiful uniform hue, and seemed as if they were two different shades, stealing the typical marvelous symmetry of a xoconai face. His ears were too low on the side of his head, their top edge barely even with the bottom of his droopy, always-sad eyes, and he always had his mouth opened into some weird mix between a scowl and a smarmy smile.

It occurred to Tuolonatl that if Matlal became the next high priest, the xoconai skull Scathmizzane affixed permanently to his face might well be an improvement.

Tuolonatl felt ashamed by her own judgment of the man for his appearance, but not too badly, for if Matlal hadn't been in a state of such continual whining, she knew that she would judge even his appearance more generously.

She turned back to Ataquixt, who motioned to the back of the church, and only then did Tuolonatl notice a bare foot sticking out from behind the block altar of the place. She moved with the other two to the altar and found a large human, the one they called Abbot Chesterfield, lying behind the stone, sobbing in pain. He had been shaved head to toe, and a thousand small cuts showed on his skin. The broken bindings on his wrists told Tuolonatl that the man had thrashed himself off of the altar, almost certainly under the extreme agony of Matlal's torture.

"The humans of this town see this man as a leader," Ataquixt explained. "If they learn of this, controlling them . . ."

"Will be easier," Matlal insisted. "They are monsters, the children of Cizinfozza. All they understand is strength and punishment."

Another scowl from Tuolonatl caused the man to shrink back from her.

"Why was he being punished?" she asked.

"Because Augur Matlal took pleasure in it," said Ataquixt.

"As an example," the augur corrected. "He is a holy man to the humans and their false god! He serves Cizinfozza."

Tuolonatl stepped around the altar and crouched down beside the trembling, crying man. She held her hand up passively, trying to calm him, but he gasped and shied away—as much as he could in his pained and broken state.

"What god do you serve?" she asked quietly.

"Scathmee . . . Scatterrme . . ." he stumbled.

"Who did you serve?" she corrected quietly and calmly. "Who was your god before you were told who you must serve?"

The man shook his head, eyes wide with terror.

With a frustrated sigh, Tuolonatl stood up and moved back to the two men.

"He said that he served Cizinfozza?" she asked, and Matlal nodded. But Ataquixt insisted, "He did not know the name."

"He said there was only one true god, the all-god, the creator of all," Matlal said.

"Did he name Cizinfozza? Did he invoke the god of darkness and death?"

"No!" Ataquixt insisted when Matlal hesitated. "None of them have. Not here, not in any of the villages we have conquered, from what I have heard."

"They are the children of Cizinfozza, by the words of Scathmizzane," Matlal insisted, trying hard to keep his voice beneath the level of a shriek, but only barely succeeding. "That they have forgotten the name, or use some other name in their strange language, is irrelevant!"

"You will stop," Tuolonatl pointedly told Matlal.

"Cochcal?"

"End your torture, of this man or any other. These are our prisoners now, and so in our care. They will not be mistreated in any way unless they take action against us."

"My great commander?" the augur asked in blank disbelief.

"In any way," Tuolonatl reiterated slowly and emphatically.

"They are the children of Cizinfozza!"

"And we are the children of Scathmizzane!" Tuolonatl shouted back in his face. "Of Glorious Gold, of the Light and the Truth and the Joy. Why would you have us behave as we would expect the children of Cizinfozza would act? Why would you have us emulate the worst of their ways?"

"We killed one in four of them in taking the town," the augur reminded.

"And these remaining have surrendered and are thus in our care. We will show them the mercy and the beauty of Glorious Gold, for the sake of our souls—and, you fool, because it will make our task easier as we press on. Would you leave thousands of desperate and angry prisoners behind as we move forward, where our numbers about them will not be enough to control them, should they revolt?"

"I would leave thousands of corpses of the children of Cizinfozza," the augur replied with conviction.

"Then you are an even bigger fool. For who will cart our supplies? Who will harvest the fields or slaughter the feed animals or dress the deer our hunters bring in? Who will care for our mounts and repair our wagons? Who will build the temples to Scathmizzane, or do you believe that we have enough mundunugu and macana to spare for such menial tasks? Our army moves by conquest, not extermination. We grow Tonoloya by gaining subjects, not corpses."

"Slaves," Matlal corrected.

Tuolonatl conceded that much with a shrug, as if it did not matter—even though, to her thinking, it most certainly did.

This was more than semantics to her, but whatever one might call these wretched, captured humans, she knew from long experience that they would be easier to control and far less dangerous if there remained something for them to lose.

She glanced back at the man whimpering and bleeding on the floor. Abbot Chesterfield had nothing left to lose. If the remaining humans of Appleby saw him, they might come to the same conclusion about themselves.

"Pixquicauh—" Matlal began.

"Is not here," Tuolonatl cut him short.

"He will arrive this morning," the augur insisted, and Ataquixt confirmed it with a nod.

Tuolonatl tried to keep a calm facade as she chewed her lip. That one would complicate so very much, she knew. His impatience galled her, but more than that, Pixquicauh did not know what he did not know about a military campaign.

There was nothing more threatening to the success of this ambitious adventure than that.

"Keep him in this place and let no others see him," she ordered both men. She looked hard at Matlal as she added, to Ataquixt, "If Augur Matlal harms the human priest again, crack his skull with your macana." She paused, noting the augur's supreme scowl, as if he were about to explode in protest.

Smiling wickedly at him, Tuolonatl then pulled her own macana from her belt and held it out to Ataquixt. "Or here," she explained, "use mine, as your hand will be my hand in the act, and if High Priest Pixquicauh is angered by the deed, let him be angry with me."

"How far into the skull would you have the teeth bite, Commander?" Ataquixt asked, in just the right tone to make the blood drain from Matlal's face, his nose seeming more that of a human than a xoconai in the moment.

Tuolonatl shrugged. "Just clean the blood and the bits of brain from the teeth of the macana before you return it to me."

Ataquixt smiled.

Tuolonatl left the church.

Out of breath from running up the tight spiral staircase in the tallest tower in Ursal, a watch turret centered in the city's southern wall and rising some four hundred feet from the ground, King Midalis crawled up through the trapdoor in the floor to join the two watchmen and the Allheart Knight who had summoned him.

With just the four of them up there, the floor was crowded, and Midalis was a bit unnerved to be pressed so close to the waist-high wall at such a height. He was glad that the tower's top room was roofed and that the corner posts were thick and reassuring.

"The south wall, my king," said Dame Koreen of Vanguard, a giant of a woman, obviously rich in Alpinadoran blood. She pointed to the spyglass in the middle of the south wall, set on a rotating base so that it could swivel enough to command a view of all the lands south of the city. An enchanted crystal, a quartz similar to the one in Talmadge's lens, offered far-sight so powerful that when he first looked through the item, Midalis could clearly see a cluster of houses nearly halfway to the Belt-and-Buckle, mountains that loomed more than a hundred miles to the south.

With Koreen instructing him, he brought the angle lower, nearer to the city, and turned a bit to the west.

And then he saw them, a line of carts and mules and desperate people carrying large packs. The refugees of the western towns he had been wondering about only a short while earlier. He couldn't make them out clearly, but enough to know that there were children among the caravan, and that they were moving with all speed.

"The poor souls," he whispered.

"Further west," Dame Koreen told him. He shifted the spyglass—too far at first, and he had to turn away and blink from the sting of the bright wall of golden light. He went back more carefully, searching the fields and forests before the wall.

And he saw them, and he knew that Aydrian had not lied to him.

"How far?" he said, standing straight and staring out with his naked eye, where all seemed calm.

"The refugees are a day's ride south," Dame Koreen explained. "The pursuers will catch them soon after that."

"So you believe that I should send out the Allhearts to rescue them?"

"A task I would eagerly accept."

Midalis glanced back at the woman, his first appointee to the knightly order. Koreen of Vanguard had served in the Coastpoint Guards on Pireth Dancard, the sentinel fortress on the islands in the center of the mouth of the great Gulf of Corona. She alone had held the docks against a barrel-boat crew of vicious powrie dwarves, striking down a half dozen of the bloody caps and suffering several nearly mortal wounds before reinforcements reached her and pulled her away. Now in her midthirties, Koreen was even stronger and better with the blade, and her skills at commanding soldiers had most of her peers whispering that she would one day serve as the garrison commander of the Allhearts in Ursal, perhaps even becoming second to the king in the hierarchy of Honce-the-Bear's military.

"Why are they not turning for Ursal?" Midalis asked, looking back out to the south, even returning to the spyglass to try to glimpse the long refugee caravan yet again. "They know we are here. Should they not be running for the safety of our walls?"

"Perhaps those in the front believe that the long line behind them will slow the enemies enough for them to get away, and that the enemies will turn for the city," Koreen offered. "Or perhaps they are too desperate to even consider where they are and where they should go, other than away from those pursuing. It is difficult to think tactically, my king, when you are dragging your children down a road just ahead of murderous pursuit."

"Tell me your advice," Midalis bade her.

"Two score knights," she said without hesitation, and Midalis knew that she had been planning this out carefully long before he had arrived. "We will turn them north to the city and form a line behind the refugees to protect them."

"Only two score?" Midalis asked. "How many enemies can forty knights fend?"

"The pursuit is not a sizable force. A forward expeditionary group, I expect, or cavalry sent out to chase down those who flee, while the main army houses and regroups in and about the captured villages."

"You assume much."

"It is how I would do it," Koreen told him, and he nodded.

"That is a lot of open ground between you and the city," Midalis remarked. "Perhaps too much."

Her nod informed him that she hadn't dismissed the possibility of this being a trap.

"Two score," he agreed after a few moments of consideration. "And do not find yourself in a pitched battle. We know not what lies beyond that shield of light, but if what I have been told proves true, we will need all the Allheart Knights and more to defend the city."

"My king, I go," said Koreen, and she dropped to the trapdoor.

"One monk for every five knights," Midalis told her. "Go to Abbot Ohwan and tell him to give over eight brothers skilled in riding and strong in the Ring Stones. Give them the fastest horses you can manage—they are there to keep you alive, but I'll lose no monks out there in the fields when their healing skills will be sorely needed here in the city."

"Yes, my king," Koreen said, her voice already distant.

King Midalis stood in the high tower, staring out to the south. The two men flanking him didn't seem to know what to do or how to react, both shifting nervously. When he noticed their unease, he offered each a smile and a pat on the shoulder.

"Eyes often on the south and the west," he said. "I will send couriers up here that you can relay news of any skirmishes." He started for the trapdoor, then paused halfway into the hole and looked back at the two. "But do not ignore the river," he instructed. "If our enemy is cunning, they, too, will not ignore the Masur Delaval."

"Aye," said one, while the other said, "Yes," and both looked to the other nervously.

"And well done," Midalis said as he departed. "You may have saved many lives with your vigilance this day."

Tuolonatl spent a long while staring into a golden mirror, studying the set of her jaw, her scars, the wrinkles about her eyes—all of it well earned. Now their god walked among them. Not the line of God King imposters, children sitting on the throne, put there by the augurs only so they could control the direction of their religion and the whole of Tonoloya more fully.

No, this Scathmizzane was the true god of the xoconai, in the flesh and riding a dragon.

For most of the people, this revelation, this god walking among them, had lifted their spirits and strengthened their faith, but for Tuolonatl, strangely (even to her), the appearance of Scathmizzane did none of that—in fact, quite the opposite.

She had been a warrior for all of her adult life—even longer! Her first kill had come at the age of sixteen and, by twenty, she had survived more than a dozen major battles and had become a legend among the macana warriors. Her reputation had only grown when she was appointed to the mundunugu lizard riders. By her midtwenties, she could not enter a room anywhere in Tonoloya without hearing awe-filled whispers whenever she passed.

She hated those whispers.

She fought out of a sense of duty and honor, not for any love of battle. She did not relish the warm fountains of blood her macana had brought spraying back upon her. She never rejoiced at seeing the light leaving the eyes of a vanquished foe.

Now came Scathmizzane, the Glorious Gold, the God of Light and Truth and Justice and Joy, and all that he spoke of was war. His every order.

She took a last look at her reflection, a reminder to her of who she was, and closed her eyes, taking a deep and steadying breath.

Pixquicauh, the high priest of Scathmizzane, had come to Appleby and was awaiting Tuolonatl at the pyramid being constructed to hold this flash-step mirror.

She spun around before opening her eyes, wanting to carry that last image in her thoughts.

"He will demand sacrifices," said Ataquixt, who had delivered the news of the high priest's arrival.

"We cannot resist his orders," she replied to the man and her other officers assembled about her. "If Pixquicauh demands a sacrifice, we cannot and must not intervene. The augurs will do as they choose."

"Matlal already has High Priest Pixquicauh's ear," one of the other mundunugu leaders warned.

Tuolonatl nodded. Of course, the sniveling fool had run right to Pixquicauh to complain about Tuolonatl's intervention and the scolding and threats she had levied upon him. She had known that would happen, from the time she had walked into the human church beside Ataquixt.

In fact, she had counted on it.

Pixquicauh would register his complaints, and so would Tuolonatl, and in this case she would be able to make a practical argument—that torturing and killing Abbot Chesterfield was counterproductive to the needs of the xoconai in this town—and not a moral one.

A moral argument, she had come to understand, would hold no sway with Scathmizzane or his high priest.

"Those of you who will remain in the towns, and for those serving you, I say with conviction, do not mistreat the humans. They will serve us, and we need that service. If they try to escape or to organize a violent resistance, kill them as you must, but do so with efficiency and, yes, even with mercy."

"Pixquicauh will sacrifice," the mundunugu said again.

She held up her hands helplessly. "I cannot speak for the augurs. They will do as they choose. But I speak for the mundunugu and the macana. The children of Cizinfozza surrendered. They are our captives, thus they are in our care. And that care will be just and decent, and any under the command of Tuolonatl who violate this order will face my wrath—and so will become the next sacrifice to Glorious Gold."

"And if High Priest Pixquicauh orders a macana to kill some humans?" the same mundunugu asked. "Or if he tells my riders to have their cuetzpali devour a human?"

Tuolonatl considered her response for a long while. She thought such a scenario unlikely, but the question was valid, and important.

"Do not disobey him," she instructed, much as it pained her to do so. "Ever. He is the mortal voice of Scathmizzane. You have my commands, and they will serve you, will serve all of us, well. Keep my orders, my advice, in your hearts, for your own sake. But if Pixquicauh countermands my commands, do not disobey him."

"Yes, Commander," the mundunugu said.

Tuolonatl could see the grimace, even as he tried to hide it, and she understood the source of it, surely. There had always been a rivalry between the proud mundunugu forces and the augurs, and the warriors too often had to choose between conflicting orders of the religious leaders and the city sovereigns.

But none of the sovereigns, even those who had distinguished themselves in military campaigns, had as yet moved beyond Otontotomi. Scathmizzane had excluded them from these early days of his campaign.

Tuolonatl noted more sour expressions about the room and knew that not all of them had come from the same place. No, she understood, some of them had nothing to do with the unending rivalry between the sovereigns and the augurs but were simply reacting to her demands for mercy. To many of her forces, even among leaders she had selected, the humans, the children of Cizinfozza, were not worthy of mercy, whatever practical gain might be found from it.

Many macana, many mundunugu, were truly relishing each and every kill.

And she could not deny them that bloodlust. She could make no moral arguments against that murderous urge or she would risk losing their loyalty.

Such a fine line she had to walk.

"Pixquicauh awaits you," Ataquixt quietly reminded.

Tuolonatl nodded and closed her eyes again, this time imagining riding her beloved Pocheoya about the golden autumn hills of northeastern Tonoloya amid the scent of ripening grapes. She found a place of calm, then brought forth the image she had seen in the mirror, the image of Tuolonatl, the great mundunugu, who had earned every scar, every wrinkle, every one of the gray strands now intermingling with her dark hair.

"Well, for the sake of all that is golden, let us not upset the mortal voice of Scathmizzane," she said, not even trying to hide her sarcasm.

She crossed the town with all of her officers in tow but entered the small, newly constructed pyramid with only Ataquixt beside her. Pixquicauh awaited her, and it was no surprise to her to see Augur Matlal standing at his side.

"Cochcal," the high priest greeted.

"High Priest Pixquicauh," she replied cautiously, surprised by the lightness in the typically dour man's voice. It was hard to determine Pixquicauh's mood, since most of his face was covered by the skull, but he did seem to be smiling behind the teeth of the upper jaw covering his own, and there was an unmistakable sparkle in his eyes, even in the shadows of the empty skull sockets set before them.

"You have assessed this town?" Pixquicauh asked.

"Of course."

"How many xoconai to handle the slaves and keep the fields and shops tended?"

"A hundred macana will properly guard," she replied.

"Half that," said Pixquicauh, drawing a curious look from the woman. "It is time to move forward with all speed," he continued. "Do you not know the jewel that is in sight of the forward lines?"

"The great city, yes," she replied. "Ursal, the humans call it."

"We will give it a proper name soon enough," Pixquicauh said.

"Soon enough?" she echoed doubtfully. She had been to the front lines, only two days before, and after seeing the truth of Ursal, Tuolonatl had designed a plan to bypass the place, leaving it besieged. She had thought to present that plan at the war council before any action was initiated. With their swimming cuetzpali, the mundunugu could take the river north of the city and command the lands in the south easily enough, but the losses in going against a fortified stone city surrounded by high walls and guarded by the finest warriors the humans had to offer seemed foolhardy. Would they leave ten thousand dead xoconai on the field about Ursal? Twenty thousand?

Would they even be able to breach those towering walls against the withering fire of archers that would surely meet them?

"Of course!" Pixquicauh replied. "Now is the time for boldness. Now is the jewel to fall to us, and let all the humans between this city and the sea flee to the water's edge and into the waves. We will break them, here and now."

"You have seen this city, then?" she asked. "I had thought you in Otontotomi."

"I have not seen it."

"It is more than you imagine," she warned.

The high priest laughed at her. "Scathmizzane has seen it. He has already prepared."

Her sigh drew a clear scowl from behind the priest's skull condoral, which, unlike the vulture skulls of the other augurs, was the facial bones of a xoconai—indeed, of the high priest who had preceded this man, an augur who had disappointed Scathmizzane and so had been melted by Glorious Gold.

Tuolonatl thought of that, then, before arguing here against what was apparently the edict of Glorious Gold. At least it seemed that way, given the obvious confidence in Pixquicauh's voice.

"Let us begin," Pixquicauh said, indicating the golden mirror that would flash-step them to the next mirror in the east, then through several more to the front lines. "The first preparations of the battlefield have already begun."

She eyed him warily. She had issued no such commands.

"You will see," he promised. "And Scathmizzane upon Kithkukulikhan has already delivered the divine throwers."

"The divine . . ." she began, at a loss.

"You will see," he said again, motioning at her more emphatically.

She walked past him, never releasing his stare from her own.

"When the city is taken, you and I will discuss with Scathmizzane your treatment of Augur Matlal," he whispered ominously. "Perhaps if you perform well in your tasks, Glorious Gold will prove merciful. Ever does he seem more generous when walking a field covered with the broken bodies of the children of Cizinfozza."

The attendants of the golden mirror turned it, catching the reflection of its sister mirror in the east. Tuolonatl stood before it, staring at her reflection as the handlers made the final adjustments.

She waited for Ataquixt to come through before taking the next magical step, and indeed, made him go first. She needed him beside her at that time, and if Pixquicauh came to realize that need, he would no doubt arrange to remove the mundunugu scout.

Soon after, Tuolonatl stood at the edge of the magical barrier of golden light, a one-way barrier that prevented the humans from looking at the gathering xoconai army but did not hinder her view to the east at all.

She saw the towers, the high wall, the solidity of this great human city. It had been designed and constructed for the sole purpose of defense. She saw the mast poles of the many ships in the river outside the northern wall, and the thin lines of smoke from the cooking fires of a thousand homes outside this western side of the wall alone.

It was as large as any of the cities of Tonoloya, and more fortified than the strongest of them. She had fought only one war in Tonoloya that had involved taking a fortified city, one not a tenth the magnitude of this one, and though she had won that battle, the losses had been staggering, so deep at one point that her attacking forces had abandoned ladders and instead just climbed the piled bodies of their dead comrades to at long last get over the wall.

Tuolonatl tried not to think about the fact that, even when Ursal was taken, the xoconai forces had hundreds of miles left to go. Every dead mundunugu or macana here would make that journey more difficult.

"Organize your legions quickly, Commander," Pixquicauh called to her. "It has already begun."

She turned to look at the high priest and respond, but she lost her voice instead, for a long line of augurs accompanied Pixquicauh—more than Tuolonatl ever would have guessed to be this far east, more than she had ever seen in one place before. Three teams of a dozen macana soldiers accompanied them, each escorting a heavy cart drawn by oxen and bearing a giant crystal, much like the great crystal obelisk in the field atop Tzatzini, except that these crystals were translucent and thickly flecked with dark gray, almost black gems.

"Divine throwers?" Tuolonatl whispered under her breath.

12

HOLY SANCTUARY

The world was a wider place than she had ever imagined, and despite the death, the danger, the approaching army, Aoleyn could not help but be charmed, full of wonderment and excitement, as the ship moved along the Masur Delaval, the great river that emptied, she was told, into a sea vaster than anything she had ever seen.

She had crossed the continent, thousands of miles, and had seen varying terrain—mountains, rivers, a desert to every horizon—and villages the like of which she had never known. She had seen a great mountain lake drained onto a desert below, revealing the structures of a long-lost, magnificent city. But still, nothing had prepared Aoleyn for Ursal, the throne of Honce-the-Bear, and no river she had crossed or rafted upon could compare to this, the Masur Delaval, a powerful and wide waterway lined with villages on either side.

"It is quite amazing, isn't it?" Sister Elysant asked, coming up beside her at the prow of the large sailing ship—another wonder to Aoleyn—now four days out from Ursal.

"I do not understand it," Aoleyn admitted. "The river flows away from the city, but there is no lake, and no river flowing into the city."

"The rivers feeding Masur Delaval are underground, beneath the bedrock of the city," Elysant explained. "It was not always this way, but those rivers were dug deeper and covered with stone by the builders of Ursal."

Aoleyn stared at her curiously.

"To withstand a siege," she explained. "You can trap the king in his city, but getting in is another matter, against those high walls. And you can't starve him out, not with a large waterway full of fresh water and fish beneath his dungeons."

Aoleyn wasn't sure that she understood—what was a siege, after all?—but she accepted the explanation with a nod.

"The Masur Delaval is more than that, too," Elysant went on. "As we move past Palmaris in the north, perhaps this very day, the water becomes salty."

Aoleyn shook her head, not understanding.

"The water of the sea, the great Mirianic," Elysant explained. "When the tide comes in, the waves can make the northern parts of the river run backwards, carrying the salty water of the sea. And the huge fish, too, some bigger than this boat."

"I would like to see this ocean," Aoleyn said, after she had digested all of that.

"Oh, you will, and soon. We'll go out of Masur Delaval and into the Gulf of Corona, then around a peninsula and to the sheltered inlet that will take us to the docks at the base of the cliff that holds Saint-Mere-Abelle."

"The church," Aoleyn said, recognizing the name.

"So much more than a church," Elysant said, leaning forward over the rail, her gaze cast ahead longingly. "The Abellican Order has been building that monastery for centuries." She looked back at Aoleyn, who was trying (unsuccessfully, she realized) to look as if she understood.

"Hundreds of years," Elysant explained. "They just keep

adding and adding to it. More rooms, more tunnels, more towers. It is the greatest structure in Honce—perhaps in the whole world."

"Like Ursal?" Aoleyn asked.

"Ursal is a great city, no doubt, but no building there can match Saint-Mere-Abelle—not the castle, not Saint Honce, not both together if you made each ten times larger! You will see, my friend."

They said no more, Aoleyn moving to the rail and staring ahead once more, feeling the droplets of the cold spray kicked up by the prow. She wanted very much to see the ocean, to see this St.-Mere-Abelle, to see everything in all the world.

She wanted to leave the xoconai army behind, leave the Ayamharas Plateau and all that she had known in the lands south of Loch Beag behind. Far behind. This had been her dream for as long as she could remember, because she knew there was a world out there, a big and wonderful world full of adventure and surprises, beyond the mountains holding the great lake, beyond Fasail Dubh'clach, the Desert of Black Stones.

She thought of Bahdlahn and felt a pang of regret. She had wanted him beside her on this journey—she still wanted him beside her. She wondered, not for the first time and not for the last, whether she had been too hasty in dismissing him.

But again, she came to that place of resolve and reminded herself that she had set Bahdlahn free of any romantic entanglements as much for him as for herself. Perhaps more for him, for he needed to grow, to learn who he wanted to be instead of becoming the image of someone else's desires.

She hoped he was safe, was sure that he was, with Khotai and Talmadge looking out for him. She hoped that he was seeing wonders as great as those that filled her eyes. She thought of Catriona, and it occurred to her that perhaps she and Bahdlahn had become something more than friends—she had seen the way the woman had looked at him, after all.

Aoleyn felt a pang of jealousy at that but then just laughed at herself. She nodded, thinking of the two of them again, and hoped, sincerely, that Bahdlahn had found more than friendship with Catriona.

Because she hoped that he was happy, that he was filling his mind with wonder, his eyes with beauty, his heart with warmth.

She hoped, too, that she would see him again. Her life would be better if she saw Bahdlahn again.

Aoleyn barely closed her jaw those last two days of the voyage, although she barely spoke a word, so overwhelmed and overjoyed was she at the sight of the ocean, its great, dark waters so wide and wild, with huge swells that lifted the boat effortlessly. She had been told about the Mirianic repeatedly, but words could not do justice to the truth of the ocean—the sight, the smell, the feel, the sense of power.

The ship stayed close to the shore on the right-hand side, the south, then turned south around towering cliffs and into a long inlet that brought them in sight of St.-Mere-Abelle, high up on a huge cliff. The monastery looked as if it had grown right out of those high rocks, with walls, square buildings, and high towers all visible.

The extensive docks, down here at sea level, were right beneath those cliffs, with only a single large door cut into the sheer rock face. Aoleyn didn't know much about battle, particularly about large-scale fights, but even she could see that no attackers could come against the monastery from this approach without suffering incredible losses.

That notion gave her hope, even more than the walls of Ursal.

The ship slid in to the long wharf, where attendants were on hand to catch the mooring lines and tie her off.

Aydrian, Brother Thaddius, and Elysant came up to Aoleyn as she watched the Ursal soldiers talking with a trio of men who came out to greet the ship. All were dressed in Abellican garb.

"You need to trust in me here and allow me to do the speaking when we are brought before the father abbot," Thaddius told Aydrian and Aoleyn—mostly Aoleyn, she understood. "The father abbot is a good and generous man, but he isn't likely to be welcoming to Aydrian Boudabras."

"Aydrian Wyndon," the man corrected.

"Let us hope he agrees," said Thaddius. "And you, my friend," he added, addressing Aoleyn, and then he paused and sighed, looking at her bare midriff, her gemstone belly ring clearly visible. "You carry upon your body Ring Stones you should not have."

"They are not your Abellican Ring Stones," Aydrian said.

"So you and she claim. Will Father Abbot Braumin agree?"

"I have never seen one of your Abellican monks on Fireach Speuer," Aoleyn replied indignantly, her voice rising. "Nor are there any stories of your Church in or about the crystal caverns where I found these stones. Now you would claim them as your own?"

Thaddius looked to Aydrian and the two shared a shrug.

"Let me speak," Thaddius reiterated, and Aoleyn noted Aydrian's nod.

"Keep your calm, my friend," Elysant told Aoleyn. "For your own sake. This is a powerful order of powerful people. They are not evil, but they are protective of the world they know."

"Viscenti," Aydrian said, and Aoleyn looked over at him, then followed his gaze to the captain of the ship, who was speaking with a middle-aged man, very slender, with angular features, dressed in fine Abellican robes.

"You know Master Viscenti?" Thaddius said, but he caught himself immediately. "Of course you do."

"Yes, it seems a lifetime ago," Aydrian agreed.

The captain motioned them over and the crew moved aside, allowing the four down the ramp to the docks first.

"I am without words," Master Viscenti said, shaking his head and staring at Aydrian.

"I did not ever expect to return to Honce at all, let alone Saint-Mere-Abelle," Aydrian replied.

"Perhaps you would like a tour of the graves of the thousands killed the last time you were here."

Aoleyn saw the pain on Aydrian's face. The man closed his eyes and took a deep breath, and it seemed to her for a moment as if he might simply topple over.

"It is good that he came," Brother Thaddius chimed in. "For he . . . we come bearing news that Father Abbot Braumin must hear, and hear soon."

Viscenti snapped a glare over at the younger monk, but his sharp visage softened almost immediately. "So I am told," he replied. He looked back to Aydrian. "I am sorry to hear the news of your mother's passing. Long will the bards sing of the heroics and heart of Lady Jilseponie. I am sorry for her loss, but I have no condolences to offer to you."

Aydrian nodded.

Viscenti's eyes went to Tempest, the legendary sword hanging on Aydrian's hip, then back to meet Aydrian's gaze, silently conveying his demand.

To Aoleyn's surprise, Aydrian unbuckled his belt and removed the sword, handing it over to the monk. Then Aydrian opened his robe, displaying the gorgeous, gem-encrusted breastplate. He began unfastening the shoulder straps.

"My helm remains in my locker, Captain," he said. "If you would be so kind as to have one of your crew go and gather it for Master Viscenti."

Before the captain even motioned, a nearby Allheart ran back up the plank.

As Aydrian removed the breastplate, Master Viscenti

reached his free hand back and a second monk placed a red gemstone into it.

Aoleyn watched carefully as the skinny monk clasped the gem in his fist, then brought the hand closer to his mouth as he recited some sort of prayer. He opened his eyes and looked at Aydrian, his gaze moving up and down. He started to turn for Aoleyn but stopped at Brother Thaddius, his eyes going wide, as he seemed to only then take note of the man's walking stick, set with six magical stones.

"Brother Thaddius?" he asked breathlessly.

"Darkfern," Aydrian said.

"I have two stories to tell," Thaddius explained. "One, of my adventures with Sister Elysant—view her robe and her staff. A tale of Saint Belfour."

The monks were all excited about that, the two behind Viscenti shaking their heads and murmuring prayers.

"And one of the west, the far west," Thaddius finished. "Farther west than we even knew existed, from what I can tell . . ." He stopped there, abruptly, but it took Aoleyn a moment to realize this, for her attention was then on Master Viscenti, whose attention, obviously, was wholly on her. He stared at her, eyes roaming up and down.

She knew the red gem he had called to. He was seeing her jewelry, and with more than a passing interest.

"How dare—" he started.

"They're not Abellican stones," Thaddius said. "It is an entirely new—"

Viscenti waved him to silence. "Remove them, every stone," the master demanded, though whether he was speaking to Aoleyn, to Thaddius, or to the brothers behind him, Aoleyn didn't know—nor did the others, she realized.

"Master, please!" Thaddius tried to intervene, but two Allheart Knights flanked him immediately, crowding between him and Viscenti and leaning into him, forcing him back.

Aoleyn felt the rage building inside of her. A stamp of her foot would shock them all with lightning and throw them aside. A gust of wind would blow them away! A fireball would—

"At ease, I beg of you," Aydrian whispered into her ear.

"They will not," she said through gritted teeth, and loud enough for Viscenti and all the others to hear.

"Temporary," Aydrian assured her. "As with my sword, and this." He removed his breastplate and handed it over to the nearest soldier. "You understand their caution." He held up his hand to keep the Allhearts back, buying time.

"I understand that they are claiming that which does not belong to them," Aoleyn flatly stated.

She saw the anger flash in the sharp-featured master's eyes, and he mouthed the word *heresy*.

"Tell me which are magical," another voice, that of Elysant, whispered into her ear. "I will remove them for you, gently, and on my word as your friend and companion, I will fight beside you to get them back."

"Aoleyn, please," Aydrian said.

Aoleyn pushed away her anger. They needed this alliance, for the sake of all the world. The gemstones were a part of her, but one that she had to relinquish if there were to be any hope of getting these priests to help in the greater cause.

The young witch nodded, her hand going to her belly ring to remove the stones. She moved her foot out, allowing Elysant to easily access her magical anklet.

Master Viscenti looked her up and down again with the garnet when Elysant had moved to his side with all of Aoleyn's jewelry, then nodded. "Now we go to Saint-Mere-Abelle," he said.

"I know every stone, intimately," Aoleyn warned. "I will have them back, every one."

"You are in no position—" he started to respond, but Aydrian stepped toward him, shaking his head and whispering something Aoleyn could not hear.

The monk looked around Aydrian at Aoleyn, his face full of doubt.

"It's true," she heard Aydrian say. "You do not understand the generosity and good faith you have just been given."

Master Viscenti turned on his heel and started for the lone door into the cliff at the back of the docks, the monk escort and Allheart Knights flanking the newcomers and pointedly separating Aoleyn and Aydrian from Thaddius and Elysant.

Into the tunnel they went, under several heavy portcullises, which all lowered behind them, and through several sets of reinforced iron doors, all flanked by sentry monks. Aoleyn didn't have to ask what the small holes scattered about the stone walls might be. She had never heard of murder holes, of course, given her background, where no structures remotely like this one could be found, but it was easy enough for her to figure out the purpose—particularly when she heard people behind those walls, shadowing their movements.

They came into a side chamber a long while later, and to a circular metal staircase that climbed up through the ceiling and far up into the heights.

It was not a direct line, and it took the troupe nearly an hour to at last exit onto the vast grounds within the castle-like monastery of St.-Mere-Abelle. There, they were met by a dozen monks and were separated, with Aydrian led into one building, Thaddius and Elysant moving with Master Viscenti toward what appeared to the huge main chapel of the place, and Aoleyn taken to a different building altogether, one that was dark and dirty, with barred windows and shackles hanging on the walls.

She was not chained, however, and the brothers who escorted her even apologized for the dingy surroundings. They sent one of their own to get her clean bedding and water and promised that she would soon be allowed to speak her defense.

"My defense?"

"For the Ring Stones in your possession," one answered. "You are no Abellican, surely, and while some who are not formally in the Church are allowed the stones, they are carefully observed."

"Those aren't your gemstones!" Aoleyn growled, but too late, for the monks had left her room and closed the heavy door behind them.

Aoleyn had only once heard a lock click before, in Ursal, but now she knew what it meant, and the reverberations of that metallic, hollow sound echoed within her and stabbed at her heart.

She moved to the one small window and peered out. The room was belowground, the window at ground level and facing east, so that even though the sun was still up, little afternoon light reached her.

Had she erred in coming east? In Aoleyn's heart, in that terrible moment, she wished that she was on Fireach Speuer, wild and free, even if alone, battling the bright-faced xoconai.

She turned her back to the wall and would have slumped down, except that the floor was muddy and smelled awful. For all she knew, she was standing among the excrement of the last person imprisoned here.

"You defeated the fossa," she told herself. "Find a way."

Aoleyn began to plot her escape.

"I feel as if you are visiting me on two separate occasions," Father Abbot Braumin Herde said to Brother Thaddius and Sister Elysant. Beside the father abbot's desk, Master Viscenti, who seemed much more at ease now than he had on the docks, gave a laugh.

"Perhaps we should finish one important matter, and then I dismiss you, and then I summon you back so that we can finish the second important matter," the father abbot went on.

"Yes, Father Abbot," said Thaddius. "But if that is to be,

then let us first discuss the disposition of our two companions. They came here at my bidding, and so—"

"The father abbot was joking," Viscenti interrupted, and an embarrassed Thaddius fell silent.

The brother felt the weight of Father Abbot Braumin's stare upon him. Thaddius took some hope, at least, from the parchments scattered and neatly weighted upon the father abbot's desk, and the three beautiful alabaster coffers set off to one side.

"You found the tomb of a lost saint," Braumin said at length. "One of the three or four greatest monks in the nine centuries of the Abellican Church. These writings before me are in the hand of Saint Belfour."

"Yes, Father Abbot."

"And you would make this other story you bring to my door paramount?"

Thaddius shuffled from foot to foot and had no answer.

"That tells me much," Braumin went on, "both about the heart of Brother Thaddius and about the weight of this second story. So, yes, we will do as you bid . . ." He paused there, suddenly, his gaze aimed at Elysant, his expression becoming one of puzzlement. "Sister?" he began.

"Elysant," she replied, her voice cracking with nervousness.

"Sister Elysant, whatever are you wearing?" the father abbot asked. "I know that you have walked a long and difficult road, but those robes hardly fit. And they are torn and threadbare. Did you not have a second—"

"They are the robes of Saint Belfour, Father Abbot," Elysant dared to interject. "Given to me by the wraith of the great man himself."

The look of absolute shock that came to Father Abbot Braumin's face surprised Thaddius.

"This is his staff, one of stone," Elysant continued, as Braumin rose and moved around his desk to approach and better inspect the young monk.

She handed Braumin the staff, and he clenched it in both hands, closed his eyes, and felt its power.

"Given to you? By the great Belfour?" the father abbot asked.

When Elysant nodded, the father abbot turned to Thaddius. "I have changed my mind. This story first and foremost. Tell me it, all of it. Tell me of Saint Belfour's . . . wraith?"

Thaddius exchanged a glance with Elysant, and on her nod, began his tale. He omitted nothing, describing in great detail the battle in the crypt and producing the gemstones he had gained from the encounter, as well as his own staff, explaining that it, too, was in the sarcophagus of St. Belfour.

He kept going, over the father abbot's attempt to end the tale there, pushing on to Appleby-in-Wilderland and Abbot Chesterfield, then to the meeting with Aydrian and the others.

"It was you who thought to bring Aydrian, King Aydrian Boudabras, back to Honce-the-Bear?" Braumin asked.

"What choice lay before me?" answered Thaddius.

"Then you believe the story that there is a great army coming for us?" Braumin held up the imprimatur of King Midalis. "You agree with Midalis—in fact, you likely helped to convince Midalis, yes?"

Brother Thaddius swallowed hard and lowered his gaze. "I did, and I do believe, yes, Father Abbot. For I have seen them, these bright-faced invaders—the sidhe, or xoconai—in all their deep and splendid ranks."

"I thought they had not gotten to Appleby."

Thaddius swallowed hard again. "I traveled with the woman, Aoleyn," he explained honestly. "We spirit-walked across the miles to the west." He stopped there when both Visconti and the father abbot gasped.

"Go on," Braumin ordered.

"I felt the exigency of the situation," Thaddius explained. "If they were not lying, or exaggerating, then of course we had to rush east to warn Honce-the-Bear. But that would mean bringing deposed King Aydrian, and with my own legacy well known . . ." He sighed and held up his hands helplessly.

"That you were once an admirer of Marcalo De'Unnero," said Master Viscenti.

"But no part of the De'Unneran Heresy," the father abbot reminded.

"I felt I had no choice," Thaddius said. "I risked the spirit-walk because I believed the stakes higher than the potential loss of my own life."

"You are forgiven that," the father abbot declared. "Your reasoning was sound—perhaps." He put a hand to his chin, his gaze scrolling from Thaddius to Elysant and back again. "What do you mean when you say that you spirit-walked with this woman, Aoleyn?"

"She led me to the sidhe."

"Physically?"

"Her spirit guided me to the sidhe," Thaddius corrected.

"You pulled the spirit from the woman's body?" the father abbot asked incredulously.

"Hardly. Aoleyn walked more easily than I!"

Braumin Herde turned to Viscenti, who merely shrugged.

"She has such command of the Ring Stones?" the father abbot asked.

"She would claim that they are not Ring Stones," said Thaddius. "But yes, her power is considerable—great, even."

"Tell me about her, both of you."

"We know little," Thaddius said.

"She is a good person, of pure heart and intent," Sister Elysant said.

"Everything," the father abbot insisted.

So they did, relating every story they had heard of Aoleyn, and every story told by Aoleyn, and every anecdote from their weeks along the road beside the woman. Elysant did most of the talking, and spoke of some quiet conversations that she had held with Aoleyn that Thaddius hadn't even known about.

When they finished, the father abbot seemed even more confused than when they had started.

"You have read these?" he asked, lifting a pile of the ancient parchments from his desk.

Thaddius nodded.

"You would go to the catacombs, then, I expect, to see what writings might have so inspired Saint Belfour to travel so far from Vanguard."

"With your permission, yes. Saint Belfour makes note of the sidhe, and of the brother whose writings sent him on his way. It would seem pertinent to the greater questions before us."

The father abbot nodded. "A fortunate coincidence," he said.

"Or perhaps no coincidence at all," Sister Elysant dared to say, and all three looked at her in surprise.

She steadied herself under those harsh gazes and continued. "It is often said that the word of God whispers most directly when it is most needed. Perhaps all of this is tied together, a moment of divine fate to warn us of the approaching danger and of how we might defeat it."

Brother Thaddius couldn't suppress a smile, and though there was a bit of condescension in it, at the woman's simplistic appeal to the supernatural, there was also a great measure of respect, counterbalancing his own doubts. Certainly, he had seen some amazing things these last months. And who, really, was this Aoleyn woman, who could use the magic of the sacred stones as easily as a bard might sing his most loved songs? Was Thaddius really being superior here, in his skepticism in light of all of that, or was he being limited by his own cynicism, which refused to accept that a—what, miracle?—might have just played out right before his eyes?

He turned to the father abbot, thinking to support his dear friend Elysant, but saw on the face of Braumin Herde that no support was needed. The man's gentle smile was sincere as he nodded at Sister Elysant.

"That robe and staff should be on display under glass along the back wall of the great nave of Saint-Mere-Abelle," he said.

Elysant winced, but then nodded. "Of course, Father Abbot."

"But it will not be," Braumin added, and he handed the stone staff back to her. "Not yet. You claim that Saint Belfour himself gave these to you, and I've no reason to doubt your tale, or your observations. Who am I to stand against the choices of a saint?"

"I am honored," Elysant said, clearly overwhelmed, her voice barely a whisper.

"You are laden," the father abbot corrected. "A great responsibility rests upon your shoulders when you wear that old robe." He shook his head. "How might it have survived the centuries?"

"There is more to it than mere cloth," Elysant said. She lifted up one tattered edge and pulled back the frayed wool to reveal a mesh of the same silvery metal that striated Thaddius's new staff, the metal Aydrian had called silverel.

"Saint Belfour is with you," the father abbot decided, "and so his spirit is with us all."

We will need it, Thaddius thought but did not say.

13

THE WALLS OF URSAL

The very next morning, Midalis found himself again running up the stairs to that tallest southern tower, this time more urgently than on the previous day. Koreen wasn't up there, of course, having led the ride to help the refugees in the south, but the king was surprised to find Abbot Ohwan waiting for him, standing beside the spyglass, his expression grim.

"Your prudence in allowing Aydrian and the others to leave may perhaps prove vital," Ohwan greeted him.

Midalis let the words digest for just a moment before rushing to the spyglass, calling upon its magical properties, and scouring the southland.

He saw it, then, the first battle of Ursal, only a few miles south of the city. Amid the dust and confusion, it took him a few moments to sort it all out, and when he did, his fears were realized. Many bodies lay on the ground in the midst of battling forces, his own horsemen against lizard-riding sidhe, and some of those carcasses were horses and some of the bodies were his Allheart Knights.

Frantically, King Midalis worked the spyglass, moving it slightly, from one small skirmish within the greater battle to another. His fist clenched when he saw a knight, perhaps Julian of the Evergreen, hack down a rider and take down the ferocious lizard, too, in one great slash.

His heart sank when he saw another of his Allhearts pulled from his horse and be immediately set upon by a pair of enemies, who let their lizards do the gruesome work of finishing the helpless, flailing soul.

The king stepped back, needing a deep breath.

"They are formidable," Abbot Ohwan said.

"How did this happen?" Midalis demanded of the other soldiers up there, a pair of women he thought to be sisters.

"Dame Koreen led the knights to the south, but the morning found a host of enemies beyond the light and north of her position," one explained.

"They informed my masters immediately and we sent magical word to our brothers escorting Dame Koreen," Abbot Ohwan added.

"She turned immediately and appropriately, my king," the lookout said. "But the enemy were too many."

"The Allhearts have left a line of dead sidhe for miles in their return," the other tower guard added. "Ten dead sidhe for every fallen Allheart."

King Midalis nodded at that and then went back to the spyglass. He had heard the pride in the woman's voice when she uttered that last sentence, and he didn't want to dissuade that appeal to valor, but Midalis knew what the lookout apparently did not: the Allheart Knights were the finest warriors in Honce, superbly trained and outfitted in metal armor by the greatest blacksmiths in the land. Few who were not Allheart wore such armor, very few. The loss of even one Allheart was a devastating blow to the defense of Ursal and Honce-the-Bear. Ten-to-one losses sounded good, but not when Allhearts were involved.

Some hope returned to King Midalis when he focused

again on the battle, for he noted Dame Koreen spearheading a wedge of knights in a more organized defensive grouping. That wedge barreled through the northernmost rank of enemies, a wall of lance and horseflesh, and to Midalis's profound relief, they broke free of the tangle.

A volley of spears chased them, but the knights, so skilled and practiced, used their shields to protect the flanks of their mounts, half-turning and never slowing.

The sidhe gave chase, but the lizards couldn't pace the horses.

King Midalis almost cheered—almost. But then he noted the number of Allhearts running free.

A dozen.

Only a dozen.

Two score had gone out.

He didn't bother to try to count the sidhe dead in this one skirmish zone alone. It didn't matter.

He had lost almost thirty of his finest, and likely more than a couple of magic-wielding priests, as well. And no mere goblin force was this sidhe army, not in skill or in tactics.

"Dame Koreen to my audience hall as soon as she arrives," he told Abbot Ohwan. "And yourself, as well."

"Yes, my king."

"Prepare," Midalis told the abbot, as he began descending the stair. "They will come at us this day."

Tuolonatl watched curiously as the augurs formed into groups, assembling in semicircles to the side and back of the strange crystals they had called divine throwers. Their line was broken only by ramps set against the back of the up-angled cylinders, leading to low wooden platforms that had been hastily constructed behind each of the throwers.

The teleportation mirror flashed repeatedly and the mundunugu commander watched a line of servants appearing, each bearing a large, roughly circular stone, then shuffling to one of the platforms, where others took the stones and hoisted each up to the landing.

Very soon, the wooden platforms groaned under the weight.

"The human warriors are in full flight and will near the city soon," Ataquixt said, coming up to her. "If we go now, we can intercept."

Tuolonatl looked out at the high, dark walls of the city, considered it for a moment, then shook her head. "What do we care for a score of riders?" she asked. "We go when they near the gates."

"The southern gates will close before we can hope to reach them . . ." Ataquixt's voice trailed off as he finished, for Tuolonatl flashed him a disappointed scowl.

"They will be busy welcoming back their valiant warriors and grieving those who did not return," she explained. "We ride near enough to get our spears over the western wall. Let us measure their response."

"Lo, he comes!" added a third voice breathlessly, and the two turned to see Pixquicauh rushing up.

"He comes?" Tuolonatl asked.

"We need not gain the measure of their response," the high priest replied. "No feigned attacks. There will be but one assault and the city will fall."

"The cost will be great. Too great," Tuolonatl argued. "We will encircle the city and take the riverbank north. The humans will have nowhere to run."

"The city will fall," said Pixquicauh. "This is the greatest city of the humans, so say the captives. Overwhelming it in a single attack will dispirit all others standing before us. Any victory the children of Cizinfozza find here, even if just in holding us back for a single assault, will offer them hope."

Tuolonatl looked all around, taking a measure of her forces. Almost half the army had arrived on the field, some forty thousand warriors, but another fifty thousand would soon enough be available, leaving one in ten behind to hold the captured towns. She didn't discount the power of forty thousand xoconai, particularly since almost half were mundunugu riders, but neither would she dismiss the height of those city walls, nor would she underestimate the fighting prowess of the humans.

Many more xoconai than human horsemen in their shining armor had fallen in the southern ambush.

"He comes," Pixquicauh said again. "I have seen it." The man in the skull condoral turned on his heel and strode away, back for the middle divine thrower.

"Scathmizzane?" Ataquixt quietly asked.

Tuolonatl could only shrug and shake her head. A single assault on a target as hardened as this seemed madness to her. She thought to that long-ago battle against a xoconai city, when the warriors had simply walked over the walls on the backs of their dead comrades. She had no doubt that dead xoconai would pile deep here, as well, but these walls were much higher.

"A single attack," Pixquicauh called back at her, as if reading her thoughts. "The human king is in there."

"Select two hundred of the swiftest riders," she told Ataquixt. "Go south of the city and pursue the human riders."

"We can intercept them."

Tuolonatl shook her head. "Pursue them. Make those within the city come to their southern wall to protect the retreat. Let us keep as many eyes turned that way as we can."

"While all the rest come through the shield of light from the west," he said, catching on.

"We haven't enough ladders yet," she replied. "Every moment the mundunugu have in holding the western wall as the macana warriors climb those ladders will be critical."

"Yes, my commander," he said.

"Stay beyond their range," she added. "Find me about the western wall when your task is completed."

Ataquixt nodded and ran for his cuetzpali, then rode off to gather his brigade.

Tuolonatl signaled to her captains and had them setting the ranks, the marching squares, the mundunugu cavalry. Normally, she would have remained there to oversee the formations, but she mounted her own cuetzpali and rode to Pixquicauh instead.

"What augurs do you give me?"

"None," he answered.

Tuolonatl looked back to the east, across the field to the imposing walls. "What do you know?"

"He comes. The city must fall quickly."

"So you have said. We will need cover. Glorious light and magical fire."

Pixquicauh nodded. "Many have died. The Glorious Gold shines brighter still, and the song of our god is in crescendo, approaching apogee."

"The divine throwers?" she asked, and he nodded again.

"You wear iron bolts about your saddle," the high priest warned. "You will wish to be far from this spot."

Before Tuolonatl could begin to ask what Pixquicauh was talking about, there arose a huge cheer from the westernmost reaches of the xoconai forces. Both Tuolonatl and Pixquicauh turned quickly, and Tuolonatl gasped, even as Pixquicauh said yet again, "He comes."

Indeed.

Tuolonatl saw him, the giant Glorious Gold, Scathmizzane in all his beauty and glory, riding fast on Kithkukulikhan. He swooped low over his gathered forces, who cheered wildly, and he held up a spear in a victorious salute.

A huge spear, Tuolonatl noted, thick and long and uniformly gray, as if it was made of a single piece of metal, or perhaps even stone, and quite unlike the slender spears of the mundunugu.

Scathmizzane rushed overhead, the cheers following him, and Tuolonatl turned back, hearing a rumbling behind.

The piled stones on the three platforms shifted and rumbled, as if the blown by the wind of Kithkukulikhan's passing.

But there had been no noticeable wind.

"Be gone, quickly," Pixquicauh warned, and he and all the priests began chanting in unison, each of the three semicircles holding hands and swaying in unison.

Tuolonatl rode back to her previous spot, noting that the back ranks of her forces were moving west, as if pulled by the wake of their Glorious Gold. She motioned to her many captains, mundunugu and macana, and lifted her own macana up high, a purple ribbon streaming from the base of its handle.

Scathmizzane was already over the city. To the south, the human cavalry was in sight, riding hard for the city's southern gates, though still far to the south. She lowered her arm slowly, not signaling the charge just yet.

"Go find Ataquixt," she told the rider beside her. "Quickly, to the south. Tell him to intercept the riders. Destroy them. Do not let them reach the city."

The woman sent her cuetzpali rushing off, and Tuolonatl again lifted her macana high.

Scathmizzane circled high above the city. She could hear the communal screams coming from behind the walls and noted arrows flying up, though getting nowhere near Glorious Gold.

He circled again, as if studying the place, and lifted his spear, the air around it bending as if it had suddenly superheated. The dragon descended suddenly, diving toward one of the two largest structures visible above the wall.

A bell began to ring.

Scathmizzane threw the spear and Kithkukulikhan swooped around and climbed furiously, chased by a hundred small missiles.

The bell rang one last time, loudly and off key—struck by

the spear, Tuolonatl realized—and then there came a loud crash from within the city.

Then came a *whomping* sound to the cochcal's left, and she turned to see the divine throwers. Rocks rolled down the ramps, into the bases of the cylinders, and then were flung away with tremendous force, fired through the cylindrical tubes and flying high and fast for the city of humans.

The augurs at all three held a singular note then, a droning command of power, and the three divine throwers shuddered with each exiting stone.

A score of stones shot out from each of the three batteries, more following, graceful lines of heavy shot arcing for the city, some high, some low. Some cracked against the wall, others clipped and bounced over, and others soared above. As they crossed the wall, those stones, like a flock of birds flying in formation, somehow swerved, moving closer together, arcing and bending in flight, heading generally for the spot where Scathmizzane had thrown his spear!

Tuolonatl didn't understand.

She looked to the throwers. The augurs ended their long note, and the last of that barrage flew away.

She didn't understand either end of this volley—the power throwing the stones or the one bending them to the target—but she collected herself to recognize that this was her moment.

Down came her macana, powerfully, and the xoconai ranks surged through the shield of light, riding and running across the long field for the human city.

Scathmizzane and his dragon came down before them, leading the charge.

Behind, the augurs again began their chant.

Before, the Glorious Gold lifted a second spear and hurled it for the city wall, then Kithkukulikhan broke upward and climbed fast. The great missile slammed into the stone and stuck there, about halfway up the wall.

The thumping sound resonated from behind and to the left, and Tuolonatl was not surprised to see three more lines of heavy stones streaming out above, some too low and close for comfort, but all speeding across the field, nearing each other more quickly this time in their swerving flight, speeding right for the area of that second huge spear.

"Sound the bells!" Abbot Ohwan instructed, calling the monks to gather in the nave of St. Honce. He rushed into the main room, most of the masters at his side, many others streaming in from the many side doors.

He began issuing orders as the bells began to sound. Some would go to the south wall to help the Allheart Knights get back into the city. Others would turn this very nave into a hospital for the expected wounded. He sent a group of monks to the secured storerooms for gemstones, mostly soul stones, and told the brothers to pray for strength.

"We will need it in these coming days," the abbot told them. "A great trial is upon Ursal. Unknown enemies have come against us. But we will turn them aside, and with King Midalis leading us, we will drive them from Honce with such certainty that they will never come against us again!"

He was hoping for a great and momentous cheer with that proclamation, hoping to rouse his brethren to greater heights of power and determination, but instead, just as he finished, the pealing bell hit a strange and off-tune note, and the whole of the giant monastery shook.

At the back end of the nave, not far from where Abbot Ohwan was standing, the ceiling cracked and broke apart, sending monks scrambling every which way, and through that break tumbled a gigantic pole—no, a spear, Ohwan realized to his horror—that smashed upon and shattered the altar.

Then came St. Honce's giant bell, tumbling and dropping to land with a dull, echoing clang.

A few brothers were hurt, but none too seriously.

"You see!" Abbot Ohwan cried, trying to save his message and their morale. "Let us go and defeat these profane monsters! To arms, my brothers!"

The cheer did begin this time, but only briefly, for then came the barrage, three lines of heavy stones slamming St. Honce, crumbling her walls. The monks fled in terror when the main tower collapsed, stumbling through the nave and onto the street.

The building's back wall buckled and crumbled into an avalanche of stone and dust, the entire structure groaning and cracking and tumbling down.

Abbot Ohwan barely escaped, and he would have been buried in the rubble had not two brothers grabbed him and dragged him across the nave and out the front doors. The trio scrambled down the stairs to the street, just ahead of the giant breath of rubble, a thick cloud of dust and small flying stones that gasped out of the destroyed building's large front doors.

Filthy and bruised, Ohwan looked back at his beautiful monastery, then around at his battered brethren, at the Ursal folk screaming and running every which way. He followed many of their gawking expressions skyward and caught a glimpse of the gigantic, snakelike dragon swimming across the sky, carrying a huge, manlike creature, a golden-skinned giant with a face red and blue.

Cries went up from within and without Ursal. Soldiers ran all about, with shouts to "Save the Allhearts in the south!" and then louder shouts for help on the west wall.

The enemy was coming. The enemy was here.

Abbot Ohwan shook away his shock at the brutal and abrupt fall of St. Honce and reminded himself that he had to lead here, that the monks had to do their part, above and beyond, to serve the folk and the king.

But he looked back to St. Honce in horror.

Most of the gemstones were in vaults in the catacombs beneath the far end of the monastery. Now, along with the brothers Ohwan had sent to retrieve them, they were buried under tons and tons of rubble.

"By Saint Abelle," he whispered under his breath.

A thumping sound, like someone beating a huge skin drum, sounded to the west. Then came the thunderous report of the second barrage, the whole of the city shaking under the pounding of the thrown stones.

"Gather where you can, in small groups," he told the brothers around him. "Help where you may. For Ursal!"

He looked to the large building beside St. Honce, the castle of King Midalis, and tried to take some solace in the fact that this man was battle-proven—indeed, was the victor in the great civil war that had torn Honce-the-Bear asunder a decade before.

Abbot Ohwan had prayed for Midalis's defeat on that dark day.

Abbot Ohwan now prayed for Midalis's victory on this dark day.

Several more human riders had fallen, but the group had proven more resilient and capable than Ataquixt and the others had expected, and more than a few mundunugu lay about the ground near the dead enemies.

The pivot of the horsemen had been brilliant, never breaking formation and moving just far enough to the east to get around the intercepting force.

And it was all her doing, Ataquixt knew, riding his cuetzpali hard to get one last throw at the woman spearheading the human force. He was moving too near the city, he realized, inviting fire from those strange throwing sticks, like a small bow held horizontally, used by the soldiers on the high wall. Those crossbows shot small arrows but at a very high speed.

Still, Ataquixt, feeling very much a failure in his inability to intercept and destroy these riders, ignored the risks.

One throw.

He hoisted the atlatl into the air, turning his mount, angling carefully. A group of his fellow mundunugu had kept up the pursuit behind the riders, spears still flying regularly, although most fell short and the others found only blocking shields.

But Ataquixt's angle was different, and he hadn't been noticed.

A pang of regret stung him. This warrior had been brilliant and deserved a better death. But how many xoconai would be doomed if he did not defeat her here and now?

He urged his lizard more swiftly ahead and closed for just a moment, just long enough to let fly. The woman was looking back, turned the other way, her shield protecting the flank of her horse.

She never saw it coming.

The javelin hit her in the small of her back, just below the breastplate. It found a seam and punctured the leather padding enough to stick in place.

The woman jolted and started to turn but faltered halfway, falling forward onto the lowered neck of her running horse. There, she held on for several strides before slowly sliding off the right side, falling hard to the ground, tumbling and bouncing.

Before he could digest that, while he was only beginning to nod grimly at the hit, Ataquixt, too, was jolted, his cuetzpali suddenly lurching and stumbling, fighting his every tug on the reins.

He looked back and saw the small arrow buried into his mount's hip, blood streaming from the wound.

A lesser rider would have been thrown in those perilous moments, as the cuetzpali thrashed wildly, but Ataquixt held his seat and finally brought the mount under control, moving it away from the wall.

He glanced back to the fallen human woman and saw another of the warriors on the ground beside her, but standing, sword and shield in hand.

The gallantry brought a grimace to Ataquixt's face. These were the children of Cizinfozza, so claimed the augurs, so claimed Glorious Gold. Thus, these were the kin of goblins, sub-xoconai, monsters more than men.

But no goblin would have moved to stand beside a fallen companion.

Ataquixt wanted to deny the truth but found that he could not.

A barrage of four javelins flew in at the man as he straddled his fallen friend, but he worked his shield with amazing grace to pick them all from the air, two of them even sticking there in that upraised shield.

In went a pair of xoconai riders, macana swinging.

The human drove his shield down across his body, angling it so that the encumbering spears had their butt ends on the ground in front of his right foot. Down and across came the sword, severing the spears up near the shield, removing the encumbrance, and up went the shield, just in time to deflect a macana swing. Out went the man's sword the other way, hooking the macana of the other passing xoconai, then diving so perfectly that it scored a hit on the cuetzpali as well. The lizard reared and dove, the rider flying over its head, sliding facedown to the ground.

After a few more barely controlled strides, Ataquixt managed to pull up his mount. He turned back to watch the fight, to call out commands to his fellow mundunugu.

Another volley of javelins went out at the human, who again deflected them with his shield—all but one, which struck him in the leg, digging in.

From the side came the wounded cuetzpali, from behind came the other mundunugu and her mount, and so Ataquixt figured the man would fall quickly.

But no. He rushed out fearlessly to meet the charge of the riderless lizard, catching it with a heavy downstroke even as it started to rear for his throat. Down went the lizard, so suddenly and so finally, and the human spun back, then dove aside in a practiced roll as the other mundunugu came in at him.

Another javelin flew in at him as he rose, slipping past the shield and striking him squarely in the chest. His fine breastplate rejected it, though the weight of the blow staggered him backwards.

On came the mundunugu, standing in the saddle and chopping down at the apparently oblivious man.

But up came the shield and down went the armored man, crouching and stabbing hard—once, then again—then retracting and chopping the back of the cuetzpali's neck.

Both lizard and rider tumbled down in the dirt.

Ataquixt vowed to never underestimate these human foes again. The beauty, precision, and strength of this one's attacks could not be denied.

Nor should they be dishonored.

Ataquixt lifted his horn and blew three sharp notes, and the charging group of mundunugu pulled up as one, some turning disappointed glances the leader's way but none disobeying.

Ataquixt signaled them to pass him, heading back to the west, to move around the corner of the city wall, out of range of the archers on the wall, and thus to join in the main charge, which had only just begun.

As eager as he was to get back to Tuolonatl's side, Ataquixt held there for a while, watching the human. He was wounded in his leg, of course, but now his shield arm, too, hung limp at his side. Even so, he retrieved his horse and walked it back to his fallen leader, and he somehow managed to hoist her up over the animal's back.

He dropped his sword to the ground and tried to unfasten

his shield, but it would not fall. He pulled off his helmet, his face a mask of anger, sorrow, and pain, and his eyes met those of Ataquixt.

The man's clear hatred challenged the mundunugu to attack, but Ataquixt, his mount hobbled, his forces moving off behind him, would not. Instead, he saluted the man and turned his cuetzpali, riding to the west.

Tuolonatl led the first wave of mundunugu riders for the wall of Ursal. They took some volleys from the crossbowmen up above, but the shaking and crumbling wall rendered that defense fairly inconsequential. By comparison, as they neared, the mundunugu lifted their atlatls as one and let fly a sweeping volley of javelins, most skimming the top of the wall, forcing the defenders down, disrupting the rhythm of the archers.

Without slowing, Tuolonatl's cavalry reached the wall and urged their cuetzpali into leaps, the riders leaning forward to keep their weight as close to the wall as possible while their sticky-fingered lizard mounts rushed upward.

Tuolonatl was among the first to reach the top, of course, and, as the cuetzpali came over the parapet, she was immediately set upon by a human soldier crashing in from the left. She drove her left leg hard into the side of her mount, urging that toothy maw around to snap and shorten the man's swing. In that moment, Tuolonatl leaned away from the swing and leaped up from her saddle, crossing her legs to set her feet opposite, left foot back. From there, she suddenly spun halfway around, her turn moving her away from the man's second feeble stab, her angle, as she circuited, allowing her to throw her full weight behind the backhand strike of her macana paddle. The man got his shield up to block, but it hardly mattered, for his feet were too close together as he tried to stay inside the angle of the cuetzpali's bite, and the weight of Tuolonatl's blow was simply too great for him to resist.

As he pitched from the wall, the cochcal flipped the rest

of the way around, fell down low, under the thrust of a spear coming from her right, then came up under it, stabbing the tip of her macana under the chin of this second human soldier. The man's head snapped back and, in the moment it took him to look back and reorient, Tuolonatl's follow-up swing came in high and wide to his right, behind his defenses, to slam against the side of his head.

He, too, fell away.

More mundunugu scaled the wall to join her, the riders avoiding the huge breach in the wall, leaving it open for the macana foot soldiers to crash into the city.

From up high, the mundunugu swept the wall and hurled their spears down into the city behind that major breach, where the shocked human defenders were trying to organize some resistance.

Tuolonatl had been in enough battles to understand that the outcome of the fight was already decided. Unless these humans had some magic or war machines she could not anticipate, the city would soon fall.

In through the wall poured the xoconai warriors, swarming onto the streets, and soon more humans were running away than were trying to stop them.

"A dragon! They have a dragon!" Abbot Ohwan wailed when he caught up to King Midalis, who was surrounded by attendants helping him to don his armor in the entry hall of the castle.

Midalis knew as well as any man alive the power of such a beast. He thought of Brynn Dharielle of To-gai and the great fire-breathing dragon she had ridden into battle against King Aydrian. The king blew a sigh. Aydrian had returned a few days earlier, and now a dragon?

Coincidence?

Or, more likely, exactly as Aydrian and the others had warned.

He didn't know what to think. The ground had been shaking fiercely and the thunderous sounds of catastrophe had swept into the castle, though muted by the thick walls. He looked to the abbot and only then noticed that the man was covered in thick dust.

"Abbot, what happened?" he asked, shocked.

"Saint Honce has fallen."

"Saint Honce? How is that possible?" Midalis shoved the hands of one attendant aside, then reached out the other way to grab his helmet from the man there. He rushed out of the castle, the abbot in tow, and stood staring in disbelief at the huge ruin beside him.

He knew the answer, or at least he thought he knew the answer.

The enemy had a dragon.

"My wife and children to the deep tunnels," King Midalis ordered the few Allhearts around him.

"They are already on their way to the secure rooms," answered an Allheart.

"No. They have a dragon. To the boat and away!"

"Saint-Mere-Abelle," one of the other knights agreed, nodding and rushing off.

"Yes, all the way to the monastery," Abbot Ohwan said.

"No," said Midalis, to shocked expressions. "No," he said again, improvising here, thinking it through. "Out of Honce altogether until we can truly determine the power of this unknown enemy."

"Vanguard?" one knight asked.

"Pireth Dancard," the king ordered. The others nodded, except for the scowling Abbot Ohwan.

"There is no greater fortress in all the world than Saint-Mere-Abelle," the abbot said. "Surely they would be safe."

"Like Ursal? Like Saint Honce?" the king replied somberly.

"Pireth Dancard is a tiny hovel next to Saint-Mere-Abelle,"

said the abbot, truthfully. "It has none of the comforts the royal family desires."

"This is no time for comfort."

"It hasn't the magical power of Saint-Mere-Abelle! A thousand brothers armed with the most powerful of gemstones. You, above all others, should understand the might."

"I do. And yes, my friend, Pireth Dancard is but a small collection of towers and castles on a patch of rocky islands. But it is in the middle of the mouth of the Gulf of Corona, surrounded by naught but water, and with all the positions protected by high cliffs so formidable that even the powries take pains to avoid the place. They can't conquer it, and they know it from bitter experience."

"Nor could they take Ursal," the abbot said dryly.

"But these enemies won't find it," said the king. He held up his hand to silence the abbot, then delivered the orders again to the knights: that his wife and two children should be out posthaste, up the river to the gulf, and across the gulf to the small fortress of Pireth Dancard.

"My king, perhaps you too should go," said Abbot Ohwan, when Midalis had barely finished.

Midalis glared at the man, angry at first but then understanding. Ohwan was only suggesting this because he wanted to be on that departing ship.

And, really, who could blame him?

Before Midalis could respond, a loud noise echoed down the street to the west, a cacophony of screams, and the king and abbot stared in surprise at a throng of people running desperately, shrieking and crying, with panicked soldiers among them.

An Allheart Knight came into view, too, riding among the crowd, weaving and trying hard not to trample anyone. He rode up to King Midalis and leaped from his horse.

"The western wall has fallen!" he cried. "The enemy, the . . . I do not know what to call them! I have never seen such beasts. They are not goblins . . . their faces . . ." He shook his head.

"The sidhe," King Midalis said, and in his thoughts he recalled the other name, the strange name. "Xoconai."

"Thousands," said the knight. "Tens of thousands. I have never seen such a force!"

"Throw wide the castle doors!" Midalis yelled. "Get them in, all of them, any of them!"

"My king, we cannot," said Ohwan.

"Shut up," Midalis told him. He turned for the stairs leading back into the castle.

"If Saint Honce crumbled so easily, do you think the castle will fare any better?" Ohwan shouted after him.

"Get your brothers to do their jobs and perhaps our odds will improve!" Midalis shouted back at him. He didn't miss the pained look that came over the man, and it made Midalis look to the side again, to the rubble that only moments before had been the beautiful monastery of St. Honce.

"I had called an audience," Abbot Ohwan said quietly. "To prepare."

"How many were lost?"

The abbot shook his head helplessly.

"Find all you can and get them inside," Midalis told him, but his voice trailed off when another Allheart Knight came into view, this one leading a horse—a horse with yet another knight lying across the saddle—and limping badly. He, too, made his way to the castle and the king.

Midalis stared at him, at Julian of the Evergreen, in disbelief. The man carried a broken piece of a javelin sticking from his knee, his leg covered in blood. His head was bleeding, too, and blood showed around the edges of his mouth. His left arm hung limply, his shield unstrapped but still there, and it took Midalis a moment to realize that, among the broken javelins stuck in that shield, one had driven right through the buckler and through Julian's arm. That spear alone was the reason the man hadn't dropped the shield.

The other knights pulled the body from the horse, removing her helm, and King Midalis knew that he had lost perhaps his finest Allheart of all, Dame Koreen.

More and more soldiers appeared among the fleeing throng, terrified and showing no signs of forming any defense, and now the sounds of the fighting grew closer.

On a nearby rooftop appeared a sidhe, riding a large green lizard and lifting a spear.

King Midalis had lost Koreen.

King Midalis had lost Ursal.

Though the battle in the walled city was going well, the fight at the river was proving far more difficult. Tuolonatl's forces had made some initial gains, cuetzpali and their riders swimming out to take the first boats by surprise.

But there were larger ships moored off of Ursal harbor, and they were crewed by veteran sailors, most from the Mantis Arm far to the east, who had spent years battling ferocious powries and were expert at defending their precious ships.

When she came upon the scene soon after the main force had driven into the city, the cochcal recalled her forces and instead set a line of macana warriors along the bank, with stacks of javelins. She had the city's docks under her control, so she would concede the waterway for now, but she wasn't about to let those crews come ashore.

For all their gains this morning, Tuolonatl did not like this moment because she couldn't control it—this was exactly why she had called for patience in attacking so powerful a target. Tuolonatl valued the lives of her forces too much for such uncertainty.

The fighting was minimal now, small pockets of dug-in humans battling fiercely. But the city itself was almost fully under control, save the one large and secure building, the castle.

Tuolonatl could afford to take her time with that structure. Scathmizzane had flown to the west and was nowhere to be found. As with the boats on the river, Tuolonatl ordered her forces not to engage the castle but to hold a solid perimeter and allow no breakout.

The mundunugu swept the fields south and east of the city. Tuolonatl tightened her noose.

With Ataquixt beside her, she rode hard back to the divine throwers and High Priest Pixquicauh. She slowed as she neared the gathering, her mouth hanging open, and she and her companion realized then that their victory hadn't been quite as overwhelming as they had previously believed.

Before them, Pixquicauh strolled about, waving his arms and extolling the beauty of Glorious Gold. The soldiers guarding the area all cheered at that, of course, but few of the augurs joined in. Many sat on the ground, heads hanging low, their condoral pulled up high or removed altogether, faces pale, hands trembling. Those few walking, other than Pixquicauh, had macana escorts helping them, while others lay on the ground, very still.

Tuolonatl rode to the high priest and dismounted. She looked all about, arms up high, silently asking what had happened.

"The unbridled power of Glorious Gold flowed through us," Pixquicauh replied, and his tone was light, giddy even. "Only I was pure enough to accept it and not resist. You see now why I am the voice of Scathmizzane, why he has entrusted me above all others."

Tuolonatl gave a slight nod, more to shut the man up on this subject than to agree.

"Are they dead?" she asked, motioning to a line of four prone augurs.

"Did you see the barrage?" Pixquicauh answered, and Tuolonatl had her answer in his poor attempt at a diversion.

"All of the augurs here will be replaced as we move on," Pixquicauh added. "The number of dead this day far exceeds all of the previous battles combined. Glorious Gold will grow stronger. The God Crystal will await our call!"

Tuolonatl narrowed her eyes. "What do you mean?"

Pixquicauh laughed at her and twirled away, calling again for cheers and prayers to the mighty Scathmizzane.

The legendary mundunugu looked to Ataquixt, who merely shrugged, obviously at a loss.

"How long?" Tuolonatl called to Pixquicauh.

"How long?"

"How long before I can use the divine throwers again?"

Pixquicauh held up his hands. "Finish your task here and let Scathmizzane and Pixquicauh prepare."

"There is a castle within the city, and ships on the river," she started to argue.

"The city is ours," was all that Pixquicauh would reply.

Tuolonatl looked to the now silent magical cannons, their platforms empty of stones. She was being asked to command the battlefield and a vast army with only half of the information. Her gaze went to the augurs, who now seemed all but useless.

These were the xoconai healers, and Tuolonatl had many wounded mundunugu and macana warriors.

Tuolonatl had seen what battlefield wounds could do when they weren't treated. She had seen the pus and smelled the pus and heard the pitiful cries of dying warriors.

A great pity, she thought, that Pixquicauh wasn't among the dead on the field.

The castle of Ursal was built near the southern reaches of the city, on higher ground. Beneath its supporting catacombs were tunnels, natural passages worked and stepped, leading down fifty feet and more to secret docks at the river level, far beneath the castle.

There weren't many floating wharves here, and not many ships—certainly nothing to match the three-masted ocean vessels out on the river. These were altered Alpinadoran longships, vessels that could be rowed as well as sailed, with folding masts to support a single square sail.

On one of these, a small one, the queen and her two children had been escorted away as the catastrophe above had begun to unfold.

"We can ferry the peasants to the eastern bank, then," King Midalis argued with his assembled Allheart Knights and officers and the few masters of St. Honce who had found their way into the castle to join with Abbot Ohwan. "Far enough to the north to at least give them a chance to outrun the pursuit."

"There are more than a thousand souls in the rooms and halls of Castle Ursal," Abbot Ohwan solemnly replied. "The vessels in here could not get more than one in ten out, and that is if we could find competent oarsmen and pilots."

"You would have me leave them?" King Midalis asked.

"I would have us, and those important for the defense of Honce, escape this unwinnable situation," Abbot Ohwan replied. "I would have King Midalis survive, so that the people who have not yet met the fury of the sidhe will know some hope, at least."

"It feels like cowardice," Midalis muttered. "I have never run from a fight."

"Of course you have," answered the abbot, and all around him gasped. "In the war with King Aydrian, you ran from Ursal, wisely so, and collected your army to win a glorious victory. This is the same thing, my king, my friend."

"We cannot hope to break out of the castle and retake the city," an Allheart Knight added, drawing a scowl from Midalis.

"You ask me to take the knights and the brothers of Saint Honce and flee to the north?" King Midalis asked, spitting every word with obvious disgust. "Who is left to defend the children and the infirm and the wounded among us?"

"No one can defend them now, my king," Abbot Ohwan said quietly.

Such anger filled King Midalis that he felt his ears burning. How had this happened? So quickly!

"The river is still open," came another voice, and Midalis turned, recognizing the speaker as Julian of the Evergreen. "It may be not so in the light of dawn. Our enemies are not stupid goblins, that much we have seen. They will close the river tomorrow, surely."

"That is why many of the ships have pulled anchor and sailed north," Abbot Ohwan added.

"It feels like cowardice," Midalis spat again.

"It is prudence," said Ohwan. "From the high towers, those overlooking the city have seen many taken as prisoner. The common folk in here have a better chance of surviving captivity than the fight our presence will bring. Let us be gone, with all the soldiers we can carry, and bid the rest to surrender when the call for it comes."

Midalis looked to Julian, the young man he had come to admire and trust, and one, he knew, who would lead with his heart and not out of any fear for his body. His severe wounds, the story of how he had turned to retrieve the body of Koreen, only confirmed that.

Julian glanced at Abbot Ohwan and reluctantly nodded.

In the dark of night, King Midalis, Abbot Ohwan, and the remaining Allheart Knights and brothers of St. Honce slipped out of Ursal through the concealed waterways, broke into the rivers through hidden doors suddenly opened, and were away along the Masur Delaval too swiftly for any serious response from the enemies in the city or those along the western bank.

The queen, the prince, and the princess were well on their way to a distant island, so they believed, but King Midalis would not go that far.

"Palmaris," he ordered, "we know our enemy better now

and know what to expect. With the large garrison there, the many fighting ships harbored there, and the brothers of mighty Saint Precious, we will turn the sidhe around and chase them all the way back to and through Ursal."

"They have a dragon," Abbot Ohwan mumbled under his breath, but King Midalis heard him, and silenced him with a scowl.

14

ALL THE WORLD IS OURS

Redshanks wandered the avenues of Appleby-in-Wilderland, his mood darker than on any day since the fall of the town itself.

He had seen Khotai that morning, crawling to the one well where the people of the town were allowed to draw water. Water had splashed everywhere.

The poor woman was in the mud.

They had taken her belt and separated her from Talmadge and the others. They had taken everything.

"Xatatl," Redshanks said, approaching a group of sidhe—of xoconai, they had corrected him, quite emphatically (and painfully).

A pair of warriors that the bright-faced invaders called macana turned and scowled at him, then began accosting him in their language, which he did not know anywhere near well enough to decipher. He understood their message loud and clear, however, particularly when Xatatl, the appointed sovereign of Appleby and usually the most reasonable of the lot, stared at him hard and shook his head.

Redshanks held up his hands and backed away, lowering his eyes and going silent as the three finished their conversation.

The two macana walked past him, one very near, and a shoulder butt sent the old frontiersman stumbling to the side.

"Fine day to yerself, too," Redshanks said to the departing warrior woman.

"You should better know your place," Xatatl said, motioning for Redshanks to approach.

"I've done all that you've asked."

"Deed and word and . . ."—Xatatl stumbled for the word for just a moment—"attitude are three different things. Align all three correctly and you will find yourself more comfortable."

"Lived in the mountains all my life," Redshanks countered with a breezy shrug. "Comfort, ye say?"

"And you will find that your example will spread to the others now under xoconai rule," Xatatl said. "Fewer will be punished, or killed."

Every instinct in the independent frontiersman screamed against that logic and made him want to spit in Xatatl's red and blue face, but he reminded himself that it wasn't about him. It was about keeping people alive until they could find some answer to this seemingly impossible turn of events.

He nodded and kept his gaze respectfully to the ground.

"What do you wish to ask of me?" Xatatl asked.

"The dark-skinned woman. She's a friend of old, and good. I'm asking that ye give to her the belt that allows her her dignity."

"All magic belongs to Scathmizzane," came a curt reply.

"Then Scathmizzane must think it good for her to possess such a gift." Redshanks shuffled nervously as he finished that argument, for when he heard the words, they sounded much worse than he had imagined.

"Look at me," Xatatl demanded, and Redshanks held his breath.

"You have been of service, but if you ever presume to tell me or any xoconai the will of Scathmizzane again, I will have the skin flayed from you. All of it."

The man nodded eagerly and apologetically. He didn't doubt that threat for a moment.

"Is there anything else?" asked Xatatl.

"Could you return her to her friends?" Redshanks dared to ask, the image of poor Khotai in the mud demanding that he try. "Or to others who might care for her?"

"The people of Appleby are concerned with their own tasks. With caring for themselves and serving their masters. They know the consequences of their failure."

Redshanks didn't have to look out to the west, to the trellis bending under the weight of the upside down hanging bodies of executed Appleby citizens.

"You are concerned with her dignity," Xatatl added. "That is laudable. The xoconai understand this. We are a people of honor. So I will help you and your dark-skinned friend."

The startling words made Redshanks look up into Xatatl's eyes.

"The woman is of no use to us. She can barely take care of herself, and there are no duties we might add to her that would be of value."

He waved Redshanks away.

The man stood staring, his jaw dropping open. "Wait, are ye saying . . ."

Xatatl waved more emphatically, and Redshanks had no choice but to leave, but every step had him glancing back, trying to decipher the dire implications of that promise. What did the augur governor mean? What had he done?

He glanced out to the west, to the bloody pergola, as the people of Appleby had come to call the bloodletting structure.

Redshanks stumbled repeatedly, trying to sort something, anything, that would give him hope. He looked up at the sky, the sun lowering in the west. The xoconai typically held their executions at sunrise or sunset, as those times seemed to hold religious significance to them. Usually, however, unless the action was in response to some event like an escape attempt or an assault on a sidhe, sunrise was preferred.

Redshanks had to hope for that. There was not enough time before sunset.

He hoped.

"Catriona is out?" Redshanks asked, after feigning a stumble and veering with the load of waterskins to bring him near enough so that only the two men would hear.

"In the south," Talmadge confirmed.

"This is madness," said Bahdlahn, who was piling wood nearby.

"Sunrise," Talmadge replied, and Bahdlahn grimaced and threw a log onto the pile.

"I know," he answered, and he did indeed. Redshanks had pushed this situation upon them so suddenly. Patience and detailed planning were not options here.

"Take heart," Redshanks whispered, continuing on his way. "They've grown comfortable in thinking that they've cowed us all."

Bahdlahn looked out to the south, through the rows of houses and down the winding lane. They had to try, but if he lost Catriona, he'd never forgive himself. She had taken a great chance, slipping out from the fields where she and some others had been working, so that she could start a distant campfire. It was an incredibly risky move, particularly since she was one of the very few in Appleby with a shaped, elongated skull. If caught, she couldn't pretend to be a newcomer here.

It was the only way, though. Talmadge and Bahdlahn had spent the day working the woodpile, stuck in the center of town with xoconai all about, and Redshanks had to be available to complete the diversion to have any chance of success—slim though that chance would be, and slimmer still since Xatatl had ordered Khotai to be brought into a tent, under guard, confirming Redshanks's belief that she would be executed.

"We have to get the belt," Talmadge whispered between exaggerated grunts, as he hoisted more wood.

"We have to get Khotai," Bahdlahn said. "And we are only two."

But Talmadge shook his head. "Not without the belt."

"We can'no."

"We have to," Talmadge said, his tone leaving no room for argument.

The startling words and the clear sincerity behind them hit Bahdlahn profoundly, for he understood that Talmadge had only said such a thing because of his deep love for the woman.

"You get the belt," Bahdlahn said, the next time his work moved him past Talmadge. "Xatatl won't be there."

"We hope."

Bahdlahn didn't even bother to respond. The whole thing seemed so hopeless and desperate to him. He thought again of that helpless moment on the ridge atop Fireach Speuer, overlooking the sacrificial ceremony of the Usgar at Craos'a'diad. This seemed no less desperate than his desire then to rush down to the doomed Aoleyn's aid.

We need more people, he thought but did not say. He knew, though, that help wouldn't be found among the folk of Appleby. They had already been broken. They outnumbered the remaining xoconai perhaps five to one, but they would never rise up.

Bahdlahn looked to the west. The sun was just about at the horizon now. Already the first calls for the humans to finish their tasks had begun.

It seemed, at least, as if the field masters hadn't noticed Catriona's disappearance yet. His gaze went to the south, then nervously back to the west, then back to the south.

The cry of her escape would go out soon.

The fire had to be seen before that!

Daylight began to wane. Bahdlahn's handler called out to him and Talmadge to be done and to get their evening water.

"Come on," Bahdlahn whispered, as he and Talmadge made their way to a line before the well.

A cry sounded and the man's heart sank, thinking it the field master.

But no! Some of the xoconai rushed to a rooftop, all staring out to the south, and moments later, others moved about among the workers, telling them to hurry and get to their cots.

They thought more unsuspecting humans were stumbling in, as Bahdlahn and his three friends had done.

Moving slowly, appearing broken and downtrodden, Bahdlahn and Talmadge neared the small house where they slept with twenty others.

Talmadge nudged Bahdlahn and directed his gaze to a side avenue, where they saw Redshanks astride his horse, trotting out to the south to set the newest trap. The xoconai hunters and riders assembled in the road were plotting their ambush.

"Take heart," Talmadge whispered, as he and Bahdlahn went into the house. "Look at them. So arrogant."

"Ximocah!" the lone guard in the house demanded, a word they had painfully learned meant "Silence."

The response was so instinctive, so sudden and improvised, that Bahdlahn's fist crashed into the xoconai's bright red nose before either Bahdlahn or his victim even realized that the punch was coming.

The warrior's head jerked back, slamming into the wooden wall, and down he slumped.

"Bahdlahn!" Talmadge said in shock.

Bahdlahn retrieved the tooth-edged paddle and checked to make sure he had not killed the xoconai. He came up with a shrug and tossed the weapon to Talmadge. "Get the belt."

"There are guards with Khotai," he replied, handing the weapon back out toward Bahdlahn.

"I don't need it," the young and strong man replied. He moved back to the door and cracked it open, then took a deep breath of relief when he discovered that the ambush party had already departed.

The fewer enemies in the city, the better.

Twilight was only then falling, the darkness hardly complete, but Bahdlahn slipped out and moved along the wall, then around the corner. He slipped from building to building quickly, gauging his position, remembering which house they had put the woman into.

He came up to the wall right beside the door and paused, noting Talmadge's movements across the way as he neared the house that had belonged to Redshanks.

Doubts flew up around him like black wings, telling him to abandon this madness.

Bahdlahn laughed them away as he considered his punch. Too late for second thoughts. He put his ear to the door and heard xoconai voices just inside.

"Don't tarry," he whispered, and he stepped out from the wall and over in front of the entry, then burst through, nearly taking the door from its hinges. He noted Khotai immediately, sitting on the floor directly across the way, against the wall.

He only registered her momentarily, though; his focus was on the more immediate problems. He snapped his elbow out the right, crashing it into the face of a woman, who went flying away, then drove it back, landing a heavy right cross on the upraised arm and chest of a man to his left.

He wanted to follow as that man went stumbling backwards, for he knew that he hadn't knocked that one from the fight, but the third, another woman, came at him, macana raised.

Bahdlahn got his arm up to block but took a heavy hit on the forearm, the weapon's teeth tearing his sleeve and skin.

He fell back a step, but only a step, and an exaggerated one, goading the warrior to follow. Then he reversed his momentum suddenly, barreling ahead as she came forward, the two crashing together in a clench.

Bahdlahn was twice her weight. He drove with his legs, tying her up, forcing her backwards. He let her get her weapon hand free, accepting another hit in exchange for looping his arms out and under hers, that he could lift her right from the ground and drive on harder. Two running strides and Bahdlahn stopped and threw out with all his tremendous strength, and the woman flew the rest of the way, slamming hard into the back wall, shaking the house.

Bahdlahn turned and saw his doom—the man coming in, weapon ready—and had no way to defend.

But the xoconai stumbled suddenly, falling forward, and he swung too soon, short of the mark. Bahdlahn used this good fortune to wade in behind the blow and snap the xoconai's head to the side with a vicious left hook.

The man went down to the floor in a heap.

But no, it wasn't merely good fortune, Bahdlahn realized, when he saw Khotai untangling herself from the fallen xoconai's lower legs.

The unbreakable woman had dived at his feet.

Bahdlahn fell over the xoconai man, yanking one arm back brutally. He grabbed his victim by the long and thick hair on the back of his head, then pulled him up and slammed him down, once, twice, thrice.

When the woman he had thrown into the wall groaned, Bahdlahn leaped up and rushed to her, retrieving her macana.

He raised it for a killing stroke.

He stood up straight and looked around, shaking his head. He didn't want to kill her, and not only for strategic reasons.

He gathered up a second macana, from the man, then hoisted Khotai in his arms.

"What are you doing?" she demanded.

"They're going to kill you in the morning," he answered. "And now they'll kill us all!"

"They have to catch us first!" Out into the deepening gloom went Bahdlahn. He hoisted Khotai over his shoulder, freeing one hand in case any came against him, and ran to the northeast, to the stables.

But he heard pursuit, a commotion behind, and knew without looking that he couldn't make it.

He growled in protest. He ran as fast as his legs would carry him.

He heard the hoofbeats behind him and knew it was over.

Bahdlahn didn't dare look back—what was the point?—as the steed overtook him. He expected an explosion of pain as a macana caved in his skull.

But the horse, fully saddled, trotted right by him, slowing to a walk.

Stunned, Bahdlahn slowed and looked back to see a solitary figure standing in the road.

Redshanks smiled at him and waved, then turned awkwardly. He had a javelin stuck in his back, hanging down behind him, the butt end dragging in the dirt. He shrugged, as if apologetically.

Bahdlahn rushed to the horse and placed Khotai over its back, then turned about, determined to rescue the valiant old man.

A second javelin arced in, driving into Redshanks's side, knocking him to the ground. He wrenched about with great effort, only so that he could wave the foolish would-be hero away.

Not too far behind came a mundunugu rider.

Bahdlahn leaped upon the horse awkwardly and held on for his life as it jumped away. He was no rider. He had no idea of what to do, other than to hold on.

Khotai shoved him back a bit and sat up in the saddle, taking the reins.

She was To-gai-ru, from the tundra lands south of the

Belt-and-Buckle. She had been riding horses before she could walk.

"The corral," Bahdlahn told her, as he tried to better steady himself on the bouncing creature.

"Where is Talmadge?" she demanded.

"Corral! Corral!"

Khotai put her head down and kicked at the horse with her one leg, weaving about the buildings to block any more throws from behind.

How relieved Bahdlahn was when they came upon the corral and found Talmadge there between two horses, holding the reins. The man ran out to meet them, immediately going to Khotai with her magical belt. Bahdlahn slipped down from the horse, staggering as he tried to regain his footing.

"The saddle isn't tight, but ride anyway," Talmadge told him, motioning to the one horse he had gathered that was wearing a saddle. "We've no time!"

"Ride? I don't know how."

"Just jump up and hold on!" Khotai yelled to him.

Bahdlahn got to the horse and went up as bravely as he could manage. He noted, then, that Talmadge had collected more than the belt, for there lay their weapons, even Khotai's bow and arrows.

"How?" he said, when the man rushed up to the remaining horse.

Talmadge shrugged and smiled. "Xatatl's house was empty." He grimaced, apparently noticing the garish wound on Bahdlahn's arm. "You should have kept the macana."

Talmadge bent and retrieved the bow and arrows, handing them to Khotai as she guided her horse to them.

"Go!" he ordered Bahdlahn.

"How?"

Talmadge slapped Bahdlahn's horse on the rump, and the animal leaped away.

Bahdlahn nearly tumbled, but he squeezed his legs and

grabbed the reins and the mane, then just hugged the animal's neck desperately. Truly he felt a fool when Talmadge, riding bareback, came up easily beside him.

"Keep going," the frontiersman urged. "They can't catch us."

Even as he spoke, a javelin flew past, and despite himself, Bahdlahn swung his head about. It took him a moment, more than one, to sort out the scene behind him.

There was Khotai, riding easily, but though her horse was chasing him, the woman wasn't facing him. She had turned right around, sitting backwards, holding nothing but her bow.

Out went an arrow, taking a xoconai right off her lizard.

Out went another.

The pursuit broke off, and the three friends rode hard out into the night.

They continued north for just a bit, until Talmadge led them to the left, the west. They weaved among the trees in the forest northwest of Appleby until they came to the banks of a small pond. There they waited patiently, and not as long as they expected, until, to their great relief, Catriona appeared on the southern bank.

Bahdlahn was the first to greet the woman, the two running hard into each other's arms. Before either appeared to even realize the action, they shared a kiss.

Bahdlahn pulled back, his face flushed with embarrassment.

Catriona snorted at him. "It took you long enough."

The young man didn't know what he felt then. He thought of Aoleyn, but only briefly, for the overwhelming sense of freedom consumed him.

They had done it. Somehow they had escaped the xoconai in Appleby.

What now?

"Redshanks," Bahdlahn said somberly.

"He fell on the road," Talmadge told Catriona.

"Dead?"

Talmadge shrugged.

"Should we go back for him?" Bahdlahn asked. "For the others? So many."

"If we go back, we dishonor them—Redshanks most of all," Khotai answered. "We must be far from this place, to tell the world what we have seen."

"Many left in Appleby are going to die," Bahdlahn said. "How can we allow that?"

"How can we stop it?" Khotai and Talmadge said together.

"Many have died already, and many more will," said Catriona. "More than we can count."

"Do we not owe it to them to try to rescue them?" Bahdlahn asked.

"We owe it to ourselves to stay alive," Catriona replied, a bit more sharply. "We owe it to the world that we stay alive and fight them when we can."

"Then where?" the young man asked.

"The road east is full of sidhe," said Talmadge.

"They march for the great city of Ursal on the river," Khotai agreed.

"A river that runs north," Talmadge said. "So we go north and east until we find it. When Redshanks talked to us about trading with Honce, those years ago, he mentioned other cities, great cities."

Khotai nodded, and so it was settled. The four didn't wait for dawn to set off. They moved slowly and steadily north, turning east only after they had put Appleby-in-Wilderland far, far behind.

Redshanks knew that he was dying, but the old frontiersman was smiling.

He could hear the distress in the voices of the xoconai around him and so knew that his friends had escaped.

He groaned and grimaced when the javelins were tugged out of him, and he was still groaning, trying to growl away the pain, when a pair of xoconai hoisted him to his feet, in the middle of the road, to face Xatatl.

Redshanks managed to recover his smile, and he offered a shrug to the augur. "I'm not apologizing," he said, his voice strained with the pain.

"I am not angry with you," the augur replied. "I salute your courage and cunning."

"Well, then, if you wouldn't mind a bit of healing."

"I promised my people a sacrifice in the morning," Xatatl said, with what seemed like an apologetic shrug. "I cannot let them down." He motioned to the guards, and they began roughly hauling Redshanks away.

"As long as it's not personal then," the doomed man said.

"Why should I be angry?"

"No, ye can't be fooling me. They're running free, and ye won't be catching horses on your short-legged lizards."

The augur shrugged. "Fool. Where do you think they can run? The world is ours."

Those words silenced Redshanks and stayed with him throughout the night, and they echoed even the next morning, when he was hanging upside down, his lifeblood pouring from wrists expertly cut by xoconai executioners.

15

DUSTY SCROLLS

"What do you know, Brother?" Elysant asked, coming under a low archway, candle in hand, to find Brother Thaddius sitting at a desk covered in parchments. Beside him sat a rolling cart, tall and narrow, with dozens of small cubbies, each holding several scroll tubes.

"I know why Saint Belfour traveled so far from Vanguard," Thaddius answered. "I know what he hoped to find."

He motioned for Elysant to come near and inspect the scroll he had open before him.

"Brother Gilbert?" she asked. "Annacuth? What is Annacuth?"

"A town, I expect, from long ago. These are very old. But look!" He unrolled a second scroll, one identified as the "First Diary of the Tomb of Unknown Ancients in the Ruins of Hertemspah."

"Hertemspah?" she asked, and Thaddius shrugged.

"But read the first line," he told her.

"*They are not masks,*" Elysant read aloud. "*We thought them masks. The red, red nose, brilliant red, bloody red,*" *with the brightest blue beside it.*" Elysant stepped back, eyes wide.

"Familiar sounding, yes?"

The woman leaned in and kept reading, silently for a bit, until she got to the end of the diary. "*Once they were mighty, so claim the poems. Once they built the greatest cities in all the lands, greater than the desert cities of Behren. They are lost to the world now. I feel a deep sense of regret. I would have enjoyed their golden temples and unusual ways. They were the Sidhe, who called themselves Xoconai.*"

"Xoconai," Thaddius echoed. "Not so lost to the world, it would seem."

"This diary dates to the earliest days of the Church. Nearly eight centuries."

"And this and the other writings of Brother Gilbert—there are seventeen entries—have been rarely examined, as far as I can determine, although the records from the early days are far from complete. Still, I can say with confidence that I am the first to look upon these in more than two centuries, and the last named in the logs was . . ."

He paused there for effect, and it worked, for Elysant leaned forward eagerly.

"Master Percy Fenne," Thaddius told her.

Elysant furrowed her brow for just a moment before her eyes grew wide. "*Who killed the goblins plenty,*" she recited.

"So, Saint Belfour and his troupe were searching for the sidhe . . . the xoconai, two hundred years ago, and now we have found them?"

"*They* have found *us,*" Thaddius corrected.

"Good fortune, then, that we uncovered the tomb in this trying time."

"Perhaps, but I have found nothing in these diaries that will aid us in the struggle if these xoconai are indeed intending to invade Honce-the-Bear. The writings are confirmation, perhaps, and with them, I might be better able to persuade Father Abbot Braumin of the impending threat, but there is so much more that we must learn." He looked around at the looming darkness in all directions in these massive catacombs, a checkerboard of small rooms walled by low arches and filled with graves, scrolls, books, and dust. So much dust.

"It is a place to start," Elysant said hopefully.

Brother Thaddius couldn't defeat her smile, and so he returned one of his own. Whatever trials might lie ahead—and he knew there would be many—he was glad that Sister Elysant of St. Gwendolyn would be by his side.

Aoleyn was more angry than nervous as the monks escorted her back to the main chapel and the audience chamber of Father Abbot Braumin. His summons had surprised her, after all these days alone in her room, with little human contact. She wasn't even certain how many days had passed!

She followed Master Visconti into the room, and when he moved aside, she was surprised to find Aydrian already in there, standing before the father abbot's desk. Not quite sure what to make of all this, Aoleyn's gaze darted all about, scanning the room for clues.

She noted three familiar alabaster coffers on the table beside Braumin's desk, and a wheeled cabinet, it seemed, set with many cubbies, all holding scrolls.

"Ah, good," Father Abbot Braumin greeted. "I trust that your stay with us has been comfortable."

"I don't like a roof above my head," Aoleyn answered. "It is a silly way to live."

Braumin furrowed his brow and looked to Aydrian, whose responding shrug and expression seemed to agree with Aoleyn.

"Well, at least many of the ceilings here at Saint-Mere-Abelle are wondrously painted, with scenes divine and inspired," the father abbot said.

"And do you think any of them more beautiful than the

tapestry painted in the sky above?" Aoleyn countered. She didn't know why she was bothering to argue over such trivialities when it would be easier, and probably better for them all, if she just let the man have his little victories. But she knew that it felt good to irk him.

The father abbot laughed. "Brilliant," he replied. He motioned to the side, and a pair of monks brought two chairs up and set them before his desk.

"Please, sit with me," he said. "I would offer food and drink, and will later, but for now, with such treasures as these ancient scrolls before me, I think not."

Aoleyn looked to Aydrian and followed him to her own seat when he took his.

She didn't like sitting. Aoleyn was much shorter than everyone in the room, and she felt smaller still as she sat there. She wondered if the monks were trying to diminish her. She took a deep breath and calmed herself. Her friends had all told her that this Father Abbot Braumin was not a bad man, and she hadn't been harmed, after all.

"What did you call these strange invaders, with their faces of red and blue?" Braumin asked.

"They call themselves xoconai," Aoleyn answered.

"*Sidhe*, I think, is also a term for them," Aydrian answered.

"Not to them. They do not call themselves sidhe, and they hold no affinity for the goblins that the people of my tribe call the sidhe," Aoleyn said. "It is a word the xoconai would consider more descriptive of us."

"Your tribe, from far in the west?"

"Yes. Usgar. I am Usgar." Aoleyn paused and considered all that had happened. "I may be the only Usgar still alive."

"I had thought that many refugees had come east with you," said the father abbot.

"Uamhas," Aoleyn replied, and Braumin furrowed his brow and looked to Aydrian.

"The folk who lived in the seven villages about the lake,"

Aydrian explained. "The Usgar lived on the mountain. She was the only one of that tribe to make the journey to the east."

"The mountain. And this was the mountain where you got these?" Braumin asked, and he held up a handful of jewelry that Aoleyn knew well. Her black eyes sparkled as she looked upon her treasures, and she had to consciously fight the irritation that tingled in her arm and hand, threatening to enact the power of her tattoo and transform her arm into that of a cloud leopard.

"Yes," she answered. "In a cave, as I told you before. A cave of crystals—many, huge and full of chips and flecks and stones."

"You know that we value these stones," Braumin replied. "To us, they are the gifts from our god. Only we know how to find them, in a place far away."

"None of you have ever been to the cave," Aoleyn said.

"We get them from a different place," the father abbot said. "To the east, across the sea."

"Then these are not yours, and not of your god," Aoleyn said, and the monks around her bristled uncomfortably. "And you are not the only ones who know how to find them. You don't even know how to find these."

"But you do?"

"I am of the Coven—or I was. We witches command the crystals of Usgar."

"Brother Thaddius believes you," Braumin said.

"Because I speak the truth."

The father abbot nodded. "Aydrian claims that you are very powerful with this magic. More powerful than many of my brethren, even."

"Most," Aydrian whispered under his breath.

"How would I know?" Aoleyn asked, glancing at Aydrian as she did.

"Aydrian says that you can access the power of the stones very quickly."

Aoleyn was growing quite tired of this leading conversation, so she lifted her right arm and grimaced as her bones cracked and reshaped, then she dropped her paw onto the edge of Father Abbot Braumin's desk. She let her claws out a bit, just to tap them on the wood.

The monks around her gasped and fell back, and even the father abbot betrayed his surprise before quickly getting himself back under control.

"Father Abbot!" Master Viscenti protested, but Braumin held up a hand to quiet the man.

"I can do the other arm as well," Aoleyn told him. "And my legs. Perhaps more."

"Please do not. And please end that," he said, motioning to her leopard paw. "It brings many painful memories to us, for there was once one among us who could so transform himself so completely."

Never blinking, never unlocking her gaze from that of Father Abbot Braumin, Aoleyn released the magic.

The father abbot breathed a sigh of relief. "What about these?" he asked, holding up the jewelry. "How fast and fully can you summon the magic within them?"

"The magic is not within them, it is within me," Aoleyn corrected, and she wasn't even sure why she had said that or how she had come to truly understand that. But she didn't doubt the observation. "I hear the song of Usgar in the stones, and that music allows me to find my way to power."

"And how quickly?"

She shook her head, not understanding.

"Not two heartbeats passed when she summoned the ice to wreck the pursuing ship," Aydrian intervened. "She is very fast with the magic, faster than anyone I have ever seen. Faster than I, when I use my armor or the lightning in Tempest."

Braumin nodded and seemed satisfied.

"This is very difficult for me," he explained. "Particularly given that it is you, that it is Aydrian Boudabras . . ."

"Aydrian Boudabras is dead," Aydrian said. "I killed him."

"Yes, so you say, and so I wish to believe. But you understand my hesitation, of course."

"Of course. I would probably be less generous to you if our situations were reversed."

"Brother Thaddius found these in the mountains south of the Wilderlands," Braumin explained, motioning to the coffers. "They are every old. And these parchments on my desk are very much older still. Brother Thaddius found these in the deep libraries of Saint-Mere-Abelle. They speak of the xoconai—and even name them as xoconai."

Aoleyn and Aydrian turned to each other in surprise, then both leaned forward, looking at the ancient parchments.

"The brothers of old called them the sidhe—isn't it interesting that such a misnomer has survived the centuries?"

"Then you know we are telling the truth," Aoleyn blurted.

"Do I? Or do I know that these are old tales that perhaps my friend Aydrian here is using—"

"You are a fool," Aoleyn interrupted, and the monks bristled. "Why would I come here? Why would I care? I am not of your people." She smiled and went on, but in her own language. "I am Usgar. I am the slayer of the demon fossa, who roamed under the blood moon, seeking its food. I am she who killed Tay Aillig, and I would do it again."

She kept going, simply telling her tale in deeper and deeper detail, and in the language of Loch Beag, so they could not understand—for the different and wholly unknown language was the whole point, after all.

Abbot Braumin looked to Aydrian helplessly, holding up his hands in confusion.

"The tongue of the high lake and the mountain," Aydrian explained.

"What is she saying?"

"She is telling her story, of who she is and what she has done."

"But she speaks ours with such fluency? How is this possible?"

"The same way I learned their tongue," Aydrian admitted. "With the wedstone—the soul stone. Aoleyn shared the mind and so learned the language."

"Possession," Master Viscenti said with a snarl, from the side of the room.

"For need and for good," Aydrian replied. "We have already been down this road, Father Abbot. There was no time for—"

"Yes, yes," Braumin agreed. To Aoleyn, he added, "Please stop."

The woman went silent, she and Father Abbot Braumin staring at each other long and hard.

"Well played," he said.

"I am Usgar," Aoleyn stated in their language, perfectly articulated. "I am from the other side of the world. I know not your church or your ways, or your claims over the magic—and I reject those. The jewelry is mine. I made it. I was right to make it. I would have died without it. We, all of the Ayamharas, would have died had I not made the jewelry."

"It's true," said Aydrian.

"And so you would not know of the danger that comes your way," Aoleyn went on, growing angrier with every word.

"I believe you."

"And the xoconai would roll over your cities and your people and leave you all enslaved or dead."

"I believe you."

"But will you even hear? No!" Aoleyn continued, her anger deafening her to the man's words. "We could have run, south over the mountains or north into the other mountains, and so we would be free, and so you would all be doomed . . ."

She stopped suddenly, staring at Braumin as his words at last registered.

"I believe you," he said again, and to Aoleyn's great surprise—to the great surprise of everyone in the room, she quickly realized—Father Abbot Braumin handed her jewelry, all of it, back to her.

"Father Abbot!" Master Viscenti gasped, and he was obviously speaking for all the other monks in the room.

"Please understand my hesitance, my fear," Braumin said. "That anyone, this man in particular, would come to us with such a tale as you have weaved . . . it is all so unusual."

Aoleyn slipped her ring on, feeling the small sting as the inner band of wedstone wire pierced her finger and filled her with the song of Usgar. Then she began working with the turquoise ear cuff.

"The belly ring, the earring, the anklet—all of it! You use the soul stone, that you call wedstone, to pierce your flesh. Why? Does this bring you closer to the magic?"

"To the song of Usgar, yes."

"Where did you learn such a thing? How did you think to turn the sou . . . the wedstone, into wire?"

Aoleyn shrugged. "I was . . . I was in the cave beneath the God Crystal. I do not . . . No one told me or taught me. I only thought that it might help. I wanted to be closer."

"And it worked?"

Aoleyn nodded.

"None of the brothers have tried this. None but I have handled your jewelry. Might I now try your ring?"

Aoleyn looked doubtfully down at the red ruby. "It makes fire," she said.

"Oh, I know, and I promise that I'll not blow up the room," the father abbot replied with a laugh.

Aoleyn slipped the ring off and handed it to him, and he placed it on his little finger, wincing as the wire poked into his flesh. He closed his eyes for a moment, his face scrunching in concentration, but then he opened them and shook his head at the onlooking brothers.

"I feel the power," he explained to the other monks. "But

no more than if I held it in my hand. I would still have to coax the magic to its full glory." He looked to Aoleyn and held the ring back out to her. "And you could use this quickly if you wanted?"

"Do you really wish to see?"

"Oh no, no!" Father Abbot Braumin said, with another laugh.

"There wouldn't be much left of your room, or of any of us she didn't protect with the other stone set in that ring," Aydrian agreed, and he, too, chuckled.

But Aoleyn wasn't smiling. The conversation had thrown her thoughts back to a cave on the side of Fireach Speuer, where she had incinerated some Usgar Tay Aillig had set about to guard her. She could almost smell again their crisped flesh, a most awful stench.

"Aoleyn?" Aydrian asked, with obvious concern, and she knew that she was wearing her discomfort on her face.

She responded by touching Aydrian's arm and holding her other hand out across the desk, and as soon as Father Abbot Braumin touched her, all three of them began to glow brightly within a shroud of white light. Aoleyn dismissed the fire-blocking serpentine shield immediately and held her hands up to show Braumin that he need not fear any fireball, as would usually accompany such a spell.

"That quickly?" Braumin asked, as much to himself as to the others, it seemed.

"I told you," said Aydrian. "The magic is not just Abellican magic."

Father Abbot Braumin sucked in his breath at that, for Aydrian had just denied perhaps the most important tenet of the Abellican Church: that the magical Ring Stones were the gift of God to the Abellicans, sent from the heavens for those who followed the word of St. Abelle. There were other types of magic in the world, of course. The earth magic of the Samhaists was well documented, and that more ancient religion seemed to be making a bit of a comeback in recent years, since the plague and the civil war had so ravaged Honce-the-Bear. Powries could resurrect through their buried hearts, and they carried a dark magic in their bright berets that toughened them and healed them more quickly.

The demons had their own magic, dark and dastardly, as did the races of alfar, both in the natural wonders of the Touel'alfar and in their hidden forest, and there was the necromancy of the Doc'alfar hiding in the shadows and peat bogs to the south.

But none of those involved Ring Stones—not directly, at least—other than the possessions of the Touel'alfar, given to them by St. Abelle himself, so said the ancient texts.

Now here was this woman, this witch, from a land thousands of miles to the west, thousands of miles away from the sea and thus from the isle of Pimaninicuit, where the monks went to gather the sacred stones every seventh generation. How could she have such gems? How could these caverns exist?

"The world is upside down," he said to Aydrian, shaking his head. "And I am overwhelmed."

"Let us hope that all of Honce is not soon overwhelmed," Aydrian reminded.

Father Abbot Braumin looked at Aoleyn directly. "I believe you. And I apologize for taking your jewels. Truly, they are treasures."

"*My* treasures," she said.

"Yes."

"Father Abbot!" Master Viscenti said.

"Are you going to keep saying that?" Braumin asked him. "Do you not see what is going on around us?"

"I hear a story, and that is all it is, until we can confirm."

Father Abbot Braumin held his hand out to Aoleyn.

"Yes, yes," an annoyed Viscenti replied. "She is a trickster with the gemstones. But have we not seen this before? Aydrian is no brother of Abelle, surely, yet he can use the stones, as could both of his parents before him."

"Jilseponie was a bishop of our church," Braumin reminded.

"She was skilled with the stones long before that," Viscenti replied.

"But how might we explain?" He motioned to Aoleyn.

"If her story is true, if she is from some distant place where crystals grow from the walls of a cave and give her these treasures, then I cannot explain it," Viscenti admitted. "But *if* is a large word, Father Abbot, and a larger possibility."

"And still, I believe them," Braumin replied.

Master Viscenti cast a glance at Aydrian, then at Aoleyn. To his credit, there was no animosity evident in his expression. He folded his hands before him and lowered his gaze, submitting to the judgment of the father abbot.

"Then the question remains of where we go from here," said Braumin. "We have to go out, and swiftly, to see if this invasion you fear is coming to pass."

"Spiritually?" Aoleyn asked. "Take great care."

"I know of your journey. Brother Thaddius told me." He slipped open the top left-hand drawer of his desk, poked about for a moment, then produced a pale green stone. "Are you familiar with this?" he asked Aoleyn, and he handed it to her.

The witch shook her head.

"It is chrysoberyl," Braumin explained. "A stone to defend the mind and soul."

Aoleyn closed her fingers about it and heard the magic within, though she couldn't quite decipher it.

"It is a shield against possession," said Braumin.

Aoleyn focused on the stone again and heard the song once more, now in the context of the father abbot's revelation. She opened her eyes, understanding, and nodded.

"You can use it, I suppose?" Braumin asked. "The magic is available to you?"

"Yes," Aoleyn answered, and no one was surprised.

* * *

"You wish you were with them," Elysant said to Aydrian. The two of them were sitting in the gallery of the large room, along with dozens of St.-Mere-Abelle's monks. At the front of the chamber, Aoleyn, the father abbot, a few of the masters, and Brother Thaddius worked with the gemstones, half of them spirit-walking out of the great monastery, the other half working with chrysoberyl to protect those going forth. Normally, a monk could utilize both the stones himself, but given the strange compulsion and power involved here, Father Abbot Braumin was taking no chances.

It was no small thing to either Aydrian or Elysant that Brother Thaddius had been selected to protect Aoleyn. The father abbot had gone out of his way to make sure that the woman felt comfortable in this most intimate of magical joinings.

"Don't you?" Aydrian replied.

"I have little affinity with the Ring Stones," Elysant admitted. "But the whispers claim that you are powerful in magic."

The king turned ranger nodded. "I am honored to be allowed in here to witness this. You were young then."

"I remember," Elysant assured him. "I was young, and very new to the order out at Saint Gwendolyn-by-the-Sea, when the De'Unnerans came. I remember."

"Yet you travel with me and sit beside me and show me such trust."

Elysant rose out of her seat and moved around to put her face very close to Aydrian's, staring him in the eye. "You were possessed and overwhelmed by the demon dactyl. We all know this. Father Abbot Braumin, friend and companion of Saint Avelyn, knows this, and if he did not believe it, you would not be here. Perhaps it is time for Aydrian to realize that many others forgive him. And perhaps it is time for Aydrian to forgive himself."

"Perhaps," he agreed, and he managed a smile. But Elysant saw his eyes and the clouds gathered there and she knew the truth of the tortured man.

She moved back around and took her seat. A group came up to her to ask about the robe she wore and the staff of stone she now carried, begging her to tell them of the experience in the crypt of St. Belfour.

There was no motion for silence in the chamber, and nothing to really watch up front—just four sitting side by side in chairs and four others hovering behind them, their hands on the shoulders of the spirit-walkers—so Elysant obliged them, weaving a tale with great inflection and drama, drawing more than a few gasps.

She was out of her seat, waving her arms as she prepared to act out the end of St. Belfour's wraith, but then she stopped short, staring across the room.

"The father abbot," she said, and all eyes swung about. Aydrian leaped out of his seat for a better view.

Up front, Braumin Herde looked to his fellow spirit-walkers. One after another, they were opening their eyes, coming back to their corporeal forms.

"Ursal has fallen," Father Abbot Braumin announced to a responding chorus of gasps and cries of "No!"

He waited, letting the protests and cries of disbelief diminish, and the prayer to King Midalis finish, before raising his arms for silence.

He added grimly, "And Palmaris is burning."

16

HE HAD TO TRY

The macana hit Midalis's shield with such weight that the king's knees almost buckled beneath him. He couldn't believe the aggression of the attackers—and that, he knew, was their advantage. They fought without fear, often leaving dangerous defensive openings, leaping high to bring their strange and strangely strong weapons down, with all of their weight behind them.

Midalis came out of the block in a stumble and threw his shield up high again, while cutting his sword out beneath the lower edge.

He had guessed right, his fine sword slamming the breastplate of the sidhe attacker. It found enough of a crease between the cylindrical wooden flaps to gouge hard into the attacker's ribs, and the warrior fell back, unable to complete her own swing, but far from finished.

That armor! It bounced when the xoconai ran, seemingly light and wholly unencumbering. It was wood-like, mostly at least, that strange stalk known as darkfern, like Aydrian's bow. A thin cylinder of wood and it could turn a clean strike from a steel sword!

The warrior seemed more angry than wounded, and she came back in with renewed ferocity, starting low and leaping high once more, trying to overwhelm her opponent.

A veteran of many battles, a middle-aged man who had never let his training lapse, King Midalis saw it coming. Instead of shying, he went at his attacker, bending low, throwing his shield above him to take the blow and turning his own sword upward. For he had seen a weakness: when the sidhe leaned forward, the light and malleable breastplate moved out from her belly.

Down she came, landing a tremendous blow once more upon his shield, stronger than the first. Down she came again, impaling herself as Midalis's perfectly angled sword slid under the lip of her breastplate, up through her diaphragm, and into her lungs.

The king rose fast and powerfully, catching her in a clench, his shield moving out to push her weapon arm back.

Their faces were no more than a finger's length apart. He looked into her bright face, into her blue-gray eyes, and saw the pain and shock, the realization of death.

He felt her fall limp in his arms and let her fall away. He wanted to let her down to the ground easily, but he had no time as another sidhe warrior quickly replaced her in the madness of battle in this Palmaris neighborhood.

In the madness sweeping all across the great city.

Palmaris was not like Ursal. It was walled, mostly, but with many parts in disrepair and many more sections of wall missing altogether, having never been replaced after the civil war a decade before. Ursal was tight and tall, with thick stone structures. Even the smaller tenements rose three stories, nearly the height of the massive wall enclosing the city proper. Palmaris was more like a hundred smaller villages all stitched together, with single-story houses of wood and thatch and stone, and even tents. It had a riverfront that extended for miles up and down the western bank of the Masur Delaval, supported by several massive sections of docks, wharves, and storehouses.

While Ursal was the seat of political and military power in Honce-the-Bear, the throne city, Palmaris served as the kingdom's largest inland port, handling the bulk of the trade from Vanguard and even from the Mantis Arm far in the east, so that the ships did not have to sail and row upriver to Ursal. The city dominated the northwestern edge of the Masur Delaval and was the largest city of Honce-the-Bear west of the river, by far, so caravans of goods came down from the Timberlands in a nearly constant stream throughout the spring and summer and into late autumn.

King Midalis was acutely aware of the importance of holding Palmaris. He had lost Ursal only a week before. To lose Palmaris, too, so soon . . . Could Honce itself survive?

Thinking of the poor souls left behind in Ursal, Midalis met the charge with renewed fury. He took a tremendous blow on his breastplate but walked through it and put his sword into the neck of the sidhe man, sending him back and to the ground, gurgling blood.

Midalis turned quickly, thinking another attacker upon him, but then realized that Julian of the Evergreen had come to his side.

"Smoke rises across the river," Julian told him. "Amvoy is under siege!"

The king's shoulders sagged with the news. The river was wide here, very wide. To even see smoke from Amvoy meant terrific fires burning.

Who was this enemy? How great their numbers?

Aydrian and his friends had not exaggerated the threat.

Midalis put it out of mind, called for his Allheart Knights to rally around him, and led them in a charge through the streets, moving through sidhe stragglers until they joined with an Allheart cavalry group.

One rider dropped immediately to offer his horse to Midalis. The king took his seat and bade a second knight to put Julian of the Evergreen up beside him.

"What is our move?" Midalis asked Julian, as the now greater force made its way along the main boulevard.

The young knight seemed uncertain.

Midalis nodded sympathetically. Most of the battles in Palmaris's history had come from within Honce-the-Bear, from across the great river, and thus the city's strongest defenses were built mostly on the docks and the warships themselves. In the case of an invasion from the west, something that had always seemed highly unlikely, since the west, the Wilderlands, was lightly populated, flight to the ships and across the river to Amvoy would be regarded as the last line of defense. Therefore, the sections of the city holding the noble houses and the monastery, St. Precious, had direct avenues to the docks, with ships always awaiting the important people and with specific assignments for passengers.

Midalis had been warned several times already, during the chaos of the day, that it might indeed come to that. But now Amvoy was obviously under siege.

Were they to flee to the ships and sail away, as he had sent his wife and children? Such a retreat meant surrendering this critical position and surrendering tens of thousands of innocents to the invaders.

"Saint Precious," the king decided, directing his forces.

Along the wide streets they went, finding less and less resistance as they neared the imposing abbey. The streets here had seen battle that morning, though, obviously so, with many sidhe bodies strewn about, burned wholly or in small areas from lightning.

The monks were proving formidable indeed.

The Allhearts gained the abbey's steps without much resistance, and the wide doors were opened, with even the horses being hustled inside.

King Midalis was led to the offices of the abbot, near the center of the large structure. There he found Abbot Ohwan of St. Honce and young Abbot Havre of St. Precious, along with Duke Anders Bire, who ruled the city, and a collection of masters and military commanders.

Their expressions confirmed to Midalis that the situation was as desperate as he had believed.

"We must flee, and must do so quickly," Duke Anders said, before a formal introduction of King Midalis could be initiated. "The fiends are swimming out of the river astride their terrible lizards and the docks are sorely pressed."

"If we do not go now, we are unlikely to escape," Abbot Ohwan added.

Midalis let the warning hang in the air, a heavy silence during which no one seemed to breathe or even blink.

Then he answered simply.

"No."

"We'll turn north to the Timberlands," Talmadge said, as he and his three companions ran for their lives along a Palmaris street. They had come into the city less than a day ahead of the xoconai army and yet they had had no idea that their enemies were so close on their heels. They had seen the invaders a couple of days previous, but far, far to the south—just a collection of distant campfires in the night.

Ever were the xoconai full of surprises.

"How are we even to get out of this place?" Catriona asked.

Bahdlahn turned to her, agreeing, just as she passed a side alley. Down at the far end Bahdlahn saw a pair of soldiers suddenly overrun by a trio of lizard-riding enemies. Enemies were all about, flanking them, before them, in every quarter of the sprawling city, it seemed.

"Bahdlahn!" Khotai yelled, alerting the man to a javelin flying down at him from a nearby rooftop.

He dove to the cobblestones, the javelin clipping the ground right beside him and painfully nicking him as it bounced away. Bahdlahn rolled about, scrambling to regain his footing, but then he paused for just a moment, seeing Khotai gliding up high into the air beside him, bow in hand, a line of arrows flying for the rooftop and the spear thrower.

On the four ran, but now the walls seemed to be closing in around them. Down a street and around a corner—then they skidded to a stop as one and reversed direction as a wall of running xoconai loomed before them, spears and macana flashing. Glancing back, Bahdlahn saw a group of people—a man, three women, and a handful of children—get plowed to the ground by the enemy rush, spears stabbing, bats swinging.

One very young boy broke free for a moment, fleeing in terror. He was looking out the side street, looking in Bahdlahn's direction as if begging the man to help him. But they caught him. A macana descended on the back of the boy's head, splitting his skull, throwing him down to the cobblestones.

Bahdlahn stumbled, his mind screaming in protest. Children! The bright-faced demons had just murdered children! Why?

He could not comprehend it, any of it. The image lingered and chased him down the next street, stealing his strength, as if he were running in mud.

His friends moved ahead of him. Another family was out in the street, children crying, desperate parents trying to herd them and get them out of the way.

Talmadge and Catriona got to them first, ushering them around the side of a building. By the time Bahdlahn arrived, Talmadge was trying to tear a plank off the base of the structure.

Bahdlahn shouldered in and grasped the board with all of his great strength. He planted his feet against the wall and pulled with everything he could manage, finally opening a way into the space beneath the structure. In went the children, then the parents, with Talmadge and Catriona fast to follow. Bahdlahn looked all about and finally spotted Khotai up above, on a high balcony.

"Come on," Catriona implored Bahdlahn.

In reply, he reset the board—it had to be done from the outside to properly cover the hidey-hole. He glanced around, ignoring the protests from Talmadge and Catriona, and ran off for a pair of fallen men.

Heartbeats later, the xoconai force charged past, sweeping the street of resistance, cutting down any who stood before them.

King Midalis, Duke Anders beside him, led the push out from St. Precious with a thunderous charge of mounted Allheart Knights. Behind them came the Palmaris garrison, supported by the Abellican monks, sweeping down the main streets of Palmaris and meeting, head-on, the same force that had tramped past Bahdlahn and the others.

In the heaviest fighting of the day, the largest pitched battle of the war against these bright-faced invaders thus far, including any of the fights in Ursal, the Allheart Knights and the Abellican monks soon sent the xoconai running.

"Keep pressing," Midalis called. "Drive them into the river! Allhearts, to me!" He motioned to Duke Anders, who nodded and took his garrison running down a side street into the next large avenue.

The knights rallied around Midalis with a grand "Huzzah!," and the force charged off once more, lighter of monks now, as so many worked to save the wounded left in the street behind. If they could engage and hold the enemies long enough, Duke Anders would sweep in from the side with his thousands and break the enemy's main force.

But the walls behind Midalis and his Allhearts closed fast as a swarm of lizard riders appeared up above them, atop the roofs. Those enemies moved back the other way, past Midalis, and began raining spears on the monks left behind, cutting them down in short order.

When Midalis turned his force around to support, the enemy force that had fled was fast regrouping ahead of them.

"Ohwan! Abbot Havre!" King Midalis cried. "Strike them down with fire and lightning!"

A few bolts did reach up at the enemy warriors. One building exploded in a fireball, the xoconai up above screaming, lizards shrieking horribly.

But many were up there, and they found their soft targets for their javelins: the monks.

Then came the main xoconai force, reversing their retreat into a second charge.

"Where are you, Anders?" King Midalis quietly asked, turning about to face the returning enemy. When Julian came up beside him, he told the knight, "Find Anders. We need him. Go!"

Off galloped the knight, down the side street. He had barely entered it, though, when a javelin flew past him. Up went his shield, just in time to deflect another javelin. As he reached the other end of the street, opening onto the large parallel boulevard, Julian pulled up short and whirled about.

"The docks!" he yelled back to the Allhearts and the monks supporting them. "Duke Anders has run for the docks!"

"Retreat!" Abbot Ohwan yelled in reply. "To the ships! To the ships!"

King Midalis spun his horse about to see the abbot and the brothers all starting for the side street.

"My king?" a knight beside Midalis asked.

Midalis spun his mount again to face the approaching army. Dozens of javelins flew out at him and his knights, and the enemies roared as one and charged.

He faced the attackers—and the starkest choice. They could not hope to win here without the support of Duke

Anders and his garrison. Even with them, the battle before them appeared daunting.

Behind him, Abbot Ohwan and the monks were fleeing. About him, the Allhearts bristled, closing ranks, dodging and blocking the missiles.

"Run, King Midalis!" Abbot Ohwan yelled from the side, the man entering the connecting street, other brothers launching lightning at the edges of the roofs to chase away the spear throwers. "For the good of Honce! Run and sail away!"

Perhaps he was right. Perhaps the best choice would be a fast retreat from this place and from Palmaris.

King Midalis thought of his wife, his children, his responsibility to the whole of Honce-the-Bear.

King Midalis thought of the folk here, the children he would leave behind, as he had left tens of thousands behind in Ursal.

He lifted his sword and looked to the Allheart Knights to either side, all grim-faced, accepting, ready.

As one, they charged—not down the side street but straight down the wide avenue, their powerful steeds crashing into the bright-faced invaders, shattering their defensive formations. On they charged, cutting lines deep into the ranks and chopping down enemies in a wild explosion of fury.

"To me! To me!" King Midalis roared above it all. He saw Abbot Ohwan pause and take note. The man surely had heard him.

Ohwan turned and fled, taking all the monks that were beside him.

Talmadge, Khotai, and Catriona crawled out from under the building, Catriona leading, scrambling desperately. She stood up and hopped all about, searching, searching, her gaze at last falling on a pile of bodies along the wall to the side of the building.

She ran, stumbling, expecting to see Bahdlahn among them.

And her guess was right, she saw, but her fears were not, for as she neared, one of those bodies rolled aside, shoved by Bahdlahn, who had buried himself beneath the dead to escape the spears of the rampaging xoconai. He pulled himself up, covered in blood that was not his own.

Catriona wrapped him in a hug.

"Where did they go?" Talmadge asked.

"There is fighting all over the city," Khotai remarked, as Bahdlahn pointed to the southwest.

"Where we should go is the better question," said Bahdlahn.

"Anywhere the xoconai didn't," Talmadge answered. He motioned for the others to follow and started away at a swift pace. They moved helter-skelter along the streets, turning down alleys, sprinting along wider ways. Their only guidance was the sounds of fighting, which they avoided.

They came into one quiet section—very quiet, and with no living people or xoconai to be seen. The structures were lower in this neighborhood, and so Khotai, with a single leap, drifted atop one house, taking in a wider view.

"What do you see?" Catriona called up to her, Bahdlahn and Talmadge rushing to nearby intersections to better watch for enemies.

"Boats," she answered. "Sails and masts." She crouched low and moved all about, looking every which way, gathering as much information about the layout of the area as possible before floating back down to the street to rejoin her three companions.

A crackle of thunder, a tremendous report, jolted them all as Khotai touched down.

"Boats," Khotai said again. "They are fighting at the docks, and great ships are sailing out."

"Fleeing," Talmadge remarked, more to himself than to the others, as they all tried to sort out their next moves.

"The monks are there," Khotai added, after a second rumble of magical thunder shook the street.

"Then they're all fleeing," Talmadge reasoned. "The city is lost." He scrambled about, starting one way, then turning back. "How?" he asked Khotai.

She motioned for him and the others to follow, then started away, weaving still, but now heading decidedly east. They paused at one wide avenue, holding back at the corner of a building and peering around to the right to see a host of fleeing enemies with armored horsemen running them down and charging along.

Talmadge, Khotai, and Catriona started across the avenue, but Bahdlahn held back, staring down the side street at the wounded and dead xoconai.

"Bahdlahn! Come along!" Talmadge called to him.

"How can we leave?" he replied, though he was moving again to join the others. "How can we just run away when so many will not escape? What of the family hiding under the house?"

"What can we do?" Catriona argued. "The priests are fleeing. The warriors are fleeing."

"Not those warriors," Bahdlahn pointed out.

"Not yet, perhaps," said Talmadge. "Or they are sacrificing themselves so that others might escape." He shook his head and pushed Khotai ahead of him, moving on toward the docks with all speed.

Around the next line of buildings, the foursome crested a hill, the river wide before them in the distance. Down below, at the end of the lane, they saw the tall masts of many ships and the full sails of others that had already slipped out into the open water. Flames roared high into the air to the left and the sounds of fighting echoed up the hill toward them.

Down they ran, coming upon a frenetic scene of running people, scrambling and desperate, and lizard-riding enemies rushing all about, trying to get to those ships that hadn't yet

departed. One large ship slipped out of port, a hail of javelins lifting toward it. On the long wharf, the invaders raced
about, running and riding, cutting down those who hadn't
managed to get aboard.

Growling, Bahdlahn started for that wharf, but then he
skidded to a stop, even fell over backwards in surprise,
when a bolt of lightning flew from over the taffrail of a ship,
shooting down the wharf, scorching flesh and wood.

"This way!" Talmadge yelled, and Bahdlahn regained his
footing and chased the others down to the right, all the way
to the right, to the last wharf before a higher dock section
supporting a large building.

A ship there was trying to get out, but fighting covered the
end of the wharf and the javelins that flew at the side of the
ship had ropes attached. The xoconai were trying to hold the
vessel in port.

Onto the long wharf ran the friends, Talmadge leading, in
between Bahdlahn and Catriona, with Khotai close behind,
springing high and letting arrows fly with every leap.

They cut through a trio of enemies who were too intent
on the action before them to look behind. Bahdlahn threw
a fourth xoconai from the dock into the dark water, then
tipped a fifth in behind, along with the lizard the female
warrior was riding.

The powerful young man scooped up a fallen macana and
ran ahead of his friends, swatting aside any who stood before him. He fought wildly, recklessly, taking hits in order to
deliver hits, and with his thick muscles, every hit Bahdlahn
scored tossed an enemy away.

They passed the midpoint of the wharf. Bahdlahn missed
a swing, and the error left him helpless against a xoconai
who leaped up high, macana raised for a killing strike.

Bahdlahn growled, thinking his life at an end, but the enemy seemed to hold up in the air just a bit too long . . . It
took Bahdlahn a moment to see the arrow stuck deep into
that one's bright face. Down he dropped, already dead when

he fell over Bahdlahn, who heaved him high and far over the side.

They came up on the back of the ship, upon the enemies trying to hold it, and one by one those lines dropped, either from the four friends dispatching the xoconai holding it or because that enemy had turned to meet the charge.

The ship slid out. Those few enemies still trying to halt it were being tugged along; a couple were even pulled into the water.

Bahdlahn sprinted to the end of the wharf, the ship sliding past him. He grabbed a woman holding a child and hoisted both up the side of the vessel, where waiting hands grabbed them and pulled them aboard.

Others ran by, stepping into Bahdlahn's cupped hands, and with a great heave, the powerful man sent them flying up to the rail and safety.

"Go! Go now!" said Talmadge, running past Bahdlahn and leaping high and far. He crashed hard against the side but caught some netting there and would not let go.

Then came Catriona, and Bahdlahn caught her in her run and heaved her up to the back of the ship as it now slid fully past the dock. She caught the taffrail, many hands grabbing and securing her.

"Bahdlahn!" she cried.

He jumped back to get a running start. He glanced back for Khotai, who came down the wharf with great springs, turning back with each hop and letting fly an arrow.

She had a javelin sticking from her side, though it seemed to be hanging in the folds of her dress rather than sticking into her flesh.

"Bahdlahn!" Catriona yelled again.

He glanced her way. The ship slid further from the dock, gaining speed.

"Leap with Khotai! The magic!" yelled Catriona.

Bahdlahn nodded, but only to silence her.

Khotai bounced down beside him, offering him her arm.

Instead, he caught her outside her grasp and then turned her past him and ran to the wharf's edge, lifting her, throwing her, shoving her far and hard so that she could not grab him.

She spun weirdly in that turn, floating with the magic of the belt and the force of the strong man's throw, out, out from the dock, out from Bahdlahn, gliding over the high back of the departing ship, now twenty yards from the edge of the wharf.

Bahdlahn nodded grimly to Catriona.

He couldn't leave. He knew that he could likely do nothing here to make any real difference, but when he looked around at the helpless innocents being cut down by the bright-faced invaders, none of that mattered.

He had to try.

17

WHEN THE SIDHE CAME

"Saint-Mere-Abelle is not like Ursal," Father Abbot Braumin said to a large gathering in the monastery's main courtyard. "There is no fortress—there is no place—anywhere in the world quite like it. Our power is in our faith, and that faith gives to us the sacred Ring Stones."

That brought a lot of nods about the gathering, but also more than a few stares turned Aoleyn's way. She was keenly aware of them, and of the fact that the father abbot's decision to give her back her jewelry had not been well received by many of the other monks.

Aydrian put his hand on her shoulder, and she turned to regard him, so impressive in his splendid silver armor and with that beautiful sword hanging on one hip. He offered her a smile and a wink.

He understood her discomfort, she knew, and he was likely feeling a thousand times the stares and intensity of those now coming at her.

She turned back to the father abbot.

"... every day," he was saying. "Construction on Saint-

Mere-Abelle happens every day. In the rain, in the snow, as it has been for almost nine hundred years, since the days of Saint Abelle himself. Always improving, always strengthening. This is our way. Look around you, my brethren." He turned a circle with his arm out wide, inviting the view of the structures and high wall.

"Is there a place in that wall that is not reinforced?" he asked. "Is there a finger's breadth the length of the barrier that has not been hardened with magical citrine?

"No, we are not Ursal, for all her might. Nor will we be caught unawares. Oh, King Midalis knew that an attack was coming, thanks to the warning brought to him by our own Brother Thaddius and Sister Elysant and these two guests." He motioned down from the platform to Aydrian and Aoleyn, and again the woman felt the stares of many upon her.

"But they in Ursal were still overwhelmed and surprised by the ferocity and suddenness and sheer size and skill of the enemy forces. Who could blame them? And I'll not make light of the power of these invaders, these sidhe, who call themselves the xoconai. But take heart, my brethren, and hold faith, for unlike the king and his Allheart Knights in Ursal, the priests here at Saint-Mere-Abelle now know exactly what to expect. In spirit-walking, we have had seen the devastation of the throne city and the unfolding tragedy of Palmaris. We have watched the enemy's approach.

"It is they, the sidhe, who will find surprise on the fields before the unbreakable wall of Saint-Mere-Abelle!"

Aoleyn started in surprise at the sudden cheering that erupted all about her. Strangely, she thought of Tay Aillig, the Usgar-laoch, the war leader of her tribe. He had given such speeches as this, though with more emotion, even rage, infecting every word.

Tay Aillig was better at this than Father Abbot Braumin, she decided. For all the Usgar-laoch's many faults, he could drive the Usgar warriors into a bloodlust that left them no room for fear or doubt.

The morning gathering began to disband then, and Aoleyn was pleasantly surprised when Sister Elysant joined her and Aydrian.

"They say the leading scout forces of the sidhe are less than ten miles to the west," she said, as the three started off across the courtyard. "The brothers have already been sent out into their holes. Are you ready for a fight, King Aydrian?"

"Aydrian. Just Aydrian," he corrected.

"Yes, of course."

"I've witnessed them in combat," Aydrian said. "Outside of a village called Fasach Crann. Do not underestimate them. These are not mere goblins."

"So I have been told."

"He ran from them," Aoleyn said, drawing a surprised look from Aydrian and Elysant. "He ran because he knew that, if he stayed, he and all the others would have been slaughtered."

"Aoleyn has fought them with her magic. Twice," said Aydrian.

"That is what they will know here at Saint-Mere-Abelle," Elysant agreed. "I am not proficient with the Ring Stones, so my role will be minimal—and better for all if I never have to raise this new stave in battle against the sidhe."

"Xoconai," Aoleyn corrected, almost reflexively. She wondered why it mattered but knew deep inside that it did. *Sidhe* was a word associated with the goblins, she figured. And these beautiful, bright-faced, manlike creatures were certainly nothing at all like goblins—indeed, they were perhaps more removed from goblins than the humans were.

That thought made her wince.

"Yes, xoconai," Elysant agreed. "Saint-Mere-Abelle is ready for them. Come, let me show you."

She led the way to a ladder, then up to a parapet not far from the monastery's main gates.

"You see?" she asked, motioning out over the wall to the long, sloping field before the great structure.

"I see grass," Aoleyn dryly replied.

"Yes, but what might it hide?" Elysant teased.

Aydrian chuckled. "Monks," he said.

Aoleyn moved to the wall and leaned out a bit, staring hard.

"The monks know well their tricks," Aydrian said to her.

"They are out there, ready to fight?"

"Oh yes," said Elysant.

"Why are you in here, then?" Aoleyn asked. "Thaddius says you are among the finest of the Abellican fighters."

"Because I fight with a staff," she replied. "Out there?"

"Magic," Aoleyn answered for her, catching on. Elysant started to elaborate, but Aoleyn hardly listened. She certainly didn't need any sermons on the potential power of the magical gemstones.

She wished that Father Abbot Braumin had sent her out there among his magic-wielding warriors. She thought to go find him and ask for permission to join.

But from far to her left, down the wall to the western side of the massive monastery, there came a call, echoing up across the courtyard.

Monks began rushing all about, out of the buildings and across the courtyards to their assigned posts. Some manned great war engines mounted on the towers. Others began setting out bedding and water and bandages on the open ground.

Elysant again led the way for her two companions, running west along the wall, hoping to catch the first moments of the encounter.

Aoleyn knew from the distant shouting that they wouldn't get there in time. She called to the gemstones of her belly ring, using the malachite to lighten her, then enacting the power of the moonstone to lift away. She flew past Elysant and Aydrian, climbing higher to see over that still distant western wall.

She heard an explosion, then saw a small ball of flames roll up into the air. Up higher she went, flying faster. She saw the dark forms out on the field, the back ranks of the enemy group.

She noted monks leaping up from holes cut in the grass, pushing aside the sod covering and standing tall, limned in glowing white light. Aoleyn knew that light well, and so she knew what was coming next.

Fireballs engulfed the areas around those monks, flames biting the xoconai and their lizard mounts. The explosions had barely ended, the flames rolling up and dispersing, before the monks lifted away in flight, speeding back toward their waiting brothers on the wall.

Aoleyn called to the song of the moonstone more powerfully, speeding ahead. More fireballs went off, more xoconai died, and those in the back ranks turned and fled.

The monks on the wall cheered.

Aoleyn set down on the parapet not far away, running to join the group greeting the returning heroes. She spotted Thaddius, who had set off one of the early fireballs, and ran to him. Before she arrived, though, she heard different yells from farther along the wall, calls for help for a monk out on the field.

She saw monks desperately trying to summon their gemstone power once again, and when she went to the wall, she understood. One of the brothers was left on the field, pitifully crawling toward the wall, through blackened grass and burned enemies, a javelin sticking from the back of his leg.

Other enemies closed for the kill.

Hardly thinking of her actions, Aoleyn leaped over the wall, flying, diving for the monk. Before she even landed, she called upon the magic in her anklet and summoned a patch of ice over the three charging xoconai riders. One tried to throw her javelin, but her lizard slid sidelong on the ice and the missile flew harmlessly aside. Another tumbled altogether, the lizard scrabbling and spinning.

Aoleyn flew past the monk, right for the enemies. The third lifted a javelin, and Aoleyn changed the song of her moonstone abruptly, adding the song of her ruby ring, using the malachite alone to keep her aloft while she sent forth a great burst of hot wind, as she had done to the witches of the Coven on that fateful day, which seemed like years before.

The javelin flew out and flipped in the air, flying back behind the thrower. That xoconai and the others, and their mounts, slid backwards across the ice patch, cowering against the stinging and biting flames in the wind. Fog rose up as the ice melted fast in the hot breath of Aoleyn's magic.

She dropped to the ground and ran to the wounded monk. Scooping him in her arms and calling on the moonstone to carry them both, she half flew, half dragged him to the base of the wall.

Down came some monks, Thaddius among them, to hoist their injured brother. The whole group moved swiftly to the side, where a small, secret door in the wall opened and others ushered them inside to safety.

Barely had she entered the courtyard, taking a deep breath to let all of the magic cease, when Brother Thaddius wrapped Aoleyn in a tight hug. "You saved him!" Thaddius whispered repeatedly in her ear, and Aoleyn only then realized that many were cheering—and cheering for her.

Elysant and Aydrian arrived soon after.

"I expect that Father Abbot Braumin will find his decisions vindicated," Elysant said.

Aoleyn just felt drained, the fury of her magic gone. A great exhaustion, emotional and physical, came over her.

She pulled back from Thaddius and looked around at all the others, some tending the wounded monk with their soul stones, others calling from atop the wall that the enemy was fleeing, still others rushing about to report the incident.

"A score dead, at least!" one called from the wall.

"Twice that number burned and running away!" yelled another.

For the first time, Aoleyn thought that maybe, just maybe,

St.-Mere-Abelle might prove strong enough to keep the xoconai at bay.

It was hard for her to take too much solace in that, however, given the images of Ursal and Palmaris that she had seen on her spirit-walk. And worse, the procession of souls she had witnessed marching slavishly to the west, to Fireach Speuer and the God Crystal, to be devoured, their life energy converted into magical power for the great demon god who led the xoconai.

She looked around again, letting Thaddius lead her by the hand across the courtyard toward the father abbot's audience chapel.

They would celebrate this small victory.

They should celebrate this small victory.

But in the larger scheme of the world, this vast monastery remained a very tiny place indeed.

Day and night over the next week, the monks kept up their vigilance and defensive preparedness, spirit-walking all about St.-Mere-Abelle, a large perimeter, watching for signs of the enemy.

But the fields remained clear.

Father Abbot Braumin sent some trusted brothers out farther to the south and out into the Gulf of Corona, and there they found some answers. Off in the south, across the inlet and St.-Mere-Abelle's docks, they found a great procession of enemy warriors, but a staggered one, with long gaps in between the legions, each of those gaps marked by newly constructed stone or wood pyramids. It took them some time to confirm that these were waypoints, places that would magically transport the warriors across great leaps of distance to the next in line. The invaders were filling the southland with these pyramids, these teleportation gates, and so they could bring their forces to bear on any critical battlefield in short order.

Nor had the xoconai fully turned from St.-Mere-Abelle, despite the quiet fields, for the spirit-walking brothers going north and west had found three of those same pyramid structures evenly spaced about the perimeter of the monastery, all heavily guarded. If the enemy turned their eyes to the monastery, they could bring a full army onto the field in very short order, all within an hour's march of the monastery.

Further north, beyond the towns abandoned by folk who were now mostly huddled within St.-Mere-Abelle, and past the limestone cliffs, where the dark waters of the Gulf of Corona and the flow of the Masur Delaval merged and blended, the spirit-walking brothers saw the ships—many ships and many more small boats—a flotilla of refugees from Ursal, Palmaris, Amvoy, and many smaller towns in between. At the point where the peninsula turned south, the ships and small boats mostly diverged, with the small craft staying on the coast and turning for the inlet to St.-Mere-Abelle but many of the larger ships staying due east, sailing for the open waters.

Running away as far as they could go.

Aydrian, Aoleyn, Thaddius, and Elysant were among the many Father Abbot Braumin sent down to support the docks, to welcome the refugees and guard against enemy infiltrators, and so the foursome were there to inspect the larger ships that came in, including one from Palmaris carrying some familiar faces.

Aoleyn's heart soared when she spotted Khotai, then Talmadge, and by the time she reached them, Catriona had joined them.

"Where is Bahdlahn?" she asked.

The three knew it was coming, of course, and they exchanged concerned looks.

"We left him very much alive," Khotai was quick to say.

"You left him?"

"He left us," Talmadge corrected. "At the docks of Palmaris. He chose not to flee with the ship. There were too many people left helpless, caught in the city as it fell. He wouldn't leave them."

"By the time we knew of his decision, we were all aboard and sailing, too far out to get back to him," Khotai added.

Aoleyn looked to Catriona and saw that the woman was holding back a waterfall of tears. Aoleyn, too, felt a lump in her throat. Was Bahdlahn dead? She closed her eyes and tried not to entertain such dark thoughts. He was a capable warrior, a clever adversary, and he knew how to hide.

She had to trust in him, she tried to tell herself, and she even silently insisted that if Bahdlahn had died, she would have somehow, mystically felt it.

"He's alive," she declared, because she, and they, needed to hear it.

"Why aren't you in To-gai?" Aydrian asked.

"The mountains crawl with sidhe," said Khotai.

"I found the pass," Talmadge told Aydrian. "And the elves and their zombies who guard it. They would have none of me or anyone else. They made it clear. And they knew."

"Knew?"

"Of the invaders—they called them the xoconai. And they insisted that the xoconai would not find them and had no business with them, and that I, that all of us, had no business with them."

"What does it mean?" Thaddius asked.

Aydrian shook his head, his face scrunched as if he had no answers.

"The news is not good from the west," Talmadge went on. "Palmaris is lost, and Ursal. The king and the Allheart Knights are, or were, in Palmaris, chased there by our enemies. The invasion is furious, fast, and huge."

"There is more," Khotai added. "Things we learned of the fall of Ursal while on the boat coming to this place. The captain meant to keep sailing, as with most of the larger ships, all the way to the east coast, perhaps even south to the kingdom beyond the mountains."

"Behren," said Aydrian and Thaddius together.

"I implored him to stop here, that we could tell the monks," Talmadge added. "I . . . we . . . didn't expect to find you here, but glad we are to see that you have survived."

The group of seven left the docks soon after, with the tall ship waiting only on the tide to return to the open waters, and the talk among the five friends from the far west centered mostly on whether they would take the captain's offer and sail far away.

Catriona, with her skull elongated to three times the normal length, garnered many curious stares as they hustled all the way to Father Abbot Braumin's audience hall.

Braumin, too, stared at Catriona in surprise.

"You are from Aoleyn's lands?" he asked the young woman, and she nodded somewhat sheepishly in reply.

"Your head," the father abbot said. "Forgive my forwardness, but your head . . . it is . . ."

"It is common among her people," Aydrian explained. "They wrap the skulls of their children to shape the growth."

"Some have two humps, others a single stretch," Aoleyn added.

"But yours is not misshap . . . altered," Braumin said.

"She is Usgar," Catriona said, somewhat sharply.

"My tribe was of the mountain, not the lake. We do not follow such a practice."

"The tribes of the lake only did it so we would not look like Usgar," Catriona said. She and Aoleyn exchanged looks and shrugs, a silent agreement that the past was truly behind them.

"It is beautiful," Father Abbot Braumin told her. "There seems to be so much more of the world than we here know. Much of it is beautiful, and much is dangerous."

"The xoconai are both," said Aoleyn.

"This is Talmadge," Aydrian told Braumin. "An old friend of mine."

The father abbot arched his eyebrows.

"Not that old," said Aydrian. "We met a few years ago, far beyond the Barbacan. It was Talmadge who showed me the Ayamharas Plateau and the wondrous Loch Beag and Fireach Speuer. It was Talmadge who introduced me to Khotai of To-gai here, and to Aoleyn and all the rest."

"Good fortune that he did, it would seem," said Braumin.

"For us, too," said Talmadge. "Aydrian showed us where to run, to both our benefit. We learned much of the fall of Ursal on the boat out of Palmaris, and we watched the sack of Palmaris. We were aboard the last ship out of port."

"We have seen the enemy, just a glimpse, but expect they are formidable," said Braumin.

"Very," said Talmadge. "Divine throwers."

Braumin and the other monks, Aydrian and Aoleyn, all stared at him curiously.

"And they have a dragon," Talmadge added.

He told his story in full, and, coincidentally, just as he was trying to explain the fall of St. Honce, another group entered the father abbot's audience chapel, led by Abbot Ohwan of St. Honce and Abbot Havre of St. Precious.

The group remained together throughout the day and long into the night, hearing the stories and discussing countering strategies.

"If they come, we will be ready," Father Abbot Braumin vowed.

His words would be put to the test the next day, when the xoconai army appeared on the field east, north, and west of St.-Mere-Abelle.

"Fair winds, my friend," Aydrian said to Talmadge that morning, down at the docks. "And watch out for powries."

"Powries?"

"You'll know them when you see them," Aydrian replied with a grin. "Though, by then, it might be too late."

Over to the side, Khotai and Catriona stood with Aoleyn.

"Come with us," Khotai said, for the tenth time.

"I can'no," said Aoleyn. "I am needed here."

"There is a wondrous world out there, I am told," said Khotai. "Away from the battles and the death."

"I will find it one day," Aoleyn promised. "I will find *you* one day."

"Find Bahdlahn," Catriona begged her, and Aoleyn nodded.

"I feel as if I should stay with you," Catriona said. "I do not run from fights."

"This isn't your fight," Aoleyn replied.

"Isn't it? They killed my people. They killed . . . they took me from Bahdlahn."

Aoleyn shrugged. "Go," she said, pointing to the ship, which was readying to leave. "Find peace and find wonder. If you stay, you would be another mouth to feed and a sword we here hope that we will not need. If we are to win this war, it will be magic, not steel, that turns the xoconai away. And so I must stay—the monks wish to learn from me and I must try to teach them." She paused and gave a helpless little shrug before finishing. "Believe me when I tell you that I wish I could just go and find Bahdlahn and fly with him in my arms to find this ship, your ship, that we could all sail together and see the great ocean and all the wonders of the world."

Khotai gave Aoleyn a long and tight hug, Catriona joining in. When they finally pulled apart, wiping tears, Talmadge nearly tackled the Usgar witch, squeezing her so tightly, so desperately, that for a moment she could hardly breathe.

"I saw you destroy that demon on the mountain," he said. "I thought you more a girl than a woman, so slight and small, and you went into that place of death and destroyed the fossa. Then you saved so many when the sidhe came, and used your magic to get us across the lake before it drained. And you stopped them again . . . Aoleyn, we are all so indebted to you."

"There is no debt among friends," she replied.

"I hope we will see you again," Talmadge said, and now his eyes were misty, too. "I hope to sail with you to the city of Jacintha in the kingdom south of the mountains. I hope to see again your face glowing in the light of daybreak as the sun climbs above the eastern sea. Truly, I am glad to know you, Aoleyn of Fireach Speuer."

Aoleyn gave him that crooked little smile and hugged him again, then stepped back and motioned.

She stood still, staring, as the three climbed the gangplank, and then she kept standing, arms folded about her in the chill morning breeze off the cold water.

She was glad when Aydrian came up beside her and draped his arm across her shoulders, pulling her close.

She felt like he was the only friend she had left in the world.

PART 3

DEMON WITHOUT, DEMON WITHIN

Tuolonatl is cochcal, the commander of the xoconai army. She was the obvious choice, as she is legend. Whenever a city of Tonoloya was threatened by rival sovereigns or by outside invaders, the first name spoken to lead the defense was Tuolonatl.

And if word came to a threatened city that Tuolonatl was leading the approaching force, the battle would likely be surrendered before it was waged.

That is the strength of reputation.

Tuolonatl was the obvious choice as cochcal, except that this war was decreed by Scathmizzane. This was destiny, a holy war, yet Tuolonatl is not devout. She is no friend to the augurs of Glorious Gold. To any of them, from all that I have learned. She doesn't speak of them with contempt only because she doesn't speak of them at all. And neither would she attend their sermons.

She is practical, though, and values the augurs among her ranks, for their healing powers if not their words of comfort and Glorious Gold.

It is curious, then, that Scathmizzane chose her to lead the great march to the east, over the mountains to conquer Tzatzini, then out from the mountains to march across the world, to conquer all who stood before us as the promise of Greater Tonoloya came to fruition, with sunrise and sunset shining on the beaches of the xoconai nation.

Scathmizzane is god. Scathmizzane is Glorious Gold.

Scathmizzane brought us the golden mirrors, that we might step a hundred miles in a single stride.

Scathmizzane brought us the divine throwers to break the walls of the great human cities.

Scathmizzane guided the march, not Tuolonatl, and indeed, Scathmizzane didn't need Tuolonatl.

Scathmizzane was the cochcal, of course!

But he chose her. He chose one who did not give prayers to him with the regularity (if at all) demanded by the augurs. He chose one who eschewed the rituals of Glorious Gold, one who, were it not for her value and reputation and the love of the common xoconai, would not be welcomed in the temples of the augurs at all, and who might well have been cast out of the more religious of xoconai cities altogether.

It pleased me when Tuolonatl was named cochcal—I know of no one who I would rather ride beside into battle. I admit my confusion as well, though now I have come to understand, and in that understanding, I feel as if I am standing on a field of shifting sands.

Because now I have come to realize that Scathmizzane selected Tuolonatl because she is not devout, not in spite of that truth.

Scathmizzane selected Tuolonatl because he knew there would be tension between her and the augurs every step of this march to the sea, and yes, I have witnessed that tension in our victories most of all. For Tuolonatl plays a longer game than the augurs can understand. In their zealotry and arrogance, they think nothing of the children of Cizinfozza and would be pleased indeed if Glorious Gold told them to simply kill every human—man, woman, or child—along our journey.

Tuolonatl would not do this, and not simply for the sake of expediency.

Tuolonatl would not do this because it is wrong.

The result, inevitably, is tension, and Scathmizzane, I have come to see, enjoys tension. Scathmizzane feeds on tension and unrest. Strife between his principal leaders does not displease him—quite the opposite.

But why?

He is a god, the unquestioned god of the xoconai. He

need not worry about any xoconai—not Tuolonatl, not High Priest Pixquicauh—ever challenging him or even questioning him. No, he does this, I believe, simply because he enjoys it.

We march to conquer the children of Cizinfozza. Of course, we must, for Cizinfozza is the god of night, the god of darkness, the god of death.

Scathmizzane is Glorious Gold, the god of day, the god of light, the god of life.

The light is good, the darkness is evil, so we are taught from our childhood days.

But now I see. Now, at long last, I understand, and all the training that you have given to me rings truer in proper context.

Cannot darkness be serene and calming?

Cannot light bring agitation and unease?

The augurs think the children of Cizinfozza irredeemable, lesser, evil. Tuolonatl knows this not to be true.

And Scathmizzane picked the old augur, Dayan-Zahn, to be Pixquicauh. Dayan-Zahn, the most devout of all. The most zealous augur, merciless in his certainty.

And Scathmizzane picked Tuolonatl to be cochcal. Tuolonatl, who is not devout. Who is not zealous, and who is merciful in her uncertainty.

Scathmizzane feeds on strife. He has ensured that the conflict will continue long after the xoconai watch the sun rise from the sea on our eastern beaches. He has ensured that the children of Cizinfozza will not be eradicated, and that the fight will go on.

Why?

Now that the answer to that question becomes clear to me, I stand on shifting sands.

But I hold an anchor, my mentor, and that anchor is that which you have given to me. For this, I am ever grateful.

Ag'ardu An'grian
Sunrise Face

18

BEND THE KNEE

"There is a tunnel," the knight reported to King Midalis. "It heads east, generally, but there seem to be several ways back above ground. We are exploring it now."

"We should leave this night," Brother Ottavian, one of the few remaining monks in the city, was quick to add.

King Midalis rubbed his face—with one hand, as the other arm was being tightly bandaged by an attending monk. He and his knights had led a gallant ride through the city, trampling and cutting down scores of the invaders. He had lost several knights in that ride, though, and barely a score remained at his side. And, in the end, for all their courage and ferocity, they had found themselves right back where they had started, caught inside the monastery of St. Precious.

Outside of that one large structure, Palmaris had almost completely fallen. Fewer and fewer were the sounds of battle echoing from remote corners of the sprawling city, and whenever a fight did start, it seemed to end very quickly.

"What think you, Julian?" he asked, looking over at the young man who had become his closest remaining advisor.

Julian pondered the question for a few heartbeats. He was stripped to the waist, tight wraps about his torso. He had taken a beating in the run across Palmaris. Thrice he had been pulled from his horse, and thrice he had fought his way back to his saddle, leaving broken sidhe in his wake. His gleaming breastplate, set on the floor beside him, showed dozens of dents from heavy blows of those strange paddles of the bright-faced invaders.

"If there is a way fully out of the city, that is the route we should go," he answered.

"Desert them?"

"We bring the people of the city nothing but greater danger," the Allheart explained. "We cannot lead them against such a force as now resides in Palmaris. I fear that our continuing presence here will press the hand of our enemy, and that hand will be tight about the neck of Palmaris's prisoners."

When he finished, he looked to the battered young man sitting next to him, a civilian and no member of the Allhearts, the Coastpoint Guards, the Palmaris garrison, or any other official military force. On that third fall, Julian had been surely doomed, caught under a trio of fierce warriors who set to pounding him with abandon. No knights had been near enough to get to him.

But those invaders had gone flying away, shoulderblocked by this man who was now sitting beside the knight, a young man of immense strength and growling bravery. He had saved Julian at the expense of his own life—or it certainly would have been at that price, except that Julian had pulled him up into the saddle behind him and charged out of that nest of enemies.

"I do'no wish to leave," the young man replied to that look.

"Nor I," Julian agreed. "But we cannot stay here. I can

guess easily enough what these merciless fiends will do to coax us out."

"They do not know that King Midalis is in here, surely," said Brother Ottavian.

Julian shrugged as if it didn't matter, and those who had been in Ursal for the previous fight all understood that it did not. Back in Ursal, he had seen the rubble of St. Honce, and so he could pretty easily guess how all of this would soon enough end. The sidhe would use prisoners, would torture and murder prisoners, to goad the force out in surrender, or they would knock the monastery down on top of the resistors.

"It pains me greatly to flee again," Midalis told them, his voice heavy, his posture one of weariness. "I think of those left behind in Ursal, the trials they must now be facing."

"I was their captive," said the surprising man sitting beside Julian, and all eyes turned to him in a moment of shocked silence.

"Here? In Palmaris?" King Midalis asked.

"In a village far west," the stranger explained. "In the lands you call the Wilderlands, a place called Appleby. I was caught there by the xoconai."

"You're from the Wilderlands?"

"I am from . . ." He paused. "I do not know how to even tell you. It would be a journey of many months for me to show you, past the mountains in the west, to different mountains, which we call the Surgruag Monadh."

King Midalis pushed the attending monk aside and stood up, moving deliberately over to stand before this surprising man.

"You don't know who I am, do you?" he asked.

"They call you King Midalis."

"But I am not *your* king."

The man shrugged.

"You walked east, thousands of miles?" Midalis asked.

"Yes."

"Who led you?"

A curious expression crossed the young man's face, as if he was trying to take a measure of the king's intent here.

"Many, and none," he finally answered. "We were a hundred and a few, fleeing ahead of the xoconai. Talmadge led us, and Aydrian."

"Aydrian?" several echoed all at once, including Midalis himself.

"Yes. And Aoleyn. I followed Aoleyn most of all. She is my friend."

"But you weren't with her when she came through Ursal," King Midalis said, and his eyes widened as the young man's face brightened.

"She is alive?" the man asked, and it seemed as if he could not draw breath.

"What is your name?" King Midalis quietly asked him.

"I am Bahdlahn."

"Friend of Aoleyn?"

He nodded.

The king turned to Julian, then looked all about, showing the gathering a knowing and warm smile. "When heroes are needed," he muttered.

"Where are you from?" Midalis asked. "What is the name of your village?"

"My people are from Fasach Crann, but I—"

"Well, Bahdlahn of Fasach Crann," Midalis interrupted, his voice steady and solemn, "on this day, in this place so far from your home, I, Midalis dan Ursal, though I am not your king, do hereby commend upon you the title of Allheart. Honorary, as you are not my subject."

He heard his knights bristling about him and turned to regard them, then nodded again when he saw that all of them were nodding in agreement.

"What does that mean?" Bahdlahn asked.

"It means that I, that we, salute you and thank you for your efforts this day, and for your courage in traveling all the way from . . . from the west, to help us in our hour of need. You do not owe me allegiance, though I hope you will give it."

The young man clearly had no idea how to respond. He looked to Julian, the knight he had saved out on the street, the knight who would not leave without him, and returned a smile.

"You were a captive in this town of Appleby?" King Midalis asked, bringing the conversation back.

"Yes."

"Tell us."

"We worked. If we worked without complaint, we were not punished."

"These sidhe—what did you call them again?"

"Xoconai."

"These xoconai, they were merciful?"

Bahdlahn shrugged. "They were not kind."

"But you weren't tortured? And none were killed?"

"Those who disobeyed or tried to run were killed," he replied. "And the few others chosen for sacrifice to Scathmizzane."

"Who is that?"

"Their god."

"On the dragon," Julian said, and King Midalis nodded.

"Were they cruel?"

"Some," said Bahdlahn. "Some not." He shrugged again. "They are not unlike men."

That answer shook all of them.

"What are you doing here?" Tuolonatl asked, when she unexpectedly encountered High Priest Pixquicauh in the command post she had established just down the wide avenue from the fortified building the humans called St. Precious Abbey.

That she wasn't happy to see him was clearly evident in her tone, she realized, as she heard her own words.

She didn't really care.

Pixquicauh and a sizable splinter of the xoconai force had continued straight east from Ursal, with Tuolonatl taking the main battle group to the north to conquer the river and the two cities, Palmaris and Amvoy, at its mouth. Her success had been swift and decisive, and she had already pushed far to the east, to another huge fortress, which was being described by many of the prisoners she had taken as the strongest fortress in the world.

She might have expected Pixquicauh to arrive there, on the field outside of the place called St.-Mere-Abelle, but not here. Not now.

Unless . . .

"The king of the humans is in that building," he replied, confirming Tuolonatl's fear that the high priest was current on the recent news. She glanced around at those xoconai closest to her, knowing there was an informant among their ranks.

"We do not know that," she answered. "I have only recently heard the same information, but it is hardly confirmed."

"Well, then we must confirm it. Conquer the building."

Tuolonatl tried not to scoff at the ridiculously casual tone of the daunting demand. "It is good that you have come, then," she said. "When can you bring one of the divine throwers here, that we might convince those inside the fortress to come out?"

Pixquicauh seemed a bit off balance at the request. "We cannot," he said.

"Why can't you? I have heard of no significant battles east of Ursal, and we'll not soon commence the attack on the great fortress in the east."

"Take the building without them."

"I will lose a thousand macana assaulting such a place," she replied. "And even then, I doubt we can get through the walls. The doors and windows are few and fortified. The humans inside have powerful magic and strong steel. If you give me weeks, my macana can, perhaps, tunnel beneath the walls to weaken them, but—"

"Weeks?" Pixquicauh interrupted, with exaggerated incredulity. "Our forces are far to the east of Ursal already! We will be at the eastern sea in days, where Scathmizzane will demand the leadership of his chosen cochcal, and you think to hold us here for weeks?"

"You would have me fill the street with dead xoconai? Give me one thrower and I will take the fortress and their king this very day."

She noted the change in Pixquicauh's posture and knew that something else was going on here.

"We cannot use the divine throwers," he finally admitted. "Glorious Gold has forbidden their use at this time. He gathers his power for a great purpose, and use of them drains the great crystal above Otontotomi."

"One throw?"

Pixquicauh shook his head.

Tuolonatl moved to the window and looked down the lane to the imposing St. Precious. She had to give the humans credit here, for they knew how to build a fortress. Had it not been for the divine throwers collapsing the monastery in Ursal upon most of the magic-wielding priests, then opening the walls, she wasn't even sure that she would have won out at that city—and certainly not without catastrophic losses.

Here, she faced a similar proposition. Mundunugu and macana could not take down the walls of St. Precious. This xoconai army had been constructed for speed and open-ground battle, and Tuolonatl had already come to understand the greatest weakness of her force: back in Tonoloya, large battles were rare and war machines were virtually unknown. The beauty of xoconai cities could not be defaced by catapults and the like, by godly decree, and so there were few fortified buildings or walled cities. This wasn't how the xoconai fought.

"Coax them out," Pixquicauh insisted.

Tuolonatl tightened up, for she understood his meaning.

"Start with the children," the high priest explained. "If you execute the adults, a king will justify it as a noble sacrifice. Minions should willingly give their lives for their king, of course. But when you start torturing children in the open street outside of that building, this human King Midalis will come forth. He is no coward, if it was indeed he who led the charges through the streets of this town."

Again, Tuolonatl was taken aback by how much information had so quickly been passed on to Pixquicauh.

The high priest looked to Ataquixt, who stood beside Tuolonatl. "Take your mundunugu and begin fetching children. The younger, the better. Bring me a hundred. That will be a good start."

"We have just tamed the city," Tuolonatl argued. "You will send the humans back into a frenzy."

"The more who die, the stronger becomes Scathmizzane," the high priest quipped. "Perhaps if you slaughter enough of the beasts, our Glorious Gold will allow us a divine thrower after all."

With a snicker that resonated with evil to Tuolonatl, the old augur turned and walked away, leaving Tuolonatl staring at St. Precious, trying not to imagine scores of little children being hung upside down and gutted.

"There are many outlets, most exiting into nondescript buildings, some into no more than hovels," the knight explained to Midalis and the others. "The main tunnel goes down to the docks but comes out under the water before them."

"The docks are heavily guarded, and the few boats remaining there are moored far out and also full of enemies," said another. "That would be our best chance, but it will be difficult."

"Their lizards are swift swimmers," the first reminded.

Midalis chewed his lip and closed his eyes. There were

several hundred people huddled within St. Precious. They had nowhere to run. Perhaps Midalis and a few of his skilled warriors and monks could get away, but not the others.

"Then we do that," said Brother Ottavian. "We fight to the boats and flee. It is the only way."

"You believe that we could free enough boats to take all of these people from the city?" Julian of the Evergreen growled.

"They can go out through the other exits and just melt in with the populace," the monk replied. "The city is lost. Their homes are lost. They are caught by these sidhe monsters, whatever that might mean for them. Our being caught beside them does them no good deed."

"The Church has grown soft since the De'Unneran Heresy," Julian said, in less-than-complimentary tones, drawing a scowl from Ottavian and several other brothers.

Midalis took it all in—no option pleased him. Ottavian's plan might be for the best, he thought, but before he could play it through in his head, he heard a voice from out in the street, calling him by name.

"King Midalis dan Ursal of Honce-the-Bear!" the speaker, a woman, called. "I would parlay with you now for the sake of your people."

Midalis led the way to the room's small windows and peered out, along with any who could crowd in for a glimpse.

A lone rider sat in the middle of the avenue, tall and beautiful, golden-skinned, with a bright red nose and brilliant blue stripes bordering it. Her hair bobbed about her shoulders, silken and smooth. Her form was lean but clearly strong and toned.

"Sidhe bitch," one knight growled.

"Xoconai," Midalis heard the young man, Bahdlahn, correct.

He had to agree with that, for this woman was no goblin. She sat on her mount, a beautiful pinto horse and no lizard, wearing a splendid breastplate of those rolled pieces of wood, all painted brightly. She carried a large black feather in her hair, sticking back from over her left ear.

"I am Tuolonatl," she said. "This city is lost to you. I will have your surrender."

The Allhearts about Midalis bristled, some cursing, one remarking, "How does this devil speak our tongue as if she was raised in Honce?"

"They are men, then," another offered. "Their faces are painted."

"It isn't paint, nor a tattoo," Julian answered definitively. "They are not men, none like we know, at least."

"Xoconai," Bahdlahn said again. "From the west, beyond the mountains."

Xoconai, Midalis quietly mouthed.

"King Midalis dan Ursal, do you hear me?" the woman called. "If you do not hear me, we will make you hear me." She turned her mount a bit, sweeping her arm out behind her to a host of xoconai.

Midalis's eyes went wide when enemy warriors moved out from the crowd, each pushing a small child before him. Dozens and dozens came forward, children crying, people along the side streets wailing.

"Do you hear me, King Midalis?"

"I hear you," he yelled back.

"You are lost. You have nowhere to run," she said. "The city is ours. We are not without mercy, but mercy must be earned. I will have your surrender, without condition."

She motioned for another rider, this one on a lizard, to come out beside her.

"Ataquixt will count to and call out each hundred. When ten have passed, if you have not come out the door of this monastery, the first child will be killed. Then another child with each subsequent hundred."

"Monsters!" said one of the knights, and the cursing began anew, along with calls for a charge out of St. Precious.

Midalis turned from the window and bade them all to silence.

"Go, flee, all of you through the tunnels," he told the knights and monks. "Find your way, fight your way."

"Not without you, my king," said Julian of the Evergreen, and a host of others agreed.

Outside, the xoconai man yelled out, "One hundred!"

"They want me," King Midalis said. "Of course they do." He searched about for a moment, then looked straight at Bahdlahn. "Tell me again, quickly, of these xoconai. They are not goblins. They do not murder for pleasure."

"They are no different than the Usgar who enslaved me," the young man answered. "They are not goblins. They are men, like us."

Midalis nodded and motioned him to silence. He paused a moment.

"Two hundred!" came the call from outside.

"The city is lost," he said. "I've nowhere to run. And I'll not watch children slaughtered without—"

"They will kill them anyway!" one of the knights claimed.

"We do not know that," said Midalis. "But we do know that they will kill them now. I have no doubt of that."

"And you cannot allow that," said Julian.

"No, I cannot. I will go out to them in surrender. Palmaris is lost. Ursal is lost."

The knights all snapped to attention. "For the king, with the king!" one chanted, others joining in.

"I will go alone."

"You will not," said another.

"You will not!" Julian echoed.

Again, Midalis called for silence.

"Three hundred!" came the call from the street.

"The monks must leave, with all the gemstones they can find," Midalis said. "Those treasures and secrets must not fall to our enemies."

"Not all of us," Brother Ottavian insisted. "For, in that case, our enemies would know of the escape. My brethren will flee with all of the most powerful Ring Stones. We will leave the minor stones here, enough for me to convince these sidhe or xoconai or whatever they are."

Midalis stared at him for a short while, then nodded his agreement.

"And I will stay and stand by my king," said Julian of the Evergreen.

"And I," another Allheart said, rising determinedly.

"And I!" agreed another, and another, and all down the line.

Midalis shook his head and moved straight for Julian. "Not you," he ordered. "You will leave, into the tunnel and into a house, any house, and you will get away from here in the dark of night and tell them. Go to Saint-Mere-Abelle and tell them. Go to Saint Gwendolyn-by-the-Sea and tell them. Go to Entel and tell them." Midalis put his hands on the man's shoulders, squaring up to him. "Go to Behren," he said. "Go and find Brynn Dharielle, who rides the dragon Agradeleous. Go and tell her, and tell the Jhesta tu mystics. You, Julian of the Evergreen, you I charge with telling the world of what happened here and what happened in Ursal."

He turned about, pulling Julian to Bahdlahn. "And take this man and tell them of the events in the west. This is my charge to you."

Midalis released Julian and moved about the room, pointing to the younger Allhearts, ordering them to go with Julian.

"Warn the world of what is coming," he commanded them all. "And keep alive that which is lost. You are the Allhearts. You serve Honce-the-Bear above all, above me."

King Midalis took a last deep breath, closed his eyes.

"Six hundred!" called the xoconai in the street outside.

"Go, my dear Allhearts," Midalis said. "Go now."

A moment of silence followed, the selected knights bristling and shifting uncomfortably, the older knights, who would surrender beside their king, all staring and nodding.

"I hate that you did this to me," Julian quietly admitted.

"I know," Midalis replied, patting him on the shoulder, then warmly hugging him. "And that is why I know you will not disappoint me." Then he whispered into Julian's ear, more quietly, "Find my queen and protect her. Promise me."

He felt the change in Julian's frame, the man relaxing, surrendering. He pushed Julian back to arm's length and saw on his face grim determination.

Yes, he had chosen correctly.

Off went the dozen selected Allhearts, the five other monks, and Bahdlahn, through the monastery and to the tunnels.

"What of the commoners?" one of the other knights asked the king.

"They surrender with us," Midalis answered. "Let us hope that the young man's description of these xoconai as more human than goblin proves true."

"Seven hundred!" came the call outside.

"Let us go and shut up that annoying fool," said Midalis, and he led the way to the front door and pushed it wide, then stepped out into the afternoon light.

"I am King Midalis of Honce-the-Bear," he announced from the top of St. Precious's large front stairway. "Do you speak for the xoconai, Tuolonatl?"

The woman on the horse nodded.

Midalis held back his knights and walked down the stairs, motioning for the woman to come to him. To his relief, she did, pacing her pinto up to the base of the steps, where she stared down at the king.

"How do you speak our tongue?" he asked.

"There are ways."

Midalis chuckled.

"I will surrender the city of Palmaris," he told her.

"It is lost to you in any case."

"But my surrender will lessen the resistance, yes?"

Tuolonatl nodded.

"Then I ask something of you in return," Midalis said.

"You are hardly in a position to bargain."

"Mercy," he said. "I ask you for mercy."

"For you?"

"I care not for me. For my gallant knights. For the brothers of the Church. For the common folk. For the children."

"You doubt me?"

"Not for a moment," he replied. He offered a smile and a helpless shrug. "Are you not relieved that I came out before your friend over there reached a thousand?"

She looked confused at that.

"A hundred, ten times," he explained. "Are you not glad that you did not have to slaughter a helpless child on the street to convince me?"

The strangely beautiful creature stared down at him from her seat, her face impassive, revealing nothing.

But Midalis had his answer, because if there was no honor in this enemy leader, she would have ordered a child murdered right then, to shatter the king's illusions and steal his hope.

But she did not. She turned her horse and started slowly away.

"Bring them out, all of them," she told him as she left. "Have them throw down their weapons and strip their armor. Any who do not will be dead before they step onto the street."

Midalis found that he didn't doubt that.

They came out quietly into the dark, wincing at every heavy footfall, every scrape of metal armor.

Brother Ottavian, who was of Palmaris and knew the lay of the land, led the way, scooting down narrow alleyways, moving ever north. That would be their best choice, they had decided while still in the tunnels, since the invaders had mostly come from the south.

Julian and Bahdlahn took up the back of the column, the Allheart looking often to the west, to the dark silhouette of St. Precious.

King Midalis was there, somewhere, in their grasp.

Julian could not imagine that his beloved King Midalis, a man who had become as a mentor and friend, would survive for long. He kept leaning toward St. Precious, veering that way for a step or two, as if being pulled by unheard cries.

Ottavian led them swift and sure, soon coming in sight of a small gate across a wide plaza, not far from the docks. A trio of xoconai milled about that gate, two sitting on lizards, the third leaning against the wall, her lizard sitting up on the top of the wall, its head very close to hers as she shared some food with it.

"We can charge right through them," one knight offered, as Julian and Bahdlahn came up to the front of the group.

"But we're very near the docks, and there are many more there who will come to any calls or sound of battle," another replied.

"Is there another way?" Julian asked Ottavian.

The monk looked all about, nervously tapping his finger against his lips. He fished in his pockets for a specific gemstone, then focused on it for a bit and held it up to his eye. Slowly, he turned his head, first toward the docks, and then back to the south, and then west.

"The docks are full of sidhe, and they're patrolling the wall," he said, his expression grave. "And there are sidhe groups moving outside the wall as well."

"Then where?" asked Julian, and the monk shrugged.

"Back to the tunnel," Bahdlahn answered, and all looked his way. "We can collapse the entryway to the side tunnel, and even if the xoconai come down into the main tunnel, they won't find us."

"It could work," one knight agreed.

"Collapsing the entrance to the side tunnel will be easy," Ottavian added, and he held up a pale orange gemstone.

The whispers began all around, as they tried to figure out how they might gather some supplies and hole up—perhaps they could strike out from their hidey-hole and sting these enemies. Perhaps they could organize a resistance among the populace.

Julian of the Evergreen put his hands over his face and rubbed his cheeks, remembering the last commands of King Midalis—orders that he go to the east and spread the warning. How much good would he really do while crouched in a dirty tunnel?

"No," he said, silencing all about him. "No. We're going out, right through that gate, fast and hard. The king has commanded us to carry the news to the east and to get those most sacred and powerful Ring Stones far from this place. What can you do to help us, Brother Ottavian? What magic have you and your brethren at your hand to get us away from Palmaris?"

The monks went off and conferred by themselves for a bit, while the knights laid plans for a sudden and brutal takedown of the three sidhe.

"Follow, and quickly," Ottavian said, rejoining the group and leading them back down the alleyway, then along a perpendicular corridor to the west, bringing them farther from the docks. He used his gemstone again at several places, Bahdlahn noted—and he knew the stone, too, for it was the same kind as in Talmadge's lens, which the man used for seeing things far away.

Finally, a long while later, with the dark of night perilously close to allowing the first tinges of dawn, Ottavian stopped them between two large buildings, once again looking across a wide avenue, to some structures to the north and to another alleyway that led to the base of the wall. Up on that wall, they saw enemy soldiers, some riding, some walking, many holding torches and others holding some magical lights that seemed like sheets of metal.

Ottavian and another brother moved to the front, checking their gemstones.

"I need one strong man," the monk told Julian, and before the knight could reply, he pointed to Bahdlahn.

Moments later, the two monks and Bahdlahn slipped quietly across the dark street, their forms blurred by the magic of Abellican diamonds, the Ring Stone that both gave and stole light. They moved down the alleyway to the wall, and there, Ottavian produced his orange stone again—like the one Aoleyn had set within the large wedstone on her hip, Bahdlahn realized.

"When I free a stone, you lift it out," Ottavian whispered to Bahdlahn. "Brother Alfonse will help lighten it that you might set it on the ground."

The monk called upon the citrine, then brought his hand to the wall and began marring the solid stone there as if it were thick clay. A few moments later, he shifted back and to the side, huffing and puffing, and motioned for Bahdlahn to be quick.

The powerful young man worked his hands into the lines Ottavian had cut and began rocking the large section of stone left and right, easing it toward him. It was enormously heavy, and Bahdlahn knew that he wouldn't easily hoist it, particularly with his fingers on the side instead of beneath it.

True to Ottavian's promise, though, Brother Alphonse then added a different magic, and Bahdlahn nodded as the stone greatly lightened. He slid it out from the wall much more easily then, catching it in his arms. Even with the telekinetic help from the monk and his malachite, Bahdlahn feared that his legs would buckle, for he was holding a section of stone three feet across, equally high, and quite thick as well, a stone that weighed more than twice his own considerable weight, easily—or would have, except for Brother Alphonse's magical trick.

Bahdlahn managed to ease it to the ground with minimal noise.

Ottavian leaned into the newly formed alcove and went right back to work with the citrine, this time digging a hole in the center of the next block, pulling out chunks of it as if they were putty and handing them back to Bahdlahn. When Ottavian came out of the wall, Bahdlahn saw that he had bored a hole right through, one large enough to allow a man to squeeze out of Palmaris and to the dark field beyond.

"Go out and hold this place," Ottavian told Bahdlahn. "We'll bring the others across with the darkness shroud."

Bahdlahn crawled in and through, rolling out onto the grass beyond. He held very still, glancing all about.

Not far from him, to the east, a xoconai warrior leaned against the wall.

Bahdlahn looked back through the hole. He thought that he could slip off into the night unnoticed, but he knew that the others, particularly the knights with their noisy armor, would never escape that sentry's attention. He thought to go back through the hole and tell them to change the plan.

He thought to run off into the night.

In the end, he was creeping—not away, no, but toward that xoconai, hugging the base of the wall, moving inch by inch.

He heard a noise behind him, back at the hole in the wall. He started to glance back but then froze as the xoconai lifted his macana paddle and moved to investigate.

Bahdlahn crouched and held his breath. He wanted to scream. He felt his sweat, felt the tiny trembles shooting through his body.

The soldier wasn't more than a step away!

Bahdlahn was shocked that he hadn't been noticed. Perhaps he was thought to be just a mound of grass at the base of the wall, or a human corpse, someone killed in the attack on the city.

That last notion brought him anger, and that anger brought him courage. Bahdlahn leaped up right before the startled xoconai, and before the enemy could lift his macana, Bahdlahn grabbed him by the edge of the rolls of his strange wooden breastplate and flung him with all of his great strength to the right, smashing him face-first into the wall.

As the stunned warrior bounced back from the impact, Bahdlahn slugged him with a powerful hooking uppercut, catching him right under the chin, lifting him into the air, and sending him flying back and to the ground.

Bahdlahn fell upon him in a heartbeat, choking and squeezing his mouth, pressing with all his weight and all his might to keep the enemy quiet and still. The sentry struggled and managed a squeak, so Bahdlahn grabbed his throat and squeezed.

The xoconai fought wildly, but the man held on. Bahdlahn knew he was choking the life from the man. He didn't want to do that! But if the xoconai called out, they'd all be cut down in short order.

The macana came up hard against Bahdlahn's shoulder, its teeth cutting in superficially. Bahdlahn shifted his considerable weight, putting more of it directly atop the head and shoulders of the sentry.

The xoconai kicked and thrashed.

Bahdlahn squeezed tighter.

The xoconai managed only a couple more stifled gasps and grunts.

Trembling badly, both horrified and exhilarated, caught somewhere between victory and horror, Bahdlahn dropped the limp form to the grass and fell back. He rose, stumbled, and would have fallen, except that Julian was there to catch him.

Bahdlahn wanted to scream, to cry, to shout in denial.

But mostly, to cry.

He had killed a xoconai. Not a goblin, he knew. Not a monster, he knew.

Julian pulled him away. The others were through the hole in the wall, and Brother Ottavian worked his citrine once more to try to cover the breach as best he could.

A pair of knights hoisted the dead sentry and off the troupe went, into the night, across the fields north of Palmaris, with the monks guiding them by using the farseeing quartz crystal and shielding them with the shrouding darkness of their magical diamonds.

The sun rose on the conquered city of Palmaris. Xoconai columns roamed the streets, ordering the citizens out of their homes, sometimes pulling them out of their homes, directing them into the streets to hear the demands of their conquerors and to learn the new reality of Palmaris.

On a high platform built on the enormous square outside of St. Precious monastery, High Priest Pixquicauh addressed them all, his voice echoed by callers set strategically throughout the city, assuring them that the fighting was over.

"We are not unmerciful," he told them. "We come with the word of Glorious Gold—you will learn the beauty of our god, the true god, Scathmizzane."

He motioned, and the xoconai ranks below moved back, revealing King Midalis dan Ursal, stripped to the waist and bound to a large pole that had been set deep into the ground among the cobblestones.

A thousand gasps echoed around St. Precious Square.

"Look up at me, Midalis," Pixquicauh ordered, and when the battered and broken man didn't immediately respond, a xoconai warrior stepped over and yanked his head back.

"Pledge undying fealty to Glorious Gold," Pixquicauh demanded.

"I pledge that I will not raise arms against—" Midalis began.

"Fealty! Name Scathmizzane as the one true god. Your god!"

Midalis stared up at him in obvious confusion.

Tuolonatl walked over and dismissed the soldier, forcing him away.

"Fealty!" Pixquicauh called down.

Tuolonatl moved before the king. "You know what you must do," she said quietly.

"I cannot," Midalis told her. "I hold faith in the teachings of Blessed Abelle."

"And you would rather die than renounce your faith," Tuolonatl said. "Yes, I know this and understand this, and even applaud this. But this is no longer about you."

"You are defeated," Pixquicauh called from above. "Pledge your undying fealty, indeed your love, to Glorious Gold!"

"No," Midalis called back, and Pixquicauh mocked him with laughter.

And Tuolonatl sighed.

"Then I will murder before you every human in this city," the high priest replied. "Each day. Every day, until they are all dead."

The crowd shuddered as one, wails and cries and shouts of protest rising, the whole thing threatening to explode.

"He is not bluffing," Tuolonatl explained. "If any now about this area try to revolt, the blood will be deep enough to cover your bare feet."

"Fealty!" Pixquicauh yelled.

Of all the awful moments of King Midalis's life, this was the worst. Even the Battle of St.-Mere-Abelle, where thousands had lain dead, paled beside the man's current turmoil.

"This is not about you," Tuolonatl told him again.

She might as well have added that Midalis's fate was already sealed in any case, and he knew as much, of course. His mind whirled, trying to suppress the fear, trying to determine the righteous course and the correct course, which seemed disparate paths indeed. Which would be the better course?

"Bring forth—" Pixquicauh started to order, moving to the front of the platform.

"I pledge!" King Midalis shouted, and he called out, too, for his warriors, for his citizens, to hold back, to hold calm.

The high priest paused and turned that hideous skull face upon Midalis once more.

"You pledge fealty?"

"Yes."

"You pledge your obedience to the xoconai, who have claimed this city as their own?"

"Yes," he said through gritted teeth—for that was the only way he could stop them from chattering.

"You pledge your love to Glorious Gold?"

The utterly defeated, utterly broken man slumped then to the limit of his bindings and quietly replied, "Yes."

"Good! Then you accept his judgment!" Pixquicauh announced. This time, he did not ask.

Time seemed to both slow down and speed up for Midalis at that terrible moment. The woman who had come to him to quietly speak with him, the great xoconai warrior named Tuolonatl, offered him a last nod, even a look of respect, then turned and walked away. A bunch of xoconai men dressed in robes swiftly moved past her and formed a circle about him.

As one, they lifted sheets of polished gold, like large shields, before them.

Up on the platform, another augur lifted a smaller sheet, holding it high and turning it to catch the morning sunlight and then reflect that beam down at the circle of augurs.

Midalis grimaced in pain as soon as the light hit the golden shields and was magnified a hundred times over in a brilliant glare that stole all other images.

The augurs began to chant and, as one, took a small step forward.

The heat intensified.

Another step. Midalis cried out in pain.

Another step, and another, and then more slowly, until the golden shields formed a solid circle about the king, and within that ring there was only light, blindingly bright, a singular white image.

And within that ring there came a singular sound: the screams of a man melting alive.

And then . . . silence, perfect silence, all about the square.

Up on the platform, the augur lowered his golden mirror. The circle of augurs moved away.

Where King Midalis had been, there was now only a crumble of blackened bones, piled in a puddle of black liquid.

"Will any choose to join him now?" Pixquicauh cried. "No? Then kneel, one and all, to the power of Glorious Gold!"

Tears and screams and shouted protests gradually gave way, the massive gathering falling to their knees.

Not all, though, the high priest saw from his high perch. "Bend the knee to Glorious Gold," he called down one last time.

More lowered. A few did not.

Pixquicauh motioned to Tuolonatl, and she sent forth her mundunugu.

The defiant humans were brought forth, one by one, and were tied to the pole, which had survived the fiery light.

The augurs repeated their gruesome ritual.

It went on for a long while, and even those taken who changed their minds were offered no reprieve. When it was done, the pile of bones at the base of the pole could be counted only by the thirteen distinct skulls.

"Go forth to your homes and your work," the high priest told the gathering, and the echoing augurs told the rest of the city. "You are the servants of Glorious Gold now, the servants of the xoconai. We are merciful masters—to those who obey.

"But know this, without any doubt," he cried more loudly.

"Know that we will kill a hundred of you for every xoconai who is assaulted."

The crowd dispersed. The sun climbed higher in the sky, a clear day.

But to the folk of Palmaris, the darkest day of all.

19

IXCHEL

Was it a dream?

Aoleyn sat comfortably, legs crossed under her, on the floor of her darkened room in St.-Mere-Abelle. She looked down at her hand and slowly unfolded her fingers to reveal two large gemstones, a chrysoberyl and a quartz.

She had requested them from Father Abbot Braumin, and he not only had complied but had given her the finest of each gem available in the monastery—likely the finest in the entire Abellican collection. He had offered her a magnificent wedstone as well, but after examining the one she kept on the chain about her waist, the father abbot had simply laughed and shaken his head, certain that he could not improve upon it.

Aoleyn had used this combination on a hunch and had found a beautiful intermingling in their magical songs. The wedstone freed her spirit from her corporeal form. The chrysoberyl protected her from the temptations of possession and from anyone else possessing her.

And the quartz, the gem of farseeing . . . With it, Aoleyn

had found the distances eliminated. She didn't fly free
across the landscape of the world in her spiritual form, as
usual. Instead, she merely thought of a place—Ursal, Appleby, even Fireach Speuer—and she was there, glimpsing,
hearing, feeling the wind.

Or was she? Was it but a dream?

The woman closed her eyes and focused on that experience, solidifying the details, replaying them, clarifying
them, committing them fully to her memory. So many things
had come at her, so fast, that she hadn't found a moment to
digest the connections among the images, the sounds, the
places.

She sent her thoughts, her spirit, north over the sea and
saw the ragtag collection of boats hugging the coast, desperate people trying to get away, to get anywhere. She felt their
thirst and hunger, the burns and blisters on their skin from
days in the sun on the open water. She knew that many, most
perhaps, would die.

She saw Palmaris, broken, with xoconai soldiers all about.
In the large square, a line of men and women marched in
shackles. One by one they were judged, and most were tied
to a pole set in the middle of the wide square, surrounded by
xoconai priests—augurs, they called them—carrying shining golden shields. A wide circle at first, but closing, closing,
the light brilliant, the glow opaque.

Aoleyn had heard the screams and felt the pain.

The magical light of the xoconai melted them!

Soon after, almost instantaneously, she stood again in
Ursal. Before her, hundreds of men scrambled to clear the
rubble of the monk's grand structure while others worked
under the direction of xoconai drivers, rebuilding.

She forcefully entered the mind of the leader of the xoconai team there and found an image of his vision. They were
building a temple, a great one like the one that had been
buried under the lake of her homeland.

They weren't leaving, ever.

She went east, following the line of the xoconai army—and how far they had already marched! Far beyond St.-Mere-Abelle, she knew, overrunning every town along the way. And before them trudged the refugees, by the thousands.

Aoleyn took a deep breath and stared down at the gemstones. Was this reality? Had she actually seen these things or was this some manifestation of her fears? Truth or nightmare?

She didn't know, and she feared it was a combination of both. And there was something more, she knew. She had felt it in the deaths she had witnessed in the city called Palmaris. The spirits of those victims had fled immediately, had swept out of the city, heading west, ever west.

Aoleyn remembered what she had seen in the west, the procession of the dead. She remembered the compulsion to join them and go with them and be . . . what?

She rolled the gemstones in her hand, terribly afraid.

Could she trust the chrysoberyl?

She knew that she had to try.

She closed her hand and closed her eyes and fell into the three songs once more.

Aoleyn moved her thoughts and thus her spirit to the west, far west. She saw Appleby and many other towns where life had returned to a new normal and the men and women labored for the benefit of the xoconai. She heard a service, a holy gathering, led by an augur and attended by dozens of xoconai and hundreds of human men, women, and children—so many children!

She cast her sight and spirit much farther and saw the xoconai city on the plateau, which had been under Loch Beag. It was beautiful—she couldn't deny that.

Graceful boats sailed about the vast lake before the place. They were like the uamhas boats she had often seen from Fireach Speuer, except many greater in number and sailing much farther out from shore. Of course, she realized, there was no lake monster lurking beneath the much shallower waters of this wide lake. Aoleyn flitted about the xoconai who were out fishing and dared to slip into the mind of one, then another, just briefly. She moved back to the rim of the great chasm to look down on the city, and now she knew its name: Otontotomi.

And within that massive pyramid in the center of the large city was Scathmizzane, the Glorious Gold. She could feel it. She could sense his presence, his sheer power, one she had felt before.

They called him a god.

Aoleyn knew better, and so she was afraid.

She turned away from Otontotomi. She looked up the mountain that had been her home.

She felt the power of the God Crystal.

Aoleyn blinked, fingers squeezing on the chrysoberyl, one running over the quartz.

Then she stood on the edge of another chasm, a smaller ravine atop Fireach Speuer, Craos'a'diad, the Mouth of God.

She stared into the abyss below, a darkness that felt as death but teemed with life—life energy, at least.

Dare she?

She wanted to let go of the song, to wake up back in her corporeal form.

But they needed her. They all needed her.

She fell from the ledge, into the chasm, down, down, among the spirits, and she heard them, she felt them, she felt what had brought them here, for it called to her, too.

The notes of the chrysoberyl sounded stronger in her mind, protecting her, keeping the compelling voices at bay.

But not the voices of those around her—a thousand, ten thousand, whispering, fearful, dead. These were not the people of her homeland, not the Usgar or the uamhas. These were the folk of the Wilderland towns and the eastern kingdom, and these were the xoconai who had fallen in the battles.

She knew that, she felt that, she heard their whispers.

And she learned.

She went to a serene cave far below the chasm and knew that she now was below the sacred lea and the God Crystal. This room, with this pool, was connected to this crystal.

To her surprise—her shock, even—she heard the song of the Coven once more. They were up there still, dancing and singing!

She floated up to the ceiling, to the vein she knew would lead to the God Crystal itself, and there she found a cacophony, a great huddled and teeming mass of spirits being sucked within, and one in particular whom she knew.

Aoleyn understood and was afraid.

Yet, one voice called her forward, asked her to join, to come into the light of Glorious Gold.

She awoke in her chamber in St.-Mere-Abelle with a start and a scream.

The door banged open and Sister Elysant ran in.

"Aoleyn!" she cried, grabbing, hugging the woman, trying to steady her. For Aoleyn was trembling wildly and sweating.

"Aoleyn? Are you all right? Aoleyn?"

Aoleyn slowly turned her head to regard her friend. Her thoughts swirled, a twisting line of images and sounds, whispers and feelings, fear and loathing and temptation.

Temptation? Recognizing that only made Aoleyn's thoughts spin even more.

"He's dead," the witch said, before she even realized she was talking.

"Who?"

"King Midalis is dead," Aoleyn stated with complete confidence.

Brother Thaddius rubbed his weary eyes, which were red and itchy from the candle smoke and the incessant dust of the catacombs. He looked around at the daunting pile of scrolls. The writings from St. Belfour's tomb had led him to the diaries of Brother Gilbert, and the log of the monks who visited those diaries—none in more than two centuries—had shown him the name of Brother Percy Fenne, who had accompanied Belfour in his travels, in his quest to find the xoconai.

That clue had steered him to seek out the signature of Percy Fenne in other logs, contemporary with his search for Brother Gilbert's diaries. He had then searched and searched, discovering references to the writings of several other brothers, but these had brought little but frustration, for they spoke not of the xoconai but of the Belt-and-Buckle Mountains, of towns and settlements, and of the Behrenese and fierce To-gai-ru they might encounter in their travels.

In those many tertiary scrolls and crumbling parchments, Thaddius had found only one more possible lead: a trio of relatively obscure references to "Brother Journey," a moniker given to a second-century monk, Master Ferdinand, who had traveled the desert dunes of Behren, south to the secret Walk of Clouds of the mystics known as the Jhesta tu, and west all the way into, and across, the high tundra of To-gai.

Thaddius rubbed his eyes again, sighed, and looked down at the table before him, at the rolled scrolls on one side, at the pots holding dozens of others, which stuck up like naked tree trunks, neglected and long dead. Only one of the hundreds of scrolls he had perused had given him anything that could prove of value, and that scroll was so decayed that he found little more than cryptic and ambiguous phrases.

He looked at his own writing, cribbed from Ferdinand's many writings.

They eat the dead and from the dead find power.

Run, do not fight, for the god grows stronger with every kill and every death!

Thaddius was fairly certain that these referenced the xo-

conai, but Ferdinand might have been writing about the To-
gai-ru! In all the scrolls, he had so far found only a single
reference that he could tie directly to the race of xoconai:

*What terrifies most about these bright-faced fiends is that
they fight without fear, they die without fear. The xoconai
are the light, their god the right . . . a candle in the darkness . . . the only truth. No other faith, not Samhaist, not
Disciple of Abelle, not Jhesta tu, not Chezhou is acceptable.
We are heathens, one and all, to be given to the giant god
of Glorious Gold.*

The monk looked around at the dusty air, at the gloom
beyond the low arches. He knew that he could spend another
year searching these vast collections. And, in that year, he
might find something of true value or perhaps nothing more
than these same cryptic references, as full of superstition as
of information.

The prospect was daunting.

All that Thaddius knew then was that he needed to go
above, into the realm of light and conversation, before he
lost his mind.

"Well, were you dreaming? Imagining? Were you really
there?" an impatient father abbot grilled Aoleyn, as they say,
in his audience in the deepening gloom of twilight. Beside
Aoleyn, Elysant put her hand on the woman's leg in support.

"I can'no know," Aoleyn admitted. "And to be sure, it
could be both, all three! But I think it true."

"Her tale is sensible," Master Viscenti interjected. "Her
description of Ursal seems true to a cowed city, and Palmaris is more freshly captured."

Father Abbot Braumin stared at Aoleyn hard. She knew
that he was studying her every inflection, every twitch, every look away and look down. She didn't wilt under that
stare, but it was no easy task, for she truly wasn't certain of

the particulars her magical journey had shown to her. She wanted to be more confident, in both tone and reality, as she understood how critical these details might prove to be.

Braumin kept staring at her, but his visage softened. "There is more," he decided. "Child, what do you know?"

Someone began banging on the door. "Father Abbot!" a monk shouted. "Father Abbot! News from the west! Father Abbot!"

Viscenti rushed over to open the door.

"King Midalis is dead," Aoleyn whispered to Father Abbot Braumin. "He was captured and executed in Palmaris a few days ago."

"Father Abbot," a younger monk gasped, huffing and puffing as he ran up to Braumin's desk.

"Brother Thigpen?" he replied.

"King Midalis," the monk stammered. "Word passed from boat to boat, called across the Masur Delaval and all the way to our docks. King Midalis is dead. They murdered him, Father Abbot! He surrendered Palmaris and they made him . . . He pledged loyalty to their god. And they killed him anyway."

Braumin wasn't looking at Brother Thigpen any longer. His stare was drifting over to Aoleyn, who nodded solemnly with every word.

"Go and rest, Aoleyn," Braumin quietly bade her. "We will need you to go forth again, I fear, and many times. The days grow darker."

"The xoconai would say that they grow brighter," Aoleyn replied, and she rose and left with Elysant, back to her room. She was soon fast asleep.

She was awakened by Elysant sometime later, when the night was still dark.

"What?" she asked, her eyes barely open. She tried to rub the weariness from them and then brushed her thick mane of dark hair from her face.

"Flashes in the north, across the field," Elysant explained.

"Master Viscenti asked for you at the wall beside the north gate."

Elysant helped her find her clothes and ushered her out, through the corridors and into the night. They moved straight across the courtyard to the north gate, to find many monks gathered there, peering out. Aoleyn climbed the steps to the parapet and was immediately greeted by sharp flashes in the north, like flickers of lightning.

"Magical," Viscenti said, coming up beside her. "We can sense it with these." He held forth a red garnet, and Aoleyn nodded and tapped the stone hanging on her left earring.

Viscenti held his hand out to the north. "What do you see?"

Aoleyn closed her eyes and summoned the power of the garnet, seeing through it, out to the north. Every flash sang a song to her.

She noted something else, too, some different magic, concentrated and powerful.

"Their magic is not unlike yours," Aoleyn said to Viscenti, when she returned from the garnet trance. "They . . . sing it differently, perhaps, but it is much the same."

"What are the flashes? Graphite lightning?"

Aoleyn shook her head. "I know not the stones, if there are any. It isn't lightning, or maybe it is some form we do not understand. They are bringing in reinforcements, I believe."

The witch looked back to the north, then surprised everyone by sitting down on the wall and fishing a couple of gemstones from her pocket. "Protect me," she told Elysant and Viscenti.

She closed her eyes and focused on the wedstone on her hip, and soon her spirit exited her corporeal body, floating up and over the wall. She heard the song of the quartz, but she didn't need it yet. Instead, she spirit-walked across the dark field, using the song of the chrysoberyl to protect herself and using the garnet as a guide.

She was not surprised to see the flashes coming from

within the loose framework of the pyramids the xoconai had hastily constructed, or to see many more warriors setting their tents outside of those pyramids.

It was the other magic, though, the less familiar magic, that drew the woman.

Her spirit moved through the ranks, then more tentatively past a group she knew to be augurs, the xoconai magic users.

She noted some new construction: high tables with ramps leading down to large cylindrical crystals. Hollow crystals, tubes smoothed inside, teeming with magical energy.

Aoleyn focused. She knew this magic, after all. Some of the spears of the Usgar warriors favored this particularly dull gray stone.

Some movements by the augurs revealed to her that they were suddenly on alert. One called for a sheet of shining gold, and when a warrior hustled up with it, the augur lit a candle and held up before the mirror.

The magical golden sheet focused and intensified that light many times over, creating a brilliant beam.

Aoleyn suddenly felt very vulnerable. She didn't understand this magic, had never seen anything like it, but she suspected that it could transcend the realities of existence, somehow, that it could show these enemy sorcerers her spiritual presence.

Aoleyn flew fast across the field, back for the wall.

A beam of light illuminated the area to the side of her, then swept her way and just past her, but then right back, as if locking on to her form!

She heard the augurs cry out behind her.

Aoleyn used the quartz, then, willing her spirit, blinking her spirit, back to the wall and her body, which she quickly reentered.

"Are you all right, child?" she heard Viscenti saying. She nodded and forced herself back to her feet.

"What have you learned?"

"They will attack," Aoleyn said. "Their warriors arrive

in great numbers." She paused and tried to sort it all out. "And there is more. We mustn't ignore their magic. It is akin to yours, akin to mine own, but there are differences. Be on your guard, all of you, for our enemies are not without tricks."

She paused again and considered the other magic, trying to make sense of the tables and ramps.

"Divine throwers?" she asked, more of herself than the others, as she considered the story Talmadge had told of Ursal's fall.

"The man, Talmadge, spoke of them," said Master Viscenti. "What are they?"

Aoleyn shook her head.

"How do they work? What do they do?"

She shook her head again, unsure.

"Catapults?" Viscenti pressed.

"I do not know what that is."

Viscenti pointed to the top of a nearby tower, to a war machine with a long arm suspended between triangular towers.

"They throw rocks," Viscenti explained. "A very long way."

Aoleyn nodded. "Perhaps."

The dawn came bright and clear, with the whisper of one word on the lips of every monk.

"Dragon."

Aoleyn and Aydrian left their side-by-side chambers together, rushing out into the courtyard, shielding their eyes from the rising sun with cupped right hands as they stared out at the fields to the north. All about them, monks pointed and rushed, many stumbling around simply because they were so afraid.

And why wouldn't they be? Aoleyn thought, for from the north, swimming in the air, came the serpent dragon, its small wings beating but seeming to do less than its snake-like body, which slithered through the air as if it were still in the depths of Loch Beag.

"Kithkukulikhan," Aoleyn said, and when she noted the gigantic humanoid sitting astride the beast, she added, "Scathmizzane."

"This is how the attack on Ursal began, so said Talmadge," Aydrian reminded, and he called to all the nearby monks, telling them to be ready for a fight.

The dragon swam closer, very high up in the sky, passing right above St.-Mere-Abelle, circling, circling.

"Surveying," Aydrian said, and when Aoleyn looked at him curiously, clearly not understanding the word, he explained. "He is taking note of the battlefield, searching for weaknesses, no doubt."

Aoleyn put her hand up to her left earring and stared into the sky, very quickly staring through the prism of the magical garnet. She noted something, some great concentration of magic, and she knew this magic. She had seen this magic out in the field.

The woman concentrated, trying to piece it all together. Stones of attraction, she knew, which could veer a thrown spear toward a specific piece of metal or could, if reversed, help deflect the swing of a sword.

She thought of the throwers, the ramps.

"No," she said to Aydrian. "No, there is more to it than that." Aoleyn rushed about, this way and that, not knowing where to begin.

"He comes!"

Aoleyn looked up into the sky again to see the dragon diving fast, swooping straight down at the monastery. She watched as Scathmizzane lifted an enormous spear—and she knew that spear to be what she had detected with the garnet.

Kithkukulikhan banked suddenly, breaking the dive, and, in that moment, the Glorious Gold hurled his spear. The huge missile, perhaps twenty feet long, flew down from on high, driving into the side of the main chapel of St.-Mere-Abelle, crashing through the stone wall and sliding in, nearly disappearing inside.

Aoleyn grabbed her garnet again and demanded the song, and before she even gathered the confirmation of the magic emanating from that spear, she began yelling to Aydrian and to all who would listen, "Get them out! Get them all out of the chapel! Hurry!"

No sooner had she finished than there came a long line of dull thuds, a continual *whomping* sound, from the north.

Monks on the wall shouted and scrambled and Aoleyn turned that way to see the sky filling with a swarm of missiles—not spears but heavy balls of stone.

No, she realized, not stone.

Metal.

Metal flying to the call of that embedded spear!

Aoleyn watched helplessly as the swarm descended, the wide-flying shots coagulating, called together, mostly, by the powerful and godly magic.

No lightning storm had ever brought such thunder. Ball after ball slammed the chapel, some close enough so that a second hit the first as it rebounded from the stone wall. Cracks became open fissures, fissures became a crumbling wall, became a collapsing roof, became a rushing cloud of dust.

Before Aoleyn could question anything, Aydrian grabbed her by the arm and hauled her off to the north, running so fast that she nearly lost her footing—and would have fallen, except that the powerful man held her up.

She tried to call out, to ask him what he knew, but just grunted and stumbled some more.

"They come! They come!" cried the brothers at the northern gate. "To arms!"

"The wall," Aydrian said to her. "Remember what Talmadge said about Ursal's wall."

Aoleyn didn't need to remember it. In her spirit-walk, she had seen Ursal's wall, breached and blasted, and now she understood how that had happened.

She put her feet under her, then did better, pulling away from Aydrian and calling upon her moonstone to fly for that northern wall. She watched the sky as she did, following the movements of Scathmizzane, and she was not surprised when he lifted a second huge spear and let fly, right for the northern outer wall, not far to the left of the northern gate.

The missile didn't penetrate the thick wall—but how Aoleyn wished it had!

No time to think of that misfortune, though. The young witch lifted higher, clearing the wall, then dove straight down, falling over the jutting spear. She grasped it and held fast, nearly swooning from the mighty notes of Scathmizzane's song.

The magic teemed. Aoleyn called to it, demanded of it.

This stone, the lodestone, could attract.

It could also repel.

So she fought its magic with her own, slowing the notes, trying to reverse the notes.

Whomp! Whomp! Whomp! she heard across the field, beyond the war calls of the charging xoconai.

She couldn't do it. She wasn't strong enough.

But then she wasn't alone. Aydrian was there. Master Viscenti was there. A dozen other brothers were there.

"Repel! Repel!" Viscenti shouted to them, all grasping the spear or, if they could not reach, grasping the hand of one who could.

The thumping continued in the north. The sky swarmed with stones, converging on the spear and on the monks, witch, and former king who held it.

The song turned, but the stones flew in.

Aoleyn gathered all her strength and screamed into the spear, demanding of it with every piece of magic she could summon. She had never dared to spiritually sing so loudly.

She felt her hand becoming a leopard paw, and her legs, too, broke and twisted into feline form. She felt herself falling, falling, becoming as one with the mighty song.

But she would not relent. She could not fail.

And still it would not be enough, she knew. She pulled out the chrysoberyl the father abbot had given to her, then put her hand over the wedstone on her hip.

Out she went in spiritual form, calling to the Abellican brothers around her, imploring them, guiding them, leading them into the song of Usgar emanating from the magical spear, compelling them to add their voices loud and strong.

The spear thrummed with power, no longer a power of attraction to metal but of repulsion.

Aoleyn returned to her corporeal form and felt as if she was in a bubble—it had all taken but a heartbeat.

A metal-filled stone slammed the wall a dozen feet behind the woman. She flinched but threw more strength into the spear. Another missile fell short and skipped across the grass, and a monk cried out, thinking he was about to be splattered.

But no, the ball hopped and weirdly turned, flying aside.

"More!" Master Viscenti demanded, but he needn't have bothered, for the song grew and grew and grew.

In midair, the flying missiles slowed suddenly and dropped from the sky, short of the mark, some even reversing direction to go bouncing back the way they had come.

Many more hit the wall to either side of the spear, a ringing, resounding, earth-shaking thunder.

But it wasn't concentrated as it had been in Ursal, and the thick wall of St.-Mere-Abelle held strong.

From up above came the reports of lightning bolts, a reminder to those outside that the xoconai fast approached. The monks ran for the gate—sheets of lightning reached out across the field beyond them, covering their retreat.

"Run!" Aydrian told Aoleyn, but instead she lifted from the ground once more, flew to him, and hugged him tightly, then rose up along the wall, coming quickly to the parapet. Aoleyn plopped down upon the ledge, her back to a stone. She wanted to rise and join in the fight, to throw her own fires and lightning, to create sheets of ice, along with the many brothers, but she couldn't even find the strength to stand. She had given everything she had to halt the song of Scathmizzane, to reverse the magic.

"Lizard on the wall!" a monk cried.

"Mine!" Aydrian answered, and rushed away. Not far to the side, Aoleyn heard her friend engaging a xoconai rider, dispatching rider and mount in short order with powerful strokes of his brilliant sword.

She heard the roar of a fireball back the other way, by the gate, and heard the cries of melting xoconai. Lightning flashed and flashed and the wall shook with every thunderbolt, and behind her, out in the field, perhaps on their lizards on the walls, she knew that xoconai were dying.

She closed her eyes and hated the world. Her leopard legs twitched, her leopard arm dropped to her side.

"Aoleyn," she heard, right before her, and she was surprised to see Master Viscenti kneeling there.

"Are you all right, child?" he asked. He lifted her arm and stroked it tenderly.

She managed a nod.

"We win the day," he told her. "They are dead on the field by the score. Most turned back when the wall was not breached."

Aoleyn nodded but hadn't the strength to do more to acknowledge the good news. She felt herself slipping away into unconsciousness.

"How, child? How could you do such . . ." Master Viscenti said, stopping with a stammer, as though he simply couldn't find the words to describe what Aoleyn had managed out there beyond the wall. He cupped her chin, and when she opened her eyes, he added, "You have saved the day, wondrous priestess of the west."

* * *

The catacombs shuddered, streams of dust falling from the ceiling.

Brother Thaddius hunched over the parchment spread open before him, protecting the valuable scroll.

He looked up as the shaking and rumbling continued and wondered what manner of catastrophe befell his brothers up above. He thought he knew, for he, too, had heard Talmadge's tales of Ursal.

The monk closed his eyes, torn. He wanted to go up there and add his power to the defense of St.-Mere-Abelle. He wanted to stand with his brothers, with his friends, to win with them or die with them.

But no, not now.

The shaking stopped. Thaddius waited a few moments, then moved back and pushed the candle back near the parchment. These new finds, contemporaneous to the return of Ferdinand, might prove important, he believed, although the implications of his findings were not yet clear to him at all.

He noted the scorn in the writings of some other brothers regarding Ferdinand's claims, particularly when the monk had spoken highly of this unknown race, the xoconai.

For Ferdinand's writings had seemingly broken a core tenet of Abellican law. Thaddius, who had once followed the teachings of Marcalo De'Unnero, understood this all too well. Ferdinand had thought the xoconai civilized and had spoken highly of their culture, from what he could glean in the writings of Master Allafous.

Ferdinand would give to these pretty goblins a place in our heaven beside St. Abelle, the master had noted in one particularly strong rebuttal. *What demon might they bring beside them, for surely it is demon magic that performs these feats of which he claims?*

"Magic, magic," Thaddius said with a sigh, for he simply

couldn't garner more from this parchment. He looked at the many rolled scrolls piled in the cart beside his desk.

It was all a puzzle, and not just a puzzle of many pieces but one where most of the pieces were broken, with bits that could not be found.

The monk leaned and listened carefully. No more dust was falling. What in the world had brought such thunder to St.-Mere-Abelle?

It had to be the divine throwers Talmadge had told them about, Thaddius decided.

He hoped he would emerge from these catacombs to find the monastery intact and still in Abellican control.

The monk put it out of his mind. His mission was clear. He carefully copied the pertinent lines, then rolled the parchment and resealed it, then went to the side cart to guess which of the many there might help him sort it all out.

Tuolonatl walked among the wounded who had crawled or been carried back to the xoconai line. She watched helplessly as augurs with insufficient bandages tried to stem the blood flowing from garish wounds or tried futilely to clean skin burned by magical fire without wiping the skin itself from the poor warrior.

Little healing magic was available on that field, for the augurs had exhausted themselves in firing the divine throwers.

She found Ataquixt, his arm broken and strapped tightly to his side. He wasn't lying and wailing, though, but sat beside the cot of a young female warrior whose upper chest was badly burned. She was trying to remain calm, and trying harder to draw breath.

"Ixchel?" Tuolonatl said, recognizing the woman, who had been named "Rainbow" because of the purplish lines where her red nose met her blue skin, a rare condition the xoconai called *tzel*.

Ataquixt nodded.

Tuolonatl recalled the battle at the wall. She had seen Ixchel and her cuetzpali scrambling up by the large gate, and now, given the wounds, she realized that she had seen Ixchel fall—though, at the time, she hadn't known the identity of the mundunugu tumbling hard to the grass.

Tuolonatl looked more closely at the woman's injured chest, listened more closely to the raspy breathing. She had seen this before. The burns were not superficial, she knew, and the young woman had to work hard to force her injured muscles to push her breath past her inner scarring. Without divine intervention, magical healing, Tuolonatl was fairly certain that the poor young thing wouldn't survive the night.

"They were ready for us," Ataquixt remarked. "They knew how we would attack and how to defeat it. This will be no easy conquest. Even the throwers failed."

"Attacking a fortress is never an easy task," Tuolonatl replied. "Attacking one full of sorcerers is more difficult still."

"How many did we lose?"

Tuolonatl shrugged. "Three hundred, perhaps, dead on the field. Thrice that number of wounded, and so another three hundred will likely die if the augurs cannot recover their powers and bring magical healing."

"Did we kill a single human?"

"I do not know."

Ataquixt sighed. He turned back to the wounded warrior and laid the hand he had been holding gently down beside her. "I need to find an augur for her," he said, standing and turning to face Tuolonatl. He meant to say more, but then he jerked in surprise, and even fell back a step, the words catching in his throat.

Cued by his expression, Tuolonatl turned about and saw Scathmizzane himself approaching, the god now back to a size still superior to, but more in line with, that of a mortal xoconai. High Priest Pixquicauh came with him.

"Move aside," Tuolonatl whispered to Ataquixt. "I will speak for your wounded friend."

Bowing and backing, Ataquixt retreated.

"My Glorious Gold," Tuolonatl greeted them, bowing low.

Scathmizzane didn't respond, other than to look past her to the gasping woman on the cot.

"Do we know when your priests will again find the power of healing?" Tuolonatl dared to ask—of Pixquicauh, not Scathmizzane. "Many more will die, I fear."

"Like this one?" Scathmizzane asked, moving past the commander.

"Yes," Tuolonatl replied. "Her burns are mortal, I expect."

The Glorious Gold stood up straight and turned to look Tuolonatl straight in the eye.

"What would you pray for me to do, my cochcal?" he asked.

Tuolonatl shifted nervously from foot to foot and cast down her gaze. "She is young and a fine mundunugu," she began quietly. "She led the charge into the western towns, and here rode through the lightning to the wall—and got up the wall—and then the fireball exploded, killing her cuetz-pali and throwing her back to the field. Her valor cannot be questioned, though she is barely more than a girl."

"And so?"

"Heal her, Glorious Gold," Tuolonatl said, and she had to swallow hard when those words left her mouth. How dare she ask a god for anything? "Or give to Pixquicauh the power to ease her wounds. She is a valuable mundunugu."

Scathmizzane moved past her to stand over Ixchel. "No doubt you see yourself when you look upon her," he said. He glanced back with a little grin.

Tuolonatl conceded that with a shrug.

Scathmizzane bent low, his face very near to Ixchel's. "Are you afraid to die?" he asked, and Tuolonatl didn't know if he was speaking to her or to Ixchel. "Is it not a blessed thing to die for Glorious Gold? Is that not the highest purpose of my mortal children?"

The wounded woman stared up at him, trembling and sweating, her blue eyes open wide.

Scathmizzane put his hand on Ixchel's face, and Tuolonatl held her breath, thinking her wish granted.

He ran his fingers down over her face, and her breathing quieted immediately and her eyes closed.

Resting comfortably, Tuolonatl thought, for just a moment, but when Scathmizzane stood back up, turned, and walked past her, giving her an unimpeded view, she realized that Ixchel wasn't breathing more easily, that Ixchel wasn't breathing at all.

"It is good to die for Glorious Gold," Scathmizzane said, walking toward some more wounded warriors.

Tuolonatl's jaw dropped open. She wanted to say something, but how could she?

"You failed," Pixquicauh scolded, moving right before her, so near that the confused cochcal stumbled back a step. It took her a moment to get past that shock.

"Failed?" she replied, her voice a whisper.

"You failed. You had the wall but were turned back."

"The wall was not broken," she retorted, regaining her voice and her fortitude. Up came her sharp glare, a look clearly threatening. "Their magic defeated your throwers. You failed."

"We did not fail, and this is good," said Glorious Gold, moving back to tower over the pair. "These are the greatest powers of the children of Cizinfozza, all together in one place. We know that now. They cannot escape."

"Their power is considerable," Tuolonatl said.

Scathmizzane laughed. "These are the greatest priests of the human kingdom. Almost all of them. Would you have expected less?"

"No, Glorious Gold. But to go against them . . . do we bring in ten thousand more? Twenty thousand? Every macana and mundunugu, and throw our full force against those strong walls? I would counsel against—"

"We will destroy them," Pixquicauh interrupted, moving right beside Tuolonatl and staring through that awful half skull at the woman he so obviously thought of as his rival for the love of Glorious Gold.

"How many would you lose on the field, High Priest?" Tuolonatl answered him, not backing down a bit, not even blinking, as she stared through those dead sockets into the man's eyes. "Half our army? It will be that, perhaps more, and perhaps futilely."

"You doubt?" the high priest shouted in her face.

"You were not there, at the wall," Tuolonatl growled back, in his face. "You did not see them reverse the magic of Glorious Gold's spear to repel your throws. You did not see the sheets—sheets, and not simple bolts!—of their lightning, or feel the heat of their fireballs."

"We will destroy them," Pixquicauh stated quietly, evenly, threateningly.

"In time," said Glorious Gold. "In time."

When Tuolonatl and her counterpart looked back to him, he waved them apart.

Tuolonatl looked past the god and back at the field, at the many dead before St.-Mere-Abelle's gates. "We cannot afford such losses."

"To die for Glorious Gold is the greatest feat of all!" Pixquicauh yelled at her, but his animated response didn't last, as Scathmizzane agreed with Tuolonatl.

"They have nowhere to run," Scathmizzane told them. "Let them have their hole, a prison of their own making—nay, a coffin of their own making. Let them watch the world around them become Tonoloya. They have nowhere to run, and if they come out, we will kill them. Build more pyramids, Pixquicauh. And set more mirrors here on the line holding them. If the children of Cizinfozza come forth from their temple, they will find an army stepping in to defeat them."

"And for now?" Tuolonatl dared to ask.

"Let us go and watch the sun rise from the eastern beaches of Tonoloya."

Tuolonatl almost reflexively replied that there were no eastern beaches of Tonoloya.

But that was the whole point, was it not?

20

SECRET OF THE GOD CRYSTAL

Bahdlahn and Julian emerged from the ramshackle building in the western section of Palmaris with the sun setting before them. Summer was nearing its end, the days growing shorter.

The two moved apart, one going north, the other south, moving shadow to shadow and making sure that no xoconai were about.

As they expected, there were none. The city had grown quiet in the last few weeks, and the conquerors had concentrated about the docks and the massive rebuilding project in the square of the ruined St. Precious. In this most remote section of town, where the buildings were lower, the folk poorer, the few xoconai about mostly patrolled the wall, making sure that the city didn't bleed needed servants.

With summer ending, though, and only the wilds out to the west, where would the folk run?

Bahdlahn waited at the edge of one winding lane, studying the shadows, looking for movement. Julian soon joined him, and the two made their way, leapfrogging from house corner to house corner, making their way east and keeping near the north wall. At a building directly north of St. Precious square, they paused, then slipped fast down an alleyway and through a concealed door that led them into a crawl space beneath a stone house.

Julian closed the door behind them and paused there, listening, while Bahdlahn silently counted the passing heartbeats.

They knew just how long it would take the xoconai lizard riders to move past this place far enough for them to slip out.

On Bahdlahn's nod, Julian quietly and carefully opened the door. He peered left and right, then went out fast, Bahdlahn close behind. Two houses down, they saw a candle in the window, just the signal for which they had hoped, and they went to the front door and pushed through without hesitation.

Their host, a woman named Cathilda, had bowls of stew set out for them, two extra places at her table, opposite the two plates she set for her teenage daughter and son. Her own setting was at the north end of the table, to Bahdlahn's right, and opposite that, at the far end, was another setting, the bowl empty.

"Donovan is at Saint Precious?" Julian asked, when they were all seated.

"Every day until long into the night," Cathilda replied. "I been luckier, working the wall. The sidhe want all of us away from the wall long before the sunlight fades."

"We don't work long hours," said the daughter, whom Bahdlahn thought to be about fifteen years old, her brother two or three years her junior.

"I feed the lizards," the son said, smiling.

"Should poison them," the daughter said.

Bahdlahn stared long and hard at the two. They weren't being badly abused, clearly, if at all, and despite all that had happened, the children (though surely not the mother) had retained their ability to smile. That was something, at least, he thought.

As soon as they had finished eating, Cathilda told her children to clear the settings and go to the bedroom, a back section of the main hall, walled by a blanket.

"What does your friend know?" Julian asked, as soon as they were gone.

"Which friend?"

"Your cooking friend," the Allheart Knight explained. They never used names of the contacts, in case Julian or Bahdlahn were caught.

"He's knowing that the meals he's making are fewer," Cathilda replied.

"Good news, then," said Bahdlahn.

"Aye, there's less of the bright-faced devils," Cathilda said. "But not all's good news. More o' their priests're here. They're building more o' those mirrors so they can bring in all the fighters they need, fast."

"So, if we're to hit them, it'll have to be a quick attack and retreat," Julian said.

"Aye, and then they'll start killing ten for every one you hurt."

Julian nodded. "Not yet," he agreed. "We'll soon know the name of every sidhe in Palmaris. We know their every patrol route, and know the new ones before they even implement them."

"What we'll need to learn is how to shut down their priests and those mirrors," Bahdlahn said, and Julian nodded.

"You heard of the attacks on Saint-Mere-Abelle?" Cathilda said.

"A bit," said Julian.

"The sidhe've been going at the walls, and they've been knocked back. Lots of the bright-faced devils killed," Cathilda said. "A dragon showed up, but . . . I hear they've stopped trying to get in."

"A siege?" asked Julian. "They'll never take the monastery. The tunnels are endless below, with chambers full of water and fish."

Cathilda pushed her chair back, rose slowly, her back obviously stiff from the long hours of work, and moved to the side of the room. From between a pair of boards, she produced a parchment, then brought it back to Julian.

"You know how much for each sidhe," she said, giving it over. "Here's the total they're cooking each day."

Julian glanced at the numbers and meals listed on the page, turning the parchment so Bahdlahn could see.

"Seems that more and more have left," Bahdlahn said, though he wasn't sure, since he didn't know how to read and had only a rudimentary grasp of the numbering system of this strange land.

"Could be ships moving back and forth to Palmaris," Julian warned. "The number of enemies here could rise quickly with a couple of ships."

"More likely shows how many o' them have marched out to the east," Cathilda interjected. "They're a long way across Honce, so say the whispers."

Julian nodded, but didn't seem convinced, Bahdlahn noted, and he understood. They didn't know how many xoconai would continue to filter into this kingdom, after all, particularly since these magical golden sheets in the pyramids allowed them to cover such distances so quickly.

Julian nodded at Cathilda, then pushed back from the table, rising and grabbing his dark cloak. Cathilda nodded and motioned to a basket in the corner, to the side of the door.

The two warriors smiled appreciatively. They knew what was in there: food for those in the forests beyond the western wall. The folk of Palmaris were supporting the resistance. Out in those woods, Julian and his fellow Allhearts (which, to him, included Bahdlahn) and the Abellican monks were assembling a fairly cohesive and powerful force. They hadn't struck, and wouldn't strike, anywhere within Palmaris yet, for fear of retribution, but they had already launched a couple of raids in the south, hitting sidhe patrols and even taking down one of the pyramids. They had buried the golden mirror in the forest and had captured one of the sidhe priests, though the zealot had killed himself by breaking free and leaping from a cliff.

They had also found some refugees, several bands, some from Palmaris, some from Ursal, some from smaller towns scattered about in the southwest.

The two left Cathilda's house and crept along now familiar avenues and alleyways, coming to the wall. They removed some bricks at the base of a nearby building, crept beneath it, carefully replaced the bricks, then crawled down into a tunnel they and their allies had dug, which took them far out from the city's northern wall.

Bahdlahn climbed out from beneath a wide-spreading oak tree, behind Julian, and there he paused, looking back at the city. For many nights after the invasion, Palmaris had seemed a dead thing to Bahdlahn, the only sounds being the occasional cries of fear and pain as the townsfolk were rooted from hiding places. Now, though, much had already returned to a state of new normalcy. Candles burned in windows and towers, torches marked the xoconai patrols, and a general glow showed the presence of the city from a long way away.

And out here in the forest, Julian of the Evergreen was quietly building an army.

"You haven't won, *deamhain*," Bahdlahn whispered into the night, and he followed his friend into the forest.

"No, they haven't," Julian agreed.

"And they haven't won that great fortress you spoke of, Saint-Mere-Abelle," said Bahdlahn.

"Of course not! And they never will."

"Then why were you troubled? I saw the cloud pass over your face when Cathilda spoke of the place. What troubled you?"

"Her reference reminded me of the tasks King Midalis put upon me. He asked me to go out and tell them."

"You have sent many couriers."

"Yes, but he tasked me. He even asked me to find his wife."

"Do you think it is time for you to go?" Bahdlahn didn't try to hide the incredulity in his voice.

"I cannot. Not now. Our work here is important. We're saving lives and making great gains—perhaps even enough so that we will be able to retake Palmaris when winter falls heavy on the land. Their numbers here are thin, too thin to hold Palmaris. If we can isolate them from reinforcements, there is hope."

"There is always hope," Bahdlahn replied with a smile. He, too, let his thoughts go out, not in search of the missing queen but for his lost friends. He was confident now that he had made the correct choice in turning away from the departing boat, in staying here to carry on the fight.

He hoped that Talmadge, Khotai, and particularly Catriona were well, wherever they might be.

And most of all, Bahdlahn hoped that Aoleyn was well.

Connebragh came down the mountainside quickly, using a crystal full of green flecks and stones to lighten her step, and another, a cat's eye agate, to see more clearly in the starlit night. She knew she was being a bit reckless here, moving quite fast and floating more than walking. Fireach Speuer was full of unexpected drops and hidden ravines—if she went over such a drop, would she have enough magical power to lessen the fall enough to avoid serious injury?

Even with those doubts, though, the woman would not slow. She had gone to the crystal caverns and had finally found the entrance, which was hidden by powerful illusions. Full of anticipation and hope, Connebragh had gone into the tunnels, hoping to find many crystals humming the many

songs of Usgar. Surely such additional magic would greatly
help her and her two companions as they continued to exist
on the edge of the great city that had been revealed beneath
the waves of Loch Beag.

Indeed, Connebragh had taken several crystals, but from
the moment she had entered the caverns, a great unease
had come over her, and as she had moved deeper into the
darkness beneath the mountain, she had found an unnatural
chill, a breeze of whispers and mourning.

The cavern was haunted, full of ghosts, and so she had
fled, terrified.

As she had rounded the western spurs of the high mountain, she had heard the song of the Coven, the voices familiar but now singing unfamiliar songs, and it had occurred to
her that they were calling to the dead.

Connebragh didn't know how she knew that, but she did.

Or maybe she didn't and it was just her terror playing on
her sensibilities.

Either way, the woman had no intention of spending a
heartbeat more than necessary up here on the high slopes of
Fireach Speuer, and she vowed with every passing moment
that she would not return.

She finally got down from the slopes to the appointed
meeting place in the tall grasses along the southwestern rim
of the chasm, in what had been a marsh when that chasm
had been Loch Beag.

The camp was there—she found it easily enough—but
her friends were not. Some sticks placed on the ground in
the shape of an arrowhead pointed the way for her.

She moved carefully, studying the ground in front of her
before every step. Many snakes lived in here—some poison-
ous, some giant constrictors, and some, the deadly, white-
furred variety, a bit of both. Giant, aggressive lizards, too,
nested in the tall grasses.

Connebragh breathed a bit easier and moved a bit faster

when she came to more open ground off to the north. She nodded, for she knew where they had gone now, and she picked up her pace even more, soon coming to a small ridge. Atop that ridge, standing amid the brush and trees, she noted two forms, Asba and Tamilee.

Connebragh moved up beside them but, before she spoke her greeting, the view before her caught her attention. Large fires burned down in the city far below.

"Bonfires," Tamilee said. "There is some ceremony."

Before she could respond, Connebragh heard a chorus of voices loud in song, for just a few moments.

"What is going on?" she asked.

"Nothing good," said Asba.

"The Usgar witches are in a frenzy of song and dance up above," Connebragh told them.

The song grew louder once more as a line of torches came forth from the huge pyramid that centered the city, and, in the glow, it seemed as if the areas before that great structure teemed with people.

"Can you look down there?" Asba asked.

Connebragh nodded hesitantly, though neither of her friends noted it. She could look down there with a magic crystal, but she didn't want to.

"Can you?" Asba asked more sharply, turning to regard her.

Connebragh nodded again, more committedly, and began fishing about her bag of crystals until she found the one full of quartz. Slowly, her hand shaking, she lifted it up before her eyes and began to sing softly.

She saw the bonfire reflected in the crystal shaft, tiny and far away, but as her song continued, that fire grew in her vision, larger and larger. She looked through and might as well have been there among the masses for a few fleeting moments—enough time for her to understand what was happening in the conquerors' city. Enough time for her to see the poor humans, children among them, being struck with those toothy paddles, over and over.

Long enough for her to see the blood. The screams filled the night—Connebragh's crystal didn't help her hear that, but she didn't need it.

"What is happening?" Asba demanded, shaking her.

Connebragh lowered the crystal and reached back to the man to steady herself. "They're killing the uamhas . . . the lake folk," she said, barely able to get the words out for her gasping. "Many. Hundreds . . ."

Connebragh straightened suddenly and looked up the mountainside, toward the area she knew to contain the sacred lea and the God Crystal.

The witches were calling the spirits of the dead. She knew that. They were directing them even as the bright-faced conquerors killed them, summoning them up the mountain and into . . . into Craos'a'diad, she realized, into the caverns below the lea, which already teemed with ghosts.

But why?

In the dusty catacombs beneath St.-Mere-Abelle, Brother Thaddius tempered the exhilaration and self-satisfaction of his expert linguistic puzzle solving with a sobering reflection on the implications he was finding in the ancient texts. These scrolls were not written as they would be contemporaneously—there sometimes were major alterations in the spelling of even familiar words, for example, and often stilted syntax.

But now Thaddius had seen enough, and enough commonality and context, to better decipher. Now he was discovering relevant facts.

This last text he had read named a place, Otontotomi. While Thaddius, of course, wasn't even sure of how to pronounce that name, he expected it sounded much like the name of the xoconai city in the far west referred to by Aoleyn. And as he read on, he found the place referred to as "the great city of golden light," a legend of the xoconai, and a place that was "drowned atop the mountains and buried beneath the sky by rains extreme."

Wouldn't that describe a city drowned under a mountain lake?

Brother Ferdinand had gone farther than To-gai in his travels below the Belt-and-Buckle. Much farther. He hadn't walked, hadn't ridden a mount, hadn't flown through the air with magical moonstones or on the back of a dragon.

"*Heca teotextli*," Thaddius read aloud. How glad he was that Aoleyn had taught him much of the xoconai language.

Brother Ferdinand's claim was that he had walked across the world on a beam of light.

Thaddius thought of the scene outside of St.-Mere-Abelle, of the pyramids flickering with what seemed like lightning.

Was this how the xoconai so quickly and efficiently moved their armies? They had come across the world with such suddenness and in such numbers, impossibly fast.

The monk went back to his reading, struggling with the smudges, the tears, the flowery font, the strange spelling of even common words. He had to decipher this, and quickly, because he believed that there was more here of great importance.

For Ferdinand was also speaking about diamonds, and diamonds created light.

Did the xoconai walk on the light of diamonds?

"The city is . . . quiet tonight," Julian said to Cathilda, when he entered her home and found her sitting alone, her children and a few others they did not know off in the side room.

"Strangely," Bahdlahn added. He and Julian had made their way to Cathilda's house quite easily—too easily. Something was wrong.

"The soldiers were all along the lane this day," the woman replied. "They took many people."

"Took?"

Cathilda shrugged.

"Why are they here?" Julian asked, indicating the other children. "You expected us."

"I thought their grandmother would have arrived for them by now," Cathilda replied. "Their mother did not return from her work. We have a deal: if either—"

Julian's nod told her that she didn't need to continue.

"Where do you think she is?" Bahdlahn asked quietly. "The mother, I mean?"

Another shrug. "She cooks for the priests. Might that they needed more for visitors. I cannot know. The grandmother will come, and very soon. She probably saw you arrive."

Julian and Bahdlahn both glanced uneasily at the door.

"She knows," Cathilda assured them. "She is part of this. More fervently than I."

"And the mother?" Julian asked, and Cathilda nodded.

Julian and Bahdlahn exchanged a look, both jumping when there came a loud rap on the door, two quick knocks, a pause, and then a third.

"That is her," Cathilda said, rushing to the door and cracking it open.

An old, small woman pushed her way into the house. Her face showed the wrinkles of a life lived long and fully. Her eyes didn't sparkle with youth, but neither were they dull with age as they darted about, scanning, taking everything in. She was tiny and hunched, with a long nose hooked by age and thin lips which she licked constantly.

"That them?" she asked.

"Allheart Knights, yes," Cathilda replied.

"Good that ye're here," the old woman said. "There's something foul afoot, and I'm knowing where to find it." She looked to Cathilda, who nodded, then motioned for the men to follow her out into the night.

The old woman moved with surprising speed and vigor, moving through alleyways she obviously knew quite well, even climbing a pile of debris blocking a long and narrow channel. Near the top, she crouched suddenly and looked back at her companions. She put one finger over pursed lips while the other hand waved for them to join her.

Bahdlahn peered over the pile, looking down another lane to the wide square before St. Precious. A large crowd had gathered there, both xoconai and human.

"Hold," Julian ordered Bahdlahn, as the young man started over the top of the pile. "We cannot go out there."

"Bah, but follow," said the old woman, and she pressed past the two, moving down the far side of the pile, skittering across the cross street and into the doorway of another building. From that door, she glanced back and waved the two men to join her.

They moved with all caution and found that the place was empty. From the other side of it, the northern wall, they had a better view of the square—and then they knew.

A xoconai augur danced and chanted and then, every so often, stopped and pointed to someone in the crowd. That person was then dragged out, pulled down to his or her knees, yanked forward over a low beam, then dispatched with a blow, or several blows, to the head.

"Is this our doing?" Bahdlahn gasped. "Retribution for our successes?"

"I don't—" Julian started to reply.

"So what if it is?" the old woman snarled, and both men looked at her with surprise.

"They warned the city of retribution," Julian reminded. "We have kept our fighting out of Palmaris for fear of—"

"Bah!" she cut him off. "So what if it is? And so be it, stripe-faced devils!"

From outside came another communal gasp as another execution was carried out.

"We should leave this place and the fields beyond, then, perhaps," said Bahdlahn.

"Bah!" the woman scolded him. "Don't ye dare. Was ye thinking it all to be easy?"

"Old woman," Julian scolded, to which she snarled "Bah!" again. Then, to the shock of both, she produced a dagger from her belt and rushed out through a broken window.

Bahdlahn and Julian ran to the window and noted her charging into the square, then pushing through the crowd. They lost sight of her but noted the jostling of her passing. Out the other side she came, running straight for the augur!

A xoconai intercepted—and got stabbed for his effort!

He fell back, dodging the subsequent wild swings from the old woman, while other soldiers rushed up, stabbing with spears.

The old woman laughed at them, even as their weapons pierced her flesh. "Swive them!" she yelled, her dying words. "Swive them all to demon hell!"

Bahdlahn fell back from the window, gasping.

"There is our answer," Julian said to him, also coming back from the window, then grabbing Bahdlahn's arm and tugging him back the way they had come.

"Back to Cathilda's?" Bahdlahn asked, as they went back over the pile and down the narrow channel.

Julian shook his head. "Not tonight. Let us be quick out of the city."

On they went, building to building, alley to alley, chased by xoconai songs and cheers and the gasps of poor people watching their fellows die.

"What answer?" Bahdlahn demanded, when they had gotten through the wall and back out into the empty night. "Do we go south? North to the Timberlands?"

"Swive them," Julian said to him, grimly and determinedly. "We fight them. We kill them."

"And they will kill us," Bahdlahn said. "Maybe all of us."

Julian stared at him, hard.

Bahdlahn glanced back at Palmaris. "And maybe all of them."

"Then they'd do it anyway," Julian said. "So be it."

Off he went, into the night.

Bahdlahn paused for a long while, looking back and forth from the receding Julian to Palmaris behind him.

He finally nodded and smiled with admiration for the old woman who had given her life for the chance of stabbing one of these merciless conquerors. Yes, he thought, better that than cowering in the quiet darkness until the macana fell, and he hoped that he would die as bravely.

"So be it."

21

HIGH PRIESTESS OF TONOLOYA?

Tuolonatl stood on the field outside a newly conquered town, looking up a long hill of grass and wind-flattened rocks to the retreating crowd of people. Atop that hill sat another human temple. St. Gwendolyn, it was called—or, more completely, St. Gwendolyn-by-the-Sea.

By the sea.

The monastery was built atop a cliff, and behind it was a drop of hundreds of feet to the black stones thrumming under the unceasing crash of waves.

The xoconai had crossed the continent. Before them, in this region called the Mantis Arm, lay the easternmost beaches. Far out beyond the waves, the sun would rise on Tonoloya, then it would climb into the sky, cross thousands of miles, and go behind a different sea on Tonoloya's western beaches.

Greater Tonoloya was right here, before them, ready to be seized.

The woman could feel the stare of angry Pixquicauh behind her—she could hear him chewing his lip behind his xoconai skull condoral. Oh yes, he was mad at her, outraged, because she had held back her mundunugu, who could have ridden their cuetzpali up that hill and caught and slaughtered the fleeing humans.

"Where will they run?" she had told him, to calm his ire. Part of her hesitancy was strategic—hundreds of refugees would put great pressure on the priests within that monastery, and Tuolonatl knew recent history well enough to realize that any advantage they might gain over these magic-wielding priests was worth pursuing.

She was still watching the retreat, the last of the fleeing humans disappearing into the huge structure, which more resembled a castle than the giant fortress they had encountered in the northwest, when she heard the cries behind her announcing the arrival of Scathmizzane and Kithkukulikhan.

The woman warrior grimaced, thinking Glorious Gold would send her army charging for the isolated temple. She had no doubt that she could defeat this one—it was nowhere near the size of St.-Mere-Abelle, and she had fifty thousand warriors on the field here. But the price would likely be disproportionately high if these priests were anywhere near as adept with magic as those they had left trapped in their walls at that other monastery.

She rubbed her chin, turned to Ataquixt and winked, and then climbed up on Pocheoya. She turned the horse about, pacing slowly to join Pixquicauh and the others on the edge of the area being cleared of warriors so that the dragon might land.

Scathmizzane was dismounting even as the dragon touched down, striding immediately toward his high priest and commander and growing smaller with each step, so that by the time he arrived right before the two, he was barely twice the height of an average xoconai, standing just tall enough to stare the mounted Tuolonatl in the eye.

"Many escaped," Pixquicauh told Glorious Gold. "We

could have caught them on the field, but they ran into the temple." He half turned, staring hard at Tuolonatl as he did, and lifted his arm out toward the distant St. Gwendolyn.

"They have nowhere to run," Tuolonatl said. "We can force a full surrender with only a single divine thrower. This temple cannot withstand such a barrage."

"We have no divine throwers here!" the high priest yelled at her.

"Then bring one," she replied, sternly and strongly.

Pixquicauh turned to Scathmizzane. "You have demanded deaths," he said. "Many deaths. A thousand more could now lie dead before us!"

"It is too late," Scathmizzane said.

"Because of her!" Pixquicauh shouted.

Tuolonatl braced herself against the expected ire of Glorious Gold, but, to her surprise, she found Scathmizzane's expression seeming quite calm and content.

"No," he told Pixquicauh. "It is too late for any killed here to offer us their power. Their journey would not be complete in time, in any case. But it matters not. We have enough."

Tuolonatl wasn't quite sure that she understood what he was talking about, but she noted that Pixquicauh apparently did, for while he threw her another sour look, he did seem to relax a bit.

"Can you not feel it?" Scathmizzane told him, told Tuolonatl, told all of the gathered xoconai army, his voice emanating strength, carrying through the air like the roar of a lion on a quiet night.

"The power!" Glorious Gold said, swinging about, striding powerfully, his giant fist clenched in the air. "Do you feel it, my children?"

A huge roar arose, and Tuolonatl noticed that Pixquicauh, too, was cheering wildly.

"What does he mean?" she asked the high priest.

He snorted at her with open derision. "We have killed enough. The crystal is empowered to glorious heights."

When Tuolonatl screwed her face up in confusion at that, he continued, "Why do you think we were told not to use the divine throwers anymore, other than the two volleys to test the strength of the great temple in the northwest? To save the magical power, you ignorant fool. Because now Glorious Gold holds the power."

Tuolonatl still wasn't quite sure that she understood everything going on here, though the pieces were falling together. She stared down hard at Pixquicauh, his claim that they had "killed enough" hanging in her thoughts. The largest battles, Ursal and Palmaris, were long behind them, and in their march east, more had surrendered or fled than had been killed. Indeed, the fights had been few and swift ever since their departure from Palmaris. The most lying dead on any field had been the xoconai killed before the gates of St.-Mere-Abelle.

But rumors had reached her ears of mass executions in the conquered lands.

She shook these thoughts away for the time being, for Glorious Gold approached once more, his smile wide, his giant steps full of energy and life.

"You will incite it," he said to Pixquicauh, and he held forth a triangular chunk of crystal—no, not crystal, Tuolonatl realized, but diamond. A huge prism that appeared to be a solid block of diamond.

Pixquicauh took it and brought it close to his heart.

"Go, my high priest," Scathmizzane ordered. "Go now, before the daylight fades, all the way to Otontotomi."

Both Pixquicauh and Tuolonatl widened their eyes at that. Such a journey would require scores of flash-steps—a hundred and more—and would carry the high priest three thousand miles away!

"Tarry not," Scathmizzane added. "You must be there to catch the sunrise. You must stand atop the great temple and find the first rays of dawn as they land upon the great crystal settled in the heights of Tzatzini."

"Catch them?"

"You will understand. You are the inciter of the triumph of Glorious Gold. None but Pixquicauh is worthy to bring me the dawn. Go."

Pixquicauh scrambled away, moving with his entourage toward a pyramid that was only then being constructed on this latest battlefield. Even with the incomplete structure, they could make the golden mirror work, and he would be on his way.

Tuolonatl sat straight on Pocheoya, trying not to wilt under the gaze of Scathmizzane.

"Tomorrow, when the sun here is halfway to its zenith, you will see the power of Scathmizzane. You will witness the most Glorious Gold."

"I will secure the village," she replied.

"Feed your warriors well. We have one more great battle before us."

"At the temple in the far northwest?"

"No, my servant. That is of no concern. Let the human priests stay huddled in their hold until they die of old age. We'll never let them out, and there is nothing they could do to us even if we did."

"And this temple?"

"You will see."

"Then where is the great battle, Glorious Gold?" she dared to ask.

"In the south, not so far. In a city the humans call Entel. When Entel falls, we will realize the completion of Greater Tonoloya. We will own the heartland sea to sea, the Kingdom of the Xoconai, the Kingdom of Light, the World of Glorious Gold!"

He turned and walked away, back to his dragon. Tuolonatl should have been comforted, for he hadn't scolded her for her act of mercy in allowing the retreat of the villagers—or for anything at all.

But she wasn't comforted. For some reason she didn't

quite understand, Tuolonatl was fearful of what the morning
would bring, of the power she would witness, and what that
power might do.

Aoleyn moved into the nave of the largest belowground
chapel of St.-Mere-Abelle. Many of the monks were in
there—this was the place Father Abbot Braumin had determined would be the gathering hall for those who would
spirit-walk from the monastery to gather information about
the lands.

Something was wrong, the young witch knew immediately. Very wrong.

She found the father abbot surrounded by some masters,
including Viscenti, who noted her approach and waved at
her to hurry over. To the side came Aydrian, as well, looking
very concerned.

As Aoleyn neared, she was able to see through the line of
masters, and then she understood. For there sat three brothers, their expressions blank, other monks working furiously
on them with various magical stones.

"Even with the chrysoberyl," Master Viscenti told Aoleyn
and Aydrian.

"What happened?" Aydrian asked.

Aoleyn answered before Viscenti could. "They were
caught by the call of the God Crystal."

"There will be no more spirit-walking," Father Abbot
Braumin said, coming over.

"I can go out," Aoleyn told him. "I have been right to the
cavern beneath the God Crystal. Its call cannot hold me."

The father abbot looked to Aydrian, who shrugged helplessly. "We have little choice, I fear," he responded.

"Perhaps," Father Abbot Braumin agreed. He glanced
back at the lost brothers. One of them had collapsed over
the table, the monks near him shaking their heads. His spirit
had fully deserted him, and he was quite dead.

"Do not go forth," Braumin ordered Aoleyn. "We cannot lose you. Not now."

The woman nodded. She wasn't afraid of going out from this place spiritually. She had been there, in the powerful thrum of the magical crystal, hearing the call in the full-throated song of Scathmizzane. She was not afraid.

But she wouldn't disobey the father abbot.

High Priest Pixquicauh came out before the dawn. The old augur, weary from his previous day of a hundred flash-steps across the breadth of the continent, looked very much his age as he ascended the long stairway leading up to the apex of the great pyramid temple of Otontotomi.

He finally reached the top, standing beside the large golden mirror that Scathmizzane had placed there, and stared out to the east, to the brightening skies. Far back there, he knew, dawn had long come, and fifty thousand xoconai macana and mundunugu stood on the field before the human temple built beside the eastern sea, prepared to witness the ultimate glory of Glorious Gold.

Tuolonatl was there. She would see it.

Pixquicauh winced. He reminded himself that he was inciting this most powerful act of Scathmizzane, and he tried to hold on to that, to suppress his envy that she, and not he, would actually witness the direct result.

The old augur turned to the south, toward the dark stones of Tzatzini, but he paused as he did so, noting some swirling brightness within the golden mirror. Tears flowed from Pixquicauh's eyes as the image brightened and became clear to him. There stood Scathmizzane, twice the height of a xoconai, holding a triangular diamond prism similar to the one Pixquicauh now carried. The whole scene came into focus, a gift from Glorious Gold. Pixquicauh saw his god, saw the dragon, saw the human temple up the hill from them. Beyond that temple, halfway up the eastern sky, was the sun, and now that orb had climbed far enough for the very tip of Tzatzini to limn with silver light.

A song came to the high priest's ears, the human witches beginning their dance about the God Crystal high on the mountain. The winds must have been favorable, he thought, for how could he hear them from so far away?

He shook his head. This was no trick of the wind. He was hearing them because Glorious Gold wanted him to hear them.

Pixquicauh lifted the prism in both hands, above his head.

The dawn's light crept down the highest peaks, and when it fell upon the human witches, the God Crystal flared with brilliant power and the prism vibrated and called to it.

A narrow and intense beam of light shot down from the mountain, striking the prism before Pixquicauh even realized its existence. From the prism, it arched up into the sky, no longer a singular beam of light. Rather, it was a brilliant, shining rainbow lifting out to the east, all the way to the east, to be caught, Pixquicauh saw just an eyeblink later, by the prism held high by Scathmizzane!

"Glorious Gold!" he cried, feeling the beauty and the power.

"Do you feel that?" Aoleyn asked Aydrian and Father Abbot Braumin. The three of them were out walking the walls of St.-Mere-Abelle on that cloudless late summer morning.

The other two looked at her curiously. She closed her eyes, focusing on the feeling. Her right hand went to the wedstone on her hip, her left into a pouch and to the borrowed chrysoberyl. She didn't call on that second gem quite yet, though. Instead, she fell within herself, into the realm of the spirit, but did not walk out of her corporeal form.

She heard it from the west, a unified cry of abject horror, thousands and thousands of voices shrieking in the final moment of existence itself. No, not voices, but pure energy—she was hearing, or feeling, the last cry of pure energy.

Energy of human and xoconai.

Shocked, Aoleyn let go of the wedstone connection and blinked her physical eyes open. She started to respond to her companions but found them gawking, staring off to the west. Following that, she saw it: a great rainbow, moving swiftly across the sky, though not instantly, as she would have expected.

Because this wasn't just color and light, she knew.

"I have to go," she told Aydrian and Braumin. "Now."

"Go?" Aydrian asked.

"Spirit-walking?" the father abbot asked at the same time, his voice clearly more distressed than Aydrian's.

Aoleyn didn't bother to respond. She now grasped the quartz with the chrysoberyl and fell fast into the wedstone, quickly freeing herself from her body and chasing the rainbow, the leading edge of which was now far to the east, diving over the horizon.

With the far-sight of the quartz, she soon saw the truth, soon saw him.

Scathmizzane, twice the height of a man, stood before the great xoconai army, facing away, facing up a long stone-and-grass hill topped by an Abellican monastery like St.-Mere-Abelle, with its back atop a high cliff overlooking the sea. The huge xoconai god, or demon, or whatever he was, held aloft a large sparkling stone, catching the rainbow within. Scathmizzane trembled with mounting power, Aoleyn could see, and he began to grow, his jaw shaking as if he was attempting to keep this godlike force within his corporeal frame.

He grew and grew and grew. Twenty feet tall and more—the size he wore when he rode the snakelike dragon that now slithered about the field behind him.

And still he trembled, his form itself blurring, flickering with sparks of magic, it seemed.

Aoleyn had once before seen the light that now shot forth from the sparkling crystal. This was a sharper and tighter beam, but with the same results. It stabbed down from the crystal in Scathmizzane's upraised hands, flashing out over the cliff top to the right, the south, of the monastery.

Scathmizzane turned the angle of his prism, lowering the ray, and when its line touched the cliff top, the grasses burned and the stone itself began to melt and spray.

Loch Beag, the woman thought—and her corporeal form back at St.-Mere-Abelle said, though she didn't realize that.

Down, slowly, came the beam, the ground beneath it roiling and spraying in protest, smoking liquid stone flying into the air.

Lower went the mighty beam of energy, moving nearer to Scathmizzane, then passing before him.

The cliff face rumbled in protest.

Aoleyn moved behind and around Scathmizzane, flying fast to the sea, out over the water. She saw the line of molten stone on the cliff face, the beam cutting through. A chunk of the cliff south of the monastery rumbled, cracked, and fell hundreds of feet to crash on the stones and surf far below. And still the molten line moved along to the north.

Aoleyn understood the inevitable result. It was like Scathmizzane was taking a large spade to cut out a semicircle of the cliff about and beneath the monastery.

With a simple thought to the quartz, the witch flashed back to the field, to find that those inside the doomed structure were figuring out their doom as well. The gates flew open wide and terrified people rushed onto the field, most running north, trying to get ahead of that destructive line of energy, some running south—all running away.

Monks magically took flight from the wall tops, scattering, fleeing in all directions except toward the giant monster.

Aoleyn could hardly force herself to bear witness. She kept trying to calculate how long it would take Scathmizzane to finish his great excavation, and how many of the poor folk would get beyond the doomed region.

It happened faster than she had thought, though, the weakened cliff face trembling, cracking, a massive chunk sliding and breaking apart. The monastery rolled over on itself, the whole of it—a gigantic slab of earth and stone and structure and screaming, doomed people—plummeting to the sea.

The giant lowered the sparkling block of diamond. The rainbow simply winked away to nothingness, and all was suddenly silent, so quiet, so eerie.

Aoleyn's spirit lingered on the field. East of her, to the south and north, those who had made it out climbed back to their feet and began running once more. Now the xoconai lizard riders went out, north and south, to catch them, while the bulk of the conquering force began to wildly and thunderously cheer.

The witch didn't know what to think or do. She had seen such power before, when the ray from the God Crystal had breached the mountains to drain Loch Beag, and she knew—she just knew—that the God Crystal had again been source.

She had never imagined that this monster had a method to take that power across the world in such a manner. Her mind whirled at the implications. She tried to fight against the hopelessness.

The field went silent, startling Aoleyn, and it took her a moment to realize that Scathmizzane had called for the quiet, his hand upraised. And now he stood, not so far from her, staring in her direction.

No, staring at *her*. Somehow, the demon god of the xoconai could see her!

"We have a guest!" he said to the xoconai woman standing beside him. That woman followed Scathmizzane's gaze, but whether she, too, could actually see Aoleyn, the witch did not know.

"She who killed Cizinfozza has come to witness our victory," Scathmizzane said loudly, his voice godly, and thousands of eyes turned in Aoleyn's direction. "Behold, my children, she who defeated my enemy and freed Tzatzini for the xoconai!"

They saw her. Aoleyn looked down at herself as panic filled her, for she felt as if she was becoming corporeal once more—not that she was flying back to her form but that, somehow, her form was being brought here, to this field, before this godlike being.

"I do not know if I should devour you or anoint you high priestess of Tonoloya," Scathmizzane said to her.

Aoleyn tore her gaze from him. With all her determination, wrought of the purest desperation, she forced herself to see St.-Mere-Abelle again, to see herself and Aydrian and Father Abbot Braumin. She felt the pull of Scathmizzane, but she fled and fought.

When she arrived back in her body, she was sitting against the parapet. Aydrian and Braumin were very near, each holding a hand, both staring with grave concern.

"Aoleyn?" Aydrian kept asking.

"Are you all right, woman?" Braumin kept asking.

"No," she answered, her voice a whisper. She was still trying to make sense of what she had seen, but what most stood clear to her was the fall of that monastery into the sea far below.

St.-Mere-Abelle was similarly perched on a high cliff.

"We cannot stay here," Aoleyn whispered. "We are all doomed."

22

ON REFLECTIONS OF DIAMOND LIGHT

"Saint Gwendolyn," Father Abbot Braumin said after Aoleyn described the abbey she had seen in her journey.

"Saint Gwendolyn-by-the-Sea," Master Viscenti elaborated.

"It is gone," Aoleyn said. "We cannot stay here." She turned to Aydrian. "It was much like the golden ray that split the mountains, and that rainbow carried it all the way from the crystal atop Fireach Speuer."

"How do you know this?" Aydrian asked, as Master Viscenti echoed, "Fireach Speuer?"

"I know," said Aoleyn. "And I know where the power came from, and it is horrible, and Scathmizzane will regain that power and more—enough to do to us here what they did to that temple, that Saint Gwendolyn-by-the-Sea."

"And what did Scathmizzane do?" the father abbot asked.

"He cut off the edge of the cliff, all about and below Saint Gwendolyn. The ground crumbled beneath the place and it fell, all of it fell, to the sea far below."

All of the monks in Braumin's audience hall began talking in excited whispers, more than one yelling a denial.

"You are certain of this?" the father abbot asked.

"I saw it. All of it. I know not how many hundreds died, but I know where they are going now."

"Going?" Master Viscenti asked.

"Their spirits," Braumin Herde explained.

"Fireach Speuer," Aydrian said to Aoleyn, who nodded solemnly.

"To the caves beneath the God Crystal, and so Scathmizzane will find of these spirits his next great power to use, perhaps against us here."

"You underestimate the power of Saint-Mere-Abelle," Father Abbot Braumin said loudly, but Aoleyn recognized that there was little conviction behind the boast.

"We cannot stay here," Aoleyn said again.

"Where would you have us go?" asked Father Abbot Braumin.

Aoleyn looked to Aydrian.

"Fireach Speuer," Aydrian answered.

"You would have us go forth and fight our way across the world?" Braumin asked.

"I do not believe that is what Aoleyn has in mind," said Aydrian, eyeing the woman.

Aoleyn locked his gaze with her own and held it fast. They both understood that they had to get back to the mountain and find some way to shut down the heinous power of the God Crystal.

But how? Aoleyn retired to her room, trying to sort out all that she knew and all that she suspected. She had barely closed the door, though, when there came a loud rapping upon it. She pulled it open to find Aydrian, with word that they had been summoned back to Father Abbot Braumin's chambers.

The masters were gathered there with Braumin and with

another, familiar face. Brother Thaddius looked pale, and when he nodded in recognition of Aoleyn and Aydrian, more than a little dust fell from his hair.

"Brother Thaddius has much to tell us," Father Abbot Braumin greeted the pair. "And much, so it seems, that would agree with your assessment, my dear Aoleyn."

"I found the writings of the man who inspired the man who inspired Saint Belfour to go south and west to try to find the xoconai," Thaddius said. "He speaks of a drowned city."

That perked up Aoleyn and Aydrian, and Thaddius nodded.

"A drowned city he names Otontotomi," the monk confirmed. "He writes that he saw this place. This long-ago monk, Brother Ferdinand, claimed to have traveled great distances on beams of light reflected in golden mirrors. He was not taken seriously by the others, but now that we have seen these mirror chambers in pyramids, how can we doubt?"

Aoleyn and Aydrian rushed over to the table, where Thaddius had spread some old parchments. They meant nothing to Aoleyn, of course, for she couldn't read the language of Honce—couldn't read at all, for that matter—but while she continued to listen to Thaddius, she noticed Aydrian taking a great interest in the lettering on the spread scroll.

Thaddius laid out his full conclusions from his investigation, that the xoconai had indeed been spoken of by the monks in the early days of the Abellican Church. As far as he could tell, though, only this one, Brother Ferdinand, would make the claim that the bright-faced race still survived, and furthermore, that he had walked among them.

"When he returned from his journeys, the other monks thought him mad, or a liar," Thaddius explained. "Many of those who had known Brother Ferdinand when he had set out from Saint-Mere-Abelle were long dead by the time he returned. They had no way to confirm his claims, for they would have had to retrace his steps, across the deserts of

Behren, across the steppes of To-gai, where the fierce To-gai-ru did not often accept guests."

"So they dismissed him," Father Abbot Braumin said. "But it would seem that Brother Ferdinand was not lying. It is amazing that such a large population and sophisticated culture could exist with so little contact for all these centuries."

"We do not travel to the west," Master Viscenti reminded. "What need have we? When are we not occupied in simply holding this kingdom of Honce together?"

"A fine point," the father abbot agreed. "Yet, still, neither did the sidhe . . . the xoconai travel east."

Aoleyn winced at that, just a bit, considering her role in ending that tradition. She had defeated Cizinfozza, who, apparently, had been holding the spirits of the dead in magical chains in order to keep Scathmizzane and his children from crossing the mountains.

Beside her, Aydrian gasped, drawing her attention and that of the others.

"By Saint Abelle," he whispered, his eyes locked upon the scroll. He glanced at Aoleyn and placed his finger on a line of text, running it across as he read aloud, "They eat the dead and from the dead find power."

Aoleyn's black eyes opened wide and she found it hard to breathe.

"What could that mean?" Master Viscenti asked.

Aoleyn hardly heard him, and she didn't listen when the father abbot and some other monks began taking up the debate. There was nothing cryptic about that line to Aoleyn. She knew exactly what it meant, and had seen it up close. She stared at Aydrian, who replied with a slight nod.

"We cannot stay here," Aoleyn said again. "We have to get there. At once."

"Brother Ferdinand hints that the light of diamonds can activate the mirrors," Thaddius told her. "He claimed that he walked on beams of light of his own making."

"This could prove invaluable in countering our enemies all about Honce," Father Abbot Braumin said. "We could move brothers and soldiers where we are least expected, where our enemies are least prepared." His voice trailed off as he studied the three at the table. "You are thinking of riding the light all the way back to the west."

Aydrian nodded. "How can we not? You heard what Aoleyn told us of the fate of Saint Gwendolyn. What then lies in store for Saint-Mere-Abelle?"

"Saint Gwendolyn?" Brother Thaddius asked. "Abbess Victoria?"

"It is gone," Braumin replied. "The cliff cut out from beneath it, dropping it to the sea, so said Aoleyn."

Aoleyn caught Thaddius's stare as he looked over at her, and she nodded. "Many got out," she offered. "Many did not."

"How could they do this?" Thaddius asked, looking to the father abbot, to Aoleyn, to anyone who might offer an answer.

"How did they sunder a mountain range to drain a high lake?" Aydrian replied.

"They eat the dead and from the dead find power," Aoleyn answered.

"We must go," said Aydrian. "We must go at once, seize their mirrors in the field beyond this place, and so begin our journey, pyramid to pyramid." He looked to Father Abbot Braumin.

"It seems reckless," he said, half shaking his head, half nodding. "Are we to charge forth and take the field?"

"Just help us get there," said Aydrian. "I will see Aoleyn through her journey."

"Just you two? Nay, the Abellican Church must—"

"I will go," Brother Thaddius offered. "I beg your leave in this. And Sister Elysant will join me." He looked up at Aydrian and Aoleyn. "We four. We will get there quickly, before our enemies can raise a defense against us."

"And we will stop them before they can do to Saint-Mere-Abelle what they did to Saint Gwendolyn," said Aydrian.

Beside him, Aoleyn nodded, though she had no idea of how they might accomplish such a thing.

She did know, however, that they had to try.

In the darkness they departed, not through the gates, which were surely being monitored, but over the wall, floating down through the magic of malachite, shrouded in darkness through the magic of diamond.

The four friends stayed low to the ground as they crossed the field, Thaddius keeping the darkness thick about them. Aydrian carried Aoleyn, for her vision was elsewhere, the woman using the song of the wedstone, the garnet, and the quartz, the former two to track and direct the movements of her friends, the latter to see their destination: the westernmost pair of pyramids the xoconai had constructed on the field.

They were more than halfway across the field when Thaddius stopped them, then moved ahead of them, taking the globe of darkness with him to shield the other three. Aydrian called to Aoleyn, and she returned to her body, blinking her eyes open as the ranger laid her down on the ground.

Aoleyn rolled over and pulled herself up to her knees, taking in the scene.

"Can you do this?" Aydrian whispered to her.

Aoleyn pulled forth the crystal filled with lodestone and nodded, to inspire confidence in herself as much as in her companion. She had two jobs here, and both seemed daunting.

She focused on the magic of the crystal, finding first the attraction to the metal clips used on the payload back at the monastery, then locating the magnetic pull of the lodestones thick in the distant xoconai divine throwers.

She fell into the song more deeply, exciting the magical energies of the small crystal, feeling the power pull against her grip as it grew in attraction to those distant magical cannons.

Aoleyn angled it high and let it fly simply by letting it go, and off it soared into the darkness. She looked at Aydrian and nodded, confident it would find the divine throwers—confident that it *had* found the divine throwers, when she heard the crack of her missile striking something across the field.

Aoleyn fell into the song of her moonstone, letting it flow fully through her form. She lifted from the ground, facing back toward the monastery, and brought a flicker to the diamond of her belly ring.

Only a heartbeat later, she heard the great creaking and *whooshing* sound, Father Abbot Braumin's promised diversion, launched from the abbey's largest catapult.

Aoleyn spotted the huge missile arching out from over the monastery wall, climbing into the night sky, soaring right above her.

She timed her next spell as she climbed higher into the air and blew forth from her magic a powerful blast of wind, a sudden tempest, just as the giant catapult payload passed above her. The wind caught the extended flaps of the missile, lifting them like wings and lifting the missile itself higher, too, extending its range.

In that jostling, some of the payload, a small mountain of enchanted celestite bits, flew out, sparkling as they tumbled across the dark sky.

Aoleyn turned to follow the huge shot's flight and smiled grimly as she noted the slight shift in the flight path, the metal rushing for the call of her distant lodestone. She and the monks had turned the trick on Scathmizzane—as he had used his enchanted spears to direct the missiles of the divine throwers, so were they now delivering this enchanted bomb into the heart of the xoconai camp!

The huge bundle tumbled and continued to spew celestite bits, each of those particles a miniature bomb all its own.

A cluster of a thousand small sparkles fell from the sky, a thousand tiny fireballs exploding on impact, with a bright flash of fiery light, shaking the ground in an earth-quaking roll of thunder. On and on it went, a thousand flashes, each a killing fireball.

"Go, go, go!" Thaddius told them, and on the ground below, Aoleyn's three friends sprinted for the sudden and violent tumult consuming the enemy camp. Elysant and Aydrian took the lead, Thaddius close behind, Aoleyn flying above them, easily pacing them, particularly since they were running across ground trembling under the barrage of magical explosions. More than once, one or another stumbled.

In the flashes and small fireballs, the woman saw the divine throwers, saw the xoconai tents, many catching fire, saw the enemies themselves, many leaping and slapping at the sharp and painful miniature bombs or at their own smoking clothes.

When she heard a voice calling out against her charging friends, Aoleyn veered off to the west and sped away, flying into the xoconai camp just ahead of her companions. She set down among the divine throwers and stamped her foot hard. The graphite of her anklet sent a rush of lightning out in a widening circle about her, stunning enemies, dropping enemies, throwing some into the air. Grimly satisfied at the destruction all about her, Aoleyn found her crystal lying on the ground beside one damaged thrower. It had served her well, and so she took it up once more and set it into the folds of the cloak the monks had given her.

In charged her friends, Aydrian cutting down a pair of enemies with precise cuts of that magnificent sword, Elysant rolling between a pair, her stone staff working in a blur of strikes and sweeps that soon had the pair tumbling and groaning.

"Take the left!" Thaddius called to Aoleyn and Aydrian, while he and Elysant sped toward the western pyramid on the right.

Aydrian, sword at the ready, rushed before Aoleyn to lead the way into that pyramid, but as they neared it, a group of xoconai came out to intercept them, javelins lifted high. The ranger growled and charged, then pulled up in surprise when Aoleyn, still in the magic of her moonstone, flew right past him, touching down.

The xoconai threw their spears, but Aoleyn threw her magic, dropping the flight and altering the song to let forth another tremendous blast of wind—filling this one with wisps of fire, as she had done to the witches of the Coven on that long-ago day.

Xoconai javelins flipped crazily and scattered back the way they had come, and the warriors, too, flew away, caught by the blast of hot wind and sent tumbling. Some crashed against the front side of the pyramid, a couple rolled and bounced past it, and another pair went rolling into the open door of the structure.

Aydrian went in behind them, sword flashing with such efficiency that Aoleyn found no threat when she came into the pyramid behind him.

"Be quick," he told her.

It wasn't hard for Aoleyn to figure out the instrument the xoconai had erected here, from simple observation and from Thaddius's notes on the writings of Brother Ferdinand. In the center of the pyramid hung a single golden mirror, tightly secured, its shiny side facing west. There was a hole in the pyramid's back wall.

Aydrian moved to face the mirror, just to the side of the hole in the wall, while Aoleyn called upon her diamond.

The witch held her breath—she heard Aydrian do so, as well—when she brought a light to that diamond. A flash in the mirror showed Aydrian's reflection clearly.

And then it didn't.

Aoleyn turned fast, to note the corresponding flash somewhere far to the west, and Aydrian was gone, had simply winked away!

The woman took his place, looked into the mirror, and called upon her diamond again.

Xoconai rushed in, hurling javelins at her, and Aoleyn reflexively closed her eyes and cried out.

But no missiles struck her, and she opened her eyes to see Aydrian standing over another fallen enemy. He had come into this place, this far-distant pyramid, ready to fight—and that was a good thing, it seemed.

The two rushed to the door of the pyramid, glancing about, locating the other pyramids in this second xoconai camp—a camp that was far from the front lines, far from St.-Mere-Abelle, and far from alert.

At the same time that Aoleyn and Aydrian were charging into one of the pyramids outside of St.-Mere-Abelle, their two monk companions were moving quickly to the other.

Thaddius let Elysant lead the way in, while he focused on the gems in his staff, particularly the diamond he would need to facilitate the teleportation. He watched the woman charge in through the opening, then gasped as enemies came at her left and right, an ambush waiting just inside.

Elysant dove into a forward roll and then came up quickly, spinning about, her stone staff sweeping across to drive the attackers back. Thaddius started to yell out to her, noting another figure creeping up at her from the shadows deep within the wood-and-stone structure.

He didn't need to yell, though, and even managed a bit of a grin, as his feisty friend brought her swing up short and pulled the staff back in close, planting the end and using it to vault into the air, throwing herself up horizontally and double-kicking behind her.

She took a hit from a macana, but nothing too serious it seemed. In return, she caught the approaching xoconai solidly with both feet, sending him flying back into the darkness.

How that fighting monk could move! As much as he loved falling into the magic of the Ring Stones, Thaddius wished that he could twist and turn his body with such grace and power.

His thoughts of Elysant disappeared, though, as a lizard-riding xoconai warrior appeared over the angled sides of the pyramid, charging down for the opening. Thaddius wasn't sure he could get in before this new foe, but he had no choice, so he lowered his head and rushed ahead.

Another enemy appeared just inside that opening, leaping forward to grapple with the thin monk. And down came the lizard and its rider.

"Sister!" he yelled, struggling with the xoconai, twisting and wriggling as the warrior tried to grab him about the throat.

Instinctively, desperately, Thaddius called to a different stone in his darkfern staff, tickling the magic, elevating the vibrations.

He got pulled aside from the entrance and lost sight of Elysant, but he heard the scuffling within, the cracking of staff and macana, the grunts of a xoconai apparently struck by the fierce monk, and then the yelp of sudden pain in Elysant's voice.

They weren't going to make it to—They had no way to get through.

Down came the lizard, the rider fast dismounting, diving into a roll that brought her right under Thaddius, taking his legs out from under him. Down he fell, and then the other xoconai warrior was atop him, one hand grasping and twisting the skin of his face, fingers poking for his eye, the other pinching hard on his throat, trying to get the man's windpipe.

Thaddius fought and writhed, one hand knifing up inside the xoconai's grip in an effort to keep the choker at bay. Just one, though, for the monk would not let go of his staff. For all his life, he knew, he could not lose the connection to those gems.

He called still to the second stone, the ruby, and felt the power within it swelling.

"Sis . . . Sister! Run!" he managed to scream, and then he screamed a second time, louder, when a lizard bit him on the shin.

He wanted to wait a bit longer!

Where was Elysant?

Had she gotten far enough away?

The lizard tugged to the side, and the monk lost his leverage. The xoconai upon him sat on him fully and then got both hands about the monk's neck, choking him.

The second enemy came back at him, grabbing at the staff. Thaddius responded by grabbing it with both hands, but that, of course, only allowed the warrior sitting atop him to squeeze harder.

The monk feared that his eyes would simply pop out of his head. Black spots filled his vision, and he felt as if he were falling far, far away.

But he still felt the mounting magic, and he added to it the magic of another Ring Stone, the third set in his staff. He tried calling out for Elysant again, bidding her to flee or to come to him, for if she could get to him, he could extend the protection.

He hadn't the time to wait for an answer, his consciousness falling away.

Brother Thaddius glowed in a white shroud of light. In their surprise, both xoconai let up for a moment, and before they could go back at him fully, a massive fireball blew out from the monk's magical ruby. Flames rolled and swept out from Thaddius, engulfing the two xoconai and the lizard, rushing into the pyramid, lighting the wood, biting the three xoconai within.

And also, he knew, engulfing his dearest friend in the world.

It was over almost as soon as it began, the flames rolling upward and dissipating. About Thaddius, the lizard screeched and thrashed, fully ablaze, the xoconai woman thrashed on the ground, burning, and the man who had been sitting upon him was up and running, flailing his burning arms, screaming awfully.

Thaddius rolled and scrambled for the pyramid opening, gaining his feet, stumbling forward and then back as he saw the burning forms within leaping about in their desperate last movements. He tried to pick out Elysant, hoping he could throw the power of the soul stone into her and save her.

He even started inside, and only stopped when he heard a sudden cracking and groaning sound. He fell back, then felt a burst of hot wind and dust blast him in the face as the pyramid collapsed in on itself.

"Elysant," the poor monk wailed, stumbling back for the wreckage. What could he do? He couldn't begin to shift this rubble, and what point would there be, anyway?

His friend was surely dead.

The howls of other enemies sent Thaddius scrambling, stumbling, limping on his bitten leg. He forced himself into the other pyramid, straight to the golden mirror. With the spark of a diamond, he saw his reflection in the sheet, then saw it fading in a second sheet, one far removed from the screams and the smoke and the smell of burning flesh.

Overwhelmed, the poor monk dropped to the ground. A strong hand caught him before he went down fully, easing him to a sitting position.

"Aydrian," he said.

"Sister Elysant?" asked Aoleyn, from the side.

Brother Thaddius stifled a sob and shook his head.

23

FASTER THAN THE SPIN OF THE WORLD

The trio executed a second flash-step, teleporting farther to the west, and then a third, without incident.

They moved out of that pyramid, creeping for the one with a mirror facing west.

"We're beyond the river," Aydrian whispered, looking to the north and the east, spotting the lights of two cities, which he identified as Amvoy and Palmaris.

The three fell silent suddenly and dropped low to the ground, noting a sudden flicker in the pyramid they had just departed. Out rushed a xoconai woman, another flicker showing behind her.

Out came another, this one on a lizard. Another flicker signaled more arrivals, and the first one out called for this camp to awaken.

Thaddius brought up a darkness globe, and the three melted away to the north, then turned back, staying low, behind cover, to watch the stirring hornets.

Two other pyramids had been constructed in this camp,

one facing south, one west, and those, too, began to flash, this time with xoconai warriors going out.

"They're trying to find us," Aoleyn realized.

"They know that we entered their magical trails back near Saint-Mere-Abelle," Aydrian agreed. "They're chasing us, or trying to surround us, or get ahead of us."

"And now they are," said Thaddius. "And so we'll be fighting with every landing henceforth."

His claims seemed reasonable, and the three looked to each other with great concern. How would they ever get near the Ayamharas Plateau and the God Crystal if the xoconai were already moving to block?

Aoleyn noted Thaddius tapping Aydrian's arm. She followed their gazes back to the south and saw, in the dark distance, flickers of light, like giant magical fireflies, flashing in various locations southeast, directly south, and southwest.

"They are awake to us," Aoleyn agreed.

The sheer number of landing locations surprised all of the companions. The clever xoconai had built an intricate and interconnected transport system here. They could move their brigades with great efficiency to many locations.

"Ursal is down there," Aydrian told them. "If the monks were to mount an attack against the conquered city, our enemies would put armies on the fields all about them, north, south, east, and west."

"Then it's good we're not attacking Ursal," Thaddius quipped.

"They know we're in their magical road," Aoleyn said. "We cannot go on, at least not now."

The weight of that reality hit them all. They had covered hundreds of miles in a few great magical jumps, but they had thousands of miles yet to go.

"I cannot believe how many of these pyramids they have constructed," Thaddius said. "If there are this many all the way back to the west, we might yet find our way through the maze. They cannot concentrate on any one."

"There won't be," Aoleyn said.

"Agreed," said Aydrian. "The xoconai are not foolish. They likely knew that we might begin using their own magic against them, as they have used ours against us. I expect that somewhere in the Wilderlands, likely near Appleby, south of the Barbacan Mountains, there will be only one or two options for us to arrive from the east. And there, in that choke point, we can expect a strong force guarding the golden mirrors."

"Unless we are quick," said Thaddius.

Aydrian shrugged but hardly seemed convinced. Aoleyn was more direct.

"It is already too late," she announced. "The word is spread to Appleby, beyond Appleby. Even as we speak, it is now being relayed in Matinee, and perhaps all the way back to the lake before the sundered mountains."

"Then we are lost," said Thaddius.

The other two didn't reply.

The morning sun over St.-Mere-Abelle found the monastery's walls lined with anxious monks who had witnessed the great cacophony of celestite fireballs the previous night, and then the singular blast, made by Thaddius or Aoleyn, they believed. The anxious brothers did not know the disposition of their assault team.

Across the way, the xoconai camp was astir, collecting their dead, tending to their wounded, assessing the damage to the tents and the divine throwers, and clearing the rubble of the destroyed pyramid.

"Mictazuma," a young mundunugu woman named Amoxt told her companions, when they lifted a heavy block and pulled it aside, revealing a broken and half-burned body.

"I will kill every human I meet," a man said, kneeling beside the body of his dead friend. "I know that Scathmizzane is a god of mercy, but mine is no more."

The others nodded in agreement.

Amoxt moved over and draped a blanket over the fallen Mictazuma, then stepped aside as two others scooped the body in that blanket and carried him from the pyramid's rubble.

"Another there," one of the searchers called out, and Amoxt led the team to what had been the center of the pyramid. The woman winced when she saw the fallen and bent golden sheet, much of it deformed and melted. She noted the outline of a leg, covered in ash, sticking out from under a heavy and charred crossbeam, and motioned for her team to begin the excavation.

Barely had they begun when Amoxt found something interesting to the side. She moved over and picked up the end of a staff, and not just any staff but one made of smooth stone that gleamed in the morning light when she brushed the soot and ash from it.

She looked back at the body, more visible now that some of the fallen stones and beams had already been moved aside.

"A human," she said with a sneer, and it took all of her willpower to not walk over and kick the body.

"A woman," another said, hooking the fallen monk under the arm and pulling her up a bit, mounds of ash falling from her. "She shows no burns."

"They have magic to protect them from their own magical flames," Amoxt reminded. "We have seen that trick before."

"Remarkably intact and unmarred," said another xoconai woman, hooking the other arm and helping to pull the human upright.

"Drag her over there," Amoxt instructed, pointing back behind her to the field beyond the burn scar. "Perhaps we'll cut off her head and stake it, to show the humans their failure."

The other two moved near to Amoxt, who only noticed at the last moment that the woman had opened an eye. She started to call out, but too late, as Sister Elysant, held up by the arms, grasped her bearers and flipped her feet forward, standing straight with suddenness and power. She let go immediately, hands forward, then hands back, chopping at sidhe necks left and right.

A subtle twist and turn of her arms, a wide-legged hop, locking her feet behind the leg of each bearer, and Elysant shoved them both hard and back, tripping them up.

She darted forward, her eyes looking wild and wide in the mask of ash, leaping for Amoxt.

The xoconai raised the stone staff in defense, but the attacking human grasped it and pulled, and leaped above it, snapping her head forward to slam Amoxt in the face, staggering her. Still she tried to hold on, but Elysant dropped, simply pulled her legs out from under her, and twisted as she fell, the rotation pulling the staff free from one of Amoxt's hands.

Elysant threw one leg behind the dazed Amoxt, set the other foot out to the side, and rose fast and hard, driving her elbow into the xoconai's chest, sending her tumbling over that trailing leg. As Amoxt fell, Elysant tugged with all her considerable strength, tearing the staff free. The woman rushed forward, hands going low on the shaft as she swung the staff like a greatsword, up and around, over and down, fending the other two, who now came at her with macanas in hand.

They were shocked and afraid, Elysant saw as they fell back, and confused—and rightly so! For how could she have survived that blast and the tumbling blocks of stone and wood?

Even Elysant didn't know the answer to that, and she wasn't about to question it then. Nay, she took advantage of her enemies' hesitance, bearing forward fiercely, rotating the staff before her in a gaudy, swashbuckling manner, then catching it with her hands shoulder-width apart and thrusting it forward horizontally. She intercepted a macana swing from the woman on her left and slipped over an attempted block by the man to the right, and as soon as her stone staff cleared his block, the agile and veteran warrior, a true disciple of fighting St. Belfour, rolled her right shoulder forward and punched out with all her strength, whacking the xoconai man across the jaw.

She heard the bone crack and figured him out of the fight as he fell away with a pained shriek.

Elysant turned and leaped past him, pulling her staff in close and out to the right, then stabbing it back like a spear to the left to drive back the xoconai woman.

That woman deftly dropped her macana and grabbed the thrusting staff with both hands, a move that would have tied up a lesser warrior, or would have at least forced the human woman, whose time was running short as other xoconai realized the attack, to surrender the staff.

But Elysant went with the pull, leaping forward, reversing her grip with her back hand to drive the staff up vertically. The xoconai's grip then worked against her, with Elysant using that as a brace to lift higher as she leaped into a forward somersault. She plowed into the surprised and off-balance xoconai woman, bowling her over backwards, landing atop her as they crashed down hard on some blocks.

Up sprang Elysant, the staff immediately put into action, swinging and stabbing, driving back the woman she had tripped, then flashing out to the side, stabbing another man in the face.

Sister Elysant felt the blessing of St. Belfour upon her, felt certain that the spirit of the legendary monk would surely approve of this small woman now wearing his robes. How she wished that she had some support here, or that she wasn't alone in the midst of an enemy camp! How she wished she could play this out, confident that she could defeat all four of these enemies.

But no, she had to run. If she wanted any chance of surviving this day, she needed to run.

So she did, gathering her bearings and leaping and sprinting away, across the camp and onto the field, shouts and cries rising all about her.

With heavy hearts and the dreadful suspicion that they had lost any chance to get to the far west quickly, Aydrian, Thaddius, and Aoleyn made their way across the fields, traveling west and keeping the distant line of the Barbacan Mountains as their guide.

They saw the continuing flashes to the south and west, further indication that the xoconai were taking no chances here and were rushing soldiers and information back to the west to protect against an intrusion and, likely, to more fully secure every golden mirror against unwanted use.

"When I was spirit-walking on the field before the doomed monastery, I felt as if I were being pulled there fully to face the xoconai god," Aoleyn mentioned early the next day, while the three were holed up in a shallow cave. "Perhaps there is a combination of stones that will allow me to bring my body to the spirit, a way to travel great distances."

"That was likely the work of the xoconai god," Aydrian replied. "And I was back at your body. It did not diminish or thin or anything else to make us believe that you were actually going there."

"There is a Ring Stone which allows one to travel great distances instantly," Brother Thaddius added. "Emerald. But only the most powerful would work, and they are almost unknown in the world. There are none that I know of in Saint-Mere-Abelle, and many there think the powers of the emerald no more than rumor."

"There are such, and I have seen one," Aydrian suddenly interjected.

"How?" asked Thaddius.

"The elves, the Touel'alfar," said Aydrian. "They possess such a gem."

Thaddius stared at him.

"How do we find them?" Aoleyn asked.

"It will take us a month and more to travel to the region of their hidden vale, and I do not know if they would help us at all. Their valley is guarded with powerful magic."

"Their cousins in the south turned Talmadge away," Thaddius reminded.

"Well, we have to try," said Aoleyn.

"A month?" Thaddius asked. "What will be left of the world in a month? What will be left of Saint-Mere-Abelle in a month?"

Aoleyn held up her hands helplessly.

Aydrian looked to the large soul stone hanging at Aoleyn's hip. "They are ever vigilant," he said. "I can go there, perhaps find them."

Aoleyn lifted the pendant out toward him and nodded. "Give me your hand," she said. "I will use the orange gem to protect your spirit while you travel."

Aydrian took a deep breath and clasped the pendant in one hand, gripped Aoleyn's hand with the other. A powerful gem user in his own right, the former king, the ranger, soon exited his body, his spirit rushing out to the north and west, to the Barbacan and the area he knew to hold Andur'Blough Inninness, the home of the Touel'alfar.

He cast about, running among the trees and across the fields, spiritually calling out for the elves, for Belli'mar Juraviel, who had given him a second chance at life by taking him in after his banishment from Honce-the-Bear.

At one point, he sensed something, some flicker, like a whisper in the spirit realm, but he found nothing substantial and saw no elves.

He returned to his body, exhausted, a long time later, and found Aoleyn still sitting before him, clutching his hand, concentrating.

"Aoleyn?" he asked repeatedly.

The woman blinked open her eyes. "Something," she said. "There is something."

Aydrian looked at her curiously, then both jumped and turned at a sudden cry from Brother Thaddius, who had gone to the entrance of the small cave. The monk fell back inside, fumbling with his pouch of gems.

"Sidhe?" Aydrian asked.

"Hardly that," came a melodic voice from just outside, and a tiny figure, barely waist-high and sporting small, translucent wings that seemed more fitting for a giant dragonfly, walked up to the cave entrance.

"Lord Belli'mar," Aydrian greeted, moving past Thaddius to stand before the leader of the Touel'alfar. "You heard my call."

"I expected it. You are a ranger now, patrolling the western lands. It would have made me reconsider our training methods if you missed an invasion of such scale. I am surprised that you did not come to us sooner."

"You know," said Aoleyn.

"Of course we know." Juraviel smiled at Aydrian. "We have rangers."

"Then you understand why I came to you," said Aydrian. "These enemies, the xoconai, have overrun much of Honce."

"The humans once called them the sidhe," the elf replied, and that set all three of the people in the cave on their heels. "Oh yes, we know them, and know them well. Once, they claimed all the lands about the Barbacan as their own. They were chased back to the far west by the goblins, who followed a demon as powerful as the one infiltrating the xoconai."

"Cizinfozza," Aoleyn breathed.

The elf stared at her curiously, making her uncomfortable.

"Who is this young woman who knows so much?" Juraviel asked.

"She is Aoleyn of the Usgar, a faraway tribe, who lived on a mountain that overlooked a large mountain lake," Aydrian answered.

Juraviel nodded and smiled, and said, "Interesting," under his breath, giving the three onlookers the distinct impression that he knew all about Loch Beag and what lay under it.

"We need your help," Aydrian implored the elf. "We need to send word to the Timberlands, to Vanguard, to Alpinador, and Behren. We need to tell Brynn Dharielle, that she can summon her dragon. The fate of the world—"

"The fate of Honce-the-Bear," Juraviel corrected, and Aydrian paused and looked at him curiously.

"Honce-the-Bear, then," the ranger agreed. "Its fate hangs in the balance."

"That is no concern of the Touel'alfar."

"How can you say that? Thousands have died. Thousands *will* die!"

"And thousands of xoconai will perish if the tide turns. Do you think the human kings will be less likely to march all the way to the western ocean when they learn of the xoconai riches? No, my old friend, son of my dearest human friends, this is no more a fight for the Touel'alfar than would be a battle between Behren and Honce-the-Bear."

"But these enemies are not humans," Thaddius remarked.

Belli'mar Juraviel shrugged as if that hardly mattered. "Are they lesser?"

That simple question brought a long moment of numbed silence.

"You intervened in the civil war of which I was a part," Aydrian argued.

"You, the child of our ranger and thus our responsibility, were demon-touched. We intervened only because of that, because it involved a demon dactyl, and because of our role in facilitating your tragedy."

"The xoconai follow a demon—you just admitted as much."

"This is larger than he who darkly prods them, and we have decided that it does not concern us. It cannot concern us. And I doubt we would be of much help anyway against the sheer size of the armies warring. We have spoken with our cousins of Tymwyvin, and they too will not interfere."

"Talmadge," Aydrian told his friends. "The Doc'alfar turned him away."

"There is a demon leading the xoconai," Aoleyn spoke up. "His darkness will cover the world."

Juraviel shook his head. "The xoconai are not demon children like the goblins, nor is the presence of a demon the responsibility of my people in this instance." He looked right at Aydrian as he said this, and the man understood. So many had to answer for the crimes of Aydrian Wyndon.

"I wish you well," Juraviel said. "But we cannot interfere. This war was long in coming, and surely to be fought as the xoconai built their great cities near the western ocean. It was only a matter of time before the humans and the xoconai did again war."

The elf bowed and turned.

"Lord Belli'mar," Aydrian blurted, and the elf looked back. "How will it end?"

"End?" the elf echoed with a helpless snort. "Perhaps the xoconai will claim the lands and push the humans of Honce-the-Bear aside and there will come a time of petty retribution and minor uprisings. Perhaps Brynn Dharielle will bring the Behrenese and To-gai-ru to the aid of Honce-the-Bear and drive the xoconai back, maybe split the land in a manner that will ensure decades of war.

"*Perhaps*, I say," he continued, seeming rather tired and saddened, "but who can know? Is the cycle of endless battle foretold?"

"But it is not your battle," Aydrian said.

"How can it be?" Juraviel answered. "The xoconai are no more the enemies of the Touel'alfar than are the humans of Honce-the-Bear. And, in any case, what are we few alfar to do against the hordes of xoconai and hordes of humans?"

Again he turned to leave, and again Aydrian called to him, turning him back.

"Am I to believe that there are xoconai rangers?" Aydrian asked.

"That is not for me to say," the elf replied. "But I will promise you that, if there aren't, it is only because they are so far removed from Andur'Blough Inninness so as to be beyond our reach."

"But the demon," Aoleyn said, coming forward as Juraviel yet again moved to leave. "Scathmizzane."

Her naming of the beast turned the elf fast about.

"Surely you would wish the beast destroyed," said Aoleyn. "For the sake of the xoconai as much as for the sake of the humans."

Belli'mar Juraviel stared at her for a long while, then nodded.

"Then help us," Aoleyn pleaded. "Get us to the far west, to the land of my home. Scathmizzane uses the power there, up on the mountain. I have to get there to stop that, to defeat him."

"You?"

"I destroyed Cizinfozza," Aoleyn told him.

"It's true," said Aydrian.

"Such a surprising child," Juraviel said. "You destroyed the demon Cizinfozza?"

"My people called it the fossa. Yes."

"Then you are the one who freed Scathmizzane to come east once more," said Juraviel.

"I . . ." Aoleyn stammered. Yes, the weight of all of this was settling on Aoleyn's shoulders, and as much as she wanted to, she couldn't deny the claim.

"Cizinfozza was evil. I didn't know," she said finally.

"Of course. How could you have known?"

"Cizinfozza held trapped the souls of the dead of my people. When the fossa was destroyed, those souls flew free, to whatever reward awaited them."

"But then came Scathmizzane, leading the xoconai," said the elf.

"And he grows powerful, so powerful," said Aoleyn. "He eats the souls of the dead and from them draws great magic—enough to destroy everything, even you. I have to stop him."

Juraviel paused for a long while, considering the surprising young woman. "What would you ask of me?"

"Take me there, with your . . ." Aoleyn looked to Aydrian.

"Tel'ne'kin Dinoniel," Aydrian said, the elvish name for their powerful emerald. "Use it, I beg. Take us to the place called the Ayamharas Plateau. At least give us a chance to defeat the demon."

The elf spent a long while staring at the three humans.

"I aided a demon once," Aydrian said. "I harbored Bestesbulzibar within me and spread its darkness and destruction. Give me this chance to help destroy the demon of the xoconai, for their sake as well as that of my own people. Give me this chance at some measure of true redemption."

Juraviel continued to stare, then reached back and produced from his pack a large green stone, larger than a man's fist, glowing brilliantly in the sunshine as the morning light streamed in through the cave opening.

"Come, all of you," the elf said. "Join hands."

When they had, Juraviel turned to Aoleyn. "Show me this place in your thoughts."

She did, and she resisted her revulsion when she felt the elf's spiritual presence within her.

Aoleyn closed her eyes. A sense of movement came over her, a trembling beneath her feet as if the world were shaking.

She opened her eyes again and saw before her the sails of boats on a wide lake and, over to her right, the towering mountains that ringed Ayamharas.

Aoleyn looked at her companions, both equally unsteady.

"I wish you well, Aydrian, and all of you," Juraviel said. "If you destroy Scathmizzane, you will do a great deed for the humans of the world, and for the xoconai of the world, and that will be a good thing."

Beside Aoleyn, Thaddius crinkled his face at that last part.

"Keep open your heart," Juraviel told him, told them all. "You will find beauty in the xoconai, perhaps, if you are able to forgive them their trespass and take the time to look."

The elf bowed and stepped back.

Then he was gone, simply gone, leaving the three on the field, a day's march from the passes that would get them up to the plateau.

She saw the wall of St.-Mere-Abelle before her, but far, far before her. Undaunted, Elysant lowered her head and sprinted on.

A javelin flew past her. She began to swerve. A second missed, stabbing into the ground so near her foot that it almost tripped her.

She felt a dull thud against her shoulder, and a third javelin bounced away.

Elysant could hardly believe it. The robe, the garment of St. Belfour, had turned the missile!

A more solid impact in her back dashed her hopes before they could begin, though, for that one hurt. That one had penetrated, a bit at least, and the woman staggered from the sudden biting pain.

She turned that stumble into a spin, letting the robe fly wide as she grabbed at the stuck javelin and yanked it free. Completing the turn, she ran on and felt the warmth of her blood. Elysant clenched her staff, heard the magic there and called to it, and felt the healing waves rolling through the weapon and into her body.

The wall was closer now. She kept running. She heard the thumping of feet not far behind and glanced back to see lizard riders closing on her.

She couldn't outrun them!

But she didn't stop and face them. She kept running, kept forcing her legs to drive her forward.

Monks on the wall began to shout at her, prodding her on, begging her to run faster.

She heard the riders closing from behind.

A lightning bolt flashed out from the wall but dissipated in the air far short of Elysant, let alone her pursuers.

The lizards were right behind her!

Elysant dove into a roll, just ahead of snapping jaws. She turned about as she came over, leaping to her feet and facing her enemies, ready to fight, with her staff presented before her.

But then they were gone, stolen from her sight by a sudden wall of orange. Flames, she realized, filling the air all around her and her pursuers, and she felt the flash of intense heat.

Confusion gripped the woman, all the more so when the fireball flared to nothingness, showing her a field of blackened grass, lizards in flames and thrashing, riders thrown and rolling on the ground desperately.

Elysant glanced to the side, to the brother who had leaped up from his concealment.

"Who . . ." he asked, appearing horrified that his blast had engulfed a fellow Abellican monk, appearing confused as to why not a wisp of flame swirled from Elysant or her robes.

It was a good question, Elysant knew, and now she had an idea that these robes, given to her by the wraith of St. Belfour, were even more blessed than she had believed. The fireball hadn't touched her—she hadn't felt anything more than the wash of warmth, though she had been standing very near the center of the blast.

"Run!" the brother told her, and he turned and sprinted toward the wall, lifting away in moonstone flight after only a few steps.

Elysant ran for the wall, more xoconai coming fast.

Up on the top of the wall, the monks cheered for her and yelled warnings when javelins flew her way.

She didn't get hit again, and lightning raining down from the wall, crackling over her, told her that her pursuers wouldn't catch her.

"The others?" Father Abbot Braumin said to her, as soon as she was inside. "Brother Thaddius, Aydrian, the woman?"

Elysant considered the question. She had lost hours, many hours. She had fallen in the night, beneath the pyramid, but now it was day.

"I know not," she admitted. "I . . . I think Aydrian and Aoleyn used the xoconai magic. Perhaps . . ." She shook her head in frustration and declared, "I know not."

The father abbot patted her on the shoulder and nodded his acceptance. "We are glad you returned to us, Sister," he said, and he stood and addressed all of the monks about her. "Now we must hope."

Elysant sat there in the courtyard before the wall for a long while, replaying the events of the previous night. She remembered the fight, more and more with each consideration. She held some hope that Thaddius had released his fireball, but what then for him, with the xoconai camp rising to meet the breach?

The woman looked at the wall and imagined the field beyond it, the xoconai camp, the pyramids, and the lands far to the west.

She prayed that her friend, a man she had come to love, had escaped.

With Aoleyn and Thaddius using the step-lightening malachite and Aydrian employing simple athleticism and training, the three easily scaled the rocky climb to the Ayamharas Plateau and began their swift journey around the western rim of the chasm containing the xoconai city of Otontotomi.

Thaddius looked in disbelief at the teeming place thousands of feet below and had to be pulled away from the rim on more than one occasion, to be reminded that their goal was before them, far to the south, the towering mountain that Aoleyn called Fireach Speuer.

As they camped under some evergreens that night, Aoleyn's spirit went forth, scouting the area ahead.

When she returned to her body, her eyes popped open wide. "We must go," she told her two companions.

Aydrian, standing off to the side, looked at her curiously. Thaddius, already almost asleep on a bed of grass, propped himself up on his elbows and yawned.

"Now," Aoleyn said.

"Enemies?" the ranger asked.

Aoleyn shook her head. "Allies. Come. Be quick."

They gathered up their possessions and set off at a swift pace, Aoleyn leading them, using the cat's eye gem set in the turquoise cuff on her left ear. With the magic of that gemstone, the woman could see in the starlight as clearly as if it were a cloudless midday.

They ran for a long way, a trip made more difficult by a chill wind that came up, a sign that autumn was nearly upon the plateau.

Aoleyn considered pausing and going out spiritually once more. She even stopped, and motioned for her friends to do likewise. But even as she reached for the wedstone on her hip, she paused, noting a natural arch formed by the branches of a pair of trees.

The woman nodded and led the way under that arch, then stopped again, not far from a tall and wide elm with exposed roots.

"Connebragh," she quietly called. "Connebragh, come out."

After what seemed like many heartbeats, a broken branch, thick with leaves, shifted aside some roots of that elm, and a person appeared from beneath the roots.

"Aoleyn?" she asked, her voice trembling.

"Connebragh," the woman said, waving her forward.

Connebragh came out of the hidey-hole cautiously, her eyes darting from Aoleyn to the woman's two strange companions—one dressed in robes, one in breeches and a cloak that was pulled in front of him but open enough to show a glint of silver from a metal breastplate.

"They are not of Loch Beag," Aoleyn said.

The other woman nodded, seeming unsurprised by that. Of course she wasn't, Aoleyn realized, for neither of her companions had misshapen skulls like the uamhas, and the only other known people about the lost lake were the Usgar—and Connebragh, like Aoleyn, knew all the Usgar.

"Tell your companions to come forth," Aoleyn said. "We are not enemies."

"Where have you been?"

"Across the world."

Connebragh stared at her with obvious skepticism.

Two others came out to stand beside Connebragh, and both gasped at the sight before them—not at Aoleyn but at the man standing to her left.

"Talmadge's friend," said the woman with the long skull.

"It is good to see you again," Aydrian replied.

"Tamilee," she said. "And this is Asba."

"Of Carrachan Shoal," Aydrian said.

"You made it across the lake, then," Tamilee said.

Aydrian nodded.

"And we kept running," Aoleyn replied.

"All the way across the world?" asked Asba.

"It seemed as much," Aoleyn answered.

"Why would you come back?" Asba asked.

"It is not good here," Tamilee added.

"It is not good anywhere," Aoleyn said grimly. "That is why we are here. We are trying to make it better."

The two uamhas looked to each other.

"And we can help?" asked Connebragh.

"Anything you know about the city and the xocon . . . the sidhe who now live here would help," Aoleyn assured her.

Tamilee nodded, then conferred quietly with her friends for just a moment before waving for Aoleyn and her two friends to follow them down under the elm. The request surprised the newcomers—it didn't seem like much of a hole, after all—but when they went down under the tree and Asba lit a torch stuck into an earthen wall, they found a large dugout chamber stocked with bedrolls, food, even rows of crude spears. Along the stone wall at the back of the chamber was a door that looked like it had come from an uamhas cottage.

"It would seem that you have a story to tell," Aydrian remarked.

"But first, let us tell you ours," Aoleyn offered, "that you will come to decide whether you should help us or not."

Connebragh nodded and plopped down upon a bed of thick blankets, then motioned for the others to find a seat as well.

They got no sleep that night. They were still talking when the first light of dawn peeked in past the leafy tree branch that once again covered the exit.

24

UNHOLY POWER

Tuolonatl regarded Ataquixt curiously when she spotted her friend emerging from the nearby tree line, astride his cuetzpali. The rider returned her gaze, offered a wave, then moved swiftly toward her. She squinted, seeking some clues about this unexpected behavior and making sure that it was indeed Ataquixt, for the sun was diving in the west on this, the second day after the fall of St. Gwendolyn. The xoconai army was well south of the destroyed monastery now, moving inland with the mundunugu, while the macana foot soldiers remained along the coast.

"Where have you been?" Tuolonatl demanded when he came up before her. She kept the anger out of her voice, but she surely wasn't pleased with Ataquixt at the moment. Soon after the fall of the monastery into the sea, Scathmizzane had directed the army's turn to the south, to sweep the land and come at the last remaining sizable city, a place called Entel, which marked the southeastern corner of the human kingdom. The xoconai had come to the eastern sea, which the humans had named Mirianic, and would watch the sun rise over the eastern border of Greater Tonoloya, but there remained one great battle.

Tuolonatl didn't appreciate the fact that, when she had looked south, she had done so without her principle scout, her most trusted advisor, who had inexplicably disappeared for more than a day now.

"Scouting, of course," Ataquixt answered.

"You left before the march. You left before you knew where we would be going."

"South, of course," Ataquixt replied. "We knew the one great—"

"And had we gone north, to sweep this region called the Mantis Arm? Or had Scathmizzane turned us again to the fortress in the northwest, the place the humans call Saint-Mere-Abelle? Where would my trusted second be in that event?"

Ataquixt assumed a pose that seemed rather uncharacteristic, and rather defiant, Tuolonatl thought.

"I was watching the force," he answered evenly. "I would be there by your side, wherever the next battle might be."

"What do you know?"

"I have come to tell you," he said. "High Priest Pixquicauh remains in Otontotomi."

"Yes."

"And Scathmizzane has headed back, through mirrors and astride Kithkukulikhan."

"Yes. This you would have known had you remained."

"You must go back there," Ataquixt insisted, surprising her. "Now."

"I must?"

"Yes, my commander, my friend. You need to go back to Otontotomi now, with all haste. I will come with you, of course, but we've little time to waste."

Tuolonatl's face spoke volumes then, screwed up in surprise.

"You have heard that our enemies have entered the pyramid flash-steps?" Ataquixt asked.

"Yes, but so have mundunugu, stepping beyond them, securing the mirrors. How did you hear of this?"

"Our enemies will get there, to the city," Ataquixt replied. "The mundunugu will not catch them. This will be decisive, and Tuolonatl must be there to make sure that it is properly decided."

Tuolonatl eyed him suspiciously. "How do you know this?"

"Because I know the web of the pyramids. I know where each was built and all the connections between them. If those who came forth from the human fortress and did battle with our soldiers kept moving when they entered the lights between the golden mirrors, they would not have been caught by those who sought to flank them and arrive before them."

"You do not know that this happened."

"I know that Pixquicauh has not returned. I know that Scathmizzane and Kithkukulikhan are fast returning to Otontotomi."

"That could mean many things."

"The humans are going there," Ataquixt said with open confidence. "Need I remind you of the rainbow and its unseen origin? My commander, my friend, the humans are not stupid. They, too, understand the source of Scathmizzane's true destructive power. Remember that we found refugees from Tzatzini far to the east, even in the city of Ursal, and we heard of more who continued to the west, reportedly to that very besieged fortress from where came the attackers seeking the web of pyramids."

Tuolonatl rested back in the saddle, Pocheoya nickering softly and swaying left and right. She was fairly certain that at least some of the refugees from Tzatzini had arrived in the fortress of St.-Mere-Abelle. Some insisted that the woman who had led the humans to the spear implanted on the wall, and had led the chanting and magic to foil the bombardment, was the same woman who had flown down the mountain and out over the lake during the initial attack, and though it had not been confirmed, Tuolonatl could not dismiss the possibility.

"We can arrive at a pyramid by nightfall and step within the limits of Otontotomi before the sun rises," Ataquixt said.

"Scathmizzane did not summon me."

"Scathmizzane gives you the freedom of your wisdom," Ataquixt said. "He need not summon you, nor would he question your arrival in the city, or back on the field outside of Saint-Mere-Abelle, or anywhere else you chose to be."

"We have one last great battle before us."

"Days from now. You can get to Otontotomi and back here in short order, long before the fight with the last large human city. You can even instruct the mundunugu and the augurs to create more pyramids to facilitate your return. I beg of you, my commander, my friend, to trust me now on this. Tuolonatl needs to be there, at Tzatzini. For the good of all. This I know."

The woman sat astride her horse, staring down at the surprising mundunugu on his collared lizard, who sat much lower to the ground. She had known Ataquixt for a long time, which made this exchange all the more surprising, for he had never asked much of anything from her. He had ever been the consummate mundunugu, following his orders perfectly, showing always the proper respect for those ranked as his betters.

He had never made such a request of her—for anything. All of this struck the cochcal as out of sorts.

But Tuolonatl would never question Ataquixt's loyalty to her.

"I beg of you, my commander, my friend," Ataquixt repeated. "This may be the moment that decides the war and determines the future, and woe to us all if wise Tuolonatl is not present at that event."

* * *

Using the cat's eye gem set in the turquoise ear cuff, and the wedstone on her hip, Aoleyn conferred the remarkable ability to see clearly in the nighttime darkness to all five of her companions as they made their way up the mountain.

Darkness was their ally now, and not limiting.

Aoleyn and Connebragh soon came to trails they knew well, and soon after that, they heard the singing of their sister Usgar witches. Over the next ridge, they saw those witches dancing in the light of the glowing God Crystal.

"They are beyond their mortal bodies now," Connebragh answered. "I hear them all the time. They dance and sing—I do not know that they even eat or sleep anymore, all these seasons since the coming of the sidhe."

"In service to the god of the xoconai," Aoleyn added, and Connebragh nodded her agreement.

"They are not even aware of the world about them," Connebragh said, and then Aoleyn was nodding.

"In service?" said the young uamhas, Asba. "Then we should kill them at once. And it will please me greatly." He hoisted his spear and started forward but only got a couple of steps before Aydrian grabbed him and yanked him back.

"What do we do?" Connebragh asked, aiming the question mostly at Aoleyn.

"They are in thrall," Aoleyn replied. "You know of my battles with Mairen, Connebragh. You know that I have fought with her before, and seriously. If I believed that she was in league with Scathmizzane and the xoconai willingly, then I would help in killing her, in killing them all."

She paused and looked toward the sacred lea. The witches were turning in small circles within the larger circular perimeter that they walked around the central crystal.

"But no, they are blameless here," she decided. "They are in thrall."

Connebragh started to respond, but Aoleyn held up her hand to stop the woman. Thaddius, too, began to speak, but the young witch hushed him as well.

She needed to think, to sort it all out. It occurred to her then that the Coven, particularly Mairen, was doing more here than exciting the magic of the God Crystal. Mairen was Scathmizzane's conduit to the crystal and to the enormous magical power below the crystal, below the lea, in the caverns of gemstones and the life energy of the newly dead.

"Before we take any action against them, let me try something," she told the others. "If there remains any part of Mairen within her, let me find it."

She took out the pale green chrysoberyl that Father Abbot Braumin had given to her and then put her other hand on the wedstone on her hip.

Aydrian grabbed her arm. "Aoleyn," he whispered, "we are at the source of godly power."

"Mairen is the link to that power."

"Then she is mightier than you can imagine."

"No, perhaps not, because Mairen does not know that she is the link."

"If I sense you losing yourself within the magic of the God Crystal, I will strike hard at Mairen and the others," Aydrian told her.

She considered that for a moment, then nodded her agreement and fell into the gemstones again, freeing her spirit—her chrysoberyl-protected spirit—from her physical body.

All was beauty and light. She had never known such a sense of harmony, of oneness. She was aware that she was less now and, at the same time, so very much more. She had no needs, none at all—not food or drink or rest or sleep.

All was music and movement, intertwined, in concert, in the sunlight, in the starlight, in light rain and thunderstorm, in flakes of snow melting as they tickled her in that other realm, the realm of the corporeal, the lesser realm.

She was here alone, a bit of a larger and singular universal beauty that engulfed her and so many others.

And here she would remain, content, blissful, forevermore.

There was no conversation here, no dialogue, save the occasional demands of Glorious Gold. There need be none, for the music was all.

But then Mairen heard a whisper, and it was not a feeling, like those godly commands, no. It was a voice, a human voice, calling to her by a name she had long abandoned, but one she still somewhat recognized.

"*Mairen.*"

Who was Mairen?

"*Mairen.*"

She was Mairen, or had been.

"*Mairen.*"

The beauty closed in around her, trying to silence the voice, she somehow knew. But the light seemed . . . thin, somehow, and the images translucent, and behind those images, Mairen saw darkness, and behind the music she heard the wails of ultimate doom.

"*Mairen . . . Mairen, come to me, come back to Mairen.*"

The woman could not ignore the compulsion. She blinked open her eyes—her real eyes, her corporeal eyes. It took her a long while to realize her surroundings, to recognize the God Crystal, to recognize her sisters, dancing still.

She knew the dance. She still felt the connection between it and the power beside her.

The lea was only dimly lit, the sun rising behind Fireach Speuer but not yet high enough for the rays of dawn to land directly upon her.

She put her hand upon the God Crystal, felt the vibrations and heard the song—but she heard it differently now, not as a part of it but as a witness to it.

And now, only now, she understood it.

Mairen trembled. Tears leaped from her eyes, dropped down her cheeks, and fell to the ground as she turned her gaze downward, trying to digest, trying to come to terms with the ultimate violation, which she now could not expel.

Anger welled within her, a primal rage beyond anything she had ever felt or known before.

She heard a twig snap under a footfall and looked up to see a small group of people coming onto the lea, over to her left.

Her breath came in gasps.

She noted a fellow witch, Connebragh. Connebragh!

And another, former, disgraced . . . her hated enemy, Aoleyn. Aoleyn!

"No!" she growled, and she tapped the God Crystal and brought forth from it an aimed wind, such a gust—as Aoleyn had done to her on their last meeting.

The group fell back, compelled by the wind, blown back into the suddenly shaking trees.

"Mairen, no!" she heard distantly, a voice thinned by the godly wind.

And then another, another woman's voice, shouting, "A dragon!"

A roar before her demanded Mairen's full attention. It was the roar of a giant being, a godlike being. She saw him then, and recognized him surely: Scathmizzane, astride the gigantic snakelike dragon swimming in the air, coming for her, for the God Crystal.

Scathmizzane, huge, giant-sized . . . but shrinking, she thought.

The high priest awakened to the sound of scrambling augurs, rushing footsteps all about his small chamber in the great pyramid of the Temple of Otontotomi. He came out of that room, pulling on his robes, and entered the immense main chamber of the building. The slanting walls of the pyramid climbed to the apex, all about him.

"What is this?" he yelled to a nearby augur, who was running fast for the open eastern door of the structure.

"Glorious Gold is come!" the man yelled from behind his vulture-like condoral, hardly slowing as he continued on his way. "Something is wrong!"

Pixquicauh mouthed that last sentence a couple of times, then, after a quick glance at his battered, tortured prisoner, Egard, he ran as fast as his legs could carry him. At last he came out onto the grand entrance pavilion outside the pyramid, some fifty feet up from the ground level of the city. Following the gazes of the other augurs on the balcony, he squinted and shielded his eyes from the sun, just then peeking over the mountain Tzatzini before him.

There flew Scathmizzane, Glorious Gold, upon the massive Kithkukulikhan. The dragon swam through the sky, rushing for the mountain, toward the God Crystal, it seemed.

Pixquicauh held his breath, his legs nearly buckling, as his gaze lingered on Scathmizzane—and then he realized that Glorious Gold was shrinking up there on the dragon's back.

His instinct screamed at him that his god's power was diminishing.

He heard in his mind the running augur's warning.

"Something is wrong."

Mairen saw him flying toward her, and in her mind she again heard the beautiful song, the call to oneness with Glorious Gold.

"*Mairen!*"

It wasn't a whisper this time. It was a shout, and she knew the person calling to her.

"*Mairen!*"

She felt the pull from the song of Glorious Gold, the path back to harmony and oneness . . .

But she knew who she was now. She recognized her personal being and heard the repeated call of her name, the reminder that Scathmizzane's compulsion was no more than an attempt to enslave her.

She shook her head. She saw Aoleyn and the others, back on the lea, not far away. Her hand went to the God Crystal again, reaching for the power.

But not for a wind. Not this time.

Instead, a ray of brilliant light, a beam like the one that had sundered the mountains, like the one that had sent the rainbow flying out beyond sight to the east, shot forth, guided by Mairen in an emphatic scream of protest and denial.

It struck Kithkukulikhan midflight, and how the dragon screamed—and dropped, straight down.

The whole of Fireach Speuer, of Tzatzini, shuddered under the weight of the impact as the dragon and Glorious Gold fell, splintering trees, cracking stones.

"Mairen, no!" Aoleyn yelled.

"No?" Connebragh cried, turning upon Aoleyn with apparent disbelief.

"The crystal consumes the souls of the dead!" Aoleyn shouted, rushing forward.

Mairen hardly heard her. She was focused on the God Crystal again, releasing its powerful beam of destruction once more, this time down the mountainside, over the rim of Otontotomi's chasm, and to the golden mirror set atop the great temple. It was instantly reduced to a molten puddle.

On Mairen's call, the beam lowered, lowered, working down the stone pyramid, cracking the stone, soon making the whole of the structure glow.

"Mairen, no! It devours souls, obliterates them to nothingness!" Aoleyn yelled.

Augurs cried out in fear and horror and ran all about, some going down the large steps of the temple, others running frantically about the pavilion in ridiculous circles, waving their arms and crying out in fear.

And others, Pixquicauh included, ran back into the structure. The high priest rushed for the alcove near his private quarters, to the personal mirror he used to communicate with Scathmizzane. He paused only briefly to look at Egard hanging there, turning . . . and smiling.

"Glorious Gold," Pixquicauh said repeatedly, as he scrambled across the large, open floor.

"This is the end," said Egard.

"Hold faith in Glorious Gold!" Pixquicauh yelled at the many augurs rushing for the exits, even as he cast a glare at the tortured human. "Believe, you fools!"

A large plop of molten stone spun the high priest on his heel. He looked up and saw the glow, and only then felt the heat rising all around him, throughout the walls of the great temple.

The stones were melting.

The huge building shuddered.

Egard laughed.

And then he died.

And Pixquicauh saw the block crush the hanging man, and it was the last thing Pixquicauh ever saw.

It glowed the color of blood in the midst of the golden city. It collapsed in on itself with a tremendous roar and a rising cloud of dust.

The mountain shuddered again.

The witches stopped dancing, all looking to Mairen, who stood beside the God Crystal, face down, shaking her head, muttering "No," over and over again.

A gust of wind hit Mairen, forcing her to stumble back from the God Crystal, and when she looked up at her assailant, Aoleyn used the wedstone to assail her with a blast of mind-scrambling energy that stunned her and left her reeling.

The other witches did nothing. All of them were standing and looking about in blank confusion. More than one fell to her knees, overwrought and sobbing.

A cry from behind turned Aoleyn's gaze, and she saw her friends all staring toward the plateau outside. Just a bit down from the lea, a huge serpentine head rose above the northern ledge. The dragon Kithkukulikhan was slithering up the mountainside, its face and side scarred, dripping ichor and dragon blood. The beast was seemingly unable to fly, but it was still very much alive.

Aydrian drew his sword and rushed to meet the dragon, with Brother Thaddius close behind.

Aoleyn wanted to go and help them face this titanic monster. She even thought of leaping to the God Crystal, or calling Mairen back to it, to strike the dragon again.

But no, she could not do that, she knew. She could never do that, no matter the cost.

25

THE EPIPHANY OF SCATHMIZZANE

The cuetzpali scrambled quickly over the rocky jags and up the steep slopes of Tzatzini. Tuolonatl and Ataquixt had ridden hard through much of the night, and now, in the light of dawn, they pressed their mounts on even faster.

They heard the windburst up above and saw the distant pines shudder under the blow. It was a magical burst, they both suspected, particularly given the location.

They saw Glorious Gold astride Kithkukulikhan, high above Otontotomi and speeding for the mountain.

They saw the beam of magic come forth from within that same windblown grove, stabbing out at Kithkukulikhan and dropping the dragon and its rider from the sky.

"Our enemies are here," Tuolonatl realized, beyond any doubt. "They have the God Crystal, the power of Tzatzini!"

The cochcal's jaw dropped open when the God Crystal fired again, a ray of brilliant light diving down over the lip of the chasm far below, melting the mirror atop the great temple, then moving down to assault the stone of the pyramid.

Tuolonatl turned back and started to urge her mount forward once more, but Ataquixt grabbed her by the arm. She looked at him incredulously.

"I fear that the world is about to suddenly change in great ways," he warned. "My cochcal, my commander, my dear friend, I pray we find our way."

Tuolonatl didn't quite know what to make of those strange words, but she merely nodded and started off. Moments later, the ground trembled again as, down below, the pyramid temple collapsed. At the same time, off to her right, she saw Kithkukulikhan, wounded but not dead, speeding up the hill, slithering about the high jags, running over the small trees with its great girth.

"Where is Scathmizzane?" she whispered, noting that Glorious Gold was not upon the dragon's back, as far as she could see. She looked to Ataquixt, who wore a grim expression, but one that seemed oddly removed from her observation.

Aoleyn gasped, startled, at the view before her: the dragon's head striking with the speed of a white-furred viper.

Aydrian dodged with an amazing sidelong leap and roll, and the dragon's head hit the ground of the plateau with such force that it jolted all of the onlookers from the ground. Then came a sudden sizzling flash, a lightning bolt from Thaddius that hit the dragon squarely in the face, in the mouth.

The beast seemed to simply ingest it, unbothered.

But Aydrian was right back in the fight, his enchanted sword with its silverel blade cutting across the side of the dragon's head as it reared once more—and actually digging in, flecking scales and slicing dragon flesh.

The dragon roared.

Aoleyn pulled a crystal from an inside flap of her cloak. It was the gray-flecked one, full of lodestone. She sent her thoughts through it, toward the dragon, trying to find some bit of the beast that would attract the magic. She sensed Aydrian's sword and breastplate clearly enough, but nothing from the dragon. Perhaps if she waited until the powerful man struck again, she could launch her missile at the embedded sword . . .

Aoleyn recognized the large xoconai who came through the pines to the left of the opening overlooking the winter plateau. All around her, the witches gasped and threw themselves to the ground—whether in fear or in supplication, Aoleyn could not tell.

Even Mairen slumped down. Unlike the other witches, though, the Usgar-righinn, the leader of the Coven, who had been the most powerful woman of the Usgar tribe, didn't seem awestruck, nor supplicant, but simply overwhelmed. She fell to her knees, tearing at her bare skin, pulling at her hair, her mouth twisting as if she wanted to scream at Scathmizzane but could not find any measure of control sufficient to formulate a curse.

Aoleyn glanced behind, noting Connebragh and the two uamhas quickly retreating into the trees.

"They understand," Scathmizzane said to Aoleyn, and his words echoed twice more, reaching the woman in three languages: that of the xoconai, that of the Ayamharas Plateau, and that of Honce-the-Bear. "They . . . you . . . cannot defeat me, because I am you. Behold Mairen, who was your better." Scathmizzane swept his arm out to his right, to the woman sobbing and thrashing on the ground. "She knows she is lost, and nothing can save her, or any of you."

Over to the side, the dragon roared—in pain, Aoleyn thought. But she did not, could not, turn away from Scathmizzane, this godlike being called Glorious Gold. She couldn't deny his beauty, the lightness about him, a seduction of hope and love.

"I am given form and name by the heart, young Aoleyn of the Usgar," he said, and still his words echoed in three languages.

He wanted everyone in the area to hear and understand.

"Open your heart and see the truth, and you will understand."

Aoleyn lowered her gaze in contemplation, and opened indeed—not her heart, but the song within the spear-like crystal in her hands.

Scathmizzane was dressed as a xoconai, with that rolled darkfern breastplate common among the warriors. In the darkfern were veins of the same metal that had been fashioned into Aydrian's fine sword.

She felt that metal now, calling to her crystal.

"I know you, high priestess of Tonoloya," Scathmizzane teased.

Aoleyn brought the song up as she brought her gaze up, staring with hatred at the being. The God Crystal beside her called to her, promising her even greater strength, but she didn't accept that invitation, and it was her power, and hers alone, that sent the crystal flying spear-like at Scathmizzane, with tremendous speed and power. It crashed through his breastplate, scattering the broken darkfern, and drove through Glorious Gold himself, right through, coming out the giant's back.

From that hole came not blood but light, beams of light, front and back.

Scathmizzane, so obviously unhurt, just laughed at Aoleyn.

Aydrian had faced a dragon before, but that beast was quite unlike this one—more formidable, in many ways, particularly since this dragon had come into the fight badly injured. Still, the serpentine attacking style of this dragon surprised the ranger and seemed far too fast for a creature of such size.

Again and again, Aydrian had to throw himself wildly to the side, or back, or shift and reverse in midstep to avoid the snapping of the dragon's huge mouth. He was scoring hits with some of his counters, and his sword, Tempest, was powerful enough for those hits to penetrate and sting. But if he was doing any real damage to the dragon, the beast didn't show it.

And the dragon was learning.

Over to the left went Aydrian, rolling, as the dragon bit at him. He had to roll again the same way when the beast swept down and around in the strike, chasing him out to the side.

Aydrian called to the gemstones in his sword and in his breastplate, growing stronger and tougher, his very form blurring to offer greater confusion and defense. He called upon graphite to send sparks arcing up and down the length of Tempest, trying to maximize his every strike.

Behind him, Brother Thaddius threw lightning bolts and bursts of biting cold at the dragon, but this seemed to be having little effect.

Back to the right ran Aydrian, pausing, reversing, then reversing again as the huge head swayed in the air far above him.

Down it snapped, and the man leaped aside again, beginning the dance anew.

He couldn't continue for much longer.

"Thaddius, I need you," he called.

The response came as a stroke of lightning searing over Aydrian's head to flash against the dragon's head. Perhaps it stung the beast, but it nearly cost Aydrian his life, for the blinding flash gave him hesitation but gave the dragon none, the fanged maw rushing down at him right through it.

Aydrian rolled and twisted, turning his hips forward, toward the dragon. As it reared, the man used his enhanced strength and considerable athletic prowess to propel himself forward, a mighty leap right into the length of the dragon.

Tempest struck hard, but if Aydrian had been amazed by the striking speed of the great beast, he now was truly stunned at how quickly the dragon coiled before him, head coming in low. To this point, the dragon had struck like a cobra, but now it seemed more akin to a viper.

Its neck uncoiled straight ahead, too fast for the ranger to react. The toothy maw closed about him and drove him back at lightning speed, playing out to the end of the dragon's length. He felt the maw closing upon him, the swordlike fangs digging into his breastplate, crushing it, piercing it, closing as if to bite him in half.

He called upon the soul stones in his breastplate for all his life, throwing waves of healing against the pressing doom.

It couldn't hold!

He felt more waves of healing—from Thaddius, he realized, when he heard the monk calling for him—but that, too, could not be enough against the bite of this giant monster.

With a determined growl, Aydrian reached his arms straight overhead, resisting the instinctive urge to grab at the dragon's massive jaws to try to pry himself free. He took up Tempest in both hands, and with every bit of power and denial he could manage, drove the sword hard into the dragon's left eye.

Ichor spewed and sparks flew as the enchanted silverel blade punctured the orb and drove deeper.

The dragon went into a rage, lifting its head and slamming it—and Aydrian—back to the ground.

The healing couldn't begin to dull the pain now, as Aydrian's bones began to snap and his tendons tore, but he didn't let go of that sword hilt, and he continued to press with all his might.

He heard Thaddius screaming for him, but the monk's voice seemed far away, receding with every passing syllable.

He knew he was dying.

He wouldn't let go or let up.

* * *

The javelin flew out, startling Tuolonatl, who turned to her companion, then quickly back, to follow the missile's flight all the way into Kithkukulikhan's remaining good eye.

The beast lay flat on the ground, its thrashes turning to trembling. The powerful human was broken in its jaws, but his hands still clenched the sparking sword with its blade buried to the crosspiece in Kithkukulikhan's left eye.

She turned back to Ataquixt in horror.

"I missed," he said with a shrug. "Perhaps I should have thrown for that one instead of the human in Kithkuku-likhan's jaw."

Tuolonatl glanced back to see a robed human priest, glowing white, go running past the dragon's head, disappearing behind its massive length. A heartbeat later came a massive fireball, exploding across the midsection of the dragon. The blinded beast gave one last shudder and lay very still. The human in Kithkukulikhan's locked jaw fell limp, arms dropping out wide to either side, head lolling back so far that his golden helmet fell free, dropping to the ground below to clang and bounce about on the stones.

Tuolonatl didn't know what to make of any of it, didn't know where to turn or how to feel—or how to consider Ataquixt and his claims. When did that one ever miss with his javelins? Was there a finer slinger in the mundunugu ranks?

It all seemed secondary, though, a moment later, when there came a bright flash of light back among the pines. Both xoconai drove their lizards swiftly ahead and saw Scathmizzane bleeding light, brilliant beams from his chest and back, as if a hole had blown right through him, releasing Glorious Gold from within.

He was laughing and seemed not in pain. He was facing down a human woman whom Tuolonatl now recognized. She was the one who had swooped down in flight over her forces at the lakeside town during the initial assault on the plateau, the one who had come out of the great fortress of

St.-Mere-Abelle to foil the magic of Scathmizzane's spear as it called the divine throwers to destroy the wall, the one who had appeared briefly on the field outside of the other human fortress as it fell into the sea. A woman Scathmizzane had taunted then as he taunted her now, calling her the high priestess of Tonoloya.

None of this made any sense to her.

"You have the weapon you need right beside you," Scathmizzane taunted Aoleyn. The xoconai god closed his eyes, and the light beams front and back faded to nothing. "Do you think there is any other way?"

Aoleyn, frozen with indecision, stared at him with hatred and tried to come to terms with her fears. This was very different from her climb into the fossa's den of death, where darkness fluttered all about her, threatening to swallow her. She was driven then by a different kind of fear, by a primal revulsion and a threat of her own death.

This was the opposite. It wasn't death and dark doom nipping at the young witch's sensibilities but a temptation of life and power beyond anything she had ever known. Yes, she could tap the God Crystal—she could feel the power thrumming there, awaiting her call—and she didn't doubt that doing so would destroy Scathmizzane. She glanced at the crystal and thought that it looker redder to her now, as if filled with the blood of the dead. She could use it to strike at Scathmizzane, to destroy Scathmizzane.

Then what? Would Aoleyn replace him?

Her gaze faltered. She glanced at the xoconai god, then back at the huge crystal.

Aoleyn shook her head. She could feel the souls below her in the caverns, trapped there, ready to be pulled through the God Crystal and obliterated, scattered to nothingness.

Cizinfozza had trapped the souls in the mountain before, and Aoleyn had felt their sensations of joy when she had freed them to go to . . . wherever it was that the freed souls of the dead might go.

And she had felt the terror of those newly trapped souls, facing nothingness.

Could she so condemn them to nothingness?

Movement to the side—Mairen coming her way, coming for the crystal.

"Mairen, no!" Aoleyn ordered, and she followed that order with a blast of wind from her moonstone, which sent the powerful Usgar-righinn stumbling, then tumbling, backwards, rolling to the edge of the lea.

Scathmizzane laughed all the louder.

"Will you fight me, then, high priestess of Tonoloya?" he asked.

"Quit calling me that."

"Perhaps you are correct. Any true being worthy of such a title would have already removed me by now, would have made the God Crystal her own."

"Removed? You mean destroyed," Aoleyn spat back, only because, in her frustration, she wanted to say something, anything, to slap at the taunting xoconai god. And why wasn't he coming at her, or throwing magic at her?

Scathmizzane was laughing yet again. "Destroyed? Foolish child, I am not a being. Do you think me afraid? I do not have the hopes and dreams and fears of you pathetic mortals. Do you not understand? I am a way, a manifestation of the desires within you all, the thoughts you cannot admit but cannot privately deny. I am as eternal as they."

"So thought the fossa," Aoleyn argued. She jumped a bit as a fireball exploded off to the side, out on the Usgar winter plateau. She glanced that way, enough to see Aydrian in the dragon's maw, to see Aydrian's sword buried to the hilt and the flames biting about the middle of the dragon's torso.

"Cizinfozza?" Scathmizzane shouted, demanding the full attention of all in the area once more. "You think Cizinfozza destroyed?"

He mocked her fully, his laughter echoing all about the lea and the pines, all across the stones of Fireach Speuer.

Aoleyn felt her rage rising, an overwhelming scream of denial. She felt the pull of the God Crystal and almost reached for it.

But no. No. No, that she would not do!

Even so, her anger demanded release, and her tattoos glowed with energy, they too demanding release.

She felt her arm transform into the leopard paw.

Then her other arm, and her legs.

And more—she could not stop it. She was falling, falling, into the tattoo's magic. Her vision changed and she thought for a heartbeat that she had fallen, for the ground was nearer. Her hearing grew sharper, the xoconai god's laughter seeming to fill her entire body.

Before Aoleyn even understood what she was doing, the woman—the gray-furred, black-spotted leopard—leaped across the lea, slamming into Scathmizzane, biting and clawing with abandon.

"Oh, fool mortal!" Scathmizzane said, laughing still. "Cizinfozza destroyed? The god of darkness awaits the whispers and shouts of humans who dare to be as gods, the cries of pride and the primacy of self."

Aoleyn's leopard claws tore at Scathmizzane's flesh, every opening expelling rays of light. He made no move to fight back or even to fend off her raking claws. He just laughed and talked.

"The whispers of envy toward those deemed undeserving of station or wealth," Scathmizzane said to her.

The leopard Aoleyn bit into his neck, tearing at his throat and tasting that light. But that could not silence Scathmizzane, no.

"The demands of satiation in excess and without effort, for money, for carnal pleasures, for power."

Aoleyn's front claws locked upon the god's shoulders, her maw clamped about his throat, and her back legs came up, claws raking wildly, peeling the flesh away, bathing that area in golden light.

"Yes, power," Scathmizzane's voice boomed, and it seemed to be coming from all around now. "The cries for power. And when the song is loud enough, then will Cizinfozza be called back to his place—or perhaps, this time, Cizinfozza will manifest among the xoconai."

Aoleyn felt a sudden intense heat, a light too brilliant to observe, and she fell to the ground, not because she had leaped away but because Scathmizzane was gone, simply gone, leaving a brilliant glow and nothing more.

Except for his voice, lingering among the ravines of Fireach Speuer. "Perhaps I will find the humans as my next servants," he warned, and the words became laughter, echoing, echoing.

But not for Aoleyn, for the departing demon Scathmizzane imparted one more thing to her, inside her thoughts, perhaps—whether it was a personal epiphany or a notion offered, she could not know.

I leave because I am done, and now my students continue my work.

26

ETERNAL BEING?

"Aoleyn . . . Aoleyn!"

She heard the call, but from far away, dulled by the blood pounding in her feline ears. Only then did the young witch realize that she was on the ground, that the being had disintegrated under her vicious rending. She spun around, taking in the scene, first noting a group of witches huddled together by the opening in the trees. Through that opening, too, she saw Brother Thaddius. Then, further around, Connebragh, who was calling to her, along with the two uamhas.

The leopard continued her turn, seeing the God Crystal and another group of witches, huddled on the ground at the far end of the lea behind it. She continued the turn to spy Mairen, gawking at her, on her knees. Aoleyn finally completed the turn to discover a pair of unexpected guests arriving at the sacred meadow.

Aoleyn instinctively leaped back to the God Crystal, and again she heard the tempting call, the promises that she could become so very powerful, that she could make of the world that which she wished.

In her head, the last epiphany of Scathmizzane echoed.

The notes of the tingling crystal sounded even more strongly when Aoleyn looked back to where Scathmizzane had been and viewed the newcomers, a xoconai man and woman astride their collared lizards.

The leopard curled her lip and snarled. Aoleyn could smell them, their blood, their trepidation.

"Kill them!" she heard from ahead and to the left, and she saw Mairen stumbling toward her—nay, toward the God Crystal.

Aoleyn didn't consciously register why, but she instinctively realized that she had to keep the powerful witch away. She hunched her hind legs, stared at the approaching woman, and gave a threatening growl.

"Kill them!" Mairen told her. "What are you waiting for?"

It was so tempting! Aoleyn's heightened primal instincts smelled the blood and the fear. She could do it so easily.

She fought the urge. She reminded herself of who she was, repeatedly calling to herself, interrupting the song of her powerful tattoo.

She felt her bones begin to crack, felt her flesh twisting and turning and tearing. One front paw became a hand once more, then the second. Her legs transformed.

Then she was kneeling on the grass beside the God Crystal, naked and trembling. She looked up, first to scowl at Mairen and warn her away and then to focus on the newcomers, her expression similarly threatening.

She came up to her knees, then shakily gained her feet.

Brother Thaddius ran up beside her and threw a robe over her shoulders, though Aoleyn hardly cared for her nakedness. There was no sense of vulnerability within the young witch at that moment, unless it was the weight of Scathmizzane's last epiphany.

"Aydrian," Thaddius said solemnly, and the woman didn't need to glance back at the winter plateau to remember the horrible scene of the dead Aydrian in the dragon's clamped maw.

"Be gone from this place," Aoleyn warned the xoconai pair.

Both held up their empty hands unthreateningly.

"You saw that?" Aoleyn demanded in the xoconai language. "The death of your god?"

"And heard, every word," the woman xoconai assured her.

"Kill them!" Mairen insisted. "The crystal is ours. I can feel its power. Kill them and destroy the sidhe city. Burn them from the mountain!"

"No!" Aoleyn shouted. "Do you not understand?"

"I feel the power," Mairen insisted. "That is what I understand."

"As do I. But do you not recognize where that power comes from? Do you not hear the silent screams of the souls trapped below?"

"What do you mean?" asked the xoconai woman, and only then, with the rhythm of the strange words coming from the mouth of this strange-looking humanoid, did Aoleyn realize that Mairen, too, had been speaking in the tongue of the xoconai, and perfectly.

"I speak of the lie of your god," Aoleyn told her. "Your Glorious Gold. He trapped the souls of the dead—human and xoconai—and from those souls, and through this crystal, did he draw the power to cut the cliff out from under the priests' fortress far in the east. Through those trapped souls do your divine throwers launch their stones, sucking the life energy, changing it to raw and destructive magic."

"It will be worth it to rid the world of sidhe," Mairen insisted.

"Mairen," Aoleyn said to her, calmly. "The souls . . . gone into nothingness. Eternal oblivion."

Aoleyn took note of the expressions on the faces of the xoconai. The woman appeared to be quite horrified; the man nodded.

"Your god is destroyed," Aoleyn told them. "The dragon is dead. The great pyramid below lies in ruin."

Then the woman, too, nodded.

"This is Tuolonatl," said the man, dismounting and stepping forward just a bit. "The cochcal of Tonoloya. She who leads the xoconai mundunugu and macana. She is a great warrior."

"Leads?" Mairen asked, her voice full of suspicion and judgment. To the side, Aoleyn translated to Thaddius.

"Then she would make a worthwhile prisoner," Thaddius said to Aoleyn, and he grasped his staff set with empowered gemstones.

"A better ally," the xoconai man unexpectedly answered— and, even more unexpectedly, he said this in the language of Honce, spoken naturally.

"Ally?" Aoleyn asked him. "You think we would trust her? Trust you?"

Thaddius looked to Aoleyn, then to the others about the lea. "Take them, now."

Aoleyn stared at the two xoconai for a few moments longer, then gradually began to nod her head.

"Do not," the xoconai man warned. "Do not fill this moment with blood. There is good to be found—"

"Good?" Thaddius yelled at him, and he presented his staff before him, the shaft suddenly sparkling with arcs of budding lightning.

"That is my spear in the eye of Kithkukulikhan!" the man shouted, stepping forward and pointing toward the dead dragon. "A spear thrown before the beast had died. A spear thrown in support of Aydrian. I am Ataquixt of Tonoloya and I threw my spear in support of Aydrian, against the mount of the xoconai god."

His naming of Aydrian gave Aoleyn sudden pause and rocked Thaddius back on his heels. How could this strange-looking being know anything about Aydrian?

"Do not let his gallant death be in vain," Ataquixt continued. "You think us enemies, and rightly so, but it needn't be. Not now. No more. Scathmizzane is gone, Kithkukulikhan is dead, the temple is destroyed—may High Priest Pixquicauh lie buried beneath the rubble."

The woman beside him slapped him on the arm, then, and demanded that he explain more clearly to her, for it seemed to Aoleyn that she was not fully comprehending the conversation in the language of Honce.

A moment later, she nodded and turned back to Aoleyn.

Ataquixt glanced about behind him. "There are likely thousands of xoconai warriors now climbing the slopes of Tzatzini," he said. "Now is the time to speak, and that time is short. Let not this moment end in blood, I beg."

"Let them come," said Mairen. "We will lay waste to them, and then to the city below . . ."

"Mairen!" Aoleyn yelled, silencing her. Then, to the xoconai, she added, "What is there to say? If your warriors attack, we will fight them, and many will die."

"You would use the crystal even after what you just claimed?" Tuolonatl asked. She took a step closer to Aoleyn.

"I do not need the power of the souls trapped within it," Aoleyn replied. She turned about and swept her arm to include the others, the witches standing up at her summons and moving toward her. "*We* do not need it. If your warriors come, they will find fire, ice, and lightning."

"From the crystal?"

Aoleyn stomped her foot, and a burst of wind struck Tuolonatl, strong enough to drive her back a step.

"No," Aoleyn answered evenly.

"It should not be used, ever again," Tuolonatl said. "It is an abomination."

"You only speak so because we control it now," said Mairen.

"Would you use it, then?" Tuolonatl asked Mairen.

Mairen started to answer in the affirmative, but Tuolonatl pressed her. "Would you, truly?"

"Mairen?" Aoleyn added.

The older witch stuttered and seemed smaller suddenly, as if the weight of all of this had suddenly descended upon her.

"What did he do to us?" she asked, looking about at her sisters of the Coven.

Mairen began to sob, as did the others, and they rushed together and hugged, needing the strength.

"What did he do to us?" Mairen yelled, coming forward from that hug a moment later.

"He possessed you and dominated you," Aoleyn said. "He tried to take everything from you. But you survived, Mairen. You found your way back."

"You showed them the way back," Connebragh said to Aoleyn.

Aoleyn and Mairen shared a long look then, Aoleyn seeing sincere gratitude there, among a bevy of other twisting and conflicting emotions. She understood. She knew what Scathmizzane had done to these poor women for all these months. Aoleyn thought of her own experiences with Brayth, her husband, on that last day of the man's life. He had violated her physically, and oh, she had been glad indeed when he had been killed by the fossa—so glad, in fact, that she had frightened herself, never imagining that she could be so elated about anyone's death.

Mairen felt that way now, as did the others who had been so horribly dominated, she knew.

"It wasn't them, Mairen," Aoleyn said, noting the two xoconai. "It was the god who deceived them, as the demon fossa so held the Usgar for so many years."

Mairen walked over to stand directly before Aoleyn. She looked past the young witch to the God Crystal.

"I feel its power," she said quietly. "Power that would cleanse the mountain of the vile sidhe."

"Your words are echoed by the xoconai when they speak of the humans," Ataquixt interrupted.

"Then the war must have a victor," Mairen quickly countered.

"Is that the doom that Scathmizzane set for us all, then?" Ataquixt went on. "Endless war and misery?"

"You speak for the xoconai?" Aoleyn asked.

The man shook his head and deferred to Tuolonatl, who nodded to Aoleyn. "I speak for many," she confirmed. "They will hear me." She glanced back through the opening in the pines, to the chasm far below and the still-glowing rubble of the destroyed pyramid. "And they will hear me more clearly now, if Ataquixt is correct and Pixquicauh, high priest of Tonoloya, lies dead beneath the rubble of the temple, as I believe."

"Then get the warriors off the mountain and keep them off the mountain," said Aoleyn.

"I want it back!" Mairen said then.

"What do you mean?" Tuolonatl asked.

"Usgar," said Mairen. "This is the home of the Usgar. I will have it back."

"This meadow?"

"The meadow, the plateau, the mountain," Mairen demanded. "It is for Usgar. It is ours. You do not belong here."

"The city below is Otontotomi, ancient heart of the xoconai nation of Tonoloya," Ataquixt replied. "It was never the domain of humans, even when the lakemen sailed the waters above it, oblivious to its presence. Perhaps there is common ground to be found here." He looked to Tuolonatl and they shared a nod.

"A truce?" Tuolonatl asked, turning back to Mairen and Aoleyn. "A truce here between xoconai and human?"

"Do you have a choice?" Mairen growled at her.

Tuolonatl shrugged. "There is always a choice. I can bring fifty thousand mundunugu and macana here to do battle. They can assail you day and night without end. You will tire. You cannot win."

"But *you* won't win, either," Aoleyn said in a leading tone.

Tuolonatl agreed. "The only possible outcome would be a tragedy on top of the tragedy."

"There are humans in the city below?" Aoleyn asked.

"Thousands," said Connebragh, before the xoconai could answer.

"Your slaves?"

"No more," Tuolonatl agreed. "No more our prisoners. If we agree to peace here, they will be freed. To come up here, if they choose, or to live among us in Otontotomi, the city below."

"Uamhas?" Mairen asked, and she didn't seem thrilled at that idea.

"Usgar?" came a voice from the side, from the lakeman Asba. "You are a handful of women and no more. Would you deny us still?"

Aoleyn looked to the older witch standing before her. "Mairen," she said quietly. "Now is our time. Now is *your* time. You are Usgar-righinn, but of a tribe that is no more. I hold no claim here. The choices are yours, but I advise you to consider the offer."

Aoleyn stepped out of the way as she spoke, clearing Mairen's path to the God Crystal. "And I accept your judgment here. I would not do this, I would not allow you the power within that crystal, if I thought you would choose wrongly. You can destroy many with the crystal, perhaps even the city below, but in doing so, you will condemn—"

"No," said Mairen, stepping to the crystal and putting her hand upon it. She shook her head, tears streaming down her face. "I know what he did." She turned sharply on the xoconai pair and shouted at them, "I know what your foul Glorious Gold did!"

Tuolonatl nodded.

"The souls. The horror. What will happen if we free them all?" Mairen asked Aoleyn. "Will our magic be gone?"

"I don't know," Aoleyn answered honestly.

"Then we will be doomed," said Mairen, again turning a scowl upon the two xoconai.

"No," Tuolonatl declared. "No, I have promised a truce here and I will hold to that, no matter the outcome."

"What would you do?" Aoleyn asked her.

"Can you free them?"

Aoleyn shrugged, unsure.

"If I held the crystal and it were within my power, I would free the souls," Tuolonatl replied. "Even at the cost of my own life."

"She would," said Ataquixt. "And Tuolonatl will hold to her word, as well."

"The mountain is mine," Mairen said to Tuolonatl. "I will rebuild the Usgar, here in this place."

"Winter fast approaches," Tuolonatl reminded.

"The God Crystal will keep us warm," Mairen said, but her voice was weak with the claim, and she looked to Aoleyn and then to the crystal.

Aoleyn, too, wondered what would happen if they released the souls. Would that be the end of magic? The end of the magic of her precious jewelry? The end of the magic that sustained the winter plateau? For no one could survive up here in the winter without the warmth of the God Crystal.

"If the power of the crystal falters fully, Otontotomi will welcome you through the winter months," Tuolonatl promised. "All of you. As equal citizens or valued guests. This, I promise."

Her words hung in the morning breeze for a long while.

"Do it," Mairen decided, looking to Aoleyn. "Do it."

Aoleyn nodded, but she wasn't even sure how she might accomplish the task. She turned to Brother Thaddius.

"How?"

The monk seemed at a loss, obviously so. He stammered for an answer for a moment, then pulled a large gem from his pouch. "Sunstone," he explained. "It steals the magic of other gems while it is enacted."

He handed it to Aoleyn.

The woman focused on it for a few heartbeats, closing her eyes, hearing the song—a most discordant and grumbling song! She opened her eyes and looked to Mairen.

"Do it," Mairen said again.

Aoleyn took a deep breath and closed her eyes again. She fell into the sunstone, coaxing its song to a powerful crescendo, then placed her hand upon the God Crystal.

The teeming power of the slanted obelisk nearly overwhelmed her and seemed to growl in opposition to the discordant notes of the sunstone. Aoleyn nearly faltered, but then found her heart and pressed on, countering the song of the God Crystal, blanking its every note with an opposite chime of antimagic.

But no, she was driven back.

"Dance," she said to Mairen, holding out a hand.

Mairen called the witches of the Coven to her side, to join hands and form a circle around the God Crystal, around Aoleyn. As one, they started to dance, turning their circles within circles, lifting their voices in song, sung in the language of Usgar and the harmony of Usgar.

Aoleyn caught the waves of energy of that building spell and channeled it through herself, through the sunstone Thaddius had given her, determinedly placing her hand back upon the crystal obelisk. Then she called upon her wedstone, moving her spirit out from her body, taking the chance.

Through the crystal she went, through its veins, to the pool room below that had, at one dark time, served as her sanctuary. She felt the spirits there, hundreds and hundreds, and called to them and bade them to fly free, though she knew not what that meant.

Then she saw Aydrian. Aydrian! He came to her, and she felt his serenity, his acceptance of his fate, and his approval.

He understood, and he who had once been possessed by a demonic being, who had once done great ill to the world because of that possession, approved.

The spirit of Aydrian led her now, showed her the way, the escape, and with the rising power of the Coven joined, the song of Scathmizzane was cleared from the God Crystal.

The struggle was not ended, though. It went on and on, like a great puzzle to Aoleyn. She hunted for the notes of the evil god and cancelled them, quieted them. Back she walked, through the crystal once more, as if cutting a trail for the dead to follow.

She was quick to her corporeal form.

A gasp, then a series of cries from around her nearly broke her concentration.

She opened one eye and perused the sacred lea. The witches danced and twirled, but she saw their sudden unease. She noted Thaddius and the two uamhas, ducking and covering, gasping and crying. She turned enough to see the xoconai pair. Tuolonatl was on her knees, seemingly in prayer, though for herself or for the dead—aye, the dead, for they were surely all about!—Aoleyn could not tell.

Standing beside the woman, the xoconai man stood perfectly straight, his arms uplifted, his eyes closed, singing. Aoleyn heard his song but didn't know the language, for it was not of Honce, not of the plateau, not of the xoconai.

She thought her eyes deceiving her, for she noted, too, the spirit of Aydrian beside the xoconai man, similarly posed.

The young witch promised to revisit that curiosity but knew it would have to wait. She now fell even more fully into her corporeal form and into the song of the witches all about her, joining them with her voice once more.

She felt the coldness permeating the lea. She knew that chill keenly from her time in the chasm, before the fall of the fossa, from the presence of her Aunt Seonagh and the other dead Usgar caught in the curse of the demon fossa.

She felt them, then, hordes of the spirits of the dead, rising from the grass of the sacred lea, from all about, from the God Crystal, too. Rising and flying away, free.

It went on for a long while.

Finally, the cold breeze fell away, replaced by the naturally chill autumn breeze of a Fireach Speuer morning.

Aoleyn staggered back from the God Crystal and called for an end to the song of the Coven. She dropped the sunstone, trembling, for it had unnerved her to her core. One hand went reflexively to her belly ring, the other settling on the wedstone on her hip.

She felt nothing.

She heard nothing.

"The crystal is dead," Mairen whispered in horror.

Aoleyn looked to Mairen, alarmed. The young witch began to speak, to agree that they had killed magic, and the looks on the faces of the other witches showed her that they felt it, too.

Had they forever killed the crystal that had given life to the Usgar tribe for generations unknown? The possibility brought a profound sadness and sense of loss to Aoleyn, which was surprising, given that she had walked away from the cursed tribe.

Still . . . Her hand fell to her belly ring. These gemstones had saved her, had given her power when she was helpless, had facilitated the course that had brought them all to this place. She wondered who she'd be without the companionship of the magical songs, what strength she'd find.

She nodded. She knew who she was, firm in her beliefs. The magic had helped Aoleyn to get there, but there she would remain, even without the magic. And so she was content.

But then she heard it.

Her hand on her belly ring, she heard the song of magic, distantly at first, but growing closer.

She felt the power of magic returning, like a growing line of torches flaring up to battle the darkness. She felt the song of her jewelry once more and lifted her arm and transformed it, through the power of her tattoo, into the paw of a leopard, just because she could.

Mairen giggled like a young girl. "It is still here," she said. "Sisters, it is still here!"

Aoleyn put her hand back on the God Crystal. It didn't teem with energy as it had with the spirits trapped below, but she could sense the song below in the caverns still, the great crystals and their magic.

"It is as it was," Mairen insisted. "Before the coming of the sidhe."

"Xoconai," Aoleyn corrected, turning to Tuolonatl as she spoke. "They are the xoconai."

Tuolonatl nodded. "Your magic remains?"

"Enough to defend this place from your armies," Mairen promised. "Bring your fifty thousand. Watch them die."

"There will be no need," said Tuolonatl. "Unless you choose to strike down upon us from on high." She nodded to the giant crystal.

Aoleyn shook her head. "That power, that cursed power brought by Scathmizzane the deceiver, is no more," she promised.

"And the truce?" Mairen demanded.

"Remains," Tuolonatl stated flatly. "I will stand down the mundunugu and the macana. Tzatzini, which you call Fireach Speuer, is for the Usgar, for the humans. I hope you will welcome those of my people who would learn of you as fully as we will welcome any humans who wish to remain in Otontotomi, or to come there. Let us here on this first battleground serve as a beacon to the lands in turmoil."

Brother Thaddius snorted—inadvertently, it seemed—drawing the attention of the others.

"War is general across Honce," he reminded. "You are so quick to call a truce," he said to Tuolonatl. "Why, then, were you so quick to lead an army to war in the first place?"

"They were led by a god," Aoleyn said.

"I would not have done so if I did not believe it in the interest of a better way," Tuolonatl answered.

"A better way for the xoconai, you mean," said Thaddius.

Tuolonatl conceded the point with a nod. "But not only—even the humans, perhaps."

Thaddius snorted.

"By our legends, the humans are the children of Cizinfozza, the god of darkness and death," the xoconai man intervened. "Perhaps goblins, or perhaps prisoners."

"As the xoconai were prisoners of Scathmizzane," Aoleyn interrupted.

Tuolonatl and Ataquixt looked to each other and shared a resigned nod.

"We were enemies because our gods were enemies, so believed the xoconai," Ataquixt went on. "Tuolonatl is the greatest warrior of Tonoloya. I follow her—nay, I love her—because she was ever called to settle the wars within Tonoloya and ever did so, while spilling as little blood as possible. She was kind to the human prisoners of the towns we first conquered. She demanded mercy from her warriors."

He smiled and walked toward the humans. "You should see the cities of Tonoloya in the far west," he said. "They are things of beauty, and ours is most often a way of peace. Is it so hard for you to consider that Tuolonatl, good Tuolonatl, honestly believed that the lands conquered by the xoconai would thrive for all, even the humans? Or that the humans, under the dark domination of Cizinfozza, would find a better way in the light of Glorious Gold?"

"The lie of your god, you mean," Mairen said sharply.

"Indeed," said Ataquixt, glancing through the opening of the pine ring. "And that is my spear in the eye of Kithkukulikhan."

"Did you?" Aoleyn asked. "Did Ataquixt believe in the goodly light of Glorious Gold?"

The xoconai man chuckled and looked back at his companion. "I believed in Tuolonatl, always and from the beginning," he answered. "I am no friend to war. I have survived a dozen battles in the march to the east, and defeated scores of humans, but not one of them did I intentionally kill."

That seemed to surprise his xoconai companion, whose jaw dropped open a bit. She stared at Ataquixt curiously, as if looking for something she had not before known.

Tuolonatl came forward, never blinking, her gaze never leaving the man. She moved beside him and took his hand in her own, then turned to Aoleyn. "Perhaps it will change," she said. "All of it, for the better of human and xoconai alike."

"Promise that it will change!" Aoleyn demanded.

"I will do what I may, but I am only one voice."

"One important voice," Ataquixt insisted. "Perhaps the most important singular voice among the xoconai. There will be strife between the city sovereigns and the augurs, between the political leaders and the religious voices. Who knows how it will play?"

"My voice will be many times more important because of what you have done here now," Tuolonatl said.

"What do you mean?" asked Aoleyn and Thaddius at the same time.

"The world, all of Tonoloya, faces an uncertain future—certainly hundreds of battles and strife, revolt, and oppression. What we—what you!—did here gives to me hope. I would not have expected your choice to forsake the power of the captured crystal, not from what I once believed of humans."

She turned to the man beside her. "But Ataquixt told me. He predicted much of this on our journey back from the east. I am glad that I listened. The truce here in this place, mountain and city, is real. As long as I draw breath, it holds. The humans in Otontotomi are free to come here or to remain, as they choose. They are not slaves, nor even prisoners. If they remain, they will have voice in Otontotomi."

"What does that even mean?" Mairen asked.

"Our city sovereigns are chosen by the people of the city," Ataquixt explained.

"The humans who stay in Otontotomi will have say in that choice?" asked Aoleyn.

"One person, one voice," Ataquixt said.

"This is my promise," Tuolonatl added. "This is my word."

Aoleyn turned to Mairen, the two silently sharing agreement. She turned to Thaddius and found he was staring at the surprising xoconai pair, his eyes full of wonderment, his posture revealing his hopes—but also his pervasive doubts.

Aoleyn turned to Connebragh and her two uamhas companions.

"You would have us ignore our hatred," Asba said to that look. "You would have us abandon our just revenge?"

Tamilee put a comforting hand on Asba's shoulder. "What would Asef want?" she whispered.

Neither of them seemed mollified or even convinced, Aoleyn realized, and she knew in her heart that, for all the pretty words spoken here, for all the apparent victory in destroying Scathmizzane and freeing the trapped souls, the attitude of vengeance and mistrust would be the norm, not the exception.

I leave because I am done, and now my students continue my work.

For all the world west, and particularly east, the road ahead remained dark and uncertain and surely would be colored red with spilled blood. Human blood, xoconai blood.

Would the priests come forth from St.-Mere-Abelle and rain death upon the xoconai with their powerful magic?

Would the xoconai fly about their pyramid portals to find the vulnerable humans and perpetuate the slaughter?

Would any of them here even survive, or would the xoconai down below, outraged at the fall of their god and the destruction of their holy temple, murder Tuolonatl and Ataquixt and scale the side of Fireach Speuer to take revenge on the god-killers?

Aoleyn felt as if she were standing on a narrow ledge high in the air, the wind growing all about her, ready to sweep her away to certain doom. What choice truly lay before her? War or peace? But no, those were not the options—would that they were!

War or a desperate attempt to begin a spark of peace, those were the options. A tiny spark in a continent dark with rage and vengeance and generational hatred.

It all seemed so utterly hopeless. She felt as if she were hugging a single warrior on the end of a charging army while the swarm of her minions charged across the battle-field to engage the other vast army. But still, for her own sake at least, Aoleyn understood that her next step, her every step, would be critical. She looked to Mairen for confirmation, for some clue.

"This is my promise," Tuolonatl said again. "This is my word."

Aoleyn sucked in her breath. If she didn't try to be that tiny spark, then who would?

"This is my promise," she replied. "This is my word."

EPILOGUE

"Stay with us," Mairen bade Aoleyn.

Another group of uamhas arrived on the plateau, the numbers swelling as more and more climbed from Otontotomi to be among the reconstituted tribe, which now was larger than it had been in the days before the coming of the xoconai, before the fall of the fossa.

Aoleyn didn't hesitate to shake her head. She had promised to remain for a bit, only to ensure the transition. If it turned out that Tuolonatl was lying or didn't prove strong enough to carry through with her promises, Aoleyn would fight with her Usgar sisters.

Such had not been the case. Down below, the xoconai city had remained quiet and orderly, and there were no more than a scattered few stories of repercussions or retribution against any humans for the destruction of Scathmizzane, Kithkukulikhan, and the temple.

It was quiet—here at least. But when Aoleyn looked out to the distant east, she recognized that she looked toward lands much less in transition in any positive way.

"My life is out there," she answered Mairen. "I would not have remained here on the mountain or about Loch Beag even before the coming of the xoconai. Even then, I had determined my road to be east, beyond the Desert of Black Stones."

"With that uamhas," Mairen said, her tone one of disapproval.

"Bahdlahn, yes," Aoleyn admitted. "He is a good man. You should consider that truth carefully now, if you hold any hope of remaining in a position of power here. Your new tribe is uamhas, Mairen, save a dozen Usgar women."

"That is why I need you to stay!"

"To hold them down and ensure Usgar supremacy?" Aoleyn asked with a chuckle.

Mairen fell back a step and stared at Aoleyn as if the woman had just slapped her.

"Open your mind and your heart," Aoleyn told her. "These are not your uamhas, and not your lessers. No good will come of you thinking that way, and less good still for you and the Coven if the lake folk come to understand that this is the truth in your heart. They have not forgotten the Usgar, Mairen, and our raids on their villages for centuries uncounted. It is they, not you, who are being most beneficent and forgiving.

"Perhaps it is only because of the few choices before them, and that this is better to them than living among those who inflicted the most grievous and recent wounds upon them. But hear me now, Mairen—and I say this as one who has no stake in the outcome—if you give the uamhas coming here to resettle reason to remember the injustice done to them by the Usgar, then they will find a new course and choice. They will be rid of you and your Coven sisters."

"And still you would leave us?"

"You, too, were victim, Mairen," Aoleyn said. "Victim of Usgar, of the demon Cizinfozza, and of the tribe grown under the demon's command. Know that. Let the uamhas know that, and perhaps you will survive. Perhaps you will even find that you enjoy the new company."

"They are so ugly," Mairen said, motioning her chin out to the side, to a woman who had two long humps on her head.

Aoleyn chuckled again. "I wonder who will lead the dances about the God Crystal, should I return here in five years," she quipped. "If it is Mairen, then I will know that she has grown. When the migration is finished, the lake folk will outnumber you and your sisters fifty to one. And if you ever desire to lie in the arms of a man again, know that it will be no Usgar. It will be an uamhas, unless you find a desire for the xoconai."

Mairen didn't appear very happy with any of that lecture. She sighed and turned away, and Aoleyn, who had been well reminded, these last few days, of why she had decided to leave Fireach Speuer in the first place, was more than happy to let her go.

"Mairen," Aoleyn called after her, halting her. "Do not convince yourself that I care more than I do, for you or for the remnants of Usgar," Aoleyn told her.

The Usgar-righinn held her pose for a long while, staring back at Aoleyn with what seemed like a mixture of anger and bewilderment.

Good, Aoleyn thought, for she understood that if Mairen and the others were to have any chance of surviving here, they needed to put their ridiculous pride and superiority aside and recognize their vulnerability.

Mairen turned away again, finally, and walked off, and Aoleyn put her out of mind. She spotted a man to side of the plateau, near the steps between the caves once used for slaves, who was neither Usgar nor lakeman nor xoconai, and she went to him eagerly.

"Aoleyn," Brother Thaddius greeted, when he noted her approach. "I had feared that you had already gone down to the city. I was told you were up there." He motioned up the stairs that led to Craos'a'diad.

"I already said my farewells to Aydrian," she replied, for the small clearing about the chasm was where Ataquixt, Aoleyn, and Thaddius had buried the ranger who had once been king.

"You are leaving, then?" Thaddius asked.

"This day," the woman answered. "Tuolonatl and Ataquixt will accompany me to the east. Will you accompany us?"

Thaddius smiled but shook his head. "I have spoken with Tuolonatl and the augurs, and they have agreed to let me stay in Otontotomi for now, to learn about xoconai history and their ways. Perhaps in the future I will return to Honce-the-Bear as an emissary of the xoconai. Perhaps I will do some good."

Aoleyn was disappointed on a personal level, for she had come to quite like this monk, but she couldn't argue with his choice. What did he have back there to rival the adventure awaiting him here?

"The vaults of Saint-Mere-Abelle should hold more truth about the xoconai, in any case," the monk added, a hint of sadness in his voice.

"You loved her," Aoleyn said, recognizing those echoes of wistful pain.

"She was my best friend in the world," Thaddius admitted. "And yes, sometimes my lover and always my love. Elysant was a beautiful heart in a world too filled with darkness, and it is my trial to forgive the xoconai for her death. I am only able to pass this trial because I know that my failure would disappoint Elysant."

"She would wish for a better way," Aoleyn agreed.

She gave Thaddius a hug, then, and kissed him on the cheek. "I hope I see you again," she whispered in his ear.

"Well, travel is now easier, if the xoconai allow, so who can know," he answered.

Aoleyn agreed with the point but still felt, somehow, that she would never return to this place and would never again enjoy the company of Brother Thaddius.

She pulled away, wiped a tear from her eye, then giggled a bit with embarrassment. She looked around, saying a silent good-bye to this place that had been her home for so long. The last time—the first time—Aoleyn had left the mountain, she had been fleeing for her life, but even then she had imagined that she would come back to this place someday.

Now, she thought not. There was nothing left here for her. She was glad that the human survivors of the xoconai war would band together into a single tribe on the Ayamharas, but her words to Mairen held truth: this region wasn't her concern or her business. She thought the uncovered and restored city of Otontotomi beautiful and interesting, but not enough to take her thousands of miles from that wider world she had found in the east.

She moved across the plateau to the point where the fall from it was highest, and there she called upon the malachite in her belly ring and let herself fall away. Then she called upon the moonstone and went half falling, half flying down the mountainside.

Aoleyn felt the same elation as she had on her first such journey, and this flight would be longer and better, she thought, for she intended to go right over the edge of the chasm and soar all the way down to the floor of Otontotomi, where Tuolonatl and Ataquixt waited.

She found them near the ruins of the great temple, Tuolonatl in deep and heated conversation with a handful of augurs.

Ataquixt walked over to join Aoleyn.

"It goes well?" Aoleyn asked.

Ataquixt shrugged. "Who can know? The augurs are not pleased. I do not think they have come to accept the changes. They argue now about where to bury High Priest Pixquicauh—or the small bit of what is left of him."

"But they are letting the people leave?"

"You have seen it, and look now to the stair, as more depart. Tuolonatl has many friends here, including Sovereign

Disu Suzu Ixil, who arrived in Otontotomi only a few weeks before the fall of Scathmizzane. She was a revered sovereign in the west, and the people here gladly gave her the seat of power for now. Thus, she controls the mundunugu and macana warriors here—unquestionably so, with the fall of Pixquicauh, who was high priest. The augurs are in disarray; they do not even know how to choose their next high priest!

"From the beginning, the planning in Tonoloya, Sovereign Disu Suzu Ixil had no heart for this war and only agreed to come this far east and oversee the transformation of this place in exchange for Scathmizzane's agreement that her garrison would serve as the city guard of Otontotomi." He winked at Aoleyn and whispered, "I believe that she thought we would lose in the east and she would then be in position to take her warriors home and command all of Tonoloya.

"She is no friend to the augurs, and she holds great respect for Tuolonatl. She will abide by the agreement forged on the mountain. Indeed, I believe she is glad of it."

Tuolonatl approached then, managing a smile at the sight of Aoleyn. "Truly, they exhaust me," she said. "They care more for the rituals of their religion than the ethics that guide it, to a one."

"Are we ready to leave?" Aoleyn asked.

The xoconai pair nodded, but Tuolonatl walked past Aoleyn, turning her gaze up the mountain, her expression wistful. "How fast the world has changed," she said. "A year ago, I thought Scathmizzane a legend, a name, an idea more than a being. And then he came to us, in flesh, and promised to us the world."

She gave a helpless little laugh.

"And now Scathmizzane is dead, and by my inaction, I helped kill my god."

"The demon fossa, Cizinfozza, is dead," Aoleyn said, coming up beside her. "I killed him."

Tuolonatl smiled as she considered Aoleyn.

"Maybe we don't need gods," she told the young witch, who nodded in agreement.

The three set off immediately, out from the city to a waiting boat, which ferried them across the lake to the next pyramid in line, the first magical step to Palmaris, where Tuolonatl would claim sovereignty, perhaps that very day, they thought.

But no, for the trio found an unexpected consequence of the changes, of the fall of Scathmizzane and the release of the trapped souls: the mirrors used for flash-stepping were not so easily accessed anymore. They could not be used at all by the xoconai gathered at the pyramid outside of the city, in fact, and only Aoleyn's powerful exercise of a diamond got her and her two companions across the miles to the next pyramid in line.

A second great step left the witch magically and physically exhausted. Her companions, too, felt as if they had finished a hard day's march.

"Perhaps this is a good thing," Tuolonatl said, as the three settled in at that last landing camp for a much-needed rest.

Aoleyn looked at her skeptically but noticed that Ataquixt was nodding in agreement.

"The individual cities and regions will find their balance more quickly if armies cannot be readily moved to join the fighting," Tuolonatl explained.

"If it holds true that only those powerful in the use of the gemstones can manage the pyramids, the situation in the human lands is greatly changed, and perhaps greatly advantageous to the human monks, who outnumber the augurs in the region," Ataquixt added.

"The changes are more an advantage to whomever holds the ground about the pyramids," Tuolonatl said. "Look how tired Aoleyn was after a mere two steps. Few will be coming uninvited to do harm." She nodded, and Aoleyn thought she seemed quite pleased by that.

And why wouldn't she be? If Tuolonatl seized control of Palmaris, as she intended, in order to change the very structure of the city to include the humans and the xoconai side by side, she wouldn't have to fear a sudden and fierce reprisal from the xoconai augurs and those who would follow them in a continued war of conquest.

It took them nearly a month before they could step before the golden mirror in the pyramid constructed on the remains of St. Precious in Palmaris. There, as with all of the previous dozens of steps, the xoconai guards snapped to attention, eyes cast downward in proper respect to the great cochcal Tuolonatl.

All of that gave Aoleyn hope. Ataquixt hadn't been exaggerating when he had introduced the woman up on the sacred lea. With every flash-step, they had found the same reception, and the deference shown to Tuolonatl was as great as anything Aoleyn had witnessed in Ursal with King Midalis, or in St.-Mere-Abelle with Father Abbot Braumin.

But it was slightly different with Tuolonatl, she thought, for it seemed to Aoleyn that the woman was greatly loved as well as greatly respected. That had been true with the other two comparisons, as well, of course, but not like this. The xoconai warriors guarding the pyramids had been so happy to simply glimpse this legendary woman. She was, to them, a great and true hero, Aoleyn thought.

Again, that gave her hope, for she was coming to believe that Tuolonatl was worthy of that respect.

"Are you sure that you will not remain with us in these important first days in the city?" Tuolonatl asked Aoleyn, as they neared the docks, soon after arriving in Palmaris. "These early moments may prove critical."

"I have seen the way they look at you," Aoleyn replied. "All of them."

"All except the augurs," Ataquixt interjected. "And I suspect that whoever has claimed the mantle of city sovereign here will not be so pleased by Tuolonatl's intentions."

"That is your fight, and one I would only complicate," Aoleyn replied. "I will go to the father abbot at Saint-Mere-Abelle with all the news from the west. They must be told. I will tell them, too, of Tuolonatl and your plans. Perhaps you will find very powerful allies in your quest to forge alliance between human and xoconai."

"I trust that you will prove a worthy emissary," Tuolonatl replied. "Your actions on the mountain showed me your heart, Aoleyn. You could have conquered the world, perhaps, with the power of the God Crystal."

"That would have been the worst outcome for all, especially me," Aoleyn answered with a grin.

Tuolonatl and Ataquixt shared that smile. "Come," Tuolonatl said, "let us find you a boat to sail you to Saint-Mere-Abelle. Know that you are ever welcome here if I am successful and claim the city as my own."

"May you reign long," Aoleyn said.

"Two years," Ataquixt unexpectedly replied to that. "And then she will face challengers, and the people of the city will decide if she should remain."

"The xoconai and the humans of Palmaris, if I am successful," Tuolonatl added.

Aoleyn had never heard such talk. It seemed too simple a concept.

The young witch stood at the taffrail of a great ship soon after, watching Palmaris recede as they made great speed along the Masur Delaval. For all that had happened, all the death and blood, all the horrors of the God Crystal and the great destruction wrought by Scathmizzane, and for all that she missed her friends, particularly Bahdlahn, Aoleyn felt strangely light and hopeful.

Perhaps some good would come from the darkness of the last few months.

But still, the epiphany of Scathmizzane lingered, mocking her optimism.

"They are all around us," the scout reported with obvious distress, gasping with every word.

Julian of the Evergreen looked to his commanders, Allheart Knights all, now that King Midalis had knighted Bahdlahn of Loch Beag. "We knew this day would come," he said to somber nods, and he asked the scout, "How many?"

"Thousands," the woman answered. "Five thousand at least. It is as if they emptied the city."

"They knew where we were and knew when to strike," Julian reasoned, for most of his forces were together here on a hill in the forest west of the city, gathered to discuss their plans for the next round of their resistance, since winter was coming fast. They had already seen the first snowfall, though it didn't amount to much and had already melted. But that wouldn't hold, and the nights were growing noticeably colder.

"Five thousand," he muttered, along with several others, all of them glancing around. Julian's fighters numbered less than three hundred here, and most of those were hardly veteran fighters, just Palmaris citizens—farmers and dockhands, fishermen and craftsmen—training with the knights in the hope of someday reclaiming their beloved city.

"What do we do?" a man in the back asked.

"We die well," Bahdlahn replied. He adjusted his breastplate, still uncomfortable in the thing, which only recently had been awarded to him by Julian, after the death of another Allheart.

"How much time?" Julian asked the scout, but even as he did so he saw the torches flaring, one after another in a line. The knight commander moved about the hilltop, following the sight, to see the whole of the hill encircled by a ring of torches.

"Riders," Bahdlahn said, from the eastern edge of the hilltop.

Julian moved beside his friend. Down at the base of the hill, he spotted two figures riding slowly across the moonlit field. They were xoconai, so he and his band believed, but they were riding horses, not the lizards they called cuetzpali.

One of the riders unfurled a flag then and began waving it about.

"Julian of the Evergreen," the other called, a woman's voice, "your soldiers within the city have all been arrested. We have captured, too, the people who housed your resistance and ferried your supplies."

Julian looked to Bahdlahn, and then around. All of his fighters were shaking their heads, frustrated and helpless.

The woman began calling out the names of the captured— names Julian knew well.

"Julian of the Evergreen," she finished, "there is no need of further bloodshed. Things have changed, across the world. Come down now and speak with us. Let us see if there is a better way."

"It's a trap," someone to the side of Julian insisted.

"Don't go," said another, and a third added, "We'll all go, and kill as many of the devils as we can!"

Julian looked to Bahdlahn.

"They have those who helped us and those we tried to help," Bahdlahn reminded.

Julian looked to his nearby knights, to the woman who served as his second-in-command, who stood scowling and shaking her head.

"Come with me," Julian said to Bahdlahn, instead. To his surprised second-in-command, he added, "If they take us or kill us, I trust that you will make them pay dearly."

"Count on it," the grim-faced woman assured him.

The xoconai riders dismounted when Julian and Bahdlahn walked down onto the field, Bahdlahn carrying a torch.

"I am Tuolonatl, city sovereign of Palmaris," the woman introduced herself.

"I have heard that name many times, though not with that title," Julian replied.

"Much has changed, in the city and across the world," she replied. She motioned to the ground. "Let us sit and I will tell you."

"You have my people," Julian said, not moving.

"They are well. They will not be harmed." She looked Julian in the eye, nodded, and added, "Whatever may happen here."

Julian and Bahdlahn exchanged curious looks, then did sit across from the two xoconai. Even after the woman started talking, Bahdlahn found himself staring at the man—staring at him in response, for the lithe xoconai warrior, who seemed not much older than Bahdlahn, had locked an unrelenting gaze on him.

"The fate of the world is uncertain," Tuolonatl began. "There will be no one leader, human or xoconai, at least not for a long while—generations, likely. Of this, I am sure."

"Curious words," Julian replied. "I suspect that you have lost a great battle."

"The xoconai have marched all the way to the sea, to the place you call the Mantis Arm," Tuolonatl said. "Even now, a great xoconai army remains encamped outside of the city you call Entel."

"You invite me to sit with you so that you can tell me of your glory?"

The woman shook her head. "Everything has changed." She looked to Bahdlahn. "You look familiar to me. Should I know you?"

"He looks like those from the west," the man beside her said. "He is from the lake, from the mountain, Tzatzini." His stare remained fixed on Bahdlahn, and he smiled, and Bahdlahn got the uncomfortable feeling that this one knew more than he was saying and that his words about Bahdlahn's origin were no guess.

"We recently came from there," Tuolonatl told Bahdlahn, "from the place the Usgar call the winter plateau, and the God Crystal. There was the greatest battle of the war fought, as summer turned to fall."

"A great battle with few combatants," the xoconai man added, "but with consequence for all the world."

"For there, Scathmizzane, the god of the xoconai, was destroyed," Tuolonatl said. "There did Kithkukulikhan, the great serpent dragon, meet its end. There was the great temple of Otontotomi destroyed, the High Priest Pixquicauh of Tonoloya buried under its stones."

Bahdlahn and Julian exchanged even more curious looks.

"You do not seem troubled by these events," Bahdlahn said.

"It is the way of things," Tuolonatl replied. "With the fall of Scathmizzane, the world's future is more uncertain, but perhaps more hopeful than before."

"You say this with the fall of your god?" Julian asked skeptically.

"I say this because my god was a lie," the woman bluntly replied. "I say this because the future is ours to determine now, of our own hearts and minds, hopes and dreams. And so I come to you not as an enemy but with the hope of alliance, of an end to the fighting here in Palmaris, at least. I am the city sovereign, but by decree and not by the will of the people of Palmaris, and certainly not by the wishes of the augurs. It had to be, but only for a short time, until the new order of things can be established. Then, if I hope to remain, it will be by huzzah and not by decree.

"In this time of transition, I ask that you come into the city and serve beside me, as my equal, a voice for the humans as I will be the voice of the xoconai. Let us build together the shining city that will become the beacon of hope for the world."

Neither man could formulate a reply for a long, long while.

"I understand your surprise," Tuolonatl said finally.

"And your suspicion," the man beside her added. "But understand that we could have easily burned you off that hill if we so chose. All of you would be dead or captured by now."

"But to what good end?" Tuolonatl asked.

"You are willing to cede half the power?" Julian asked. "You have everything under your control, and I am to believe that you would surrender that advantage?"

"Yes."

"Why?"

"Because Scathmizzane is destroyed, and I am glad of it. Yes, I could kill you here, along with all of your warriors and all of those within the city who helped you. This very night could bring the end of your resistance. But to what gain? Would the remaining humans in Palmaris then accept us? Or would they hate us even more, giving rise to another resistance, and another after that?"

She shook her head and blew a long sigh. "I have seen too much war. I have heard too many cries of the dying on the cold fields. I do not think we are so different, xoconai and human, Julian of the Evergreen. In the human cities we have entered, I have seen the same things I knew in the xoconai cities of Tonoloya." Her voice lowered. "I am not a young woman. I would have my legacy be that of one who brought our peoples together, not as one who slaughtered thousands."

"He was a god," Bahdlahn blurted. "What happened there in the west? How could he be killed by so few?"

"By one," Tuolonatl answered. "Scathmizzane was destroyed by a young woman, fearless and mighty with magic, who became a leopard and tore him asunder."

Bahdlahn sucked in his breath, his eyes going wide.

"A human woman?" Julian asked.

"What woman?" Bahdlahn asked at the same time.

"Her name is Aoleyn," Tuolonatl declared. "Aoleyn of Fireach Speuer. She is my friend."

Aoleyn stood along the wall of St.-Mere-Abelle, staring out to the southeast, to the wider waters beyond the sheltered inlet that held the monastery docks. She glanced back behind her to a small chapel. The Abellican leaders were in there, debating the future of the Church, of the kingdom, of the world.

Father Abbot Braumin Herde had listened to her attentively, and she had recounted the events of Fireach Speuer and of Palmaris as faithfully as she could manage. She had also advised the father abbot and those others about him to focus on Palmaris, on the great xoconai Tuolonatl, who hoped to change the world.

The young witch crossed her arms over her chest, bringing her cloak in closer against the cold autumn wind, and also as a shield against the fears within her. They had listened to her, yes, but Aoleyn wasn't sure that they had heard her. She had barely finished telling them of her departure from Palmaris when one of the masters had posited that they could use the disarray there to their advantage. If they could just sneak into the city enough brothers armed with potent gemstones, might they take and secure the docks quickly enough for a fleet of soldiers to arrive and sweep the place clear of the invaders?

She was thankful that such talk had been mostly quelled, and by a man whom Aoleyn considered an unlikely ally. The sharp-featured, sharp-tongued Master Viscenti had urged caution and had advised that they at St.-Mere-Abelle take a patient view of Palmaris, to see whether the situation would improve, and perhaps even spread to the eastern banks of the river and the sister city of Amvoy. Viscenti had argued that it was not insignificant that this Tuolonatl and her designs, however misguided and doomed, would keep a sizable number of enemy warriors tied up in the cities, while the monks of St.-Mere-Abelle faced more pressing problems confronting the land, like the huge force then encamped just outside of Entel, the last holdout city.

His wink to Aoleyn as he finished had made her think, or at least hope, that Master Viscenti was hoping for more than a delay of the dire and inevitable battle in Palmaris.

Still, Aoleyn felt silly for even considering the bubbling optimism that had brought her back from the west. By all reports, there was fighting between humans and xoconai all across Honce. In some areas of the northern Mantis Arm, battles waged among humans alone, even, with rival lords more than eager to fill whatever power void offered them some personal gain.

The words of Scathmizzane reverberated in Aoleyn's thoughts and followed her through every moment of every day. The demon's claim that he was a manifestation of darkness in human or xoconai hearts and not some separate corrupting entity rang true to her, as did his prediction that he or Cizinfozza (or probably any of many others, she figured) would always be ready to return.

Had they ever really left?

I leave because I am done, and now my students continue my work.

"Aoleyn?"

The young witch spun about at the familiar voice, and despite all her worries, a huge smile erupted on her face at the sight of Sister Elysant. The monks on the dock had told her that Elysant had returned and was well, but having the confirmation, having the woman before her, overwhelmed Aoleyn with relief and gratitude. She opened her arms wide and caught Elysant in a great hug, and they held on to each other for a long while.

"You have heard the tales?" Aoleyn asked, when the sister stepped back from her.

"He is alive? It is true?"

"Brother Thaddius resides among the xoconai in the distant city of Otontotomi, on the plateau of my old home," Aoleyn answered. "He will learn of them, of their history and ways. I expect he will remain there for much of the rest of his life."

Elysant nodded. "I hope to go to join him."

Aoleyn smiled warmly at the thought. "He would like that, and the xoconai would welcome you, I believe."

"Do you think I can get there?"

"Are you powerful with the gemstones?"

The monk shook her head. "I've no affinity for them."

Aoleyn considered it for a bit. "Perhaps we can convince Father Abbot Braumin to send a group of monks, envoys to foster peace between xoconai and human."

Elysant seemed surprised by that suggestion. "Perhaps Aoleyn will take me," she said.

Aoleyn's purely reflexive expression in reply was not the answer the young monk was seeking, surely.

"If the father abbot gives me leave to go, I mean," Elysant stammered.

"I'll not return there," Aoleyn said. "It is not my place. But I will stand beside you to speak with Father Abbot Braumin and convince him that such a journey would bring hope and perhaps enlightenment to the world."

Elysant stood staring at her for a long while, until finally an accepting smile began to crease her face. "I must go back to my duties," she said, rushing up and giving Aoleyn another, far less crushing hug.

"I am glad that you have returned."

"And I am glad that you are alive," Aoleyn said, "after the story Thaddius told us of your fall."

"It is surprising," the woman replied. "And there is much

to the tale that he does not know. After Vespers this night, sit with me and I will tell you, and you can tell me all about your journey to the west."

"I would like that," Aoleyn answered sincerely.

Elysant nodded, rushed forward to give Aoleyn another hug, then skipped away along the wall and gracefully slipped and then stepped down the nearest ladder.

Aoleyn turned back to the dark waters and back to her dark thoughts. Elysant's survival gave her courage against those thoughts now. It seemed impossible, given Thaddius's recounting, but here she was, very much alive and well, by all appearances.

Yes, the days ahead were dark—darker than she had imagined when she had started back from the Ayamharas Plateau. This war, these wars, were going to last for a long, long while, she believed, given all that the monks had just told her. Even if she could steer the Abellican Church correctly, even if Tuolonatl's dreams for Palmaris came to reality, the struggle would continue, for these were wars for land, for riches, and for power, stoked by revenge and wounds still fresh.

Racial wars, religious wars, and wars of opportunism.

Aoleyn blew a long and deep sigh and lifted her gaze farther out to the east. Talmadge was out there, somewhere, Khotai and Catriona beside him.

What of Bahdlahn?

The mere thought of her oldest and dearest friend, her first love, her great confidant, had tears welling in the young witch's dark eyes.

"Be alive, Bahdlahn," she whispered, her voice dissipating fast in the cold autumn wind.

Bahdlahn hustled to keep up with the graceful Ataquixt. The xoconai went over the wall of Palmaris so quickly that

Bahdlahn feared his companion would be long out of sight before he ever reached the top.

He caught a grip and pulled himself up, throwing his foot out to the side to set it on the stones, then paused and relaxed, more carefully picking his descent, for Ataquixt stood on the darkened field just to the side, waiting.

"How did you do that?" Bahdlahn asked, when he stood beside the mundunugu warrior once more.

Ataquixt flashed him that easy smile, one that Bahdlahn had seen many times of late. For some reason that Bahdlahn could not understand, this man, the trusted advisor to Tuolonatl, had befriended him and was staying quite close.

"Practice and training," Ataquixt replied. "You will learn, but it will take years, not mere days."

Bahdlahn shrugged and chased Ataquixt off into the darkness. He wasn't sure where they were going, only that Ataquixt had promised him an important mission this night. Bahdlahn figured they likely were out hunting for more refugees to welcome into the city, as that had been the typical adventure he and Ataquixt had shared these last couple of weeks.

"You always speak in riddles," Bahdlahn called after the man. "Or in promises of the distant future!"

"If I told you everything, then what would be the fun, for either of us?" the xoconai asked.

Bahdlahn couldn't suppress a chuckle. For all of his complaining, he was very pleased with his new friend. Julian of the Evergreen was now busy beside Tuolonatl, the two of them reordering the city to better serve human and xoconai alike. Even the Allheart Knights and some of the augurs had fallen in line with the idea of peace and compromise here in Palmaris, ideas they hoped to export to Amvoy soon enough, perhaps even before the first real snows of winter.

Bahdlahn was surprised at the attention Ataquixt was showing him. The man was very important to Tuolonatl, clearly, and certainly would command a high position in the city.

Why, then, would he waste his time with the likes of Bahdlahn of Loch Beag and Fireach Speuer, who was not a great warrior—certainly no real Allheart Knight—and was no leader of any faction in Palmaris?

Why?

He was still wondering this when he caught up to the fleet-footed xoconai along the forest trail, in a place where it widened into a small clearing.

Ataquixt stood facing him as he approached, waiting for him.

"You have been in many fights?" Ataquixt asked.

Bahdlahn slowed and stopped a few strides from the mundunugu warrior, caught off guard by the curious question.

"A few," he answered cautiously.

"Are you confident with a weapon?"

Bahdlahn shrugged, not wanting to tell the truth. He had seen lots of battles over the last few months, of course, but he had never trained with any weapon, beyond what Julian and the other knights had offered him in these weeks outside of Palmaris.

Ataquixt turned his gaze from Bahdlahn to the ground at the man's side, to one of the curious paddles the xoconai employed as favored weapons.

"Go ahead," Ataquixt told him.

Bahdlahn stooped and retrieved the weapon, lifting it in the moonlight, running his fingers over the jagged edges, both sides set with real teeth from some fierce animal. The paddle was very light and very balanced, he realized, when he gave it a couple of easy swings.

"It is a macana," Ataquixt explained, and Bahdlahn nodded at the familiar word. "The foot soldiers of the xoconai are named after that weapon."

"Then you are a macana."

"No, I am mundunugu, a rider."

"Ah, yes, those lizards."

"Cuetzpali, and we think of them as friends."

"I wouldn't share a meal with one," Bahdlahn muttered.

"Are you ready to learn?" It was a surprising question, and Bahdlahn looked up from the weapon to see Ataquixt approaching, macana in hand.

"Learn?"

"Do not be afraid to strike me hard," Ataquixt said. "Swing with all of your strength and fury."

The words alarmed the man. What was this about? Was Ataquixt planning to kill him out here in the night? Had it all been a lie?

"But I will not," Ataquixt promised, leaping in suddenly and snapping off a sidelong swing, which Bahdlahn blocked awkwardly.

"That hardly seems fair," Bahdlahn said, trying to remain calm and trying to sort through this confusing turn. If Ataquixt had wanted to kill him, the xoconai was going out of his way to make it harder, after all.

"It is more than fair, for I will strike you many times and you will never get near to hitting me," said Ataquixt. "Come, fight, and fight well. Let me make a warrior out of you."

Bahdlahn, still full of questions, didn't move.

"You would not want to disappoint Aoleyn when next you see her," Ataquixt teased. "Do you not fear that she will prefer the company of a great mundunugu like Ataquixt to that of a servant like Bahdlahn?"

Bahdlahn leaped forward, swinging wildly and missing badly. He stumbled as he overbalanced, drove his front foot into the ground to abruptly stop, then spun about to see the mundunugu standing off to the side. How had he gotten there so easily?

"In control, Bahdlahn. Never let your anger guide your swings."

The man moved in more cautiously this time, his macana

held up before and beside him, vertically, in his right hand. Bahdlahn faked a swing, then another, sliding his right foot out to the side and then following with his left.

Ataquixt turned with him, then came forward suddenly and snapped off a trio of strikes, first across, right to left, then a fast backhand, and then the third, which stopped the second swing short and prodded the macana straight ahead suddenly and unexpectedly.

Bahdlahn, leaning far back to avoid the first slash and stepping out of range of the backhand, had planned to come right in hard behind the second swing, and even started to do so. But the macana tip slammed him in the chest, hard, taking his breath away. He reacted with a sweep of his arm, bringing his own weapon across to swat Ataquixt's macana aside.

He hit only air as his opponent suddenly dropped low. Bahdlahn felt the macana against the inside of his leading left leg, stinging him and then slapping across as he tried to rebalance, stinging the inside of his right knee.

"Ataquixt!" he called, or started to call, for the mundunugu rolled past him. He tried to turn to keep up with the movement but got hit rather hard in the middle of the back, and when he did get around, bringing his macana to bear, Ataquixt struck it hard, once, twice, and a third time, nearly tearing it from Bahdlahn's hand.

"Fight better!" the xoconai demanded, and his fourth strike easily slipped past Bahdlahn's weapon to slap him hard on the side of the head.

Bahdlahn reeled.

"You will learn," Ataquixt promised. "Are you not impressed?"

Bahdlahn leaped at him, but the mundunugu began moving in a manner that Bahdlahn had never seen before. His right foot was forward, toes facing Bahdlahn, but his left was back, bearing most of his weight. Shoulders turned, Ataquixt held his macana more like one might expect of a thin sword, pointed out before him. As Bahdlahn advanced, the xoconai retreated, right foot back to plant, left foot dropping, and all the while he remained in perfect balance, his head and shoulders and weapon bobbing not at all.

Bahdlahn waved his macana before him, but there was no opening. He aimed for the extended macana and repeatedly thought he had a hit on it, but Ataquixt gracefully dipped or rolled each time.

Spurred by frustration, Bahdlahn charged faster and swung harder—hardest of all when he was sure that he would strike the weapon and send it flying from Ataquixt's grasp.

He whiffed badly and stumbled forward, and with a speed so sudden that it didn't even make sense to Bahdlahn, Ataquixt reversed his retreat into a sudden, fast-stepping charge. Three quick steps, legs never shifting their angle or balance, ended in a sudden thrust of the macana right into Bahdlahn's throat.

The man staggered backwards, gasping for air.

"It is beautiful, is it not?" Ataquixt asked

Bahdlahn couldn't have found the voice to answer even if he had so desired.

"It is a dance, my friend," Ataquixt said. "A fight is a dance, and one of fluidity and balance."

Bahdlahn's vision blurred. He grasped at his throat with his bare hand and finally managed to gulp down some air. Just as he tried to halt his retreat and set some defense, he felt the impact of Ataquixt's macana striking his own with surprising power, sending it flying away.

"Stop! Stop!" Bahdlahn pleaded, holding up his hands, turning his head defensively, wholly overmatched.

"Admit the beauty!"

"I do!" he cried in response, stumbling back another step. He held there, crouching, his hands out defensively before him, staring through the blur at Ataquixt, who stood barely two strides away.

"Would you like to learn to fight like that, Bahdlahn of Fireach Speuer?" Ataquixt asked. "Do you think it beautiful, truly?"

"Yes," Bahdlahn answered, then felt a sudden sting in his neck. He reached up and slapped at it reflexively, thinking it a wasp.

He was surprised when he brought his hand before him and found he was holding a small dart, its needle tip wet with blood. He looked at Ataquixt incredulously.

"The world needs you to learn," Ataquixt told him.

"Learn?" Bahdlahn couldn't follow. His thoughts spun and swirled.

"It is called *bi'nelle dasada*," Ataquixt told him. "The dance, I mean."

Bahdlahn hardly deciphered the words. They rolled about in his head, jumbling.

"Remember the beauty, Bahdlahn, and forgive me this deception. Know that I am your friend, and know that, when we meet again, we will fight again to test our skills, and you will fight well."

Bahdlahn couldn't reply. He shook his head, trying to find some stability here, trying to shake aside the darkness that seemed to be closing in on him.

Ataquixt stood right before him. Or was it Ataquixt, he wondered, for the form was just a blur.

He fell to his knees. He fell to his face and lay very still, and the world turned to darkness.

"You did well, Ag'ardu An'grian," he heard another voice, one that flowed through his thoughts like a soft breeze through the trees.

"I am honored by your trust," he heard Ataquixt answer, as the world fell toward silence, "Lord Juraviel."